Also by Beverly Barton and available from Center Point Large Print:

Dead by Midnight
Dead by Morning
Don't Cry

This Large Print Book carries the Seal of Approval of N.A.V.H.

W9-BFN-645

DISCARD

STEVENS MEMORIAL LIBRARY
NORTH ANDOVER, MA 01845

DEAD BY NIGHTFALL

Center Poi
Large Pri

BEVERLY BARTON

Lg. Type
F
Barton

DEAD BY NIGHTFALL

CENTER POINT LARGE PRINT
THORNDIKE, MAINE

This Center Point Large Print edition is published
in the year 2012 by arrangement with
Kensington Publishing Corp.

Copyright © 2011 by Beverly Barton.

All rights reserved.

The text of this Large Print edition is unabridged.
In other aspects, this book may
vary from the original edition.
Printed in the United States of America.
Set in 16-point Times New Roman type.

ISBN: 978-1-61173-265-8

Library of Congress Cataloging-in-Publication Data

Barton, Beverly.
  Dead by nightfall / Beverly Barton. — Center Point large print ed.
  p. cm.
  ISBN 978-1-61173-265-8 (library binding : alk. paper)
  1. Large type books. I. Title.
  PS3552.A76777D46 2012
  813'.54—dc23
                                          2011038000

In memory of Walter Zacharius,
with great respect, admiration, and affection.
Thank you, Mr. Walter,
for always making me feel special
whenever I visited Kensington Publishing.

In Memoriam

For sixty-four years she blessed the world with her vibrant personality, passion for life, and a love for her family that was unsurpassed. Her great beauty both inside and out was unquestionable. Her heart was always open and full of love. She had a witty sense of humor and mind that thirsted for knowledge. She loved old movies, poetry, good food, great books, and an eclectic array of music. Her career as a *New York Times* bestselling author gave her many adoring fans the world over who supported and helped make her dream career possible. She was the epitome of a true Southern lady who was loved and admired by all who knew her.

Beverly, Mom, Grammy . . . memories of you and your love will fill our hearts with each passing day until our souls are reunited.

"I love thee with the breath, smiles, tears, of all my life!—and if God choose, I shall but love thee better after death."
—ELIZABETH BARRETT BROWNING

Our beloved wife, mother, and grandmother
Beverly Marie Inman Beaver

"The hero path . . . where we had thought to find an abomination, we shall find a god; where we had thought to slay another, we shall slay ourselves; where we had thought to travel outward, we shall come to the center of our own existence; where we had thoughts to be alone, we shall be with all the world."

—JOSEPH CAMPBELL (Mythologist)

PROLOGUE

Ciro Mayorga deserved to die. In truth, the sadistic bastard deserved far worse. If there was any justice in this unjust world, he would have suffered untold misery for years on end. He would have been beaten and starved, hunted like a wild animal, and then forcefully sodomized before being utterly humiliated and tortured until he begged for mercy.

Rafe Byrne believed in the old biblical eye-for-an-eye type of justice and had made it his life's mission to dole out payment in kind for the unforgivable sins that men such as Mayorga had committed. It had taken him sixteen years to hunt down and eliminate four of Malcolm York's closest friends and associates, the men York had so often entertained on Amara. Tanaka, Di Santis, Klausner, and Sternberg.

And now Rafe had captured Mayorga.

The fifty-year-old Spaniard sweated profusely. Rivulets of perspiration ran down his throat and across his flabby bare chest. The distinctive brand between his nipples, a bright pink against his olive skin, no doubt still burned like hell, as did an identical brand in the center of his back and on each butt cheek. The smell of charred flesh temporarily overpowered the scent of fresh hay and manure. Blood dripped from the numerous deep welts crisscrossing his body, back and front, from neck to ankles. The still-hot branding iron and bloody whip lay at Rafe's feet, both objects used in exacting some small measure of revenge.

Suffering the torment of the damned, Mayorga whimpered continuously between agonized cries and pathetic pleas.

His pleas fell on deaf ears.

The naked man hung by his bound wrists from the rafters in the horse barn, his carcass dangling like a side of butchered beef. As Rafe approached him, Mayorga's bleary gaze struggled to focus on the weapon in his tormentor's hand. In a useless attempt to escape the inevitable, he struggled to free his raw, rope-burned wrists. Knowing the fate that awaited him, he screamed in terror. No one else, save God and the Devil, could hear the man. And only God, the Devil, and Rafe were present when Rafe used the sharp, serrated knife to castrate the demon whose soul was destined for eternal damnation.

CHAPTER 1

Maleah Perdue pulled her Chevy Equinox in behind Nic Powell's black Cadillac Escalade, parked, and hurriedly jumped out of her SUV. She and Nic had spent some wonderful girlfriend weekends here at Nic's sprawling mountainside cabin in the Smoky Mountains. Happy times. Not like today when she had come here to lend support and comfort to her dearest friend. It had taken Maleah longer to say good-bye to her fiancé than she had planned. But knowing she might not see Derek again for days, perhaps weeks, she had taken time for a long, romantic good-bye before leaving Griffin's Rest to follow Nic into her self-imposed exile. She understood Nic's reasons for putting some distance between her and her husband, for wanting to be alone to sort through her feelings and decide what she was going to do about her shattered marriage. However, leaving the safety of Griffin's Rest put Nic in danger, a risk she had been willing to take to get away from Griff. Maleah would have gone with her earlier today, but Nic had insisted on her staying with Derek since the two of them had only recently fallen in love and were newly engaged.

Maleah was grateful that Derek had understood and supported her completely when she had told him that Nic shouldn't be alone with no one nearby except a bodyguard keeping watch outside her cabin.

"Right now, Nic needs you," Derek had told her. "We'll have plenty of time to plan our future together once the Powell Agency is no longer under attack from some crazy madman."

Maleah rushed up the steps and across the cabin's wide porch. She knocked on the front door. No response. She knocked harder and repeatedly. Nothing.

"Nic? It's me, Maleah. Please, let me in."

Silence.

Maleah turned and surveyed the area around the cabin. A warm summery breeze flitted through the treetops, swaying the tall, skinny pines. Somewhere in the distance, bushes rustled and wild creatures stirred. Several birds soared overhead and a dog's howl echoed through the hollows below the mountainside house.

And then it hit her.

Spinning around, she stared at the two SUVs parked in the driveway. Two vehicles. There should be three. Where was Cully Redmond's Hummer? For that matter, where was Cully Redmond, the Powell agent sent to follow Nic and protect her?

"Nic!" Maleah screamed as she pounded on the door. Frantic with concern, she grabbed the door handle and much to her surprise, it gave way and the door opened.

Not locked!

Without a moment's hesitation, she reached inside her holster and removed her pistol. Gun in hand, Maleah entered the cabin and hurried cautiously from room to room searching for Nic.

The house was empty. She located Nic's unopened suitcase inside the master bedroom closet. The door leading from the living room out onto the back deck stood ajar. She eased outside, keeping her back to the rough-hewn log walls, and made her way carefully from one end to the other. No sign of a single soul.

Where was Nic? Where was Cully?

Something was wrong. Badly wrong.

Damn it . . . damn it!

Why hadn't she tried to talk Nic out of leaving the safety of Griffin's Rest? Why had she let her best friend leave without her?

Maleah pulled her phone from her jacket pocket, hit the programmed number, and tried to control her frazzled nerves as she waited.

Deep breaths. Don't panic. Think positive thoughts.

"Hey, Blondie," Derek said. "Are you there all safe and sound?"

"Yes, I'm fine. I got here about five minutes ago. Derek . . ."

"What's wrong?"

"Nic's not here. And neither is Cully. Nic's Escalade is parked in the drive, but there's no sign of Cully's Hummer. I've checked the house and there's no one here. And Nic's suitcase is in the closet."

"Get out of there now," Derek told her. "Put your butt back in your car and—"

"We have to do something. We have to find Nic."

"We will, but it may not be safe for you to stay there. Come back to Griffin's Rest. I'll handle things from this end."

"Griff will go ballistic when he finds out," Maleah said. "Oh, God, Derek, what if—?"

"I'll talk to Sanders first. We'll get some operatives out there to do a complete search for Nic and Cully. But I want you back here ASAP. Understand?"

"Yes, I understand. I'm leaving now." She choked down her tears as she walked back inside the cabin. "She's not dead. Please tell me she's not dead."

"She's not dead," Derek assured Maleah. "Nicole is far more valuable alive than she is dead."

Damar Sanders clutched the house phone with his meaty fist. "Yes, I will inform Mr. Powell. Thank you for acquiring the information so quickly, Mr. Mitchum."

"Dreadfully sorry the results were not what you wanted," Thorndike Mitchum, the head of the

Powell Agency's London office, said. "But at least we now know the man's true identity."

"Yes, of course. Mr. Powell will be in touch with further instructions very soon."

Within minutes of ending the conversation and settling the receiver onto the phone base in his office, Sanders heard the doorbell ring. As he walked swiftly toward the foyer, he encountered Barbara Jean guiding her wheelchair down the hallway.

"I will see to our visitors," he told her.

He could tell by the way she looked at him that she knew something was wrong, but she simply nodded, turned around, and wheeled back down the hall.

Barbara Jean Hughes was his assistant, his dear friend, and his lover. During the past few years she had become an essential part of his life. He admired her and respected her and counted on her understanding and support.

When he reached the foyer, Sanders paused for a moment, squared his shoulders, and mentally prepared himself for what he suspected was more bad news. Since Griffin's Rest was on red alert, the security at the entry gates and throughout the compound had been reinforced. No unauthorized personnel entered or exited. Whoever their visitors were, they had passed inspection and had been allowed entrance.

Sanders opened the door and found two

uniformed officers standing there, somber expressions on their young faces. The taller of the two, a freckle-faced guy who could not be a day over twenty-five, introduced himself and his fellow officer. "I'm Deputy Josh Taylor and this is Deputy Chris Meyer. We would like to speak to Griffin Powell."

"Mr. Powell is not available. May I help you? I am Sanders."

"We need to speak to whoever is in charge of the Powell Agency," Deputy Meyer said.

"I am second-in-command at the agency." Sanders took several backward steps and said, "Would you gentlemen please come in."

The officers entered the foyer. Sanders closed the door behind them.

"The Sevier County sheriff's department notified us of an accident—a single-vehicle wreck—that occurred in their county today. The driver of the vehicle found in a ravine was Cullen J. Redmond. His ID showed that he was an agent for the Powell Private Security and Investigation Agency."

Sanders's stomach knotted painfully. "Is Cully—?"

"I'm afraid Mr. Redmond is dead," Deputy Taylor said.

Sanders tensed. If Cully was dead that meant Nicole was without protection. Griffin had assigned Cully as Nicole's bodyguard and sent him after her when she'd left Griffin's Rest this morning. His instructions had been to follow her from Douglas Lake to her cabin retreat in Gatlinburg and guard her with his life. Nicole had known Cully was right behind her, so why, when he had not arrived at her cabin, had she not called Griffin's Rest to find out what had happened to him?

"You said Cully was killed in an accident?"

"No, sir. I said he had been involved in a single-vehicle accident." Deputy Taylor shifted his feet nervously and cleared his throat. "Mr. Redmond died of a gunshot wound. A direct hit to his head is what we were told."

Sanders took a couple of seconds to absorb and correlate the information. Cully had been shot in the head. Murdered. Assassinated. He had been sent to protect Nicole and now he was dead.

Managing to put aside his fears for Nicole and his personal grief over the loss of a valuable agent and a fine man, Sanders faced the young officers. "The Powell Agency will cooperate with the Sevier County sheriff 's department in every way possible. And we will contact Cully's nearest relative, a sister in Louisville."

"Thank you, Mr. Sanders. You and Mr. Powell have our deepest sympathy," Deputy Meyer said.

Sanders escorted the two young men outside, shook hands with both, and watched until they got in their car before he returned to the house. After closing and locking the door, he stood in the foyer for several minutes, deciding how to handle this situation. And then he went to find Derek Lawrence.

Derek and Sanders met on the stairs as Derek headed down, intending to find Sanders and tell him about Maleah's frantic phone call. The moment Sanders saw Derek, he stopped and the two men stared at each other. Derek instantly sensed Sanders had bad news for him. But what could possibly be worse than the news that Nicole Powell was missing, as was her bodyguard?

"Were you looking for me?" Derek asked.

Sanders nodded. "And you were coming downstairs to speak to me?"

"Sure was." Derek glanced past where Sanders stood four steps up from the foyer and in the direction of Griff's study. "Is he still in there?"

"Yes. He has not come out since Nicole left this morning."

"I have some information that he needs to know."

"As do I," Sanders said.

"But you and I need to talk first."

"Agreed."

By unspoken mutual agreement, they met in the foyer and went straight into the living room where they would not be disturbed.

"You first," Derek said.

"Two deputies left here a few minutes ago. They

came to tell Griffin that Cully Redmond was involved in a single-vehicle accident." Sanders paused, allowing Derek time to assess the info and respond.

"Is he dead?" If Cully had been hurt in an accident, perhaps Nicole was with him at the hospital. *Please, God, let that be what happened,* Derek prayed.

"Yes, he is dead, but he did not die from injuries in the accident. He was shot in the head."

"Son of a bitch."

"You need to contact Maleah immediately and warn her that—"

"Maleah is on her way back here," Derek said.

"But Nicole—?"

"Nicole is not at the cabin. Her Escalade is parked in the driveway and her suitcase is in the closet, but she's nowhere to be seen."

Sanders remained silent for a full minute, his dark eyes unfocused and his sturdy, compact frame totally rigid. Then he took a deep breath and said, "We must work under the assumption that whoever killed Cully has taken Nicole. Do we agree?" He looked Derek right in the eye.

"We agree."

"And Griffin must be told as soon as possible."

"Absolutely."

"I believe I know who murdered Cully and kidnapped Nicole."

"How could you possibly know?" Derek asked.

"And please don't tell me that it was Malcolm York."

"The real Malcolm York is dead."

"Then who?"

"Anthony Linden."

"But Linden is dead. Luke Sentell took care of that unpleasant chore."

"I received a call from Thorndike Mitchum shortly before the deputies arrived. The expedited autopsy and DNA testing on the body we assumed was Linden's showed that the man Luke killed was not Anthony Linden. He was a man named Neal Hinesley, who, like Linden, is on Scotland Yard's Most Wanted list."

"We should have known Linden was too smart to get caught. He brought in Hinesley, switched places with him, and set him up to kill or be killed when Luke found him," Derek said. "He's a clever bastard. And if he has Nic . . ."

God help Nic. Nic had discovered only yesterday that she was pregnant. A fact that her husband didn't know. She had shared the news with Maleah, as women often do, because they were best friends, and Maleah had told him.

"If Linden kidnapped Nicole and if he was hired by the man who is calling himself Malcolm York, then odds are he is planning to take Nicole to his employer. After months of attacks on Powell agents and their families, Linden has captured the prize."

"We don't know who this pseudo-York really is

or where he is," Derek said. "If he does have Nic, we also have no idea what he will ask in exchange for her life."

"We will know soon enough," Sanders said. "I am certain that it will be only a matter of time until he contacts Griffin."

Nicole's head throbbed unbearably. She struggled to open her eyes. The first attempt failed. Dear God, she felt as if she'd been drugged.

On a flash of fear-induced adrenaline, her eyelids popped open and her heart rate shot off the charts. Muted gray darkness surrounded her. The steady hum of an engine droned in her ears. She bolted upright and quickly realized that she had been lying on a bed.

Whose bed?

And just where the hell was she?

Checking to make sure she wasn't bound and gagged, Nic extended her arms on either side of her and raised them up and over her head. She lifted first one leg and then the other. After swallowing hard, she whispered aloud, "What happened to me?" and blew out a relieved breath when she heard the sound of her own voice.

She wasn't bound or gagged. And other than the mother of all headaches, she wasn't in any pain. So what had happened to her and how had she wound up unconscious and confined in a room with no windows or—?

As her eyesight began to adjust to the murky light coming from beneath what she assumed was a door, she surveyed her prison, listened to the thrumming of a loud motor, and sensed the vibration of a moving vehicle. This wasn't a room, not in the strictest sense of the word. It was a cabin. But she wasn't in a car or on a bus or a train.

Nicole suddenly realized that she was on an airplane.

But not the Powell jet.

Think! Damn it, Nicole, think!

Shards of memory returned to her, the sudden unexpectedness like an excruciating blow to the gut. She remembered now. Her husband had been lying to her for years, every day—every hour, every minute of their marriage. He and his dear old friend Yvette Meng had been lovers. He could have fathered the child Yvette had given birth to nearly seventeen years ago.

Griff's child.

What about my baby!

Nic wrapped her arms around her midsection, her open palms spreading instinctively across her still-flat stomach. She had discovered that she was pregnant only a few days before Griff had confessed the ugly truth about his past. Yvette had been forced to give up her newborn shortly after birth, never knowing whether it was a girl or a boy; and she, Griff, and Sanders

24

had been searching for the child all these years.

As if they were a row of unbalanced dominoes, her memories fell into place, one quickly toppling the other. She had fled her home at Griffin's Rest despite her husband begging her not to leave him, to stay and give him time to make her understand why he had not been completely honest with her. But she had fled, unable to bear the sight of him. Even knowing that someone had targeted Powell Agency employees and their families, she had refused to stay with Griff where she would have been safe. Foolishly, she had believed that, together, she and her bodyguard could protect her from whatever danger threatened everyone associated with the agency.

She had been wrong. Dead wrong.

Too late she now realized that her wounded pride had not only put her life in danger, but the life of her unborn baby.

Shortly after her arrival at her Gatlinburg cabin, high in the Smoky Mountains, a man had walked in on her, informed her not to expect help from her bodyguard, and then introduced himself.

"I'm Anthony Linden."

"That's not possible," she had told him. "Anthony Linden is dead."

"Yes, I know. And so is Malcolm York. And yet here I am, in the flesh, come to take you to see another dead man. Mr. York is eager to meet you."

Nic managed to stagger up and onto her feet.

Still feeling slightly disoriented, she recalled that her abductor had overpowered her and injected her with some type of drug that apparently had rendered her unconscious. She had tried to resist, but had known she didn't dare risk a physical altercation that might harm her unborn child. But what if the drug had harmed her baby?

Taking one careful step at a time, Nic walked toward the door, felt around in the darkness until her hand encountered the latch, and then opened the door.

She stood at the threshold, the shadowy gray cabin behind her and a brightly lit lounge in front of her. The sole occupant of the lounge sat in a leather swivel chair facing her, a glass of what looked like red wine in one hand and an unnerving smile on his clean-shaven face.

"I see you've finally awakened," he said, his tenor voice edged with only a hint of a British accent.

"Where am I, Mr. Linden?"

"Please, there's no reason for formality, Nicole. You may call me Tony."

Nic scanned the interior of the plush lounge in what she assumed was a private airplane. "Where am I, Mr. Linden?" She repeated her question.

"At this precise moment, we are somewhere over the continental U.S., heading south."

"You've kidnapped me."

He shrugged. "I'm simply assisting you in

26

accepting an invitation from your soon-to-be host."

"An invitation from someone you refer to as Malcolm York, a man we both know is dead."

"You believed me to be dead, too," he reminded her.

"Yes. Luke Sentell killed Anthony Linden in Harpenden, a town in Hertfordshire, England."

"Sentell killed a man he believed to be Anthony Linden. In due time, after an autopsy is performed, your husband will realize his prized gladiator slew a lesser mortal."

Nic's mind whirled with the possibilities. Yes, it was possible that Anthony Linden, an assassin who had been hired to kill various people associated with the Powell Agency, was still alive and that this man was who he said he was. But the real Malcolm York was dead. Griff and Sanders and Yvette had killed him.

"Even though he was already dead, we chopped off his head," Griff had admitted to her. "We had to make sure."

"Believe what you will," her abductor told her. "But soon you can see for yourself. Mr. York is eager to meet Griffin Powell's wife."

A shiver of foreboding rippled through Nic's body.

Whatever lay ahead for her, she knew one thing for sure and certain—she would do whatever she had to do to stay alive and keep her baby safe.

27

CHAPTER 2

"This is our fault," Yvette Meng said. "We should have insisted that Griffin tell his wife about everything that happened on Amara. She had every right to know the complete truth before she married Griffin."

Sanders stared at her with fathomless dark eyes, not a flicker of emotion showing. "It was Griffin's decision to make, not ours."

"Lying to her by omission created problems from the very beginning. And the very thing he feared would happen if she ever learned more about his past has happened. She left him."

"We have far more to concern us than the state of Grif-fin's marriage," Sanders reminded her.

"Yes, we do. Nicole's life is in danger."

"As well as Griffin's sanity and possibly his life and ours."

"We cannot think of ourselves," she told him as she reached out and gently grasped his arm.

The moment she touched him, she felt him tense and sensed his need to guard his emotions and hide his thoughts. Her empathic abilities were directly linked to touch. As if separated only by a thin veil between her mind and another's, she could feel what they felt, hear fragments of their thoughts, even view glimpses of their past, present, and future, although that ability was the weakest of her various psychic talents.

"I know how much you lost on Amara," Yvette said, keeping her voice little more than a whisper. "And I know that we owe Griffin our lives. I love him, as you do. And I fear for him. But we will stand by him through whatever lies ahead."

Sanders jerked away from her. "You talk as if there is no hope for Nicole, as if she is already dead."

Yvette gasped. "No, no, you misunderstood. Surely, you know me better than that. Yes, Nicole and I have had our differences, but . . . Griffin loves her. If necessary, I would give up my own life to save her."

Sanders's hard expression softened to his normal stoic appearance. "You must cancel your plans to fly to London tomorrow. Under the circumstances—"

"Yes, of course." Yvette could not help wondering if there was a connection between Nicole's kidnapping and the letter Griffin had received this morning . . . a letter from a man who called himself Malcolm York. A letter Griffin had shared with her and with Sanders. And with his wife.

Dear Griffin,

I hope this letter finds you and your wife well. Give Mrs. Powell my sincerest regards. And please give my regards to our beautiful, delectable Yvette. I think of her so often, of the two of you and dear Sanders, too. Ah, what wonderful times we shared on Amara. How I wish we could all be together again, as we were then.

I have been fortunate not to have spent all these years alone, to have been able to keep a part of Yvette with me. She is almost seventeen now. I gave her a little red Porsche for her sixteenth birthday. She calls me Papa and adores me as I adore her.

I believe I've been selfish far too long by keeping her all to myself. Being a generous man, I have decided to share her with her mother. If Yvette would like to meet her daughter, tell her that she can find Suzette at the Benenden School in Kent. As you can imagine, I've spared no expense on her education. You will find her to be as beautiful and brilliant as her mother and as strong of heart as her father.

Sincerely,
Malcolm York

Was this young girl, Suzette York, truly her child, the baby Malcolm York had taken from her only moments after she gave birth?

Yvette had prayed for a miracle all these years. That she would someday find her child alive and well. Griffin had searched the world over trying to locate her baby, but whatever Malcolm had done with her—or him—it was as if the child had never existed.

"You do realize that this girl is most likely not your child," Sanders said, voicing her own thoughts. "This pseudo-York sent that letter not only to torment all of us, but also because he knew Griffin would have little choice but to reveal the truth to Nicole."

"But if there is even the slightest chance that she is my child . . . " Tears welled up inside Yvette, tightening her throat and misting her eyes.

Sanders reached out, obviously intending to touch her shoulder, but instead he formed a hard fist and dropped his hand to his side. She did not need physical contact with Sanders to know that he was thinking of the child he had lost, an infant buried in his mother's arms on Amara.

"This man who has assumed Malcolm York's identity knows how much you want to find your child," Sanders said. "He will use that to manipulate you. He has already used the letter he sent as a weapon against Griffin and Nicole. That letter forced Griffin to admit to his wife that he could be the father of your child. And that letter also accomplished something nothing else could have. It prompted Nicole to leave Griffin and the safety of Griffin's Rest."

"But we all know that Griffin may not be the father of my child, that there were others . . . "

31

Yvette avoided remembering the past as much as possible, but doing so was unavoidable when she thought about her child and the way in which that sweet innocent baby had been conceived. "Even if we discover that Griffin is the father, Nicole would have no reason to be jealous of her."

"Do you truly know Nicole so little that you would believe such a thing about her? Nicole is not jealous of your child."

Yvette lowered her head and closed her eyes. In the beginning, she had believed that the woman Griffin had chosen as his mate would understand and accept the unique relationship that Griffin, Sanders, and she shared. Yvette had hoped that she and Nicole would become dear friends. But secrets from their past had doomed any hope of a friendship between Nicole and her, just as those same secrets had created problems of trust in Griffin's marriage.

"Nicole is jealous of me, but she shouldn't be. Griffin does not love me in that way. He never has."

"Nicole knows that. She did not leave Griffin because she is jealous of you. She left him because he lied to her."

"But he lied to her to protect her."

"Did he lie to her to protect her or to protect himself?"

"Perhaps both," Yvette said.

From the very beginning of their marriage,

32

Nicole had suspected that in the past, Griffin and Yvette's relationship had not always been plutonic. But she and Griffin had sworn to Nicole that they had never been lovers. In the truest sense of the word, that was true. Being lovers implied the two parties had chosen of their own free will to make love with each other. But neither she nor Griffin had been willing sex partners. They had been forced to perform, just as she had been forced to have sex with numerous other men, by an amoral, sadistic madman.

Malcolm York.

Her husband.

Griff stood staring out the window, his thoughts focused forty miles away on the mountain retreat he had given Nicole as a Christmas present. When she had opened the gift box that he had halfway hidden under the tree behind stacks of larger gifts and found the deed and a set of keys, she had jumped up and thrown her arms around him. He could almost feel her hugging him, could almost feel her soft mouth planting kisses all over his face. He ached with wanting her, needing her. When he had purchased the cabin as a surprise, he had envisioned the two of them spending quiet days and nights alone, just the two of them in a world where only they existed. He had never imagined that the cabin would become Nic's sanctuary away from him, a secluded refuge where he was the one person who was not welcome.

If only she hadn't run away. If only she had stayed so he could have made her understand why he hadn't been totally honest with her. She believed he had lied to her. Hadn't he? No, he hadn't lied when he had told her that he and Yvette had never been lovers. But that truth was based on a mere technicality. No, he and Yvette had never been willing lovers, but they had been sexual partners, forced to perform like rutting animals.

If only he had told Nic the complete truth about his past before they married, the truth about everything that had happened on Amara, about the complexity of his relationship with Yvette.

He now faced a difficult decision. Torn between his desire to go to Nic and beg her for a chance to make things right and fulfilling his promise to Yvette to accompany her to London tomorrow morning, Griff cursed with frustration.

"You're a damn fool," Griff said aloud. Allowing himself to be torn between the two most important women in his life these past few years was what had brought him to this point. Nic had left the safety of Griffin's Rest and his marriage was in jeopardy because of his own stupidity. He had failed to prove to his wife that she always came first, that no one was more important to him, that if he ever had to choose between his love for her and his devotion to Yvette, he would choose her.

But what had his actions proven to Nic?

That you're a selfish, egotistical bastard who thinks you can have everything your way, that there is no reason for you to be forced to choose between Nic and Yvette.

It wasn't too late.

He couldn't lose Nic.

Sanders could fly to London with Yvette in the morning and accompany her to the Benenden School in Kent. Yvette felt certain that once she saw Suzette York, spoke to her, and touched her, she would know if the girl was her daughter. They could run DNA tests later to prove or disprove his paternity. Whether or not Yvette's child was his, he would do all he could for the girl, if indeed Suzette was the baby York had taken from Yvette.

But nothing—not Yvette or her child—was more important to him than Nic. While Yvette traveled to London in the morning, he would drive to Gatlinburg, and when he arrived at Nic's cabin, he would get down on his knees and beg his wife's forgiveness.

Sanders asked Yvette to allow him to speak to Griffin alone. "As soon as I explain to him what has happened, he will become irrational with anger and fear. He will blame himself and also blame you and me. You cannot help him. Not at first. He will see you only as a part of the problem."

35

"As much as I want to help him, I know that you are right."

"Once he has vented his frustration, he may need you then. He will be in unbearable pain, perhaps more pain than he can bear alone."

Then and only then would Sanders allow Yvette anywhere near Griffin. Not only for Griffin's sake, but for her sake, too. Under any other circumstances, he would never ask Yvette to link with another person and absorb some of their pain, to suffer for them. But this was Griffin's pain they were talking about and he was the one exception to the rule.

"If only we could have spared him this. If only I had tried to persuade Nicole not to leave. I was so wrapped up in my own needs, my desire to rush off to England to meet Suzette that I—"

"We must deal with what has happened, not concern ourselves with what we should or should not have done."

Yvette nodded. Tears glistened in her almond-shaped, Eurasian brown eyes. Her shimmering black hair, neatly tied with a red silk ribbon into a loose ponytail, hung down between her slender shoulders. Small and delicate and utterly feminine, she was without a doubt one of the most beautiful women on Earth. How ironic that someone so physically perfect could be so emotionally flawed and spiritually tormented. Inside that exquisite outer shell existed a deeply

36

wounded soul, a creature capable of great compassion, sympathy, forgiveness, loyalty, and friendship, and yet incapable of the most basic of all human emotions. Yvette Meng was unable to love.

Sanders understood. Even now, he was not sure that the tender emotion he felt for others was truly love. He believed that he loved Barbara Jean as much as he could love another person. He knew that he cared for Griffin and Yvette, that on some level he loved them and would lay down his life for either of them. But like Yvette, a part of him had died on Amara all those years ago, the part capable of true and abiding love. Love that brought joy to one's soul.

Of the three in their unholy Amara triad, Griffin had been the only one given a miracle.

He had fallen in love with Nicole.

Glancing over Yvette's shoulder, Sanders saw Derek Lawrence approaching. The Powell Agency's profiler, formerly with the FBI, had been hand-picked by Griffin himself, and the two men had gradually become friends, enough so that Griffin had brought Derek into his inner circle. Only a handful of people knew anything about the missing ten years of Griffin Powell's life or when, and why the three of them—Griffin, Sanders, and Yvette—had forged the deep bonds that united them. Derek Lawrence knew the basic facts, which was far more than most people ever knew.

"I spoke to Maleah," Derek informed them. "She's on Douglas Dam Road and just turned east onto one-thirty-nine. She should be here in less than half an hour."

Sanders simply nodded before he asked, "Did you send Holt Keinan to Sevierville to handle the Cully Redmond situation with the sheriff's office?"

"I did," Derek replied. "And I sent Ben Corbett to Louisville to personally inform Cully's sister about his death."

"Good. Good."

"For now, all our bases are covered." Derek glanced at the closed door to Griffin's study. "Are you two doing this alone or do you want me to—?"

"I will speak to Griffin," Sanders said.

Derek cast Yvette a sidelong glance. She kept her eyes downcast and said nothing. Sanders knew how much she wanted to go with him, to step in immediately and try to help Griffin. But she would do as he had asked, no matter how difficult for her.

"Are you sure you don't want backup?" Derek asked. "I wouldn't want to walk into that lion's den without a whip and a chair."

"Sanders knows what he's doing," Yvette assured Derek. "He understands Griffin far better than anyone else."

"I guess he does—doesn't he?—which means

he has to be concerned that, once he tells Griff that Nic is missing and presumed kidnapped, Griff just might shoot the messenger."

Sanders ignored Derek's warning, fully aware of how Griffin would react when he delivered the news of Nicole's possible abduction. Without delaying any longer, he reached out and knocked on the door.

"Go away," Griffin called from inside the study.

"It is urgent that I speak to you," Sanders said. "It is about Nicole. I have news—"

All within a couple of seconds, the lock clicked, the handle turned, and the door opened. Griffin stood just over the threshold, the room behind him dark except for a glimmer of dying twilight coming through the study windows.

"What about Nic?" Griff asked, his gaze glued to Sanders.

"May I come in?" Sanders didn't hesitate. He moved forward and Griff stepped back inside the study.

Sanders closed the door behind him.

"What's going on?" Griffin asked. "What's wrong?"

"Cully Redmond never reached the cabin in Gatlinburg. He was shot and killed while en route and his Hummer veered off the road and into a ravine."

"And Nic? Does she know about Cully? Has Maleah arrived at the cabin?" Griffin stormed toward the door. "I'm going straight there now. Call her and—"

"Nicole is not at the cabin."

Griffin stopped dead still and turned to face Sanders. "Where is she? Did Maleah take her somewhere else?"

"When Maleah arrived at the cabin, Nicole's Escalade was parked in the driveway and her suitcase was in the master bedroom closet, but . . ." Sanders paused for a brief second. "Nicole was not there. We don't know where she is, but we suspect that she has been abducted by Anthony Linden."

Griffin stared at him with an incredulous look in his eyes. "Anthony Linden is dead. Luke Sentell—"

"Thorndike Mitchum contacted me less than an hour ago," Sanders said. "They managed to do a rush job on the autopsy and the DNA testing. The man Luke killed was not Anthony Linden."

For several minutes, Griffin stood there staring at Sanders. And then like a wild animal brought down by a hunter's deadly shot, Griffin Powell roared in excruciating pain.

Rafe Byrne escorted the five-nine, luscious blonde through the entrance of the private dining room in the River Restaurant at the Savoy in downtown London. His date was none other than the infamous stage and screen star, Cassandra

Wilder, and she, not he, had been invited to this exclusive party hosted by Sir Harlan Benecroft. As luck would have it, he had known Cassie for a number of years, having deliberately cultivated her acquaintance because he had once seen a newspaper photo of her with Sir Harlan. Rafe was a patient man. He had no problem biding his time and waiting for the right opportunity. And his casual relationship with Cassie had finally paid off when in a recent telephone conversation, she had mentioned tonight's dinner party at the Savoy.

"If you're in London next week, you simply must accompany me, darling. I'll be the envy of all the other women."

Cassie couldn't have known what her offhand invitation had meant to him. He had been searching for a way to gain entry into Benecroft's elite circle of friends, hoping that Yves Bouchard would be among them. Bouchard was a wily old fox who kept a low profile and had proven impossible to locate. But if luck was on his side, Rafe just might meet the elusive billionaire tonight.

"I have no idea who the other guests are," Cassie admitted in a quiet whisper as they entered the dining room. "I so hope one of the royals is here. I've fancied meeting a prince for ever so long."

Upon close inspection, Rafe saw that the table was set for twelve. A quick scan of the people

41

present told him that he and Cassie completed the party and were apparently the last to arrive. As that nefarious toad, Sir Harlan, rose from his seat at the head of the table and waved a cordial welcome, Rafe steeled himself in preparation for what lay ahead this evening. Every instinct he possessed urged him to go in for the kill, to rip out the old pervert's heart, and feed it to his guests.

Harlan Benecroft had grown older, fatter, and balder with age. He had to be at least seventy by now. Age spots dotted his round, ruddy face and not even the elegant cut of his expensive tuxedo jacket could camouflage his wide girth.

Did he still prefer pretty young girls who had just reached pubescence? Girls of eleven or twelve with small newly blossomed breasts and their virginity intact?

There had been a time when Rafe couldn't have been in the same room with Benecroft without vomiting. And even now, the sight of the man sickened him.

With iron control over his emotions—anger, hatred, revulsion—Rafe managed to nod and smile when their host urged them to take their seats. In his role as a gentleman, Rafe assisted his date and then pulled out the chair beside her. Once seated, he ran his gaze quickly around the table, concentrating only on the men, the two older men in particular. He had not seen Yves Bouchard in person for more than sixteen years, not since Bouchard's last visit to Amara. And there were no recent photos of the man. None.

Would Rafe actually recognize Bouchard?

One of the two older men, he dismissed immediately when he heard him speak to the woman next to him. His accent was decidedly Scottish. And his eyes were blue, not brown.

"I believe that Ms. Wilder needs no introduction," Sir Harlan said as he focused his gaze on Cassie. "But, my dear, perhaps you would like to introduce your young man to the other guests."

As all eyes turned to Rafe, his heart stopped beating for one gut-wrenching moment when the white-haired man with the neatly groomed gray mustache and Vandyke looked directly at him. Yves Bouchard, in the flesh.

Got you, you son of a bitch. After all these years, I've finally found you.

Cassie reached over and laid her hand atop Rafe's. "Sir Harlan, please let me introduce my date for tonight, my dear friend, Leonardo Kasan."

CHAPTER 3

Derek paced the hallway as he and Yvette waited outside Griffin Powell's study. Whenever he heard a shout or a crash, he paused to exchange concerned glances with Yvette, who stood serenely at the end of the corridor, her head bowed and her hands folded in a prayerlike gesture. For what seemed like the hundredth time, Derek checked his wristwatch. Although it had been barely twenty minutes since Sanders had gone into the study with Griffin, it felt more like twenty hours. The horrifically painful roar Griffin initially released had sent chills through Derek's body. Then several minutes later, silence had replaced the sound of unbearable pain. But only momentarily. One loud crash had followed another and then another, interrupted by periods of ominous quiet. And then Griffin had begun bellowing at the top of his lungs. His loud, gruff voice resonated with anguish, his words of remorse and self-condemnation clearly audible through the closed door. And all the while, they heard the soft, steady drone of Sanders's calm voice interspersed throughout Griff's ongoing savage tirade.

Derek could only imagine what was happening behind that closed door. If he were in Griffin's position, if Maleah was missing, presumed kidnapped by a deadly assassin, how would he have reacted?

A strange silence interrupted Derek's thoughts, a lingering quiet that signaled a conclusion. The door eased open and Sanders stood there looking as if he had survived a vicious battle, his facial features drawn and haggard, his gaze a blank stare. After he stepped out into the hall, leaving the door open behind him, Derek glanced into Griffin's study, a room he now barely recognized. In his tortured rage, Griff had destroyed the beautifully elegant and classically masculine room he had personally designed for his private use. Every stick of furniture—tables, chairs, ottomans—had been overturned. Only the large, sturdy Jacobean table remained upright, but the surface had been swept clean, the items scattered about on the wooden floor. Shattered lamps littered the Persian rug, as did the porcelain figurines that had once lined the mantel over the massive rock fireplace.

Yvette walked toward Sanders, her steps increasing in speed as she neared the study entrance. She paused in front of Sanders and waited for him to speak.

Derek suddenly sensed that his presence was superfluous. At this moment, there was nothing he could do for Griff. Sanders had done his part. Now, it was Yvette's turn. Without a word being spoken, Yvette and Sanders passed each other as he left Griff's study and she entered. When Sanders approached, Derek was still staring into the ransacked room, watching as Yvette walked up behind Griff, whose back was to her, lifted her arm, and placed her hand on his shoulder.

"She will help him," Sanders said.

Derek nodded.

"We have a lot to do," Sanders told him. "It

may well be tomorrow before Griffin is able to take charge again. In the meantime, I will need your assistance to address certain urgent matters."

Snapping out of his trancelike state, completely absorbed by the way Yvette doubled over and groaned in pain as she struggled to hold on to Griff. When she dropped to her knees, her hand clinging to Griff's leg, Derek forced himself to face Sanders.

"Yvette can do more for him now than you or I." Sanders reached behind him and closed the door. "But there is much you and I can and must do as soon as possible."

"Maleah should be here anytime now," Derek said. "You work up the game plan and we'll expedite it immediately."

"The first order of business is to assign agents to go to the cabin and search for any clues that might tell us what happened to Nicole." Sanders motioned for Derek to follow him as he moved down the hall, away from Griff's study and toward the foyer. "I need to tell Barbara Jean what has happened. She is waiting in our quarters. While I fill her in on the situation, will you please get in touch with Saxon Chappell and send him to Gatlinburg? And see if you can get in touch with Shaughnessy. Ask him to return to Griffin's Rest as soon as possible. If . . ." Sanders cleared his throat. "If it were to become necessary for us to subdue Griffin, Shaughnessy is the only agent we have who has the physical strength to help us do that."

"Anything else?" Derek asked.

"Get in touch with headquarters and have all available personnel called in and put to work tracking every airplane, boat, bus, and train that left the region in the past eight hours."

"Airplane departures should be the top priority," Derek suggested. "In all likelihood, if Anthony Linden abducted Nicole, he would have a private plane waiting to take her out of the country."

"Agreed." With a curt nod of his shaved head, Sanders walked briskly away, through the foyer, and down the hallway that led to his and Barbara Jean's quarters at the back of the mansion.

Derek headed toward the state-of-the-art-equipped office suite there at Griffin's Rest. He had taken only a few hurried steps when the front door opened and a voice called out to him.

"Derek!"

He turned, sighed with relief at the sight of the woman he loved, and rushed toward her as she raced straight into his arms. He hugged her to him before capturing her face between his open palms and kissing her long and hard. When she broke away and sucked in a deep breath, he grasped her hands and held them between their bodies.

"I am so damn glad to see you, Blondie."

"Yeah, you just made that perfectly clear."

Maleah tried to smile, but the effort failed. "Has there been any word on Nic?"

"Nothing."

"How's Griff?"

Derek grimaced. "Not good. Sanders told him that Nic is missing and Cully is dead. Now Yvette is in the study with him."

"If it wasn't for that woman—"

"Don't." Derek squeezed Maleah's hands. "Now is not the time to assign blame. We have to work together to keep Griff halfway sane and to do everything possible to locate Nic and bring her home."

With her lips pursed in reluctant, silent agreement, Maleah bobbed her head affirmatively.

"And for now, I think it's best if Griff doesn't know that Nic is pregnant," Derek said.

"Oh, God . . . " Maleah softly butted her head against Derek's shoulder. And then she stopped and looked up at him. "I know Nic. If she weren't pregnant, she would fight tooth and nail, but she's at a disadvantage because she is not going to do anything to jeopardize her baby's life." Tears gathered in Maleah's hazel-gold eyes.

He grasped her shoulders and shook her gently. "We have things to do. Go wash your face, pour yourself a stiff drink, and pull yourself together."

She offered him a fragile smile. "I'm okay." When he gave her a skeptical once-over, she told him, "Really. I'm fine. Let's get to work. Just tell me what I need to do first."

Rafe Byrne had used numerous aliases over the years; Leonardo Kasan was one of many. Since he had walked out of the London hospital over sixteen years ago with a face even he hadn't recognized, he had never once used his real name. He had been born Raphael Byrne, his lineage an equal mix of Irish and Italian, but that name meant nothing to him now. As a boy, he had dreamed of becoming either a priest like his uncle Stephano or an artist like his grandfather Byrne. Those dreams, along with every other worthwhile thing in his life, had been brutally and irrevocably stolen from him. First by Malcolm York. And then by York's special guests who had visited Amara for sport and pleasure, hunting young men in their prime by day and amusing themselves sexually in the evenings, each in his own way.

To say that he had hated York was a vast understatement. Malevolent to his very soul, York had taken a sweet and innocent boy with a kind heart and gentle spirit and turned him into a savage animal. On the island of Amara, Rafe had joined the other "perfect" specimens in York's dungeonlike prison, men and boys such as he who had once been normal human beings. He had been thrown into a world he had never known existed, into a dog-eat-dog world where one motto ruled supreme: Kill or be killed.

If not for a man named Griffin Powell, Rafe

would not have survived even the first month on Amara. He owed Griff his life. But there were times, those lonely, soul-searching moments when a man cannot hide from himself, that Rafe wished Griff had never intervened. For three years on Amara, the angelic boy who dreamed of devoting his life to God had endured every aspect of hell here on Earth. And for the past sixteen years he had existed for one purpose. He had become a brutal, merciless fallen angel, a weapon of vengeance and punishment. He killed in the name of justice and had never asked forgiveness from the God who had forsaken him.

"Leo, please let's go with the others." Cassie Wilder tugged on his sleeve, her touch jerking him abruptly from his memories. "Harlan knows the most decadent places in London where all sorts of wicked things go on."

"If that's what you would like to do." Rafe slid his hand down her back to rest in the curve of her spine, playing his role as her attentive date. "Is the entire dinner party going?"

"I don't think so. Just a few of us."

The group mingled in the private room, several saying their good-byes with air kisses and insipid mock hugs, while others lingered, apparently eager to follow Harlan Benecroft to whatever den of iniquity he planned to visit.

"You two simply must join us." Harlan came over and draped his hefty arm around Cassie's shoulders. "I know this delicious, exclusive club where the entertainment is marvelously titillating."

"We wouldn't miss it for the world," Cassie assured him as she snuggled against Rafe. "Leo is such a darling about doing whatever I want to do."

"A man must never give a woman everything she wants." Yves Bouchard joined the conversation, a wide smile on his aging pretty boy face. "You must remember that a woman wants a man to be a man and never a doormat."

Rafe forced a phony, amused laugh. "I am always prepared to learn from an older and wiser man."

Bouchard searched Rafe's face for any sign of sarcasm and apparently seeing none, he laughed as he slapped Rafe on the back. "I believe I'm going to like you, Kasan."

"The limousine is waiting," Harlan said. "Come, children, the night is young and full of promise."

Rafe kept his arm around Cassie's waist as they joined Harlan's small group of fun-seekers. On the deepest level of his being, two emotions stirred to life—revulsion and anticipation. The moment Bouchard's hand touched him, Rafe had cringed, wanting nothing more than to kill the man on the spot. The last time Bouchard had touched him . . . But anticipation outweighed the revulsion. After over a decade and a half of searching for the elusive billionaire, he had

51

found him. It was only a matter of time until he sent the son of a bitch to meet his maker.

Patience.

Over the years, he had cultivated the invaluable qualities of perseverance, patience, and self-control.

Rafe was one of six who entered the elevator with Harlan. Cassie and a bone-thin, middle-aged brunette were the only two women in the group. And the way the older woman kept eyeing Cassie, made Rafe suspect she was a lesbian. He knew for a fact that Cassandra Wilder swung both ways and proudly boasted to the press about her sexual exploits as a bisexual woman. Bouchard, though cordial with the others, seemed disinterested in the two women, in Rafe, and in the other three men.

Once ensconced in Harlan's limo, the group of seven settled back as their host popped a fresh bottle of champagne and filled their glasses to overflowing. Rafe sipped the sparkling wine while the others devoured theirs. He occasionally nuzzled Cassie's neck and laid a possessive hand on her knee, all the while subtly observing the others.

Twenty minutes later, the limo pulled up at the back of a dark warehouse near the Thames. A slightly inebriated Harlan exited first. His guests followed his lead like ducklings waddling behind their mama. After removing a key from his pocket and unlocking a heavy metal door, their host entered the building and led them down a dimly lit corridor to a service elevator. As the clanking elevator ascended, the sound of music and laughter drifted downward from the loft area.

When they reached the top level, two naked, muscular black guards opened a set of double doors to reveal the private club.

Heavy, room-darkening drapes covered all the windows, cocooning the massive loft in shadowy warmth. The diffused lighting, soft pinks and vivid reds, created a mysteriously wanton atmosphere. Small stages set up at ten foot intervals around the outskirts of the huge room surrounded the crowds of onlookers, men and women of various ages and races. On eight of the twelve separate podiums, one or more performers participated in some type of sex act for the entertainment of the club's patrons.

Rafe had seen this type of club before and knew that for the right price any of the performers could be bought—for the night, the week or indefinitely.

Around the world, people were bought and sold as if they were livestock, some sold into servitude, some into sexual bondage, and others as prey in hunting games for bored sadists who no longer found hunting wild animals a challenge.

He knew only too well the nightmarish hell in which these boys and girls, who ranged in age from preteens to young adults in their early twenties, existed. That world was populated by rich and powerful perverts such as Harlan Benecroft and Yves Bouchard, a world created and perpetuated by men such as Malcolm York. A world from which he had barely escaped with his life. A world that had robbed him of his innocence, his dreams, and his very soul.

This time when he entered the dark underbelly of society, Rafe Byrne entered as a predator, not as the prey. He would keep up the ruse for one purpose and one purpose only—to lure Yves Bouchard into a trap from which he could not escape.

After their brief conversation, Anthony Linden had escorted Nic back into the sleeping quarters of the private jet, instructed her to sit on the bed, and once she was seated, had taken her photo using his mobile phone.

"Your husband will want proof that you're alive and well."

Alive maybe. And for now, she was as well as she could be under the circumstances. But more than once during the flight, she had fought the urge to throw up. If she did vomit, she would pass it off as nothing more than motion sickness. She intended to keep the fact that she was pregnant a secret from her abductor. If Griffin Powell's wife was worth a king's ransom, what would Griff's wife and child be worth?

Having gone over half a dozen different scenarios during her seclusion, Nic had come to the conclusion that until they reached their destination and she acquired more information, she couldn't devise a workable plan of action.

Suddenly she felt the plane begin to descend. Was the pilot preparing to land? Surmising that at least three or four hours had passed since she had awakened from her drugged sleep and found herself on the plane with Linden, Nic tried to think of exactly where over the U.S. they might be. Linden had said they were traveling south. If he had been telling her the truth, then calculating four hours plus however many hours she had been asleep, they could be about to land somewhere in Mexico or Central America or even on one of the Caribbean islands. If she was allowed to talk to Griff, she would find out a way to give him a clue to her whereabouts, assuming she could figure out where they were.

As the plane continued its slow, steady decline, Anthony Linden unlocked the bedroom door and motioned to her. "We'll be landing shortly, Nicole. It's time for me to prepare you for departure."

A short time later, she understood what he'd meant by preparing her. Within minutes of their arrival at only God knew where, Linden yanked Nic to her feet, pulled her hands behind her back, bound her wrists, and then quickly gagged and blindfolded her. With a tight grip on her upper arm, he guided her off the plane. The moment the warm air swooshed around her, Nic sucked in a deep breath. Almost hot except for the balmy breeze, the weather was decidedly tropical. Linden hadn't been lying. They had flown south.

Once her feet hit solid ground, she was all but dragged away from the plane and to a waiting vehicle. Not a car or truck. As the driver, who hadn't spoken a word, jerked the gearshift into reverse and backed up, Nic realized she was seated beside someone—probably Linden—inside a jeep. No seat belt restraint, just the tight grip of a large, hard hand manacled around the back of her neck. Keeping quiet and staying alert, she breathed in the scents and listened to the sounds. She might not be able to see where she was, but she could use her other senses.

She knew only that they were south of the continental U.S., possibly in Mexico or even farther south in one of the Central American countries. She had no idea exactly where Linden was taking her or what awaited her upon their arrival. But she did know that she was a hostage, that she had been kidnapped because she was Griffin Powell's wife, that she was soon to be the guest of a man who called himself Malcolm York. And she suspected that the odds of her coming out of this alive were slim to none.

CHAPTER 4

Shortly before dawn, Griffin Powell emerged from his study, an unconscious Yvette in his arms. He had survived the past few hours and come through the darkest moments of his life solely because of Yvette's sacrifice. After learning that Nicole was missing, probably kidnapped by Anthony Linden, Griff had gone mad. The magnitude of his anger and frustration, coupled with his guilt and anguish, could have destroyed him. He had been on the edge of the abyss, inches from taking an irrevocable plunge. He would have lost his mind had Yvette not used all the power of her unique psychic talents to absorb enough of his emotions to restore his equilibrium. Long ago, she had saved him in a similar manner. He owed her not only his life, then and now, but his sanity.

If only he had explained everything to Nic. If only he had been completely honest with her from the very beginning.

"Sanders!" Griff shouted his best friend's name. Sanders was far more than a good friend; he was Griff's right-hand man and his most trusted confidant.

Within seconds, four people appeared, each rushing toward him. Shaughnessy Hood's hulking form moved with amazing speed and he reached Griff's side before Sanders, Derek, and Maleah.

Griff looked at Shaughnessy as he placed Yvette in the six-foot-six bodyguard's huge arms. Then he turned to Sanders. "She needs someone with her until she regains consciousness. Send for Meredith Sinclair. Tell her it's urgent. She'll know how to help Yvette."

"Meredith is with Luke Sentell," Sanders reminded him. "They're en route from Paducah, Kentucky. She went with Luke straight from London to return Michelle Allen's niece to her parents."

Griff grunted. He remembered now. The child, barely seven years old, would have needed a woman's tender care after the ordeal she had been through recently. Abducted by Linden from the safety of her own bed, whisked off to England, and held hostage as a means of forcing her aunt to do a madman's bidding, Jaelyn Allen had been rescued by Luke Sentell, with Yvette's protégée, Meredith, assisting him.

"Yes, of course, I remember now. As soon as Meredith returns to Griffin's Rest, send her directly to Yvette," Griff said. "In the meantime, choose another of Yvette's students to stay with her, preferably someone with the ability to soothe her."

Sanders nodded. "That would be Blythe Renshaw."

"Then send for her immediately and once that's done, join me in the office. I assume you've already begun—"

"Agents have been dispatched to the cabin and one to speak personally with Cully Redmond's sister," Sanders said. "All available personnel have been called in to headquarters in Knoxville and the wheels set in motion to obtain all possible info."

After assuring Griff that he had followed procedure without any delay, Sanders left to do as he had been instructed.

Griff called out to him, "Send in the house-cleaning crew to clean up in there." He inclined his head toward the utterly destroyed room.

Sanders paused and listened. He nodded once before walking away, without uttering a single word or giving a quick backward glance.

Griff then told Shaughnessy, "Take Dr. Meng upstairs to one of the guest rooms and stay with her until Ms. Renshaw arrives."

With the utmost care, the gentle giant of a man held Yvette as if she were made of spun glass as he immediately followed Griff's orders.

"You two, come with me," he said, sliding his gaze hurriedly from Derek to Maleah. "Once I place several calls to my contacts in D.C. and around the world, we will begin receiving a tremendous amount of information. Ninety-five percent of it will be worthless. It will be up to us to figure out which five percent can actually help us locate Nic."

Griff forced himself to look directly at Maleah, to face her and accept her wrath. No doubt at this very moment, she hated him almost as much as he hated himself. Maleah Perdue was his wife's best friend. She had stood by Nic, shared confidences with her, and possibly knew her better than anyone on Earth. Knew her even better than he did.

"I'm going to find her," Griff swore to Maleah.

She stared at him, tears moistening her eyes, her teeth clinched tightly. He sensed that she wanted to physically attack him, to claw his eyes out, to damn his soul to hell.

Mercy God, didn't she know he was already in hell?

Derek Lawrence grasped Maleah's hand.

"And we're going to help you find her," Derek said. "We're a cooperative team working together for the duration of this all-out manhunt. We have one goal—find Nicole and bring her home safely. Nothing else matters."

Morning sunlight poured into the room like melted butter over hot pancakes—soft, warm, and golden. As she roused from sleep, Nicole blinked her eyes several times, all the while her mind slightly muddled. At first, she wondered why Griff had opened the blinds when he usually kept the room dark until after they were both awake.

Still in that relaxed state between sleep and becoming fully alert, she turned over in bed and ran her hand out in search of her husband.

She was alone in bed. Griff must have gone downstairs already. He would bring her a cup of coffee soon, sit down on the bed, and give her a morning kiss.

Nicole's eyes snapped open wide.

She was not home at Griffin's Rest. This was not her bed. Griff was not downstairs.

After flipping over on her back, Nic gazed up at the white ceiling. In the quiet stillness of the room, she listened and heard the delicate hum of a motor. Easing herself into a sitting position in the center of the large king-size bed, Nic glanced up and down and then circled the entire room. A large ceiling fan with palm leaf–shaped blades rotated slowly, sending whiffs of cool air downward. The twenty-by-twenty-five-foot room, tastefully decorated with ornately carved dark furniture—four-poster bed, highboy, and large chest—was in direct contrast to the pale white and cream drapes, bed linens, and brocade material covering the armchairs and the chaise longue.

Where am I?

And then, once again, it all came flooding back, her memories like a tidal wave. Her abduction from the cabin in Gatlinburg. Her conversation with Anthony Linden aboard the private airplane. Being bound, gagged, and blindfolded upon arrival before being transported via a jeep to—? Where was she?

Linden had guided her from the jeep onto a boat. At that point everything was fuzzy, but she vaguely remembered being carried inside a building and . . . And what?

Damn it, he had drugged her again.

While sitting blindfolded on the boat, she had felt a sharp sting on her arm. Now, she realized that sting had been caused by a hypodermic needle. Apparently after she had fallen into a semi-unconscious state shortly before the boat docked, Linden had removed the gag and the blindfold and untied her wrists.

Nic scooted to the edge of the bed, slid her feet off onto the floor—her bare feet—and stood on the highly polished wooden floor. Someone had removed her shoes. She glanced down at herself and gasped. She was completely naked.

Who had undressed her?

What, if anything, had Linden—or anyone else—done to her?

Seeing a large gold-framed cheval mirror in the corner of the room, Nic ran straight to it and inspected herself from head to toe. No blood. No bruises. No sign of being abused. But then she had been unconscious. With cautious deliberation, she ran her fingers over her mound and between her thighs. Nothing there to indicate she had been violated.

As she searched the room for an exit—a way out—she discovered a luxurious white marble bathroom, a balcony overlooking an inner courtyard—lush with greenery and flowers, a pool in the center—and one locked door. Draped on a pink padded hanger on the back of the bathroom door, as if it had been placed there just for her, she found a cream satin robe. Without hesitation, she jerked it off the hanger and put it on, eager to cover her nakedness. Just as she knotted the satin belt around the robe, she heard the sound of a door opening and closing.

Her breath caught in her throat. Garnering her courage, she forced herself to walk out of the bathroom and back into the bedroom. Not knowing who had entered or what she would find, Nic stopped suddenly the moment she saw the dark-skinned woman, dressed in a colorful muumuu, carrying a large silver tray.

"Good morning, missus." The woman smiled at Nicole before she placed the tray atop the large table between the two armchairs.

"Who are you?" Nic tried her best to keep her voice calm, not an easy task considering the predicament she found herself in at the moment.

"I am called Lina," the woman replied. "You want I pour tea now?"

"No," Nic said and then added, "No, thank you."

"You want I make bath now?"

"No." She walked straight toward the woman

63

who appeared to be in her early twenties. "Lina, I want you to tell me where I am."

Lina looked at her as if she didn't understand the question. "You are here at Sea View." She pronounced the two words as if one, sounding like zee-few.

"Sea View? Is that the name of the town or this house?"

"You are hungry," Lina said, obviously ignoring Nic's question. "I bring you fresh fruit, tea, and bread. You sit. Eat. You feel much better."

"I feel fine." Nic skimmed her hands over her body from neck to waist. "Did you undress me?"

Her large brown eyes wide, Lina stared at Nic and shook her head.

"You didn't undress me? Then who did? Who took off my clothes?"

"Your clothes?"

"My shirt." She patted her upper torso. "My pants." She slid her hands over her lower torso. "Who took them off ?"

Lina smiled. "I take. You rest good."

Nic sighed with a combination of relief and frustration. The girl's accent sounded neither Spanish nor French. She had no idea what Lina's native language was.

"Where is Mr. Linden?"

Lina's expression changed immediately, going from warm and friendly to somber and quiet.

"Mr. Linden, the man who brought me here. Where is he?" Nic repeated her question.

Without saying another word, Lina hurried away from Nic. She beat her fist against the door and called loudly, "I go now." The door opened instantly. Nic rushed across the room as Lina walked out into the hall, but before she could follow the woman, a muscle-bound man with dark hair, beard, and mustache closed the door in her face.

Nic pressed herself, forehead first, her open palms following, against the wooden door. She curled her hands into fists and beat repeatedly against the locked door. After venting her vexation, she pushed aside her anger and fear and faced the facts. At the present moment, there was absolutely nothing she could do to free herself. There was no point in wasting her energy on useless emotions. In order to survive today and in the days ahead, she would be forced to adapt. She had to stay alive. And she had to protect her unborn child.

Lifting herself away from the locked and guarded door, Nic marched straight toward the silver serving tray. After taking a seat, she removed the covers from the dishes and poured herself a cup of hot tea. She was hungry. She hadn't eaten anything since yesterday. That wasn't good for her or her baby. Even though she was slightly nauseated, she forced herself to eat. First a piece of the delicious bread that she smothered with butter and jelly. After finishing off the bread and first cup of tea, she picked up a fork and speared a chunk of fresh pineapple.

All the while she nourished her body and the child inside her, Nic tried to remember everything from the moment she had left the airplane until she had been drugged and later locked in this room. She thought about the sounds she had heard, the scents she had smelled, the feel of the road beneath the jeep. The road had been bumpy, as if it were gravel or even dirt, and filled with potholes. Apparently the plane had landed somewhere on a private airstrip out in the middle of nowhere. There had been no distinct sounds or scents coming from a town or even a village they might have passed through on their journey from the jeep to the boat. She recalled only ambiguous nocturnal sounds, the feel of hot, muggy air and the smell of ripe vegetation. Nic suspected they were somewhere tropical, somewhere more than four hours from Knoxville, Tennessee. The warm, balmy breeze and the scent of saltwater suggested that they were near the ocean. A heavy floral perfume blended with the feel of humidity against her skin added weight to her supposition that they were in Mexico, Central America, or the Caribbean.

Lina's accent had not been Spanish. Did that mean Nic could rule out being in Mexico or Central America? Yes? No? Maybe? Not necessarily?

Because she suspected that Lina's native tongue was a bastardized version of other languages, Nic's gut instinct told her that she was in the Caribbean, on one of the islands where some type of either French patois or Creole Papiamento was spoken. Then again, Lina could have been transported from her original home and might even be a captive forced into servitude.

Did it really matter where she was? For all she knew, they could be on an uncharted, private island or in the jungles of Central America somewhere. Her suppositions could be wrong. Besides, what made her think she would ever get the chance to talk to Griff and manage to send him a coded message concerning her whereabouts?

"Raphael . . . my sweet boy . . . " Yvette murmured the words in her half-awake, half-asleep state.

She sensed his presence as if he were nearby, close enough to reach out and touch him. But he wasn't there beside her. She had dreamed about him, her dream a memory of long ago. Choosing not to open her eyes, she allowed the image of his face to appear inside her thoughts, the face of an angelic boy, the face of a teenage Raphael, not the transformed face of the twenty-year-old who had emerged from the London hospital.

If only we could have done more to help you. We offered to take you with us, but you refused. We knew what you intended to do and neither

Griff nor Sanders nor I tried to stop you. Would it have done any good if we had tried harder?

The first time she had held the frightened boy in her arms, she had known how pure and sweet and innocent he was. She had felt the goodness inside him, the gentle spirit that struggled to stay alive, and the kind heart that refused to die despite the torment he endured every day. He had tried to be strong and brave, to show no fear and survive without losing his own humanity.

In the beginning, he had been unable to hide his thoughts and feelings from her, his very soul an open book, easily read. And from the very beginning, she had not told Malcolm the complete truth about Raphael, knowing the truth would help her husband destroy the boy. In time Malcolm had become obsessed with Raphael and took particular pleasure in torturing him. His physical beauty lured two of Malcolm's frequent guests on Amara to ask specifically for Raphael whenever they visited, men who preferred boys in their teens to adult males or females of any age.

Why are you tormenting me, Rafe?

In her heart, Yvette knew that Raphael no longer existed. Although his body had survived and escaped, his heart and soul had died on Amara. Rafe Byrne existed, out there somewhere, a man on a mission, a heartless, soulless creature.

Yvette opened her eyes to see a concerned Blythe Renshaw hovering over her. Blythe, sparkling with an effervescent loveliness that went beyond her physical appearance to encompass every aspect of her being, smiled warmly when she saw that Yvette was awake.

"How do you feel?" Blythe asked.

"Tired. But that is quite normal." She held out her hand. "Please, help me to sit up."

Blythe grasped Yvette's hand and assisted her. "Are you hungry? Ms. Hughes said to let her know when you woke up and she'd bring something for you."

Slightly woozy, Yvette gripped the edge of the mattress as she slid her legs around and settled both feet on the floor. "I'm not hungry."

"Do you need anything? What can I do to—?"

"Stop fussing," Yvette said. "Sit back down. I'm fine. Really." She looked directly at her protégée, one of six gifted young people who possessed special psychic talents and had come to her for understanding and guidance. "Blythe, did I talk in my sleep? Did I say something, anything you could understand?"

"You mumbled, but I couldn't understand most of what you were saying. Only a few words."

"And those words were?"

"A name. You called out a name several times."

"What name?"

"Raphael."

"What else did I say?"

Blythe flushed. "You said, 'My sweet boy.' And

69

you said . . ." Blythe cleared her throat. "You said, 'Let me hold you and kiss you and take away the pain.' "

"Thank you for telling me." She could see that Blythe was curious. Everyone who knew Dr. Yvette Meng knew there was no special man in her life, no husband, boyfriend, or lover. And as far as most knew, there never had been anyone special. "Raphael was someone very dear to me many years ago."

Yvette forced herself to stand despite feeling desperately weak. She had to rebuild her strength as quickly as possible. Griffin needed her. She intended to use every means available to her, and that included her protégés, in order to help Griffin and the others find Nicole.

"You need more rest," Blythe said as she rushed to help Yvette.

She clutched her student's arm. "I need you to do something for me, something that under ordinary circumstances I would never ask."

"You know that I will do anything for you."

Yvette clung to Blythe. "Are you willing to allow me to drain your energy, to take it from you?"

"You want to . . . ?"

"It will take me days to recover otherwise. At this very moment, I am on the verge of fainting." Yvette swayed unsteadily on her feet. "Once I lose consciousness again, I don't know how long I will sleep. I am needed now. Do you understand?"

"Yes."

"Then may I take your strength and energy?"

Blythe's face paled. "Yes, of course. Do what you must."

Yvette tugged on Blythe's hand and they sat on the bed side by side. Within moments, the two had connected. Mentally, emotionally, psychically.

Once she had absorbed enough of Blythe's youthful energy to restore herself to a normal state, Yvette knew what she had to do first. She had to convince Griff that finding Rafe Byrne needed to be a top priority. She had sensed Rafe's presence for a reason. In some as yet unknown way, Nicole's disappearance was connected not only to the pseudo-York, but to the boy who had become a killer of monsters and by doing so had become a monster himself.

He shuddered with release, his entire body on fire with passion as he climaxed. Melting his body into hers, he clung to the woman lying beneath him, savoring this moment, allowing himself the pretense that they loved each other. The first time they had been forced to have sex, she had been the one to comfort him, to hold him after he lost his virginity, to promise him that he could survive the humiliation.

"Be strong, sweet boy," she had whispered in his ear. "I will not share your secrets with him. I will protect you."

• • •

Rafe Byrne's eyes flew wide open as he awoke from the fragmented dream. A dream of the boy he had once been and the woman who had taken his virginity and stolen his heart.

Sweat dampened his bare chest and moistened his face. He didn't want to remember her, didn't want to feel anything tender and loving, not even in his dreams.

During his years on Amara, as he grew from a naïve boy of barely seventeen into a tormented young man of twenty, the comfort she had given him became a mutual give and take. It had become something they shared, something he had believed that she cherished as much as he did.

In time, he had fallen in love with her and had lived for those precious moments they shared alone. Usually, they had an audience of lascivious men, titillated by observing them perform. Sometimes her husband demanded a private showing. He would sit in the dark and watch. And then there were those rare occasions when it was just the two of them, when she had been instructed to "read his mind." In those quiet, gentle moments when they made love—and he had foolishly believed she loved him—he had known that he could endure anything as long as he could be with her. The beatings. The deadly hunts. Even the brutal rapes.

But in the end, once Griffin Powell and Damar

Sanders killed Malcolm York and his henchmen and they had escaped from Amara, he had lost her.

How can you lose something that was never yours?

She had cared about him, had helped and protected him, but she had cared for all the others, too, especially Griffin Powell. She had helped Griffin, protected him, and in the end had enabled him to destroy her husband.

She had no more been in love with him than she had any of the other men her husband forced her to have sex with for either his amusement or to gain information.

Their sexual encounters had not been love-making. Not to her. He had been a fool to ever think otherwise. If she had loved anyone, it had been Griffin. And in the end, it had been the giant blond warrior who had saved her from her husband.

A part of him hated Griffin, as irrational as it was for him to feel such animosity toward a man who had saved his life time and time again. But on some level, he still felt as if Griffin had taken Yvette away from him.

That's not true and you know it. You chose not to go with them, not to be a part of Yvette's life. She no more belongs to him than she belongs to you. Whatever she felt for Griffin or for you years ago on Amara, she belongs to no man now.

The body lying next to Rafe stirred and flung a long, slender arm across his chest, her movements rustling the silk sheets. He glanced at the woman, seeing her clearly in the sunlight shining through the row of windows in the bedroom of Cassandra Wilder's loft apartment. The woman lived up to her name—Wilder—in and out of bed. She was insatiable, like a bitch in heat.

Rafe stretched languidly, wondering what time it was. Probably noon or later. They had not returned to Cassie's place until nearly dawn.

As he turned from Cassie, intending to get up, find his clothes, and discreetly leave before she awoke, he felt another warm body lying next to him on the opposite side of the bed. He reached out and ran his hand across the darkly tanned body of the brunette Cassie had chosen at Harlan Benecroft's private club—Body Parts—and brought home with them. Cassie had paid for the woman's services, for her to become the third party in their ménage à trois.

The dark-haired woman whose name he didn't remember, if he'd ever known it, sighed heavily and cuddled against him. He stared at her, admittedly enjoying the sight of her voluptuous breasts, the curve of her waist, the tempting waxed V between her slender thighs. She was young. Probably no more than twenty. How many years had she been a prostitute, a sex slave owned by one of Sir Harlan's contemporaries?

He couldn't waste his time or energy on feeling anything akin to pity for her. He couldn't save her. He wasn't in the business of rescuing others. This girl, like Cassie, meant nothing to him. They were a means to an end. They were his intro into Harlan Benecroft's world. And he needed Benecroft to believe he was a rich and powerful man who didn't care how he made his millions or how much it cost him to appease his sexual appetites. Cassie had led him to Benecroft and Benecroft had led him to his ultimate target—Yves Bouchard.

Rafe lifted himself up and over the luscious brunette, landed quietly on both feet, and picked up his scattered clothing on his way to the door. Later, he would order Cassie two or three dozen roses and wait until the florist delivered them before he called her.

Body Parts was only the tip of the iceberg as far as sex clubs went. What he needed now was access to the best of the best, the darkest, most perverted slave markets, the places that Yves Bouchard frequented on a regular basis.

CHAPTER 5

By midafternoon that day, Griff had become totally absorbed in spearheading the manhunt for Nicole. Utilizing her special abilities to absorb his emotions while at the same time infusing him with her own strength and energy, Yvette had given him what he needed most at this time—to function in a somewhat normal manner. He could not change the past, couldn't undo what had been done. But what he did now, today, and tomorrow and the next day, could mean the difference between life and death for Nicole. He had to find her and rescue her. The alternative was unthinkable.

He had two choices. Succumb to his emotions again, which would render him completely useless. Or he could focus on what had to be done.

He had chosen the latter.

Nic was still alive. He was certain of that. If she were dead, he would know, somewhere deep in his soul.

And as long as she was alive, there was hope. He clung to that knowledge, aware that it was his lifeline, the only thing keeping him from sinking into madness.

The Powell Agency headquarters in downtown Knoxville, housed in the Powell Building, was seventy percent staffed and by tomorrow morning would be fully staffed with every employee in place. He had set up three shifts so that the agency would be completely active around the clock. Holt Keinan would remain in Sevier County to monitor the sheriff 's investigation into Cully Redmond's death and Nic's abduction. Ben Corbett had arrived in Louisville and had informed Cully's sister about his death. After he had done whatever the family needed him to do for them, Ben would return to Griffin's Rest.

Griff had half his agents, including those employed around the world, on standby, all of them ready to begin a universal search for Nic. He was in hourly contact with Thorndike Mitchum, who headed their London bureau and oversaw the agency's satellite agencies throughout Europe, Asia, and the Middle East. Mitchum had assigned a number of agents to locate and tail Harlan Benecroft, on the off chance he might in some way have a connection to the pseudo-York and therefore to Anthony Linden. They had no real proof that Linden had kidnapped Nic, but the consensus among Griff's associates was that in all likelihood Linden had abducted her. And the odds were that Linden worked for the man who called himself Malcolm York.

Brendan Richter, one of Powell's top agents and a former Interpol officer, had contacted old friends with the world's largest international police organization. Working under the assumption that Anthony Linden was alive, Linden was once again placed on Interpol's Most Wanted list, as was Malcolm York's old friend, Yves Bouchard. Unfortunately, Harlan Benecroft, York's cousin, had managed to stay just under the ICPO's radar. Benecroft was a worthless piece of trash, an old pervert who dabbled in various illegal activities, but managed to keep his involvement undetectable by law enforcement. Unlike the real York and his peers, Harlan Benecroft had not made most of his millions illegally. He had inherited the family fortune, presumed to be worth in the neighborhood of half a billion U.S. dollars.

At Griff's request, Sanders had put in calls to numerous contacts from Hong Kong to Johannesburg, with one objective in mind. Locate and contact Rafe Byrne. Their Amara comrade, whom they had not seen in sixteen years, had proven to be an invisible man. If not for hearing, through mutual associates, about the deaths of certain men over the years, men who had been frequent visitors on Amara, they would never have known if Rafe was dead or alive. Apparently, he was still very much alive. Less than a month ago, the slaughtered body of Ciro Mayorga had been discovered in an old horse barn in Argentina.

If anyone could find the pseudo-York, it was Raphael Byrne.

But first, they had to find Rafe.

Lost in thought, at first Griffin didn't hear Barbara Jean speaking to him. Only when she reached up from her wheelchair and touched his arm did he realize she was there.

"I'm sorry. What did you say?" Griff asked.

"You haven't eaten a bite since breakfast yesterday morning and then only toast and coffee," Barbara Jean informed him, a maternal censure in her mild voice. "You'll be no good to yourself or anyone else if you pass out from hunger."

He knew she meant well, that Barbara Jean looked out for everyone there at Griffin's Rest like a mother hen. If he didn't eat something soon, she just might try force-feeding him.

"I promise I'll eat."

"Fine. I've brought in a tray of sandwiches and put on fresh pots of coffee." She nodded to the two coffeemakers on a table in the back of the office suite, both now brewing a steady stream of hot, black coffee. "Take a break soon." She glanced around the room and said, "All of you. No one touched the lunch that Mattie and I prepared."

"How about we stop and eat in shifts?" Griff suggested.

"Fine. As long as y'all eat." She looked pointedly at Sanders.

He didn't respond verbally, but did make eye contact when he nodded.

Barbara Jean waited until Griff poured himself a cup of coffee and picked up a sandwich before she wheeled out of the office. After downing a sip of coffee and taking a bite out of a ham-and-cheese sandwich, Griff realized he actually was hungry. Derek, Maleah, and Sanders soon joined him at the refreshment table set up in the back of the office. The other three agents—Shaughnessy Hood, Brendan Richter, and Everett Dawson—continued working.

Griffin wolfed down the rest of the sandwich and then poured a second cup of coffee. He caught Maleah Perdue staring at him. Sensing she wanted to say something to him, he looked directly at her.

"Go ahead," he told her. "Let me have it."

Maleah glared at him, her anger barely restrained. She clenched her teeth tightly. Griff figured she really was going to let him have it with both barrels. Hell, he wished she would. He deserved it.

But before she managed to compose herself enough to say anything, Derek reached out and placed his hand in the center of her back. Griff noticed Maleah relaxing, the tension in her body easing and the strained muscles in her face softening.

"Maleah knows that we all want the same thing," Derek said. "Nothing else matters now except finding Nic and bringing her home."

"Derek's right," Maleah finally said, then slammed her coffee mug down on the table and walked away, straight to the door and out of the office.

"She doesn't hate me any more than I hate myself," Griff told Derek.

"She doesn't really hate you. She hates what's happened. She loves Nic. She's worried sick and she's holding on by a thin thread." Derek looked directly at Griff. "The same way you are."

• • •

Lina had delivered the makeup bag and clothes an hour ago. The panties, bra, sundress, and sandals were all expensive designer items. When Nic had tried to question Lina, she had seemed confused. Apparently the young woman understood very little English. Or she had done an excellent job of pretending she didn't. Either way, Nic had gotten no useful information from her.

When Lina had offered to brush her hair and apply her makeup, Nic had declined.

"You hurry. Not keep him waiting."

"Don't keep who waiting?" Nic had asked.

Lina had shaken her head, then said, "You be ready." She grabbed Nic's hand. "Yes, please."

Sensing the woman's fear, Nic had asked, "And if I'm not ready when he comes to get me, what will happen to you?"

Lina had shifted her gaze nervously right and left. "If I am bad"—she lowered her voice to a whisper—"I must be punished."

Every instinct Nic possessed urged her to rebel and demand that Lina join her, for the two of them to go up against Lina's oppressor, to take on their mutual enemy. But common sense quickly reined in Nic's immediate response. "You don't need to worry," Nic promised. "I'll be ready."

And so here she was, wearing a calf-length, bright yellow sundress with white leather sandals and pale yellow underwear, her hair neatly brushed, and her makeup applied sparingly. She was ready. But for whom? And for what?

With each passing minute, Nic grew more nervous as one frightening scenario after another flashed through her mind. She didn't know what, if anything, had happened to her while she'd been drugged, but she chose to believe she had been left alone to sleep. She had no idea what might happen to her today. The only thing she knew for sure was that Anthony Linden, the man suspected of being the assassin hired to kill Powell agents and members of their families, had kidnapped her. She had no doubt that if he was ordered to kill her, he would not hesitate.

But Linden could have easily killed her at her Gatlinburg cabin yesterday. Whoever Linden worked for, the person issuing the orders, didn't want her dead. At least not yet. She had been abducted because she was Griffin Powell's wife and the mysterious "he" intended to use her to make Griff suffer. Would he torture her? Would he subject her to untold humiliation and physical torment? If "he" was the pseudo-York and anything like the real York had been, then he was capable of terrifying atrocities. Hadn't he already hired Linden to murder six innocent people associated with the Powell Agency? Hadn't he, by holding her seven-year-old niece hostage, forced a Powell agent to kill one of Yvette's psychic protégés and ordered her to kill Maleah Perdue?

A man such as that was capable of anything.

Sitting quietly on the edge of the chaise longue, doing her best to steel her nerves and prepare herself for whatever might happen, Nic jumped as if she'd been shot when the bedroom door opened.

Anthony Linden, freshly shaved, his bald head smooth and shiny, his white slacks and shirt slightly wrinkled, entered the room. "Good afternoon, Nicole. I trust you've been provided everything you need."

She rose to her feet and faced him. Surveying him from head to toe, she realized several things all at once. He was a sturdily built man in his early to midforties, muscular and fit. He wore no disguise, allowing her to see the real man. Since she would be able to identify him, it was highly unlikely he would allow her to live.

"You're really quite a beautiful woman," Linden told her. "Dressed and undressed."

Nic's stomach clenched. He had seen her naked. Had he done more than look at her?

She hated the way he smiled at her, cocky and self-assured, with a hint of mockery. When she glared at him, her contempt no doubt visible in her expression, he laughed.

"You are not my type, Mrs. Powell," Linden assured her. "Some men may like the statuesque Amazon warrior type of woman. I prefer a smaller, less fierce female."

Nic glared at him.

"Your virtue is intact. Lina undressed you. All I did was enjoy the scenery. Besides, you are off-limits, except by special permission from our host."

"And who is our host?"

"You will find out in due time. He's eager to meet Griffin Powell's wife."

"Griffin Powell's estranged wife."

"Your choice, I believe, not your husband's. A decision you made after he received a letter informing him where he could find Yvette Meng's long-lost daughter."

"You seem to know a great deal, Mr. Linden, for a mere employee."

"Please, I insist you call me Tony." He held out his hand, which she ignored. "Our host would like for me to give you a tour of this house and the grounds and allow you to observe one of several pastimes available to his guests."

"Do I have a choice . . . Tony?"

"No, Nicole, you do not."

"Then by all means, give me a tour. The sooner that's done, the sooner I'll meet our host, right?"

After giving her another unnerving smile, he called out to the guard in the hallway. She walked up beside Linden, but refused to touch him. When the door opened, he escorted her out into the hall, down a long corridor, and straight to a double set of stairs leading down to the ground floor level of what appeared to be a rather large mansion.

"There are nine bedrooms in this twelve-thousand-square-foot house, one of many around the world owned by my employer," Linden told her as he led her through the marble-floored foyer, into a huge parlor, then a dining room that easily seated a dozen people, and out onto the patio and pool area that she could see from her upstairs bedroom.

"You may use the pool whenever you like or you can sunbathe in one of the lounge chairs." Linden raked his gaze over her breasts. "I have no doubt that your lovely olive skin tans beautifully."

He was flirting with her, playing host as if she were a willing guest, and prolonging the inevitable for a reason. She suspected that he was deliberately trying to lull her into a false sense of security. If so, there could be only one reason—he wanted whatever happened next to surprise her, perhaps shock her or even scare the hell out of her.

Meredith Sinclair, Yvette's most gifted protégée, and Luke Sentell, the Powell Agency's from Black Ops agent, arrived at Griffin's Rest shortly before six that evening. The moment she arrived, Griff sent Meredith upstairs to Yvette, explaining to her what was needed. He had then taken Luke into his den and shut the door.

"Sanders contacted us while we were en route from Paducah," Luke said. "I assume you have no word about Mrs. Powell yet?"

"No, nothing," Griff said.

"Tell me what I can do."

"Your expertise will no doubt be needed more later on, but for now, you can contact anyone and everyone you know who might be able to help us. Even the smallest bit of information could help locate Nic."

"I understand. I'll start immediately. I can make several phone calls, but I can gain more info out in the field. I should leave tonight, if at all possible."

"Let Sanders know what you need and he'll see that you get it. You'll report in to me or if I'm unavailable to Sanders or Derek Lawrence."

"I'll need a line of credit and—"

"Tell Sanders how much and he'll transfer the funds in the morning," Griff said. "Spend whatever is necessary. There is no amount too high to pay for the right information."

"And no action off-limits."

"Absolutely. Do whatever needs to be done." Griff had just given a trained killer, albeit trained by the U.S. government, carte blanche to kill. "While you're gathering info, see what you can do to help Sanders locate a man who was on Amara with us. His name was Raphael Byrne then. He has probably been using various aliases the past sixteen years. Sanders can give you all the information we have on him."

"Do I need to know why we're looking for Mr. Byrne?"

"Because he could be our best chance, maybe our only chance, of finding the man who calls himself Malcolm York. We all agree that odds are the fake York orchestrated Nic's abduction."

When Linden opened the double doors in the foyer, the doors that led outside to the front of the mansion, Nic held her breath. Was there any way she could escape? The armed guards outside the doorway gave her the answer—no way in hell. While she halted on the expansive veranda, Linden walked ahead of her, down the three steps to the yard, and then turned and held out his hand.

"Come along, Nicole. There is a great deal to see before nightfall."

And just what happened at nightfall?

She remembered Griff telling her that Malcolm York's hunts always stopped at the end of the day and if a kill had not been made earlier, one of the wounded human prey was singled out to be killed at nightfall.

When she hesitated, Linden frowned. "I would prefer not having to force you. If that becomes necessary, it won't be pleasant for either of us."

Reminding herself that far more than her own life was on the line, Nic went down the steps and directly over to Linden's side. He smiled.

"Good girl. I have to admit that your compliance has surprised me. I had expected you to put up even more of a fight than you have."

"Don't mistake cooperation for weakness," she told him.

He lifted his brow and stared at her. "Duly warned. Now come along. I'll show you where the prized stock is kept before we join the others in today's hunt."

Nic forced herself to keep moving, to stay at Linden's side without betraying any sign of emotion. He had to know that she possessed some knowledge of Griff's experiences on Amara and therefore had some idea what to expect. But like a little boy eager to show off his new bicycle, Linden hurried her along, away from the house and down a long, winding, brick walkway. All the while he softly hummed a rather pleasant tune. A building that vaguely resembled an open-air pavilion stood at the top of a nearby hill. Mentally and emotionally preparing herself for whatever she might see, Nic didn't slow her pace as she followed Linden up the steps set into the hillside that took them all the way to the large, thatch-roofed structure. She wanted to stop, to turn around, and run away as fast as she could. But she didn't run.

Do what you have to do. Stay strong. Show no weakness.

As they approached the huge dirt-floored hut, she noticed several armed guards patrolling the area. Linden guided her from one large wooden cage to the next, each of the first four empty.

"These four are taking part in today's hunt," Linden said. "It's a small party today. Only six hunters."

She stopped and stared at the empty cages. Her own husband had once lived inside a cage as these men did.

"Come along. I'll show you the two lucky bastards who weren't chosen for today's adventure."

The two remaining cages were occupied by young men, both bearded and dirty, their hair touching their shoulders, their pants and shirts in rags. She forced herself to look at them, to really see them, and reminded herself that this was what it must have been like for Griff on Amara. One man lay on the dirt floor, his scrawny body curled into a fetal ball, his eyes closed, and a soft moan coming from deep in his chest. The other man wore a set of leg irons and wrist manacles, the two connected to restrict his movements. When Nic stopped in front of his cage, he stared straight at her.

"Come to feed the animals?" he asked.

His question startled her. She jerked back and away from the cage.

He was tall and still somewhat muscular, despite being much too thin. His cheeks were sunken and she could count his ribs. But there was fire in his brown eyes, a blaze born of anger and hatred and a will to live. She recognized that look only too well.

"I'm not here by choice either," she told him.

"Then God help you."

By the end of the day, approximately twenty-eight hours after Nicole Baxter Powell had disappeared, the Powell Agency's all-out manhunt for her was fully operational. Every resource known to man had been employed. Every contact Griff, Sanders, Luke Sentell, Brendan Richter, and Derek Lawrence knew, on even the most superficial level, had been utilized. The resources of the FBI, the CIA, Scotland Yard, MI6, and Interpol had been unofficially placed at Griffin Powell's disposal. There wasn't a law enforcement or government agent in the Free World who wasn't interested in apprehending Anthony Linden and anyone associated with him.

Maleah had set aside her anger, realizing that venting her feelings toward Griff would be counterproductive to the goal they shared. Besides that, she didn't doubt for a minute that there was nothing she could say that Griff hadn't already said to himself. He knew the part his duplicity had played in Nic's present fate. He blamed himself, as well he should, for what had happened to her.

Derek came up beside her and whispered in her ear, "You're staring daggers at Griff again."

She glanced at Derek, her brand-new fiancé, with whom she wanted to spend the rest of her life. Under normal circumstances, they would be discussing wedding and honeymoon plans.

"I'll try not to throw any more daggers his way," Maleah said.

Derek draped his arm around her shoulders. "It's not all his fault, you know. He begged Nic not to leave Griffin's Rest. You have to lay part of the blame at her feet. If she had stayed here—"

Maleah whipped around, her quick move knocking Derek's arm off her shoulders, and glared at him, barely able to believe what he had just said.

"You men are all alike. You stick together, defend one another, even when you know something is your fault." The more she said, the louder her voice became so that by the time she said, "If Griff hadn't lied to Nic over and over again about his relationship with Dr. Fragile Flower Meng, she wouldn't have felt that she had no choice but to leave here."

Suddenly, you could have heard a pin drop in the office suite, and Maleah realized that everyone had heard her infuriated outburst. When she glanced around the room and made eye contact with the other agents, they looked away. Sanders turned his back to her as he concentrated completely on the computer screen in front of him. Only Griffin Powell didn't flinch or back down as he met her gaze in a straightforward manner.

"Griffin lied by omission," Yvette Meng said from where she stood in the open doorway,

Meredith Sinclair directly behind her. "He deeply regrets that he was not completely honest with Nicole before they married. He should have explained more fully the complexity of our past relationship." She emphasized the word *past*.

"Yeah, I'd say he should have explained the complexity," Maleah said, so upset that her voice trembled. She realized she was on the verge of tears. "Especially one major complexity, namely a child that he may have fathered."

"Blondie, don't do this." Derek looked at her pleadingly.

"No, don't stop her," Griff said. "Everything she's said is true."

Derek went around the room quietly, almost unnoticed, until Maleah realized that he had ushered everyone toward the door and that Yvette had entered alone and gone to Griff's side. Damn it, she had allowed her emotions to control her actions. Her outburst had served no purpose other than blowing off some built-up steam.

"I suppose I should apologize for making a scene," Maleah said.

"It's all right. You're Nic's best friend," Griff told her. "I know where all that anger is coming from and you're justified in—"

"Justified or not, I swear it won't happen again."

Just as she swore to keep a lid on her temper and deal with her animosity toward Griff, she caught a glimpse of Derek in her peripheral vision as he walked over and stood behind Sanders, who had apparently summoned Derek. Maleah turned her head just enough to see that Derek was looking directly at Sanders's computer screen. A startled expression crossed his face. He shut his eyes for a moment and laid his hand on Sanders's shoulder.

"What's going on over there?" Maleah asked.

Sanders swiveled his chair around and stood up beside Derek. The two men faced her just as Griffin and Yvette responded by turning around to see what was going on.

Sanders looked squarely at Yvette. "Stay with him" was all he said to her.

Derek and Sanders stepped aside before Derek said, "The Powell Agency just received confirmation that Nicole is alive. We've been sent a photo of her."

Griffin stormed across the room, Yvette barely managing to keep up with him. He stopped in front of the computer where Sanders had been working and stared at the photograph there on the twenty-one-inch monitor. Maleah peeked around Griff's shoulder and gasped when she saw a picture of her friend lying on silk sheets in the middle of a king-size bed. Nic was sound asleep. And she was also as naked as the day she was born.

Before anyone had a chance to completely digest the implication of the nude photograph, Griff rammed his big fist into the computer screen.

CHAPTER 6

Griff plowed through his concerned friends and employees, bolted out of the office suite, and charged down the hall, the picture of Nic, naked and vulnerable, forever burned into his brain. He had shaken off Yvette's comforting hand as she tried to connect with him. He didn't want her to ease his pain. The others had called out to him, but he hadn't heard a word they said. A bloody rage roaring inside his head drowned out every sound except an accusatory inner voice telling him that everything was his fault. Nic's kidnapping was his fault. Anything that happened to her was his fault.

After Amara and the years when he had diligently pursued claiming Malcolm York's fortune for his widow—for Yvette—he had avoided all but the most superficial relationships. And when he had returned to the United States a billionaire, with a mysterious past, and had become one of the most sought-after bachelors in the South, he had lived up to his reputation. He had gone through women as if they were a disposable commodity, keeping his affairs on a purely physical level and avoiding any emotional attachments. His actions had not been as selfish as others might assume. By not allowing himself to become emotionally involved, he was not only protecting himself, but the women in his life.

Beneath his expensive tailor-made suits, Griffin Powell was a beast with deadly survival instincts, instincts honed to perfection during his four years on Amara. When your life depended on acquiring the skills necessary to stay alive, you either adapted and became as cunningly diabolical as your captor or you died. Griff was a survivor. He had done whatever was necessary to stay alive and in the process became a dangerous wild animal.

And then FBI Special Agent Nicole Baxter had come into his life. Fiercely dedicated to her job, she had immediately disliked the CEO of the Powell Private Security and Investigation Agency because he didn't play by the rules.

They had locked horns more than once, both stubborn, neither giving an inch.

Griff had taken great delight in ruffling her feathers whenever possible. Although he had found her attractive—what man wouldn't?—he had realized the attraction wasn't mutual. Or so he had thought. The first time he kissed her, he should have run like hell. He should have protected her. He hadn't. He had thought he could handle his feelings for her, control them, and keep them from getting out of hand. But once he had made love to her . . .

Falling in love with Nic and having her love him in return was Griff's miracle. Did a man have the right to ask for more than one miracle in a lifetime?

If so, he was willing to make a deal with God, on whatever terms the Almighty required.

Griff flung open the French doors that led onto the patio and stopped long enough to draw in huge gulps of the refreshing breeze coming in off the lake. Gazing at the fading gold embers of the day spreading across the water, Griff thought about how many evenings he and Nic had shared here on this patio.

The pain he felt was unbearable and yet he had no choice but to bear it.

He lifted his gaze from the beautiful and serene lake to the evening sky, afire with the approach of twilight.

"Punish me," he said aloud. "Don't punish Nic. Name your price, God, and I'll pay it."

He sensed rather than saw or heard someone behind him. He wanted to shout at them, demand that they go away and leave him alone.

No one could help him.

"What will you do if God will not bargain with you?" Sanders asked as he came up beside Griff.

With his gaze still focused heavenward, Griff replied, "Then I'll make a deal with the Devil."

They stood side by side for several minutes in the peaceful solitude of the warm summertime evening.

"He wants to torment you," Sanders said. "He sees your love for Nicole as a weakness, one he intends to take advantage of while he holds her hostage. You must prove to him that he is wrong, that your love for her is your greatest strength, not your greatest weakness. Do not let him win this mind game he wants to play. No matter what happens, no matter what he does, you must not lose hope that you will find Nicole and rescue her."

Griff turned and looked directly into Sanders's black eyes. "I have no idea how you survived after you lost your wife and child. If I lose Nic . . . "

"You will not lose her. She is alive. That is all that matters. We will find her and bring her home. You must believe this."

" 'We will find her and bring her home.' " Griffin recited Sanders's positive words. He had to believe that he could save Nic. The alternative doomed him to a hell from which he could never escape.

Stay strong, Nic. Stay alive. I swear I'll find you no matter what I have to do or how long it takes.

As Linden escorted Nic from the pavilion housing the caged men, she glanced over her shoulder and made direct eye contact with the manacled prisoner. Despite his circumstances, he remained rebellious and determined, unlike his fellow inmate who apparently had succumbed to hopelessness. She sensed that the chained man possessed the same indomitable spirit that had kept Griffin alive on Amara.

If only she could help him.

"Thinking of your husband?"

Linden's question momentarily startled her.

"Yes," Nic said. "I'm thinking about how he killed Malcolm York and the guards who worked for him."

She looked at Linden and smiled.

He stopped and stared at her, apparently surprised by her comment. Recovering quickly, he returned a smile and said, "I'm afraid Griffin Powell's tales of glory are exaggerated. Malcolm York is very much alive."

"If you believe that to be true . . . Tony"—she emphasized the use of his given name—"then you're delusional. The man you work for is no more the real Malcolm York than I'm the real Queen of England."

"Believe what you will, but in good time you'll find out the truth."

Linden gripped Nic's arm as they continued their trek downhill. When they reached the bottom, she expected him to return her to her luxurious prison cell inside the house. He didn't. Instead he guided her away from the house and along a winding path through an overgrown garden area. Within minutes, the path cleared and she saw what lay ahead—a group of hunters, dressed in camouflage and with rifles strapped to their backs, formed a circle around something lying on the ground.

Nic's gut tightened.

"Unless one of the hunters managed to make a kill during the actual hunt, a single man was chosen for execution at the end of the day, usually the one most severely wounded during the hunt or whoever had been the easiest to capture. At the end of every hunt, one man would be dead by nightfall."

Griff's words came back to her, warning her about what was, in all likelihood, about to happen.

"On average, York hosted at least six hunts a year. That forced him to continuously bring in new stock. He paid top dollar for young men from around the world who were in their prime, and if they excelled in any way, they were all the more coveted."

"Gentlemen," Linden called to the hunters, "Mr. York has invited a very special guest to join you this evening."

All eyes turned on her. Nic had not felt this vulnerable since she had been at the mercy of psychotic serial killer Rosswalt "Pudge" Everhart, four years ago. Except for an occasional nightmare, she had managed to put that grueling ordeal behind her and live a normal life.

She had not backed down from Pudge, had held her own against him, and had eventually escaped. By God, she wasn't about to cower in front of these sadistic bastards.

Holding her head high as the hunters leered at

her, she studied each of them as she moved her gaze from one to another. Five men ranging in ages from their forties to their seventies, three Caucasian, one Asian, and one Black, surveyed her from head to toe, apparently liking what they saw.

"This is Nicole." Linden shoved her forward toward the circle.

She stood rock solid, every muscle in her body rigid, her nerves jangling, her shoulders squared, and her determination to stay strong unwavering.

The hunters separated just enough to allow her to see inside the circle. She stifled a gasp as she stared at the bloody man lying on the ground at their feet. Apparently he had been shot more than once, probably during today's hunt, and had lost a great deal of blood. Wounded and weak, suffering horribly, he moaned quietly. One of the men, the youngest of the three white men, lifted his foot and kicked the dying man, and when he cried out in pain, the hunter kicked him again and again.

Nic tried to shut out the sound of the man's screams while the other hunters watched her reaction to their comrade's cruelty.

"The bidding starts at twenty-five thousand," a voice from out of nowhere proclaimed.

As the hunters shouted their bids, a small, thin man wearing a white suit appeared and oversaw the auction. When all was said and done, an auburn-haired man in his midfifties outbid the others, offering a quarter of a million dollars for the prize.

Nic wasn't sure what the prize entailed or if she was part of the bounty.

"York used all of us as prey in the hunts," Griff had told her. *"And the younger, prettier men, some only boys, were always used for sex. And some, usually the biggest and strongest, were used by those whose pleasure came from inflicting pain. York provided whatever his guests wanted, either on Amara or at one of his other estates. Men, women, and children. It didn't matter to him what happened to the people he had abducted. He didn't care as long as they could be used to make money for him."*

The real York might be dead, but his namesake apparently was following in his footsteps.

Nic fought the urge to run, knowing full well she wouldn't get twenty feet before Linden or one of the male guards overpowered her. Or maybe one of the hunters would shoot her.

Bracing herself for whatever happened next, she watched in horrified shock when two guards dragged the dying man through the dirt to a nearby tree. Unable to stand on his own, the man fell over and only the guards' quick actions prevented him from landing face-first at their feet. While one guard braced the man against the tree, the other guard tied a rope around him, binding him securely. And then Mr. Auburn Hair grasped his high-powered rifle in his gloved hands, aimed at the target, and fired repeatedly, effectively blowing a large hole in the victim's chest.

Sour bile rose from Nic's stomach, burning her esophagus and throat. Nausea threatened her iron-willed control.

Don't vomit. Damn it, don't show them any sign of weakness!

Clamping her mouth shut, she clenched her teeth.

Breathing deeply through her nostrils, trying to repress the ever-increasing queasiness, she thought she had succeeded.

Until . . .

Smiling triumphantly, Mr. Auburn Hair hung his rifle over his shoulder and marched toward the dead body bound to the tree. Another guard, one Nic hadn't even noticed, came forward and handed the conquering hero a leather-sheathed object approximately twenty inches long. Nic wanted to look away, but she forced herself to watch while Mr. Auburn Hair removed a large machete, the stainless-steel blade at least thirteen inches long.

Nic closed her eyes then and prayed.

"Open your eyes, Nicole," Linden whispered in her ear, his mouth so close that his warm breath fanned the side of her neck. "He expects you to watch."

Who was "he"? Mr. Auburn Hair? The pseudo-York? Or the Devil himself?

The first machete slice cut through the ropes binding the dead man to the tree. His mutilated body slumped and fell forward, the ragged tatters of what was left of his back clearly visible. And then Mr. Auburn Hair lifted the machete and in one forceful swipe, chopped off the man's head.

A celebratory chorus of hearty male shouts echoed in Nic's ears. Retching, she turned her head and vomited. Before she managed to regain her composure, Mr. Auburn Hair, the bloody machete clutched in his right hand, grabbed her arm with his left hand and yanked her against his sweaty chest. His crazed brown eyes looked straight at her as he flung the machete straight down, the blade boring into the soft earth, before he grabbed her around the neck with both hands and pressed his wet lips against her mouth.

Griff wasn't sure how long he had been outside walking around alone after his brief conversation with Sanders. But when Derek caught up with him, twilight had faded into nightfall, the first stars blinking in the late-evening sky. He had left the house, followed the well-lit path along the lake, and then ventured onto the gravel lane that wound around past the old boathouse. He knew every square foot of Griffin's Rest and loved this private sanctuary, his safe haven, guarded night and day.

If only Nic had stayed here. If only his duplicity

hadn't forced her to run away from him.

"You can go back and report in to the others that you found me alive and somewhat sane," Griffin said as Derek approached, the beam of his flashlight hitting Griff mid-chest.

"You should be thankful that you have people who give a damn about you," Derek told him. "Barbara Jean is fretting. Yvette hasn't spoken a word since you stormed out. Maleah has cursed your very existence, but mostly she's been crying and I've been trying to console her. Although Sanders has kept himself busy manning the agency's search, his concern is obvious."

"That's one thing I've always liked about you, Derek. You've never been afraid to speak your mind."

"I didn't come looking for you to check up on you for the others or to give you a piece of my mind, though God knows you need it." Derek stopped when he and Griff stood face-to-face, less than five feet separating them. "Information has started coming in. I thought you might want to know that a small private jet owned by Kroy Enterprises took off from McGhee Tyson this morning, supposedly heading to Miami. The flight manifest, not easy to come by as you know, stated two passengers, a Mr. and Mrs. Nick Baxter."

"God damn son of a bitch!" Griff felt the precarious control on his rage slipping. "Kroy Enterprises? K-r-o-y spelled backward is York.

And Mr. and Mrs. Nick Baxter? He deliberately used Nic's name. He wants me to know he has her. He's taunting me."

"He wants to rattle you," Derek agreed. "At this point, you have to know that, more than anything else, he wants you to suffer and he's going to turn the screws every chance he gets."

"Who the hell is he and why does he hate me so much?" Griff had made his share of enemies, but he couldn't think of anyone who would resort to sending an assassin to murder his employees and members of their families and to kidnap his wife.

No one other than Malcolm York.

But York was dead. He and Sanders and Yvette had killed the bastard sixteen years ago. Men didn't rise from the dead, especially after you chopped off their head.

"It isn't Malcolm York," Derek said. "He may call himself York, but he's not the original."

"No, but I'm beginning to believe he's a damn good carbon copy."

"Come back to the house and show the others that you're okay. Eat supper and go over the info we've collected so far." Derek motioned toward the path leading back to the house.

"Did the Kroy Enterprises plane land in Miami?" Griff asked.

"Nope. And all we know is that it went south, past Miami."

"I'd lay odds that son of a bitch has his own

little private island somewhere in the Caribbean."

"My thoughts exactly. And Sanders agreed. That's why we're searching now for a list of all privately owned islands in the Gulf, in the Atlantic, and in the Caribbean."

"Something's not right about this." Griff fell into step alongside Derek as they headed toward the house. "It's as if he wants us to find out where Linden has taken Nic, as if he's issuing an invitation for us to follow."

"Don't read too much into this. I have a good idea where your mind is going. He is not going to kill Nic, at least not yet, not until he's made you suffer a lot longer than just a day or two."

"Then he thinks he's leading me into a trap."

"Only if the man is a fool. He has to know the kind of firepower you'd bring with you."

Griff paused midstep and looked right at Derek. "Can you work up a profile of the new Malcolm York based on what little information we have?"

"Using the info we have, what we know about the original York, and utilizing my expertise and instincts, I can put together a tentative profile. Then I can add to it as we learn more about him."

"You think he's trying to mimic the real York?"

"Yes, I do," Derek said. "Actually, I think he idolizes York, maybe even wants to be him. He holds you responsible for York's death and he's intent on punishing you."

"Then he is as insane as the original."

"Brilliantly insane and diabolically evil, just as the real York was."

"What I want to know is who the hell is he?" Griff said. "And why has he waited sixteen years to bring Malcolm York back to life?"

CHAPTER 7

Although Nic's basic instinct urged her to fight, she forced herself to endure the man's slobbering kiss and made no protest when he slid his bloody right hand down her dress and grabbed her breast. When he squeezed roughly, she clenched her teeth to stop the moan, trapping it in her throat. Mr. Auburn Hair shouted something to his fellow hunters as he released Nic and shoved her in front of him. The other men laughed.

"We will finish this in your room," he told her in heavily accented English. Trying to focus not on what this man intended to do to her, but on maintaining some semblance of control over her fear, Nic followed his instructions and led him toward the two-story stucco mansion.

As he talked, telling her in lurid detail the fun they would have tonight, Nic decided, from studying his accent, that her would-be rapist was Dutch.

Big freaking deal. So he's Dutch. How the hell

does that help you? If you can't figure out a way to stop him . . .

She had no weapon. She might be able to overpower him, but there was no way she could escape from the house. What would Linden do to her if she somehow managed to either knock out her attacker or even kill him? She was in a no-win situation. If she wasn't pregnant, if she didn't have another life to consider, she'd find a way to kill the son of a bitch and then take her chances.

On the climb up the stairs, Mr. Auburn Hair repeatedly slapped her on the butt and when they reached the door to her bedroom, he clutched each buttock in his hands and squeezed so forcefully that Nic knew he would leave bruises on her butt. No doubt by morning, she would be black-and-blue.

When she opened the door, Nic's mouth gaped open when she saw Lina standing there completely naked. She smiled at Mr. Auburn Hair.

"I bring wine for celebrating." She motioned to the open bottle of red wine on the table and the three half-filled glasses.

"You must be a bonus," Mr. Auburn Hair said. "Two for the price of one." He threw back his head and laughed, and then reached out, grasped the bodice of Nic's sundress, and ripped it down to her waist. Instinctively, her hands flew up to shield her breasts barely covered by the sheer lace bra. He slapped her hands away and ordered her to undress.

Nic hesitated. Feeling Lina's gaze on her, she looked at the other woman. Lina picked up two glasses of wine and walked toward the mighty hunter. Nic watched as Lina offered a glass to the man. Grinning as he scanned the woman's beautiful young body, he accepted the wine, lifted his glass, made a toast in his native language, and put the glass to his lips. He gulped down half a glass, then wiped his mouth with the back of his hand and motioned for Lina to come closer. When she did as he had commanded, he poured the remainder of his wine over her chest, from neck to waist, threw the glass onto the nearby bed, and immediately began licking the rivulets of merlot staining Lina's high firm breasts. The girl's fingers tightened around the stem of her wine-glass as he suckled her.

Nic watched in frozen horror.

Lina looked past her attacker, her eyes speaking volumes as she stared at Nic. While Mr. Auburn Hair licked and bit his way downward to Lina's belly, the girl lifted one hand and motioned to Nic. At first Nic didn't understand, but when she tugged on her torn sundress, Lina nodded, and Nic knew the girl was telling her to take off her clothes. Reluctant to strip, Nic debated what to do, but decided to trust Lina, who had no doubt faced this situation on numerous occasions. While Mr. Auburn Hair clawed Lina, Nic removed her sundress, her transparent lace bra and matching bikini panties.

With the skill of an experienced courtesan, Lina guided Mr. Auburn Hair toward the bed. He staggered once, then fell into the bed, laughing as he pulled Lina down on top of him. As if suddenly remembering Nic, he glanced across the room and motioned for her to join them.

Dear God, she couldn't do this. She was no meek lamb who would go willingly to the slaughter.

When he ordered her to come to him, his speech slightly slurred, Nic forced her legs into action and slowly made her way toward the bed. As Nic drew near, Lina slid down over Mr. Auburn Hair's penis, taking him inside her.

"You great lover," Lina told him as she began riding him.

While Nic stood at the edge of the bed, waiting, but for what she didn't know, Mr. Auburn Hair grunted with release. Not until Lina crawled off him and stood up did Nic realize that he was not simply resting after sex, but that he was unconscious.

"What happened to him?" Nic asked. "Did he have a heart attack?"

"Wine." Lina smiled.

"The wine?" Realization dawned. "Oh my God, you drugged the wine."

"His wine, yes."

"You did this for me, didn't you? Oh, Lina,

you've bought me some time, but at great cost to you. How can I ever thank you?"

"I am whore since thirteen," Lina said.

"Oh, Lina, I'm so—"

Lina held up her hand in a Stop motion. "He sleep all night. You"—she pointed to Nic—"and me"—she pointed to herself—"in bed when he is awake."

"Yes, I understand. If I'm in bed with him and he doesn't remember what happened, he might believe that we had sex. But what do I do if he wants sex in the morning? We can hardly drug his orange juice."

"He will not," Lina said. "He cannot."

"He can't?"

Lina stuck her index finger straight up, and then folded it in half.

Nic almost laughed. "The drug you put in the wine not only knocked him out but . . . " Nic mimicked Lina's finger gesture.

"Old medicine from island," Lina said. "Plants grow here. I make and hide."

Nic saw Lina in a whole new light. Not as a pitiful victim, a sex slave doomed to endless humiliation and abuse, but as a cunning young woman who had not completely surrendered control to her masters. She didn't fight in an obvious way, but in a very subtle, very careful way. Nic had just learned a valuable lesson from her newfound friend.

• • •

Griff finally left the office suite around four that morning, went to his study, and eventually fell asleep on the sofa sometime after five. When he woke, his left shoulder ached where it had pressed awkwardly against the sofa arm, and he felt groggy and slightly disoriented. Sitting up, he folded the upper half of his body toward his knees and stretched his neck, shoulders, and back as he stared down at his feet. He lifted his hands, placed them on either side of his head, and rubbed his temples.

He needed coffee.

Barbara Jean would have coffee in both the kitchen and in the office. All he had to do was go to either place for a much-needed caffeine boost. But he dreaded leaving the quiet haven of his private den. His friends and employees meant well, their actions coming from sincere concern for his well-being and their love and respect for Nic, but he couldn't bear the looks of pity in their eyes.

Coming up slowly onto his feet, Griff clutched the back of his neck and massaged the sore muscles. As much as he would like to, he couldn't hide away in here all day. Staying alone in his study, thinking about Nic, imagining what she might be experiencing, wouldn't help her. All it would do was drive him crazy.

Griff walked across the semidark study, shards of morning light slipping through the shuttered windows. He opened the door and walked out into the hall. The buzz of a wide-awake and active household met him the moment he emerged from his seclusion. As he neared the kitchen, the smell of coffee brewing and bacon frying lured him closer, but when he heard the drone of female voices, he paused, his hand on the kitchen door.

You're going to have to eat and sleep and interact with others if you have any hope of staying sane while you search for Nic.

He shoved open the door and walked into the kitchen. The voices he had heard belonged to Barbara Jean Hughes, Maleah, and Griffin Rest's longtime cook, Mattie Glover. All three women turned and stared at him.

"Morning," he said as he headed for the coffeemaker.

"Did you get any sleep?" Barbara Jean asked and then motioned to Mattie, who immediately filled an empty plate with bacon, eggs, hash browns, and a couple of biscuits.

"Yeah, I got some sleep." Griff poured the hot, black brew into a mug, lifted the mug to his mouth, and savored the first sip.

"Sit down and eat," Barbara Jean told him as Mattie set the overflowing plate on the table.

"Yes, ma'am." Griff placed the UT orange mug beside his plate, pulled out a chair, and sat across from Maleah, who lifted her gaze to meet his.

"How about you? Did you and Derek get any sleep?" The couple had gone upstairs to bed around three this morning, an hour before he had sought solitude in his study.

"Some," she replied. "Derek's in the shower. He'll be down soon."

Griff eyed the food in front of him.

"I took it upon myself to call Charles David last night before I went to bed," Maleah said. "I thought he should know that Nic is missing."

Griff snapped his gaze up from the breakfast plate and met Maleah's hostile stare. "Right. Yes, of course. He did need to know. Thank you." Griff hadn't given Charles David, Nic's younger brother, a thought.

"He's going to take the first flight out of San Francisco this morning."

"Then he's coming here?"

"Eat now, talk later." Barbara Jean cast Maleah a scolding glare.

Maleah downed the last drops in her coffee cup, scooted back her chair, and stood. Just as she walked over and put her cup in the dishwasher, Shaughnessy Hood came barreling into the room.

"Good. You're up." Shaughnessy looked at Griff. "Sanders wants to see you right now. He has a lead on where Linden may have taken Nic."

Without giving his breakfast another thought, Griff shot to his feet and hurried out

114

of the kitchen. Shaughnessy lumbered along behind him, his size sixteen shoes pounding against the wooden hallway floor.

As they rushed to the office suite, Maleah caught up with them. Sanders met Griff at the door. He held up several computer printouts.

"There is a privately owned island, off the coast of Belize, south of Mexico, in the Caribbean Sea that could be where Linden took Nicole," Sanders said, and without taking a breath added, "I contacted the deputy prime minister personally, explained the situation, and he agreed to cut through all the red tape. The information we needed just came in a couple of minutes ago. The title for the island shows that it is owned by Kroy Enterprises."

"Kroy again," Griff said. "Do you have the exact location?"

Griff's heartbeat strummed inside his head. They could be in Belize in a few hours. Was it possible they had actually found Nic so easily, that there was a chance they could bring her home today?

"Shelter Island consists of nine acres of heavily wooded land and is located northwest of the Cat Cayes range. There is no landing strip on the island, so unless Linden took Nicole there by helicopter, he had to have taken her by boat."

"Do we have anyone in Belize?" Griff asked as he rammed past Sanders and went straight to his desk.

"We have several freelance operatives we can trust."

"I want to know if and when a private jet owned by Kroy Enterprises landed in Belize or Mexico or—"

"Rett's handling that now." Sanders glanced at Everett Dawson who was at that moment on the telephone.

Griff scanned the office, saw that Sanders, Rett Dawson, Shaughnessy, and Maleah were the only people in the suite. "Where's Luke Sentell? He hasn't left yet, has he?"

"Luke hasn't come up to the main house this morning. I assume he's still asleep down at the bunkhouse," Maleah told them.

"Get him," Griff said, his voice deadly calm. "I need him to postpone his trip to Europe."

Maleah turned and immediately left the room.

They could wait to gather more info, to be absolutely certain that Nic was being held captive on Shelter Island, but Griff wasn't willing to postpone doing what his gut told him to do now. Yeah, sure, they could be walking into a trap. Or the mastermind behind Malcolm York's resurrection could have planted the info leading them straight to Shelter Island as a decoy. Linden could have taken Nic anywhere. For all they knew, she could be halfway around the world by now.

Before Mr. Auburn Hair began to rouse, Nic slipped into the robe hanging on the bathroom door and tossed Lina the matching gown. While

Nic poured the contents of the wine bottle into the commode and flushed the merlot, Lina kept watch over the sleeping hunter. Just as Nic came out of the bathroom, a loud knock rocked the heavy wooden door seconds before Anthony Linden swept into the room, a package under his arm. He glanced from Nic to Lina and then at Mr. Auburn Hair, who rolled onto his back and mumbled incoherently, apparently coming out of his drug-induced sleep.

"It would appear you two wore him out." Linden grinned at them. "Neither of you look the worse for wear." He walked over to Nic, ran the back of his hand down her back, and into the V of her robe. "I find the bruises on your neck exciting. I'm sure other men will, too."

Nic cringed at his touch. Bastard!

"Lina, leave us," Linden said. "Go to your quarters and pack. You'll be leaving the island in less than an hour."

They were on an island. She knew it. That was the reason she had been transported from the airplane to a boat. Apparently there wasn't a landing strip on the island.

Lina hurried from the room without a word of protest or a backward glance at either Linden or Nic. Once the door closed behind the servant girl, Linden turned to Nic again. The way he ogled her made her uneasy.

Mr. Auburn Hair grunted, kicked back the

covers to reveal his naked body, and cursed loudly as he tried to sit up.

Linden lifted the small package from under his left arm and handed it to Nic. "Fresh clothes. Shower now while you can and get dressed." He glanced at the grumbling man who struggled to get out of bed. "I'll take care of our guest."

Nic didn't hesitate. She grabbed the package and ran into the bathroom. If only there was a lock on the door. But there wasn't. Either man could easily barge in on her. But Linden had said for her to take a shower while she could. Did that mean it could be a while before she got the chance again?

After removing the robe, she hung it on the back of the door, and then turned on the shower and stepped under the lukewarm spray. Working quickly, she washed her hair before she soaped, scrubbed, and rinsed her body. In less than five minutes, she had bathed, towel-dried her hair, brushed her teeth, applied deodorant, and dressed in the skintight jeans and cotton T-shirt Linden had provided. No bra. No panties. Not a good sign.

She stood in front of the wall of mirrors above the double-sink vanity and inspected the bruises on her neck. Mr. Auburn Hair had choked her when he'd wrapped his hands around her neck as he kissed her.

Last night, she'd gotten lucky, thanks to Lina. But Linden said they were transferring the young woman off the island today. Did he suspect what she'd done to Mr. Auburn Hair? Or were her services simply required elsewhere? When Lina went away, Nic would lose her only ally on the island.

She walked over to the closed door and listened, wondering what was happening in the bedroom. If Mr. Auburn Hair had caused a ruckus, she hadn't heard it while she was in the shower. She cracked the bathroom door just enough to peek into the bedroom. It appeared to be empty. There was no sign of either man. She eased the door open and walked out of the bathroom.

Alone in her gilded cage, Nic slumped down on the chaise longue, a sense of hopelessness weighing down on her. She was on an island, probably somewhere in the Caribbean, but she had no idea exactly where. Could she reasonably expect Griff to find her? Yes, damn it, if it were humanly possible to locate her, Griff would do it. At this very moment he was using every resource available to the Powell Agency to search the world over for her. She simply had to stay alive, to do whatever was necessary to keep herself and her baby safe until Griff came for them.

But between now and then, what was going to happen to her? If not for Lina, Mr. Auburn Hair would have raped her last night, probably more than once. Was he only the first of many men she would be expected to service? Last night, she had been nothing more than part of the hunter's package deal—winner take all, and that included a woman for the night. How many more would there be? And how would she deal with them without Lina's help?

Nic closed her eyes. "Please, God," she whispered, "help me stay strong. Help me survive. Keep my baby safe."

Malcolm York looked out from the wall of windows in his penthouse suite in Mayfair. The lovely view of Hyde Park had been one of the reasons he had leased the two apartments that covered approximately ten thousand square feet, which was quite enormous for this area of London. A local real estate magazine had boasted that these duplex penthouses could well be the most impressive penthouses in London, possibly in the entire world.

Malcolm liked owning impressive things. This penthouse was only one of his many possessions, including his garage of automobiles, his yacht, his stable of Thoroughbreds, the castle in Scotland, a ranch in the U.S. and a number of private islands around the world. Although his international business concerns required that he occasionally travel, he preferred spending most of his time here. But quite soon, a matter of the utmost urgency would require him to leave for a rather extensive period of time. He had finally managed to obtain the means by which to even an old score, to at long last exact overdue revenge against his most grievous enemy.

Despite his eagerness, he knew that he must be patient. *All good things come to those who wait.*

In due time, he would introduce himself to Nicole Baxter Powell, but until then, Linden would take very good care of her. The man had his instructions. Malcolm wanted Griffin Powell's wife to be introduced to every aspect of the businesses that had made him a billionaire and learn firsthand how her husband's vast wealth had been accumulated. Money that Powell and Sanders and Yvette Meng had stolen. They were all three murderers and thieves. However, he knew that Yvette and Sanders were now, as they had been on Amara, nothing more than Griffin Powell's accomplices.

Malcolm smiled at the thought of his archenemy moving heaven and earth trying to find his beloved wife. Nicole was the carrot he would dangle in front of Powell, giving him hope that he could find her and save her.

False hope.

But in the days and weeks—perhaps even months —ahead, he would enjoy himself immensely as he brought Griffin Powell to his knees and made him beg.

As laughter bubbled inside him, Malcolm checked the time. His personal assistant had been sent to pick up his guest and bring him here for a visit. As if on cue, Yves Bouchard stepped from the private elevator entrance into Malcolm's luxurious apartment. Having delivered her employer's guest, Martine took the elevator back down to the ground floor.

With open arms, Malcolm met Bouchard and encompassed his compatriot in a welcoming hug. As they broke apart, Malcolm said, "I am so pleased that you accepted my invitation."

"Surely you do not think I would come to London and leave without seeing you."

Bouchard could be charming when he chose to be, but Malcolm knew, perhaps better than anyone, what a ruthless bastard his old friend really was. But who among his friends did not have a few flaws?

"Will you be here in London for long?"

"A few more days," Bouchard said as he followed Malcolm into the massive dining/living room area that spanned the length of the building. "I dined with Harlan last night. He mentioned that you were planning a hunt sometime soon. I don't hunt as much as I once did, but if you will be personally hosting the event, I would like to be included."

"Of course, of course. Without question, your name always heads the list when I host a hunt. And you are always welcome to bring a guest with you."

Malcolm indicated for Bouchard to sit beside him when he stretched out comfortably on the thickly padded leather sofa. "I am working on the details to make this hunt one my guests will never forget. It has been years in the making, so be patient, my friend."

"Perhaps you will give me a *petite* hint." Bouchard indicated a miniscule measurement by bringing his thumb and forefinger almost together. "What will make this hunt unforgettable?"

"The grand prize and the prey will be one and the same," Malcolm said. "The winner may do with her as he wishes. He may kill her or keep her alive for his own pleasure until he tires of her."

Bouchard's brow furrowed. "What could possibly make this woman so valuable? She is only a woman."

"But she is not just any woman. She is Griffin Powell's wife."

CHAPTER 8

Within an hour of Sanders's initial report, Griff had assembled his team—the men who would go with him to Belize. In a closed meeting, which included Derek and Maleah, Griff laid out the plan and opened the floor for discussion. The Powell jet was at that very moment being prepared for their trip, two of the four pilots on the agency's payroll en route to Griff's private airstrip, which was closer to Griffin's Rest than McGhee Tyson. In another hour, they would be headed south, but in the meantime, info was being gathered in Belize and an advance team of two men had been sent to Shelter Island. Their orders were to scope out the setup and report in, all the while remaining invisible to the island's inhabitants. The Powell jet would land at Phillip S.W. Goldson International Airport in Belize City where a rental car would be waiting to whisk them off to Belize City Harbor. Arrangements had been made for two boats to be readied for their arrival.

"We will be in constant contact with Derek and Maleah," Griff said. "They will be in charge while we're away. All info they receive from our Knoxville headquarters will be combined with the updates coming in directly to Griffin's Rest.

We will be exchanging info with them throughout this mission."

"By the time we land in Belize City, our independent operatives who have been sent to Shelter Island should have a preliminary report, including photos," Sanders said. "They should be able to advise where the safest point of entry to the island will be and what precautionary measures we need to take."

"We will split into two units, each a three-man team," Griff told them. "Luke and Shaughnessy, you'll be with me. And Rett, you and Holt will be with Sanders."

Luke and Rett were former Special Forces. Shaughnessy and Holt were expert snipers. Griff was a graduate of the Malcolm York hunting school. Sanders, a former Gurkha, had taught Griff how to outsmart his opponent, how to fight and kill without reservation, how to survive despite the high odds against him being able to stay alive on Amara for more than a month or two at best.

If Nic was on Shelter Island, Griff and his team would bring her home.

"Gentlemen, we will leave Griffin's Rest in"— Griff checked his wristwatch—"fifty-three minutes. The flight to Belize City will take approximately five-and-a-half hours, which will put us there by midafternoon and on Shelter Island by late afternoon. For now, take care of any business you need to attend to. Any other questions or concerns can be addressed during the flight."

One by one the agents exited the office suite, leaving Griff alone with Sanders, Derek, and Maleah.

"Perhaps you and I should go over what the day-to-day duties of being in charge here entails," Sanders said to Derek.

"And I'd like to speak to you privately," Griff told Maleah.

While Derek went with Sanders over to his desk, Griff indicated for Maleah to join him at the conference table. He pulled out a chair for her.

"I need for you to personally take care of several things for me," Griff said.

"All right. What do you want me to do?"

"First, I'd like for you to send someone to meet Charles David's flight and when he arrives here, I want you to personally bring him up-to-date on the situation. Answer his questions truthfully. And if those answers put me in a bad light, so be it."

"Yes, sir."

"I don't have time to deal with Yvette and her desire to go to London as soon as possible. I want you to convince her not to go, to stay here at Griffin's Rest where she will be safe. However, if it becomes necessary, post bodyguards with her twenty-four-seven. Do whatever you need to do, but don't let her leave here."

"I don't like the idea of playing Dr. Meng's jailor, but I will."

"Thank you."

"Anything else?"

"Arrange for a medical team to be on standby in Belize and another in Miami. If Nic needs medical attention before we arrive back here, I don't want any delays."

"I'll see to it immediately." Maleah pushed back her chair and stood.

Griff reached out and grasped her wrist. "If I could go back and change things, I would." When she tugged on her wrist, he released her.

"Look, I know it's not all your fault," she told him. "And I know you love Nic. But—"

"But I drove her away from Griffin's Rest by not being completely honest with her."

"Go to Shelter Island, find her, and bring her home safe and sound and you and I are good. Got it? But if anything happens to her, if . . . if she doesn't come out of this in one piece, then consider me your worst enemy."

Griff sat and watched her walk out of the office. He wanted to tell her that she was wrong. She could never be his worst enemy. After he'd killed Malcolm York sixteen years ago, Griff had become his own worst enemy.

Nic had spent the entire morning in her gilded cage, alone except for when an old woman, probably at least seventy or older, had brought in a bowl of fresh fruit and a bottle of water. When Nic tried to talk to the woman, the woman had looked at Nic with sad eyes and shook her head. After hurriedly stripping the bed down to the mattress, the woman had gathered up the bed linens and left.

For the past hour, Nic had heard a great deal of noise, some coming from inside the mansion, but most of it from outside. She had wondered if the hunters were leaving the island or if the man who oversaw the day-to-day running of the estate was bringing in a fresh batch of slaves. And that's exactly what they were—slaves. The men confined in the pavilion on the hill and used as prey in the hunts and the women brought here to provide sex for the guests.

And that's what you are now, too.

Unless Griff found her soon, or if by some miracle she managed to escape, her life would soon become a living nightmare. She couldn't count on Lina or someone like Lina to save her a second time.

Nic opened the windows that overlooked the patio below and heard the rumble of vehicles combined with the sound of men shouting orders. Something was happening. She just didn't know what. The patio and pool were empty. Not a soul in sight.

Suddenly, she heard the *rat-a-tat-tat* of repeated gunfire, as if someone was using a semiautomatic rifle off in the distance. Was the island being invaded? Had Griff found her and was coming to rescue her? Or had there been another hunt scheduled for today? Had one of the brave hunters just killed another defenseless man?

At the thought of another captive being hunted down and killed, Nic remembered the man in the cage she had seen last night. The tall, somewhat muscular man with the hate-filled brown eyes who, despite his predicament, had exuded pure raw rage and a determination to live. Although there was no physical resemblance, there had been something about him that reminded her of Griff. Perhaps it was nothing more than Nic sensing that the man and Griff were kindred spirits, men who fought with every ounce of strength within them until the bitter end.

Where are you, Griff ?

I need you.

She laid her hand over her flat belly. *We need you.*

I'm going to fight for my life and the life of our unborn child. I'm going to try to be as brave as that dark-eyed man in the cage up on the hill, as brave as you were on Amara.

I know that you will find me, that you will never give up. Knowing you're fighting for me at this very minute, doing everything possible to locate me, is what will keep me from giving up hope.

Nic closed the windows, walked across the room, and slumped down on the chaise longue. After leaning back, she closed her eyes and said one more prayer. *Please hear me, God. Please.*

When Griff's image appeared in her mind, she almost cried. Keeping her eyes shut, hoping to hang on to the image as long as possible, Nic concentrated very hard. If only she possessed mental telepathy, she would send Griff a message. She would tell him she loved him. And then she would do her best to tell him where she was. But as far as psychic gifts went, Nic had none. Zero.

Zip. Nada. Did any of Yvette's protégés possess such a gift? Nic had no idea. Maybe Meredith Sinclair did. Hadn't Griff mentioned something about the girl being exceptionally gifted?

How about sending me a message, Meredith? Let me know what's going on back at Griffin's Rest.

Yeah, sure, what were the odds of that happening? But despite admitting the absurdity of Meredith being able to send her a telepathic message, Nic managed to smile. She smiled because thoughts of home comforted her.

But was Griffin's Rest really home? Had it ever been? Hadn't she always felt like a visitor, someone passing through on her way somewhere else?

Loud voices outside her bedroom jerked Nic back to the reality of the moment. The door flew open and Anthony Linden burst into her room. She rose to her feet and faced him.

"Come on," he said. "Let's go."

"Go where?" When he grabbed her arm and pulled her toward the door, she demanded, "Tell me where you're taking me."

"Damn it, woman. Just do as you're told. Come with me now!"

Rafe sat alone, his laptop balanced on his thighs, in his apartment at Catherine Place, adjacent to the Rubens Hotel in London. Renting this type of luxury apartment instead of staying in a hotel room suited his needs. It afforded him more privacy and yet allowed him to take advantage of all the hotel amenities. He never remained in one place long enough to make buying a house or an apartment practical. Once or twice during the past sixteen years, he had considered purchasing a house in some out-of-the-way, back-of-the-beyond area, but what would have been the point? He could never put down roots, could never live a normal life. Living like a gypsy, always on the move, was part of the price he paid to achieve the goals he had set for himself when he had walked out of the hospital, here in London. On that day, he had left behind every semblance of the boy he had been before Malcolm York took him to Amara.

Standing, he stretched his arms over his head and brought his hands together, linking them as he slid them downward to cradle his neck. He had spent most of the afternoon and early evening concocting plans and making arrangements for the upcoming weeks. Through various phone calls and a number of e-mail exchanges, he had acquired updated public knowledge and private information about Harlan Benecroft and Yves Bouchard. Gathering info on Benecroft had been relatively easy. Since Sir Harlan was no longer directly involved in the major illegal businesses and had never been a major player, he managed to present himself to the general public as nothing more than a wealthy, slightly eccentric old man. In certain circles, his deviant behavior was considered the norm and no one thought less of him because he indulged in his perverse appetites. Yves Bouchard was most definitely a horse of a different color. Bouchard had been and still was a major player in drug and human trafficking. He had been on Interpol's Most Wanted list for a number of years, but had eluded capture by keeping a low profile. It would require the utmost cunning and finesse to trap a man who had outsmarted law enforcement around the world. And it would take patience. But now that Rafe had seen the man face-to-face again, had spoken to him, had been given a personal introduction, it was only a matter of time before Rafe would weave the web that would ensnare the famous and elusive *Le Ravisseur.*

Discontinuing his neck massage, Rafe made his way across the room to the bar-table set up by the staircase, picked up a bottle of water, and removed the twist-off cap. Although a variety of liquors adorned the top of the ornamental serving tray, he chose simple H2O. He seldom drank, opting to do so only in very select circumstances. Whenever someone noticed his near-teetotalism, which surprisingly wasn't all that often, he simply implied that he was an alcoholic. He wasn't, of course, but it was a convenient lie that no one questioned. Rafe did not often drink or smoke or do drugs and not because he lived by some strict moral code. His body was a machine, part of his arsenal of weapons that assisted him in his life's mission. In order to fine-tune his body, to keep it in prime condition, he generally abstained, just as he maintained a healthy diet, exercised his body and his mind on a regular basis, and got eight hours of sleep whenever possible.

His all-night adventure with Cassie Wilder was far from the norm for him. The three-way he had shared with Cassie and the bosomy redhead had relieved a great deal of sexual tension, but more importantly, it had convinced Cassie, and any "friends" who might inquire, that he was a sexual venturer, a man interested in far more than the ordinary. He had hinted to Cassie that he would like to explore more places like Body Parts, other clubs for a very select clientele.

Rafe sipped on the water as he climbed the stairs to the second-floor bedroom. He had learned from past experience that if he tried to rush things, impatience often resulted in failure. He would eventually get around to taking care of Sir Harlan, a mere piss-ant among giant cockroaches, but Bouchard was the last name on his list. Of course, there was no written list. The record of offenders was entirely mental, locked away securely inside Rafe's head. The list was nothing more than memorized names and faces of the men who had frequented Amara on a regular basis, the men who had been Malcolm York's intimate friends and colleagues. All six men had at one time or another participated in the hunt, Rafe often one of the captives used as prey. And two of the six had always requested Rafe be made available for their sexual pleasure. He had killed the four—Tanaka, Di Santis, Klausner, and Sternberg—in the order in which he had located them. But he had deliberately put Ciro Mayorga and Yves Bouchard at the end of his list, singling them out for special deaths.

After sixteen years of being the hunter instead of the quarry, he had become a stranger to himself, the ghost of a human being, a creature capable of inflicting the kind of cruelty that he and the others on Amara had suffered.

He set the bottle of water on the bedside table, opened the door that led outside, and crossed over to the small terrace. The heart of Westminster surrounded him—the lights and sounds and smells—although here on the quiet residential street the sensory distractions were diluted.

The hunt had begun now, starting with the private dinner at the Savoy the moment he saw Bouchard, and would proceed slowly and carefully to its inevitable end. As much as he wished it otherwise, Rafe knew that he would take great pleasure in torturing and eventually killing *Le Ravisseur*.

• • •

The Belize City Harbor shimmered like a multicolored jewel in the late-afternoon sunlight. Rows of buildings painted in a variety of colors ranging from pink and turquoise to a soothing yellow lined the boardwalk. Numerous sailboats, naked masts stretching skyward, floated languidly on the surface of the calm blue water. Not even a hint of a breeze stirred. No wind at all. Overhead the azure sky canopied the harbor and spread out over the Caribbean Sea.

Griff noticed a fishing boat returning to the harbor, dories stacked up on deck. On several of the recently docked boats, the fishermen were busily stripping their sloops of outboard motors and sails.

"This is the place," Sanders said. "We are to ask for Martinez and Pitts."

At this time of day, there were only a handful of patrons in the restaurant, and none of them, all seated in the bar, paid much attention to the six foreign visitors who entered, two at a time. Sanders approached the bartender, spoke to him briefly, and motioned to the others.

In the back room of the harbor restaurant, Griff and his agents met with the reconnaissance team who had explored Shelter Island. The two men had returned several hours ago with a full report and photos. Several beer kegs, two large beverage coolers, and a couple of floor-to-ceiling wine racks took up more than a third of the small storeroom. A stocky, dark-haired man in black jeans and black T-shirt came out of the shadows and introduced himself as Juan Martinez.

Griff extended his hand. "Griffin Powell."

Martinez shook Griff's hand. "Three-fourths of the island is wooded, sparsely in places. There are several small buildings and an open-air pavilion on a knoll overlooking the main house. That U-shaped main house is approximately nine thousand square feet and has two levels and an enclosed courtyard. There was no way we could get inside the house. It's heavily guarded."

"If she's on the island, she'd be inside the house," Griff said.

"How many guards are there?" Luke Sentell asked. "What's the head count? How many residents? How many soldiers, how many servants, and how many guests?"

"We counted a dozen guards." The second recon guy came forward, a digital camera in his hand. "They were all male and looked to be in their twenties. My guess is that none of them are well trained, but they were carrying around plenty of firepower—M16s."

Plenty of firepower was right. The M16 had a magazine capacity of thirty rounds, with a twelve to fifteen rounds per minute sustained rate of fire and a point target of nearly 2000 feet. The gas-operated, air-cooled, shoulder-fired, lightweight assault rifle had been used by the U.S. military for more than thirty years. York's guards on Amara had been equipped with M16s.

"You must be Pitts." Luke's gaze locked with the darkly tanned blonde, his hair buzzed short and his muscles bulging, his impressive biceps revealed by the short sleeves of his gray T-shirt.

The guy nodded. "On our way there, we met up with a couple of cruisers we believe may have just left the island. Since we were aboard what appeared to be a fishing boat, I figure they barely noticed us."

"The thing is," Martinez said, "there seemed to be a lot of activity on the island. It was as if they were cleaning up, storing things, burning some stuff. We saw a couple of big fires."

"Any idea what was happening?" Luke asked.

Pitts shrugged. "No way to tell in the time we had to scout out the area, snap some photos"—he held out the camera to Griff—"and get off the island without being detected."

Griff studied the camera, quickly figured out how it worked, and brought up the first photograph, apparently one taken when Martinez and Pitts had first landed. Zipping through more than two dozen pictures—buildings, the main house, guards, a couple of attractive young women, and an old woman, probably a servant, Griff stopped the slide show and stared at the photo on the screen. His gut tightened.

"What's this?" he asked as he held out the camera for Pitts to see.

"That's an open-air pavilion," Pitts replied. "There were six cages. Five were occupied."

For a split second memories of another island half a world away flashed through Griff's mind. Cages. Dark, dank, dungeonlike holes. Screams in the night. Pleading cries. The scent of blood and urine and feces.

Sanders took the camera from him and glanced at the photo that momentarily had held Griff spellbound. Without a second look, Sanders handed the camera back to Pitts. "Sentell and Dawson may have a few more questions before we head out." He looked at Luke. "I want us on our way in fifteen minutes."

"Yes, sir," Luke replied, and then motioned to Rett Dawson, who joined him in a hasty tête-à-tête.

While Luke and Rett talked to Pitts and Martinez, gathering pertinent info in order to plan their strategy, Sanders issued orders. "Shaughnessy, you make contact with the medical team here in Belize and the one in Miami and make sure they're ready in case we need them. And Holt, you check on the boats, make sure they're exactly what I ordered and that they're ready now." He looked at his wristwatch and quoted the time. "We'll join you in exactly fourteen minutes."

The two men immediately left the storeroom. Sanders moved to Griff's side and said in a low whisper, for Griff's ears only, "Remember one thing—all evidence to the contrary, the real Malcolm York is dead."

CHAPTER 9

Logically, Yvette understood that her first priority should be to help Griffin find his wife. And she fully intended to do everything within her power to assist in the search for Nicole. But Yvette's heart pulled her in a different direction. Every maternal instinct she possessed demanded that she go to the Benenden School and meet Suzette York. Face-to-face. Perhaps mother-to-daughter. She truly believed that if she could see this young girl, speak with her, touch her, she would know the truth. For nearly seventeen years, not one day had passed that she hadn't thought of her child, that she hadn't wondered if she had given birth to a girl or a boy, and if her baby was still alive.

As much as she needed Griff, had counted on him being with her when she met Suzette, she had been forced to turn to Sanders. Before he had left with Griffin for Belize, she had asked him to approve a request to headquarters that the Powell Agency gather more information about the Benenden School and about one particular student.

"I will authorize the agency to begin an immediate investigation," Sanders had assured her. "But in the meantime, while Griffin and I are gone, you will remain here at Griffin's Rest. I want your word that you will not leave here."

Reluctantly, she had agreed. "I will remain here until either you or Griffin can accompany me to England."

"I am glad that you see the wisdom in remaining where you are safe."

And so she had made a pact with Sanders, one he trusted her not to break. But waiting proved to be almost unbearable. She had spent the day alone as much as possible, doing her best to avoid her six young protégés with whom she shared her home. Thankfully, the house was quite large, and the student quarters were located in a separate wing from her private suite of rooms.

Half an hour ago, she had received a file, via an e-mail attachment, from Powell headquarters, which she had read quickly and then printed so that she could reread it. As of yet, there was no information on Suzette York, just a detailed report on the Benenden School. In a nutshell, the account detailed the school's long history as one of the premiere English boarding schools for girls, stating a number of illustrious alumnae, which included Anne, Princess Royal, as well as Olympic medalist Georgina Harland, and Academy Award–winning actress Rachel Weisz.

Whoever Suzette York was, her benefactor, be that a parent or a guardian, had made certain she would receive the best education and social opportunities his money could buy.

"You do realize that this girl is most likely not your child." If only she could forget Sanders's warning, but despite her heart's yearning for Suzette to be her child, she had to admit that it was highly unlikely.

With her promise to Sanders forcing her to stay at Griffin's Rest, there was nothing she could do except wait. Wait for the next report from Powell headquarters. Wait for word from Sanders or Griffin about the rescue mission to Shelter Island. Wait and hope. Wait and pray.

She should be doing more than waiting. She had promised Sanders, hadn't she?

"If there is any possibility that Meredith could give us something to go on, something that would help us locate Nic . . ."

If only her own psychic abilities could be activated without human touch, but her strong empathic gifts required contact with the subject. She could sense another's pain and even help ease that pain by taking it from them and suffering it for them. She could delve inside a person's thoughts and feelings and could even see glimpses of their past and present through interpreting their thoughts.

But her own "clair" skills, such as clairvoyance,

clairaudience or clairsentience, were minor and of little use to her. Of all her protégés, only one possessed the unique gift of psychometry, only one who could possibly use her talent to help in the search for Nicole.

Having been forced, completely against her will, to use her own psychic abilities for Malcolm York's evil purposes, Yvette seldom requested that any of her students put themselves in danger in order to help with a Powell Agency case. Griffin had always understood and had allowed her to keep her work with her students completely separate from the agency's business. Only when rumors gradually began propagating in European underground circles about a man named Malcolm York had Griffin requested the voluntary services of her most gifted protégée. And it was that same protégée that Yvette had summoned to her office.

Meredith Sinclair, her hair a riot of red curls, her freckled face void of makeup, stood there in the doorway, a concerned expression on her plain little face. "You sent for me?"

"Yes, please come in. I need to ask you for an enormous favor."

When Meredith entered the office, Yvette closed the door and invited her student to sit on the sofa.

"This is about Nic Powell's disappearance, isn't it?"

Yvette nodded.

"What can I do to help?" Meredith asked as she

sat on the edge of the sofa, folded her hands together, and rested them in her lap.

"You are aware that Griffin and Sanders have taken a group of highly trained agents, including Luke Sentell and Rett Dawson, to Belize," Yvette said.

"Yes."

"There is a chance that Nicole is being held on a privately owned island off the coast, somewhere in the Caribbean Sea. If she is, they plan to rescue her." Yvette paused for a moment, collected her thoughts, and then said, "Sanders asked me to speak to you and ask if you will use your skills to try to locate Nicole. If it turns out she is not on the island . . . "

"Why didn't Mr. Powell ask me himself ? I would have thought, considering that he has not hesitated to ask for my help in the past, he would—"

"Griffin has been and is under a great deal of mental and emotional stress. I'm sure that if he doesn't find Nicole on the island, he will consider his options and asking for your help will be one of those options. I believe that if you will allow me to assist you, we can, at the very least, find some clues that will help locate Nicole."

"Then I'm willing to do as you ask."

"Thank you. And I hope you have no objections to my asking someone else to be present. It is quite possible that as an empath I will go under

143

with you, and if that happens, we will need someone completely grounded as a safeguard, someone who can bring us back safely."

"You know best," Meredith said. "You are the master. I am the student."

"For now, yes." Yvette lifted the telephone from its base, dialed the number, and waited.

"Hello."

"Would you please come here as soon as possible? Meredith has agreed to try to help locate Nicole. I will act as her guide, but we need a—"

"Give me ten minutes," Barbara Jean Hughes said. "I'll find Maleah and have her drive me over there."

The boats Sanders had arranged for their use were Ribcraft 6.8 models, with twin 90HP Honda engines. The boat's overall design allowed for high speed and maneuverability regardless of the conditions. Martinez and Pitts piloted the two RIBs, each containing a landing team of three.

Shelter Island was almost perfectly round and possessed a small cove ideal for landing their boats, but that site was guarded, no doubt 24/7. Despite the steep drop-off about a hundred feet from shore, they had chosen an unguarded landing site on the other side of the island. Leaving Martinez and Pitts, both heavily armed, to guard the boats and act as backup if needed, the others began the dangerous trek into the thick mangroves. When they reached the inner circle of the island, they found that the land had been cleared of smaller trees and underbrush. Without having to fight their way through the thickets, they could reach their destination faster, but without the cover the woods provided, they were easily visible to anyone watching.

When they were within binocular range of the outbuildings, the two teams separated, planning to circle their objective and meet up at the main house. Griff hated this island, every sound, every scent, every square inch. It reminded him too much of Amara.

"We're seeing no signs of the island's inhabitants." Rett Dawson radioed the info five minutes later. "What about you?"

"Nothing," Luke told him. "We're approaching the open-air pavilion and I see no sign of any guards."

"We're preparing to check the outbuildings. There's no one stirring. It's too damn quiet. I don't like it."

As they climbed the knoll leading up to the pavilion, a hard knot formed in the pit of Griff's belly as a sense of déjà vu threatened to suffocate him. For one painful heartbeat, he couldn't breathe.

"Good God." Shaughnessy halted at the top of the rise, his gaze fixed on the cages inside the pavilion. "I've never seen anything like this."

I have, Griff thought. *A lifetime ago on an island in the South Pacific.*

Two cages were empty. The other four contained one man per cage, each bone-thin, lifeless body riddled with bullets. Blood streaked the prison bars of the four cages and soaked the earth around the bodies.

"Why kill them in their cages?" Luke voiced his question aloud.

"Easier to kill them than to transport them," Griff said.

"And they could not risk leaving them behind," Sanders added.

"You think they've evacuated the island?" Luke asked.

"The hunters are gone," Griff replied. "The overseer and servants could still be here, but my gut instincts tell me that no one is left on the island."

Before Luke could respond, Rett Dawson radioed again with an update.

"We found a headless body at the foot of a tree a few yards back. And we're seeing more dead bodies—at least five—scattered about as if they were shot wherever they stood."

"We found four bodies," Luke said. "This is beginning to look like a full-scale massacre."

"Tell Rett to meet us at the main house, but take every precaution," Griff said. "There could still be some guards around or they could have booby-trapped the house."

Griff tried not to think about the possibility that they would find Nic among the dead, that she could be lying inside the house, her body ripped apart by bullets.

Sanders exchanged a glance with Griff, each aware of what the other was thinking.

The two teams, their weapons defense ready, approached the house from opposite sides. A couple of bodies, one of an old woman and the other of a young boy, lay on the veranda, each a god-awful bloody mess. The heavy wooden front doors stood wide open as if whoever had come through them last had been in too much of a hurry to bother closing them. Luke approached the open door, inspected the area, and then cautiously entered the house.

He called back to the others, "Griff, you, Shaughnessy, and Holt stay outside. Rett, you and Sanders come with me."

Griff started to protest, but common sense kicked in and he understood that Luke had ordered him to stay outside just in case they found Nic. If she was still here, she was probably dead. But they had no proof that she'd ever been here. It was possible this entire island had been set up as nothing more than a decoy.

Unable to erase the thought that Luke might have discovered Nic's body, Griff died by slow degrees as they waited. And waited. He wanted to pray. Tried to pray. But he couldn't form the words. If there was a God, which he doubted, then that higher power didn't give a damn about him or Nic or any of the poor, pitiful bastards lying in shattered heaps all over this fucking island.

Whether five minutes had passed or an hour, Griff couldn't be certain. All he knew was that when he saw Luke coming down the stairs and into the foyer, he finally managed to pray. *Please, God, don't let her be dead.*

"She's not here," Luke called the moment he saw Griff. "There's no one here."

Griff closed his eyes. *Thank you, God.*

Sanders clamped his broad, thick hand down on Griff's shoulder. He opened his eyes and looked at his old friend.

Luke came up to Griff, dug something out of his pocket, and held it in his open palm. "Does this look familiar to you?"

Resting there in the center of Luke's big hand lay a gold circle, a simple wedding band. Griff grasped the ring, looked inside for an inscription, and when he saw the initials GP, his heart stopped.

"It's Nic's wedding band. She had my initials put inside her band and her initials are inside mine."

Bound, gagged, and blindfolded once again, Nic managed to keep her balance as Linden dragged her from the boat onto shore. She had no idea where they were, but she suspected that they wouldn't be here for very long. From time to time, Linden issued orders in English, Spanish, and another language that Nic didn't recognize. She heard grumbling male voices—no female—and the steady tromp of feet, her own included.

Linden stopped abruptly, hauled her to his side, and lifted her up and onto a seat. Another jeep? Probably. The vehicle slipped along over the bumpy road, a road Nic thought no doubt led to the same airstrip Linden had used two days ago. Dear God in heaven, had it really been only two days ago? On Sunday morning, she had arrived at her Gatlinburg cabin. By late that day, they had arrived on the island. If her calculations were correct, this was Tuesday.

The vehicle slowed, stopped, and then Linden helped her down and out and onto her feet. As he guided her up the steps and onto the airplane, she heard shouting, followed by rapid gunfire and someone swearing loudly.

She wanted to scream, "What happened? Did they kill someone else?" But despite the nausea in her belly and the trembling through her body, Nic boarded the plane without protest. Once on board, Linden shoved her down into a seat and buckled the safety belt around her.

"Sit there and behave yourself," he told her. "Once we're in flight, I'll take off your blindfold and remove the gag."

Nic sat quietly, being a good little girl, wondering how long it would take Griff to figure out where Linden had taken her. How many hours, days or weeks would it be before he stormed the island and discovered all those dead bodies? All those poor, pitiful people the guards had murdered. If she was lucky, when Griff searched the house and grounds, he would find the little present she had left behind, just for him.

While Linden had been ushering her through the foyer and toward the front door, Nic had managed to fiddle with her wedding band and engagement ring and deftly remove both. As she had walked past a lace-adorned, mahogany entry table, she had inched close enough to drop her wedding ring, praying that it would land quietly. It had barely made a sound as it fell onto the handmade lace table runner.

Chapter 10

Maleah stopped the Dodge Grand Caravan in front of Yvette Meng's home, shut off the engine, and turned around to face Barbara Jean where she sat in her wheelchair in the back of the modified minivan.

"I don't like this," Maleah said. "I don't completely trust Dr. Meng."

Barbara Jean sighed softly, wishing she could help Maleah see past her resentment for Yvette and become fully aware of what a truly good soul the woman possessed. "Yvette wants to help locate Nic. What could possibly be wrong with that?"

"On the surface, nothing. But it certainly would clear the way for her if Nic never comes back, wouldn't it?"

"Maleah! What a terrible thing to say, to imply. . . " Barbara Jean leaned forward from her position behind Maleah where the center seats had been removed to accommodate her wheelchair. She reached over and laid her hand on Maleah's arm. "You've allowed Nic's doubts about Yvette to cloud your judgment. If Yvette and Griff had wanted to be together, they could have been years before Griff and Nic met."

"Just because Griff didn't want her doesn't mean she didn't want him."

Barbara Jean shook her head. "Yvette isn't in love with Griff. She cares for him and for Sanders as one would their brothers."

"As a general rule one doesn't have a child fathered by someone who is like a brother."

"You are determined to dislike and distrust Yvette, aren't you? Can't you put yourself in Yvette's place, imagine what it was like for her to be forced to have sex with numerous men, to become pregnant and not know who had fathered her child? Griff is only one of several men who may be the father."

151

"All right. All right. I'm not being fair to her. So shoot me."

"You're worried about Nic. I understand. But blaming Yvette really isn't fair."

"I know. There's more than enough blame to go around, isn't there? If Griff had just told Nic the truth before they got married or anytime in the past three years, Nic wouldn't have left here. If Nic had stayed at Griffin's Rest where she was safe and hadn't run away to her cabin to lick her wounds, she wouldn't be missing. If I had gone with her when she left—"

"You might be missing now, too," Barbara Jean told her. "There is no point in thinking about 'what ifs' at this point. We have to concentrate on doing what we can to find Nic and to help Griff."

"And you think that Yvette and Meredith Sinclair can conjure up some spell that will reveal to them where Nic is?"

"I think that it would be foolish not to take advantage of every possible avenue open to us." Barbara Jean held up the tortoiseshell-handled hairbrush she had brought with her. "Once Meredith handles this brush, she may pick up on something. She may sense where Nic is now and what's happening to her."

"This is all too much like voodoo to suit me."

"Maybe it is, but if using voodoo would help us find Nic, wouldn't you be willing to use it?"

"Sure I would. I'd do anything to find Nic and bring her home."

"I believe that Meredith has a rare gift and she is willing to use it to see if she can in any way connect with Nic."

"I hope you're right about her. I hope she can dream a dream or pick up on Nic's energy or can experience an alternate reality where she sees where Nic is."

Before Barbara Jean could respond, Maleah opened the driver's side door of the silver minivan. She got out, rounded the front of the vehicle, and using the remote, opened the passenger-side sliding door. The ramp deployed from the bottom of the sliding door, allowing Barbara Jean to maneuver her wheelchair out of the Grand Caravan, down the ramp, and onto the half-moon driveway in front of Yvette's home.

"Want me to go with you?" Maleah asked.

"I think I can take it from here." She smiled up at Maleah. "You should get back to the main house. Saxon will be returning from the airport with Nic's brother at any time. You need be there to meet him."

Maleah nodded. "I promised Griff that I would be the one to explain what happened and bring him up-to-date on the situation."

"Don't paint Griff as the bad guy," Barbara Jean said. "All of us need to pull together, not let our differences of opinion pull us apart."

"I don't intend to say anything against Griff. Charles David can draw his own conclusions. It's not as if he wasn't already aware that there was trouble in paradise."

Barbara Jean knew it was useless to say more. Maleah, Lord love her, was a stubborn little mule who felt duty-bound by her friendship with Nic to do what she thought was in Nic's best interest. For the time being, that included disliking Yvette and blaming Griff.

"I'll call you when I'm ready to return to the main house."

"Okay." Maleah gave Barbara Jean a hesitant smile. "Good luck with Dr. Meng and Meredith. I hope they actually can do something to help us find Nic."

Maleah and Derek met Nic's brother in the foyer and welcomed him to Griffin's Rest. Charles David Bellamy was tall, muscular, dark-haired and dark-eyed. He resembled his older sister so much that they could easily pass for twins. The first time Maleah met him, she had thought that it was a pity such strikingly beautiful features were wasted on a man.

"Here, let me take your bag." Derek reached out and took the black vinyl suitcase from their guest. "I'll run it up to your room and make sure Inez's got everything ready."

Maleah offered Charles David a reassuring half

smile. "Come on into the living room and I'll fill you in on everything."

Without hesitation, he followed her; and when she indicated they should sit on the sofa, he followed her lead.

"When you called me last night, you said that Nic had left Griffin's Rest Sunday morning and that you followed her up to the Gatlinburg cabin later, but when you arrived she wasn't there."

"That's right. I should have gone with her, but she insisted I stay here. Griff sent Cully Redmond with her, in a separate car. Cully followed Nic and was to act as her bodyguard while she was away from Griffin's Rest."

"You explained all of this in our telephone conversation." Charles David looked straight into her eyes. "Nic went to the cabin, but when you arrived she wasn't there. This Redmond fellow was shot and killed while en route to the cabin. You suspect that Nic was kidnapped by a man named Anthony Linden, a man who has murdered six people associated with the Powell Agency. Now, what I want to know is, with a man like that on the loose, why would my sister leave the safety of Griffin's Rest?"

There it was, the inevitable question that Maleah had been dreading. How could she possibly answer him truthfully without condemning Griff?

Griff had told her, *"Answer his questions*

truthfully. And if those answers put me in a bad light, so be it."

"Griff tried to talk her out of leaving," Maleah finally managed to say. "So did I, but you know our Nic. When she makes up her mind about something . . . In retrospect, I wish I had gone with her when she left Sunday morning, but she insisted that I stay here with Derek because we're newly engaged and—"

"Congratulations."

"Thank you."

"But you decided later to follow her to the cabin, right?"

Maleah nodded. "I'm sure Griff wishes he had kept her here even if he'd had to lock her up and throw away the key." *There. I defended Griff. Conscience clear.* "We're all feeling guilty that we didn't do more to persuade her to stay here."

"Why did she leave?" Charles David asked again. "She must have been upset about something to feel the need to get away from Griffin's Rest, to go alone to the cabin when she knew—"

"She was upset. She needed to get away and think about some things without any distractions." Maleah swallowed hard. "Sunday morning, Griff revealed to her certain facts that he had never shared with her, things about what had happened to him and Dr. Meng and Sanders on Amara. I'm sure Nic has told you something about that, but . . . There is no easy way to say this, so I'm

156

just going to say it. Dr. Meng was forced to have sex with a lot of different men by her psycho husband who controlled Amara and its inhabitants. Griff was . . . he was one of the men. And she had a baby that her husband took from her right after it was born and she and Griff have been searching for the child all these years and . . . " Maleah paused for breath.

"And Dr. Meng's baby, the child she and Griff have been searching for, could be Griff's child. Is that what he told Nic?" Charles David closed his eyes and tightened his jaw, so obviously doing his best to control his emotions.

She wanted to tell Nic's brother to go ahead and cry or scream and curse or run his fist through a wall, to do whatever he needed to do to relieve the anger.

"Yes," Maleah said. "I think Nic could have accepted the news about the child if Griff had been totally honest with her about his relationship with Dr. Meng. He had sworn to Nic that he and Dr. Meng were never lovers."

"And technically, they weren't," Charles David said.

"That's right," Derek agreed as he entered the living room. "I'm sure that once Griff finds Nic and brings her home, they will be able to work through whatever problems—"

"If I know my sister, right now she regrets having left Griffin's Rest," Charles David said.

"But as far as Nic and Griff being able to work through their problems when he finds her, I have my doubts. Griff should have told her everything long before now. The secrets he's kept from her are what created their problems. And if anything happens to Nic, I'm not sure I'll ever be able to forgive him."

"Amen to that." She didn't realize she had spoken aloud until Derek shot her a damn-it-Maleah glare.

"Where is my brother-in-law? Did he send you two to—?"

"The agency received information that led us to believe that Nic is possibly being held on a privately owned island in the Caribbean Sea," Derek explained. "Griff took an experienced team with him on a search-and-rescue mission."

Charles David's eyes misted with unshed tears as he looked from Derek to Maleah. "Will you be honest with me, Maleah? What are the odds that they'll find Nic alive?"

Oh, God. Oh, dear God. Maleah couldn't bear the thought that Nic might already be dead. She had kept telling herself that if Linden had kidnapped Nic, he had been following Malcolm York's orders. And if the namesake of Griff's nemesis from Amara was behind Nic's disappearance, then maybe—just maybe—he would keep Nic alive and dangle her life in front of Griff, using her to lure Griff into a deadly trap.

"I honestly don't know," Maleah admitted. "But I have to believe that she's still alive and that Griff is going to find her and bring her home."

When she glanced at Derek, he shook his head subtly. Was the gesture a warning or a plea? Did it really matter? She knew what he was asking her not to do, could almost hear him saying, "Don't tell Charles David that Nic is pregnant."

Nic wondered how long Linden planned on waiting before he removed her gag and blindfold. They had been in flight for quite a while, but she knew she couldn't accurately estimate the time. Under the circumstances, every minute seemed endless, every hour an eternity. As much as she wished otherwise, she had no control over what was happening to her, and that knowledge both frustrated and frightened her. The great, freaking unknown lay before her, its insidious, foreboding tentacles wrapping themselves around her mind, creating wide-awake nightmares she fought to control. She could be raped, tortured, and killed. She could be set loose to run for her life while a group of crazy millionaires and billionaires hunted her for sport. She could be tossed from the plane. She could be sold into slavery and become some despot's sex toy. The horrifying possibilities seemed endless.

Whatever fate awaited her, she felt relatively certain that Malcolm York was the all-powerful puppet master who would be pulling the strings. Did York already know what he intended to do to her? Was she simply part of some elaborate plan he had concocted? Or were his plans for her fluid and unformed, his decisions made on one whim after another? Either way, she had no doubt that York had one major objective—lure Griff into a trap by using her as bait.

Someone sat down beside Nic. She felt them, smelled them, sensed his presence and knew it was Linden.

"I apologize for keeping you in the dark this long." He chuckled as if he found his comment amusing. "I've been busy. Arrangements to be made. Orders to be followed."

Nic squirmed in her seat, but didn't make a sound.

Linden's fingers grazed her cheek as he reached around her to untie the tightly knotted gag. When he yanked it from her mouth and then completely off, she sucked in huge gulps of unrestricted air. Breathing so deeply made her lungs ache, but it was a good pain.

"I told Mr. York that you've been quite cooperative," Linden said as he undid her blindfold and removed it. "I didn't tell him everything." Linden leaned close, his mouth at her ear. "Lina will be severely punished for helping you. I have personally seen to that, but there's no need for Mr. York to worry himself with such trivial details, is there?"

Nic opened her eyes, blinked a couple of times, and turned to look straight at Linden. "You're a sadistic son of a bitch, aren't you?"

He laughed. Lifting his hand, he grazed his knuckles across her cheek again and then down her neck. "You intrigue me, Nicole Baxter Powell. I feel certain that Mr. York will find you as intriguing as I do."

"Just when am I going to meet Malcolm York?"

"Soon. Be patient."

"What's the holdup? I thought he was eager to meet me."

"He is. He is. But he's made all these interesting plans for you. He wants to give you time to become acclimated to the situation, to find out for yourself that you are completely at his mercy, that he owns you body and soul."

Nic stared at Linden, hating him with every fiber of her being, but hating the pseudo-York even more. "And just what plans does Mr. York have for me? More of the same? Being awarded as a prize to another victorious hunter?"

"Mr. York has a series of games he wants you to play to keep him entertained and also to help you adjust to your new position as his property. The game on Shelter Island was only one game and you've played it now. We'll be moving on to something new and even more fun."

"I can hardly wait."

Linden laughed again. "I find it interesting that you haven't lost your sense of humor yet. But you will, Nicole. You will. Before long, you won't be uttering any sarcastic remarks. You'll be begging for mercy."

Nic tugged on her bound wrists. "How about I start now?" She held up her hands. "Please, take these off. I promise I won't try to scratch your eyes out."

Linden grabbed the back of her neck and jerked her toward him until they were nose-to-nose. Her breathing quickened. Damn it, she had waved a red flag in front of this raging bull. He threaded his fingers into her hair, tightened his hold, and yanked hard. Pain shot through her head and brought tears to her eyes.

"I would like nothing better than to beat you until you couldn't open that pretty little mouth except to moan and groan."

If her hands weren't tied . . . If Linden wasn't armed . . . If she wasn't afraid retaliating would endanger her baby . . .

"Who knows, maybe when Mr. York finishes with you, he'll give you to me. Something for us to look forward to. Right, Nicole?"

He eased his fingers from her hair and his hand from around her neck. "But for now, you're safe from me."

She stared at him, hoping he noticed the defiance in her eyes. She needed for him to know that even if she didn't put up a physical fight, she was not defeated. Linden was wrong about York owning her body and soul. They could use and abuse her body. They could even kill her. But her soul belonged to her and she would never relinquish possession. No matter what.

Before she realized his intention, Linden unbound her wrists. While she rubbed the raw flesh on first one and then the other, he unsnapped her safety belt, grabbed her arm, and pulled her out of the seat and onto her feet.

"Mr. York has arranged a surprise for you." Linden shoved her in front of him. "You remember the way to the sleeping quarters on this airplane, don't you?" When they reached the private cabin, Linden opened the door. "Go on. Go inside and see what's waiting for you."

What sort of surprise? Nausea churned in her belly. Overwhelming fear ate away at her resolve to stay strong. *You can't escape. You have no choice but to face whatever unknown terror is waiting for you.* She squared her shoulders and said a prayer for strength and endurance as she tried to prepare herself. And then she took a deep breath and walked into the bedroom.

The area was dimly lit, so after Linden closed and locked the door, it took her eyes a couple of minutes to adjust completely to the semidarkness. She scanned the room from floor to ceiling, from side to side, and then the length from end to end.

Something stirred in the far corner.

Something large and hairy rose up from the floor and stood on two feet.

When the beast came toward Nic, she screamed.

CHAPTER 11

"Thank you for agreeing to help us." Yvette exchanged a cordial expression with Barbara Jean Hughes.

"I'll do anything I can to help find Nic." Barbara Jean lifted a tortoiseshell hairbrush from her lap and offered it to Yvette. "This is Nic's. She used it every day."

"And yet she didn't take it with her to the cabin."

"There was no need. She has an identical vanity set there."

Yvette nodded. Staring at the hairbrush, she hesitated taking it from Barbara Jean. She had learned not to touch others, not even in a friendly handshake, unless she knew beforehand that she could block that person's energy. Otherwise, a simple swipe of her hand against theirs could result in an unintentional invasion of their privacy. In the years she had known this kind, understanding woman, they had gradually built a fragile friendship, one sustained by the fact that they never discussed the past that Yvette shared with Sanders and Griffin.

"It's all right. I don't mind if you touch me." Barbara Jean extended her hand farther, holding out the brush for Yvette to take.

Being careful to avoid any skin-to-skin contact, she cupped the back of the brush and cradled it in her hand. But even without touch, with only the hairbrush acting as a conduit between them, Yvette sensed a momentary flash of emotion from the other woman.

Pity. Sympathy. Uncertainty. And a hint of curiosity.

Yvette shivered. The uncertainty her friend felt was understandable, as was the curiosity. They knew the basic facts concerning each other's lives, but they had never shared confidences. The pity and sympathy Barbara Jean felt were both for Yvette. She wanted neither from Barbara Jean or anyone else.

"You will stay, yes?" Yvette asked. "It is not necessary for you to be here, but I would appreciate your being near in case we need your assistance."

"Please stay, Ms. Hughes," Meredith said, her hazel-green eyes expressing resignation, accepting the fact that her participation was crucial.

Yvette knew, possibly better than anyone, what courage it took for Meredith to allow her psychic talents free rein. Although she had been with

Yvette for a number of years now and was an adept and eager student, she had not yet learned to control her remarkable gifts. It could take many more years of training for her to acquire that ability.

Yvette motioned for Barbara Jean to move her wheelchair opposite the sofa. "Are you ready?" she asked Meredith.

The young psychic nodded and when Yvette sat on the sofa, she took her place beside her. Yvette handed Meredith the hairbrush.

"Take your time. Don't force anything," Yvette instructed. "Let it come to you." When Meredith took Nic's hairbrush, clutched it in her hand, and brought her hand upward to rest against her chest, Yvette touched her. She gently patted her fingertips up and down on Meredith's shoulder and sensed an instant connection. *I will safeguard you. If you go in too far, I will bring you back without hesitation. Trust me to take care of you.*

Meredith took a deep breath. *I trust you completely.*

Yvette broke the connection, knowing it would only hinder Meredith's descent into a realm of transcendental awareness where she must go alone.

While Meredith held the brush against her heart, her eyes wide open, her expression solemn, Yvette glanced across the room at Barbara Jean. They exchanged a brief look before each focused their full attention on the woman who suddenly closed her eyes and whimpered softly.

"She loves him so, . . ." Meredith lifted the brush and cradled it against her cheek. "Secrets. So many secrets. Please, tell me. Don't shut me out."

"Yes, Nicole loves Griffin, but she knows he has kept secrets from her," Yvette said. "Go past that moment, try to leave Griffin's Rest, see if you can leave here and follow Nicole."

Meredith's head swayed slowly from side to side and then she slumped forward, her chin coming to rest on her upper chest. "Lies," she murmured. "Lies. You lied to me. Damn you! I hate you. I hate her. I hate knowing you had a child with her."

Tears spilled from Meredith's closed eyes and poured down her cheeks. She gasped for air between deep sobs. She doubled over in pain, wrapped herself in a hug, and keened with soul-wrenching pain.

"Oh, dear Lord," Barbara Jean said so quietly that Yvette barely heard her.

Yvette placed her arm around Meredith's trembling shoulders and while comforting her, she reached out and pried the tortoiseshell hairbrush from her death-grip hold. After she tossed the brush onto the floor, she rubbed Meredith's back with soothing circular motions.

"You will be all right. Release the pain. It is not yours."

Yvette continued talking to Meredith, bringing her slowly back from the brink, absorbing some of Nicole's emotional agony that had possessed Meredith. The intensity of Nicole's emotions, transferred through contact with an object Nicole used on a regular basis, had dragged Meredith swiftly and completely to the epicenter of the other woman's pain.

Eventually, Meredith settled quietly. Her breathing returned to normal and she opened her eyes. "She was in such terrible pain." Meredith stared at Yvette. "She doesn't truly hate Griffin or you. She hates the way she was lied to. She hates the way the revelation of those secrets made her feel."

"I understand," Yvette said.

"I didn't help, did I? All I sensed was Nicole's pain and anger before she left home. It was as if her emotions were completely centered here at Griffin's Rest." Meredith's eyes widened with realization. "I need to go to her cabin, to where she was when she was taken. If it's possible for me to connect with her there, I may be able to follow her to where she is now."

"I'll make arrangements for us to go to Nicole's cabin first thing in the morning."

"No," Barbara Jean told them. "Neither of you can leave Griffin's Rest. It's too dangerous."

"We have to go," Meredith said. "I truly believe it's the only way I have any chance of locating where she is."

"It may be unnecessary," Barbara Jean reminded them. "Griffin and Sanders and the others may be rescuing Nic at this very moment."

"I sincerely hope they are," Meredith said. "But if—"

"If Griffin does not find her, then we will go to the cabin," Yvette said. "I'll talk to Derek and Maleah and explain the situation. I'm sure I can make them understand."

"Don't be afraid," the man told Nic. "I won't hurt you."

With terror immobilizing her body and another scream dying in her throat, Nic stared at the tall, half-naked man standing less than five feet from her. His upper torso was bare, revealing a broad chest and wide shoulders. Despite being much too thin, his body still maintained a semblance of the muscular frame that he had once possessed. Streaks of grime and sweat stained his leather-tan skin and the loose-fitting khaki slacks he wore were faded, ragged, and tied at the waist with a piece of rope. His dirty and matted dark hair hung to his shoulders. A strong scent of body odor wafted across the room. The man stank.

When he made no attempt to come closer, Nic relaxed her tense muscles as she looked into his brown eyes. At that moment, she realized where she had seen this man before, and his presence here on the private plane puzzled her.

"You were on the island," Nic said. "I saw you in one of the cages. You—you spoke to me."

"You told me that you were there against your will just as I was." Fury and frustration edged his deep baritone voice. "You do know that they killed the others."

"Yes. I heard the gunfire and I saw some of the bodies."

"It seems that you and I were kept alive for a reason," he told her, his country Southern accent unmistakable.

"Do you have any idea—?"

"Why they didn't kill us? Why they've put us together on this airplane? I don't know, but you can be sure whatever the reason, it won't be good for either of us."

"Linden—the man who abducted me and took me to the island—told me before he forced me into this room with you that Malcolm York had arranged a surprise for me."

"Ah, Malcolm York, our benevolent benefactor." A quirky smile twitched the man's lips.

"You know Malcolm York? You've met him?"

"I don't know him. And I haven't exactly met him, but I have seen him."

"Where? When?"

When the man inched closer to Nic, she backed away, instinctively wary of his intimidating glare. As if realizing her distrust, he stopped immediately.

"I've been one of York's multipurpose captives for quite a while, probably close to a year now, although I've lost the actual count. They've moved me around from place to place. York has been on hand for one of the hunts and both of the arena fights I took part in."

"Arena fights?" Griff had never mentioned anything about arena fights on Amara. Had this been another secret he had kept from her?

"Think Roman gladiators." He grunted with disgust. "Only with two unequal, oftentimes untrained, opponents fighting to the death."

"Are you saying that you've been forced to—?"

"Kill or be killed. Yeah. Something I can be proud of, right? I'm tough enough to have survived by killing a couple of poor bastards who wanted to live as much as I did."

"Who are you?" Nic studied his hairy face, his beard and mustache sun-streaked brown and as dirty as his long, tangled hair. He looked every inch a wild man, except for his intelligent brown eyes. "Why were you taken prisoner?"

Twenty years ago, Griffin Powell, star quarterback for the University of Tennessee, slated to be drafted by the Dallas Cowboys, had mysteriously disappeared shortly after college graduation. The real York had personally chosen Griff because the men he handpicked for Amara were the best of the best in their fields. Always young, most of them in their prime. Griff had been a star athlete. What was this man's claim to fame?

"Does my name really matter?" he asked.

"It does to me."

"I could ask you the same question. You're a beautiful woman, but you're older than the usual women they abduct as sex slaves." He surveyed her from head to toe. "Judging from your physique, I'd say they plan to use you in the arena."

"Linden kidnapped me less than seventy-two hours ago. I have no idea how they plan to use me in the future, but last night I was handed over to the winner of the hunt. I was one of his prizes, along with the privilege of chopping off his quarry's head."

"I'm sorry you were raped." He inclined his head toward the locked door. "I think that may be what the man you call Linden had in mind when he put you in here with me. They think that if they treat us like animals, we'll eventually become animals."

"A servant girl named Lina saved me last night," Nic confessed. "She drugged the man and this morning, he didn't remember what had happened."

He chuckled to himself, the sound barely audible. "Good for Lina."

"No, bad for Lina. I don't know if Linden sent her away for punishment or if he had her killed."

"My name is Jonas."

Their gazes met and locked.

"I'm Nicole."

He held out his big, dirty, battered hand. Without hesitation, she grasped his hand and shook it firmly.

When he released her, he kept his gaze focused directly on her face. "I won't ever intentionally hurt you, Nicole. But there may come a time, when I won't have a choice. They can force you to do things you don't want to do."

"Like kill someone or be killed yourself. Like being forced to have sex in front of an audience. Like thinking and acting like an animal in order to survive."

"You seem to know an awful lot for a woman who's been held captive only a couple of days."

"I was aware of the type of man Malcolm York is before I was taken hostage."

He cocked his head at an angle and narrowed his gaze. "You're a cop, aren't you? Some sort of international—"

"I used to be a federal agent," she told him. "What did you used to be?"

"I was a NASCAR driver."

"Jonas . . . " She mentally repeated his name. Realization dawned. "You're Jonas MacColl. You're not just a NASCAR driver. You're *the* NASCAR driver. Oh my God, you were in a plane crash nearly a year ago. The plane went down over the Atlantic somewhere and none of the bodies were ever recovered."

"That plane might have crashed over the

Atlantic, but it went down without me in it," he said. "I did a little too much celebrating one night and when I woke up the next morning, I was on a plane all right, one headed straight for hell, not the bottom of the Atlantic. Since I have no memory of anything except getting drunk, I figured that last drink was drugged."

"And you were chosen because you were the best of the best."

Malcolm York's trademark, choosing the cream of the crop.

"Yeah, so it would seem. So, Nicole, what's your claim to fame?"

"My claim to fame?" Nic said. "I'm Mrs. Griffin Powell."

The call they had been waiting for came in at nightfall. Sanders contacted them from the Belize City airport shortly before takeoff. But the news was not what they had hoped and prayed for from the moment the Powell team left Griffin's Rest that morning.

"We arrived too late," Sanders had told Derek. "We were correct in assuming Linden took Nicole to Shelter Island. Unfortunately, before we arrived, he had already whisked her away and they are, no doubt, en route to a new location. We assume there had been armed guards on the island. We found only dead bodies. They did not leave a single person alive."

Maleah had taken the news badly. Although she had known from the get-go that the odds were against the Powell team finding Nic so quickly. Derek dreaded to think what condition Griff would be in when he returned home.

All they could do now was regroup and move on, utilizing all their available sources for more information. The agents in the field would be turning over every slimy rock they found, searching for what might be hidden underneath. Each of them, those on the A-team here at Griffin's Rest, had a specific job. Sanders had to keep Griff under control, if at all possible. Yvette Meng's psychic gifts and the special talents her students possessed would be used to help locate Nic. Maleah would coordinate all the incoming information, sort through it, and decide what was useful and what was not. And he would do what he did best. Profiling.

Derek had spent most of the day working on a profile of the pseudo-York. By combining what little they knew about this mystery man with the information he had obtained about the real Malcolm York, Derek was putting together a sketchy composite. He took into account the very real possibility that the pseudo-York possessed wealth and power equal to that of the original York. If so, that meant he really was the one issuing orders to the psychotically evil Anthony Linden. Evil was not really a scientific evaluation, but nevertheless it perfectly described men such as Linden and the pseudo-York.

"They're here." Maleah nudged Derek as she roused from the sofa, removing his arm from around her shoulders as she bolted to her feet.

He reached up and grabbed her wrist.

She looked down at him and said, "What?"

"Give the guy a break, will you? Don't jump on Griff with both feet the minute he walks through the front door."

Frowning, she jerked away from him. "Give me a little credit, will you? I'm still pissed at Griff, but I'm thinking more rationally now. I realize he's probably been beating himself up all the way back from Belize. I know that more than anything in this world, he wanted to bring Nic home with him."

"We all need to give him a wide berth. He'll probably be acting a lot like a badly wounded bear. One wrong word and he could go berserk."

"I need to know what happened on Shelter Island," Maleah said. "You told me that Sanders didn't go into much detail, but that he was certain Nic had been held on the island before they arrived."

"If I promise to find out all that I can tonight and share it with you when I come up to bed, will you go on upstairs now?"

"You don't want me to see Griff, do you?"

"No, honey, that's not it. I don't want Griff to

see you. You don't have a poker face. Despite what you say, you still blame him for what happened to Nic, and when he looks at you, all he'll see is your accusatory expression."

"Accusatory expression? You're kidding, right?"

"Blondie, please."

"Oh, all right. But if you don't find out everything that happened and why they're so sure Nic was on the island, I'll—"

"I swear." He crossed his heart, and then reached up and swatted her butt. "Now, go upstairs."

When she turned and marched toward the open double doors leading from the living room into the foyer, he got up and followed her. Just to make sure. When she reached the foot of the staircase, she paused and glanced over her shoulder.

"Don't you trust me?" she asked.

"With my life," he replied. "But that doesn't mean I'm not aware of how sneaky you can be."

When the front door suddenly opened, Maleah didn't wait around to ask questions. Without saying a word, she raced up the stairs. Derek released a thankful breath. The very last thing Griffin Powell needed was to have to face his wife's best friend.

Sanders entered the house first, an advance guard, his dark gaze sweeping across the foyer. Massive shoulders slumped, head down, Griffin returned to his home, a defeated warrior. Derek waited silently for either Griff or Sanders to speak first. Neither said a word. Griff never looked Derek's way. He lumbered out of the foyer and down the hall toward his study. By then, the other four members of the team had made their way, one by one, into the house, Shaughnessy first, followed by Holt and Rett, with Luke the rear guard.

"I suggest you all get a good night's sleep," Sanders told the men. "Meet me in the office tomorrow morning promptly at oh-eight-hundred."

Since it was already after one A.M., the guys would be lucky to get five hours' sleep. No one tarried. Everyone, except Luke, left immediately. They would spend the night in the five-bedroom building referred to by everyone as the Powell bunkhouse, located a mile from the main house, Griff had had it built to provide comfortable accommodations for the agents when they worked at Griffin's Rest.

"Will you need me tonight?" Luke asked Sanders, his gaze traveling down the hallway toward Griff's study.

"No, I don't think so. I believe I can handle things here," Sanders replied and then he glanced at Derek. "If you want to wait for me, we can talk when I return."

"I'll wait," Derek said.

Sanders nodded.

Luke and Derek watched as Sanders walked away, down the hall, heading straight for Griff's study. Luke turned to leave.

"Hold up a minute, will you?" Derek called to him.

He paused just as he reached the front door.

"Dr. Meng wants to take Meredith Sinclair to Nic's cabin in Gatlinburg tomorrow morning. She believes Meredith might be able to somehow connect with Nic and possibly be able to locate her."

"Damn," Luke grumbled.

"Griff gave specific instructions that Dr. Meng is not to leave Griffin's Rest. But he didn't say anything about Meredith. She can't go alone, and since you two have some sort of rapport, I thought you could drive her to Gatlinburg and—"

"Do you plan to run this by Griff first? He still wants me to get in touch with my various contacts in Europe as soon as possible."

"I hadn't planned on running this by Griff. I figured it would be one less thing for him to have to worry about," Derek said. "Besides, if Meredith doesn't come through for us with any useful information, then Griff won't have gotten his hopes up for nothing. Right?"

Luke glowered at Derek, but he said, "Yeah, right."

"Then you'll take Meredith to Nic's cabin in the morning?"

"Against my better judgment, yeah, I'll take her. Tell the little psychic fruitcake to be ready at six o'clock sharp. I'll pick her up over at Dr. Meng's place."

CHAPTER 12

The private plane had landed sometime during the night. Exactly where, Nic didn't know. Someplace warm. Maybe another tropical paradise? Two armed guards had entered the bedroom, manacled Jonas MacColl, and dragged him away while Linden had watched.

"Time to deplane," Linden had told her. "Come along, Nicole. People are waiting for us."

"Where are they taking him?"

Linden's lips had twitched with amusement. "Liked the hillbilly race car driver, did you? Don't worry. You'll be seeing him again."

She had expected to be blindfolded and gagged and had been surprised when Linden escorted her off the plane without either. But now she knew why. Except for the lights lining the runway, it was pitch black, which suggested a private airstrip. Since she had lost track of time—when in hell, one lost track of time. It passed much slower than in the real world, so she couldn't be sure how far they might have traveled. Her guess was not more than six or seven hours. But in which direction had they flown—north, south, east or west? For all she knew, they could now be back in the U.S. somewhere or in South America or on another island in either the Atlantic or the Pacific.

Wherever they were, she assumed that they had entered the country illegally. Linden rushed her off the plane and straight to a waiting car instead of taking her through an airport terminal.

He shoved her into the backseat of a black sedan, an older-model vehicle with tail fins and heavy with the type of chrome that hadn't adorned automobiles in more than fifty years. The side windows in the car had been darkened, making it impossible to see out or to see in. Except for the driver—and all she could see was the back of his head—she and Linden were alone.

She wanted to ask him a dozen questions, but knew he wouldn't answer even one. Keeping her guessing apparently was part of the fun for Linden and his employer. Had Malcolm York instructed Linden to build the tension, to allow her to imagine the worst, to put the fear of God into her? If so, then he had succeeded in his task. By her very nature, she was a fighter, but considering the fact she was pregnant, surviving was far more important than showing her captor how tough she was.

"You're very quiet," Linden finally said.

She didn't reply.

"Suit yourself." He chuckled. "I'm sure your husband will have a great deal to say when he finds out just how chummy you've become with another of Mr. York's guests."

Nic clamped her mouth shut to keep from blasting Linden. She wanted to scream that not a damn thing, other than conversation, had gone on between Jonas MacColl and her. But common sense overruled emotional reaction. In order for Griff to find out about Jonas, either Linden or York would have to contact him.

Okay, so let's say that they contact Griff. Will they ask for a ransom? Will they promise him my safe return in exchange for something they want from him? Or do they plan to call Griff simply to torment him?

During the ride from the airstrip to their destination, Linden kept needling Nic, trying to get a rise out of her. But she managed to remain in control and that seemed to piss him off, which delighted her.

When the old car came to a stop, Nic sucked in a deep breath and willed herself to be brave. Someone opened the car door on Linden's side and as soon as he got out, he reached into the backseat, grabbed Nic's arm, and hauled her out and onto her feet.

She might not know what country she was in, but by taking a good look at her surroundings, she knew Linden had brought her to a small, isolated harbor. Poorly lit, the rickety wooden wharf and the scattering of gangling, ramshackle buildings appeared totally deserted, except for two outback motorboats, each manned by a couple of armed guards.

Just as Linden urged her to move in front of him, onto the weathered pier and toward one of the boats, she heard another vehicle that looked like an older-model Lincoln drive up and stop. When she glanced over her shoulder, she saw a large black man emerge from the front seat, open the back door, and pull someone from the back of the car. Before Linden forced her to turn around and one of the guards helped her on board the first motorboat, Nic recognized the other prisoner. Jonas MacColl, securely shackled, struggled to walk toward the pier. When he tripped and almost fell, his jailor rammed the butt of his rifle into Jonas's ribs. Nic bit her bottom lip to keep from crying out.

"Aren't you happy that your new friend will be going with us?" Linden sat down beside Nic in the boat.

She simply met his curious stare head-on, revealing no emotion with her silent response.

In her peripheral vision, she could see the black guard shoving Jonas into the other boat before he climbed aboard himself. Three men to guard one shackled prisoner? Were they that concerned that Jonas might escape? Or had he proven himself to be such a badass that they were actually afraid of him?

The motors roared to life and within minutes the boats sped out of the secluded old harbor and zoomed toward the sea. Were they being taken to another island, another private hunting club where men were stalked and killed as if they were animals and women were used as sex slaves?

There ahead of them, out in the ocean, bright lights blazed on the horizon. Were they the lights of a small coastal town? A nearby island? Or were they coming from—? It was a yacht! An impressive-size ship, at least a hundred feet long.

Did the yacht belong to Malcolm York? If so, was he on board, waiting for her?

Rafe did not own a car. He either rented or leased, but never under his real name, always under a pseudonym. The basalt black metallic Porsche Cayman had been leased under the name of his present incarnation, Leonardo Kasan. He found the name amusing in a bizarrely twisted way. Leonardo and Kasan had been two of the most sadistic guards on Amara. To this day, he could plainly visualize the brutally vicious Kasan who took great pleasure in beating the prisoners. Big, muscular, with a black beard and mustache, Kasan had starred in many of Rafe's worst nightmares. And Leonardo, the short, stocky little prick, had marched around with his M16, firing at will, laughing as his shots forced a captive to dance or cringe in fear. And nothing had made him happier than being assigned to kill a weak, sick, no-longer-useful slave.

Kasan and Leonardo had been executed, but not by his hand, something he would always regret. Griffin had killed Kasan. Hand-to-hand combat in which Griff had gutted Kasan. And Sanders had taken out Leonardo with a single bullet square between his eyes. At least Rafe had been able to see that kill.

He had no time today to reminisce, to waste on memories that would never leave him. Today would be spent preparing for the future, putting his plan to infiltrate Yves Bouchard's exclusive circle of friends into action. As with each of his previous plans, this one would take finesse and infinite patience. Lucky for him he possessed both.

He had chosen Le Gavroche for lunch today because it was not only one of his favorite restaurants in London, but also because Sir Harlan would expect to be wined and dined at nothing less than a two-star Michelin establishment. And Rafe's aim was to please, to kiss his ass, if necessary, in order to ingratiate himself to the old buzzard and gain entry into that decadent, perverted social set that included Bouchard. Choosing a three-star restaurant might have been interpreted as trying too hard and may have sent up a red warning flag. Rafe included subtlety in his arsenal of useful skills, along with patience and finesse.

Aware that Sir Harlan expected punctuality in others, Rafe arrived at 43 Upper Brook Street precisely at ten till one for their one o'clock lunch date. Dressed in the appropriate attire of a successful businessman—tailored suit and silk tie—he entered the brick building that housed the luxurious restaurant. The establishment possessed a gentleman's club atmosphere. He found Sir Harlan had already arrived and been seated at their table.

The moment Rafe approached, Harlan Benecroft greeted him with a smile. "Good to see you again, my boy." He glanced around the room. "Absolutely marvelous choice for lunch. I adore excellent French cuisine."

"As do I, Sir Harlan." Rafe sat across from his guest.

"Please, drop the 'Sir.' I am simply Harlan to my friends and I feel quite certain that you and I are going to be great friends. I sensed it the moment Cassie introduced us."

"Thank you, Harlan. And since we are destined to be great friends, you must call me Leo."

When Harlan laughed, Rafe laughed.

Oh, yes, we are going to become the best of friends.

Their maître d', a bespectacled young woman,

greeted them with a warm smile. Rafe noticed that at a nearby table the waiter gladly translated the French menu for a young couple and even made several recommendations. At another table, when a lady left, no doubt to go to the restroom, a staff member neatly folded her napkin.

After they ordered, a lobster salad with mangos and avocados for Rafe, they settled back to sip on the wine Harlan had requested—Barrel Selection 2003, Low Yield Roussanne, Domaine de Sainte Rose.

"You know the story behind the name of this restaurant, don't you?" Harlan studied Rafe, aka Leonardo, carefully, eagerly waiting his reply.

Suspecting that Harlan hoped he would respond negatively, and would love to enlighten him, Rafe said, "Actually, no, I haven't heard the story."

Harlan's wrinkled face lit up as if a spotlight had just hit it. "You know, of course, that Le Gavroche means urchin in French. Yes?"

"Yes."

"Gavroche was a character in *Les Misérables*. The original painting of the little ragamuffin, who gave this divine restaurant its identity, was presented to the Roux Brothers, the founding chefs, on opening night."

"And when was opening night?" Rafe asked as if he gave a good goddamn.

"April of 1967. A little before your time, eh, Leo?"

Again, when Harlan laughed, Rafe laughed.

"I am told that it was quite a night, with three American movie stars among the guests. Ava Gardner, Robert Redford, and Charlie Chaplin."

"You must have an incredible memory." A little flattery. Not too much, but suitable for the moment.

Harlan beamed. "So I am told, especially for a man of my years."

"A young man such as I would consider himself fortunate to learn from a man of your vast experience."

Squinting as he focused his gaze directly on Rafe, Harlan studied him for several unnerving seconds before he said, "I believe you actually mean that. And if you do, then my dear Leo, I will be more than happy to become your most willing teacher."

Feeling as if he had dodged a bullet, Rafe gave a mental sigh as he lifted his glass and said, "To our future as friends as well as student and teacher."

For the next hour, Rafe enjoyed the delicious meal, topped off with a dessert of Omelette Rothschild, an apricot and Cointreau soufflé, while he spun a simple, succinct tale of his life and shared confidences with his newfound friend. Years ago, Rafe had invented histories for each of his pseudonyms, including the wealthy playboy, Leonardo Kasan, who enjoyed fast cars and loose women and dangerous walks on the wild side.

Harlan seemed interested and apparently easily convinced by Rafe's practiced lies. Another talent Rafe had perfected—lying.

After Rafe took care of the bill, he escorted his mentor outside, shook the older man's hand, and thanked him for the pleasure of sharing lunch with him.

"The pleasure was all mine," Harlan said. "We must do this again soon."

"Most certainly."

As Harlan turned to walk away, he paused, glanced back at Rafe, and said, "Leo, would you be interested in joining me and a few friends at my home for . . ." He cleared his throat, then grinned wickedly. "For dinner and after-dinner entertainment on Saturday evening? That is, of course, if you're free."

"If I find I have a conflict in my schedule, I will cancel the previous engagement," Rafe said. "I look forward to joining you and your friends for dinner and especially for the after-dinner entertainment."

The relatively short drive—about an hour—from Griffin's Rest to Nicole's Gatlinburg cabin seemed longer. Meredith wasn't good at making idle chitchat and since she and Luke Sentell had very little in common, she had tried her hand at casual conversation. After several attempts at discussing mundane subjects such as the weather, the state of the national economy, and his favorite sports team, she stopped trying so hard. He was no more in the mood to pass away the time talking than she was. Of course, knowing him as she did from past experience, she should have realized that he was acting as her escort and bodyguard out of duty and not because he wanted to be with her.

She doubted that anyone really knew the man. She certainly didn't.

You've worked with him, you as a psychic consultant and he as your keeper. You are not friends. You are little more than civil acquaintances.

She often sensed that he disliked her. She knew he hated babysitting her, a term he used to describe having to look after her when she agreed to help on a Powell Agency case. The had joined forces most recently in the rescue of Jaelyn Allen, former Powell agent Michelle Allen's seven-year-old niece who had been kidnapped by Anthony Linden. Several times during the days they had spent in England searching for the child, she had thought maybe Luke was beginning to like her just a little. After all, he had given her the very first nickname she'd ever had.

She had asked him, "Luke, why did you call me Merry Berry?"

She knew that in the past, he had called her a lot

of other names, mostly behind her back. But he had called her Merry Berry almost affectionately, the way a guy would his kid sister.

Is that how he sees me, like a clumsy, slightly nutty—?

"Earth to Meredith," Luke said.

"Huh?"

"You were off in la-la land, weren't you?"

"I was just thinking about us," she admitted.

"Us? There is no us."

"Of course there is. There's you"—she pointed at him—"and there's me." She pointed at herself. "That's us. We're here in this car together, working on a case together again, which means there most certainly is an us."

Luke groaned. She knew what that meant. She had heard the identical sound and seen that God-help-me expression on his face repeatedly while they'd been in London only days ago. Odd how it seemed longer.

"Okay, okay. I concede that there is an us," Luke told her. "Now pay attention."

"To what?"

"To what I'm about to say."

"All right."

"We'll be at Nicole's cabin in a few minutes. I need to set up some ground rules before we get there."

"What sort of ground rules?"

"The kind of rules that will keep you safe,

keep me sane, and if trouble shows up, hopefully will keep us both alive."

"Do you really think we could be in danger?" Meredith asked.

"Probably not, but considering the fact that Powell Agency employees as well as members of several employees' families have been murdered recently, I don't intend to take any chances."

"If Yvette had come with us—"

"That was never an option," Luke said. "But you don't need your mentor in order to perform. You can soar off into the wild blue yonder all on your own."

"Yes, I can, but you know only too well that if I fly too far off into the wild blue yonder I run the risk of not being able to fly back home unless someone is there waiting for me, to guide me back safely."

Luke didn't comment. Instead he kept his gaze glued to the winding mountainside road leading higher and higher above downtown Gatlinburg. Meredith sat quietly, tried not to think about anything in particular, and occasionally glanced out the window, noting the sparsity of cabins and chalets as the forest grew dense and the paved road turned into a gravel lane.

When Nicole's cabin came into view, Meredith's eyes widened at the sight of the glass and log structure that seemed to be hanging off the side of the mountain. No wonder Griffin Powell's wife had chosen this place as her private sanctuary.

Luke parked the agency-owned sedan, a late-model Chevy Impala, in the drive, shut off the engine, and turned to Meredith. She faced him, waiting for the first of what was sure to be many commands.

"The agency has kept guards up here, out of sight, since Nic went missing," Luke explained. "That means we can get out and roam around without worrying too much about our safety. But just because we have people watching our backs does not mean that we're a hundred percent safe. Understand?"

She nodded.

"We're going to get out now. You're to stay with me and not wander off by yourself. Take all the time you need to look the place over. Stay outside or go inside whenever you want. I'll follow you. When you pick up on something, tell me what you need for me to do." He waited for her response,

but when she said nothing, he asked, "Are you ready?"

"I'm ready."

He got out of the sedan and by the time she opened her door and stepped onto the driveway, he was at her side. Despite his skepticism and surly attitude, Luke Sentell's presence made her feel safe. She knew that he would kill to protect her, that his military background made him more than qualified to be her bodyguard.

Trying to ignore Luke's larger-than-life energy, Meredith strolled up the driveway, taking her time, hoping to pick up on something related to Nicole. When she reached the steps leading to the cabin's front porch, she turned back and retraced her steps, all the way to the Impala. And then she headed to the cabin again, stopping halfway to pick up a couple of large pebbles from the gravel drive. She closed her eyes as she enclosed a rock in each hand.

Nothing. No flashes of light. No images. No reaction whatsoever.

She tossed the pebbles aside and headed straight for the porch. The moment her feet hit the porch's wooden floor, her body tightened as if struggling to bear a heavy weight. An image zipped through her mind. A dark figure carrying something. She stopped dead still, trying to concentrate, trying to hold on to that fleeting image. But it was gone.

"You picked up on something?" Luke cupped her right elbow.

With his hand on her arm, she should have been able to connect with him, to sense what he was feeling at that very moment, but she sensed only a strong barrier, one that kept her out of Luke's head.

"It wasn't anything much," Meredith told him. "I think I saw a man. He was carrying something in his arms, but it happened too fast."

"Can you get it back, try to see it more clearly?"

"Things don't work that way. I've been working with Yvette, trying to learn to control my abilities, but although I've made some progress, I still have only a small amount of control over what happens."

She walked the length of the front porch. Nothing. Not even a glimmer. "I'd like to go inside now."

Luke pulled a key ring from his pocket, chose a key, inserted it in the lock, and opened the door. Meredith hesitated for a moment before she stepped over the threshold and into the huge great room that included a two-story foyer leading into a twenty-five-by-twenty-five-foot area lined on two sides by floor-to-ceiling windows. Moving slowly and carefully, she began running her hand over one piece of furniture after another. As if seeing everything in supersonic speed, she gained miniscule glimpses of silhouettes, bodies in motion, and briefly felt one emotion after another —joy, sadness, loneliness, love, anger, fear. She tried to concentrate on the fear, hoping to connect with whatever Nic had been feeling when her abductor had kidnapped her. But the harder she tried to force the connection, the quicker the images evaporated.

After more than two hours of exploring the large cabin inside and out, Meredith had to admit defeat. She sat down in one of the chairs in the great room, heaved a deep, disappointed sigh, and told Luke, "I sensed Nic's fear and I picked up on something I can't describe other than to call it evil, but I'm not connecting to Nic. I have no idea who kidnapped her or where she is now."

Luke slumped down in the chair opposite her. "Don't beat yourself up about it, Merry Berry. You did the best you could."

She shot to her feet. "I need some fresh air and a couple of minutes alone. Please."

"I'm not letting you go off by yourself. I told you—"

"Just let me go out on the back deck for a few minutes. You can stand in the door and watch me. I feel smothered, as if the walls are closing in on me."

"All right. Go ahead. But I'll be watching you every minute."

Meredith crossed the great room, opened the door, and walked out onto the deck overlooking the vast expanse of lush green valleys and clear blue sky. She walked from one end to the other and then stopped, reached out, and laid her hand on the wooden railing that encompassed the deck. The moment her hand touched the top of the railing an overpowering sensation burst inside, a deep maternal need to protect the life growing inside her.

Oh my God! Meredith could not shake the feeling of her body nurturing a child. And in that moment she knew without a doubt that she was experiencing exactly what Nicole felt when she had stood right there on the deck three days ago.

"What is it?" Luke called from the doorway. "Are you all right?"

She tried to answer him, but couldn't. She was so completely engrossed in the amazing sensation of being pregnant that mere speech was unnecessary and at the moment, unimportant.

Suddenly, her body began trembling, and it took her a full minute to realize that Luke had grabbed her shoulders and was gently shaking her.

"Meredith . . . Meredith . . . " He repeated her name several times. "Snap out of it."

"I'm fine," she told him. "Really, I'm all right."

"What is it? What happened? You picked up on something, didn't you?"

Nicole Powell is pregnant.

"Nicole stood right here and looked out over the mountain. She was . . . sad and worried and . . . " Meredith faced Luke. "I'm ready to leave now."

"It's okay. You can't hit a home run every time you go up to bat," he told her, apparently assuming she was disappointed in not picking up Nic's "scent."

CHAPTER 13

Nic stared at the items on the silver tray the guard had delivered to her room. Several covered dishes, a small pot of what smelled like coffee, a glass of orange juice, and a stack of buttered toast. When she had asked her waiter-cum-jailor where she was, he had looked at her and shaken his head. She didn't know if he didn't understand English or if he had been ordered not to speak to her.

What did it matter? It wasn't as if knowing where she was would change one damn thing. But Nic knew one thing for certain—she had landed in the lap of luxury. She was aboard a yacht as luxurious and elegant as Griff's own 140-foot *Nicole*. When he bought the yacht, Griff had promised her a long cruise, but life had interfered and one thing after another had postponed their trip. Now, here she was taking a cruise, not as a bride on a romantic voyage, but as a prisoner, held under lock and key. With the closets full of designer-label clothes—in her size—and the bedroom suite almost decadent in its beauty, Nic felt like a bird in a gilded cage.

"Make yourself at home here in these quarters," Linden had informed her when he had locked her in sometime during the wee hours of the morning. "Mr. York has spared no expense to provide you with only the very best."

The very best life had to offer had been what she believed she would have with Griff. Marriage to a man she loved with every fiber of her being, a man who loved her just as passionately. A business that they could share, righting wrongs, assisting people in desperate need of help, using their wealth—Griff's billions—to make the world a better place. And a family, children born out of their deep love for each other.

Had it been nothing more than a foolish dream?

Oh, Griff, why didn't you tell me the truth? Why did you keep such an important part of your past a secret from me?

During their three-and-a-half-year marriage, she had given him numerous opportunities to explain about his unique relationship with Yvette. But whenever she had brought up the subject, he had given her the same rhetoric. He, Yvette, and Sanders had been prisoners of a madman named York, each of them forced to do horrible things in order to protect one another and to survive. The three of them had killed York and Griff had chopped off the man's head. They were united for all time by the shared nightmare of their past. He loved Sanders as if he were his brother and Yvette as if she was his sister.

However, he had left out one small detail about his relationship with Dr. Meng. He had neglected to tell Nic that while being held prisoner on

Amara, he had been forced to have sex with York's wife, the oh so fragile and helpless empath. And one other slight detail that he had never bothered to mention was the fact that he could be the father of Yvette's child.

Nic curled up on the pale green brocade sofa, wrapped her arms around herself, and wept softly. Allowing herself to cry while she was alone, with no one to see her, would release the buildup of anger and frustration and fear that had accumulated since the moment she had come face-to-face with Anthony Linden at her cabin in the mountains. Had it been four days ago? He had kidnapped her on Sunday morning. The next day she had awakened in a mansion on an island somewhere. That had been on Monday. Right? And then the day after that, after Lina had saved her from Mr. Auburn Hair, Linden had taken her away, and locked her in a room on the airplane with Jonas. Had that really been last night? If so, then this was Wednesday, the beginning of Day Four, but only three full days since she had been abducted.

Poor Lina. Was she still alive? Or had Linden had her killed?

And where was Jonas? They had brought him aboard sometime this morning before dawn, only minutes before Linden had escorted her to her palatial suite. Had he been given a decent room, a chance to shower and shave, and a decent meal to eat? Or had they locked him away in some dark hole in the bowels of the yacht? Was he still dirty, ragged, and bound in shackles?

Nic wiped her face with her fingertips as she rose to a sitting position and then stood and drew in a deep, cleansing breath. If she could have helped Lina, she would have. If the opportunity arose where she could help Jonas, she would. But for now, she had to be selfish. She had to think of herself and her baby and put their needs first.

Eyeing the silver tray on the table near windows overlooking the deck, Nic decided that she should eat not only now, but whenever she got the chance. She needed nourishment to keep up her strength and her baby needed nourishment to thrive. Not knowing what even the immediate future held, she didn't dare squander any opportunity.

Nic walked across the room, opened the drapes covering the windows, and glanced down at the table. She slipped off the paper cap on the glass of OJ, lifted it to her lips, and downed every drop. There, that would hold her until after she took a shower and changed clothes. Once she finished bathing and dressing, she would eat every bite she could hold.

A flash of movement outside on the deck caught her eye. A crew member or another "guest" had just strolled by outside her cabin. There was no point calling out to him. If he was another prisoner, he was as helpless as she. And if he was a crew member, he worked for York.

Oh, Griff, where are you? I'm going to do everything I possibly can to take care of myself and our baby. But I need you to do everything you can to save us.

But if Griff couldn't find her, if he didn't rescue her, what then?

Then I'll do whatever I have to do to stay alive and protect my child.

By the time they arrived back at Griffin's Rest, Meredith had decided what she should do. She had allowed Luke Sentell to believe that she hadn't picked up on anything significant about Nicole at the Gatlinburg cabin, so he hadn't questioned her silence during their return drive. He had assumed her not being able to gain any insight into Nicole's abduction had disappointed her. She hadn't corrected that assumption. After all, she actually was disappointed. She had hoped that she would pick up something that might help them locate Nic. But what she had sensed while standing on the deck at the cabin, she wished she hadn't. She now possessed Nicole's most intimate feelings, sacred information, and had felt a mother's deep love for her unborn child, had for a few brief moments known what it felt like to be carrying a baby inside her body.

202

When they drove through the front gates and up the long drive toward the main house, Meredith realized that Luke would take her back to Yvette's home, the sanctuary where she and Yvette's other students lived.

"If you don't mind, I'd prefer to walk from here," she told him. "I need some time alone. And . . . " *Think of a reasonable excuse for why you need to go inside the main house.* "And I promised Barbara Jean that I would stop by and see her when we got back."

"Okay." Luke pulled up in front of the house and stopped, never questioning her honesty.

By the time he opened his door, she had already flung open her door, hopped out, and stood in the driveway. "No need for you to get out." Glancing back at him, she faked a smile. "And thank you for taking me to the cabin."

"Yeah, sure."

He stared at her as if trying to figure out what made her tick. Before his intense gaze totally unnerved her, she waved good-bye, slammed the car door, and rushed up the front steps. Luke drove off to park the car inside one of the numerous slots in the garage terminal. After rushing inside the house, Meredith paused in the foyer, breathed slowly and evenly until her heart rate returned to normal, and then focused on locating the person she needed to see.

Where are you? Where are you?

As she concentrated fully on the task, the answer came to her quite clearly.

You're not alone.

I need to speak to you alone, just the two of us.

I'm going outside on the patio off the living room. Come there as soon as possible.

Staying focused on the mental link she was trying to form, Meredith made her way through the living room and out onto the patio without encountering anyone. Staying close to the house, her back to the outer wall, she waited. Somewhere in the distance the hum of a boat motor rumbled from the far side of the lake. Birds chirped. Squirrels and chipmunks and a variety of other small woodland animals scurried about through the nearby forest. Voices carried on the air, the sound a muted mumble. For the vast number of people, it was just another beautiful summertime day in northeastern Tennessee.

A ripple of awareness forewarned Meredith. She sensed the other woman's presence. And then the French doors opened and Maleah Perdue walked out onto the patio. Meredith slipped into the sunlight and approached the woman she had psychically summoned.

"Oh, hello," Maleah said. "I didn't know anyone else was out here. I just suddenly had this overwhelming urge to come outside for a breath of fresh air."

"It's a beautiful day, isn't it? It will be autumn

before we know it. That's my favorite season."

"Yeah, mine, too." Maleah stared at her. "I thought you and Luke were going up to Gatlinburg this morning, to Nic's cabin."

"We were. I mean, we did. We've already been there."

"Quick trip."

Meredith nodded.

"Look, if I'm disturbing you, I can take a walk down by the lake and leave you alone," Maleah said.

"No, you're not disturbing me. Not at all. As a matter of fact, you're just the person I wanted to see."

Maleah stared at her inquisitively. "Really? What about?"

"I gave it a great deal of thought all the way back from the cabin, trying to decide what to do. Being in possession of someone's thoughts and feelings is a great responsibility, one I usually try to avoid. Heading the list of Yvette's most important lessons is learning the ability to block other people's thoughts and feelings. But in this case, I knew Yvette and Griffin expected me to use my talents to do what I usually try not to do."

"For heaven's sake, will you stop rambling and just tell me what you're trying to say?"

Startled by Maleah's aggravated outburst, Meredith clamped her mouth shut and froze to the spot, her gaze glued to the other woman's flushed face.

"I'm sorry," Maleah said. "I didn't mean for that to sound so hateful. Sometimes I say what I'm thinking without running my thoughts through a censor."

"It's all right. Really. I have a habit of rambling."

"Please, go on with what you were trying to tell me."

Meredith nodded. "At the cabin, I wasn't able to pick up on anything much about Nicole's abduction and nothing about where she was taken, but . . . " She swallowed.

"But what?"

"I did sense some of Nicole's thoughts and feelings before she disappeared."

"And?"

"And after much consideration, I decided that I had to speak to someone whose first allegiance isn't to Griffin Powell, but to Nicole. That ruled out Yvette, of course, and Sanders, and because of her loyalty to Sanders, Barbara Jean. And I wasn't sure about Derek, but I knew you were the one person—"

Maleah grasped Meredith's shoulders and gave her a gentle shake. "Just say it."

"Did you know that Nicole is pregnant?"

Maleah's face turned pale. "How did you—?"

"She didn't tell Griffin, did she?"

"No, she didn't. Before she had a chance to tell him her good news, he dropped the I-could-be-the-father-of-Yvette's-child bombshell on her."

"You haven't told him she's pregnant."

"No, I haven't told him."

"Does anyone else know?" Meredith asked.

"Derek."

"Why haven't you told Griffin?"

"If you think it's because I blame him for what happened to Nic and don't believe he has a right to know, then you're wrong," Maleah assured her. "The man is half out of his mind as it is worrying about Nic. How do you think he'd feel if he knew she was pregnant?"

"You and Derek are trying to protect him."

"Yes, we are. And I want your solemn promise that you—"

"It is not my place to share Nic's most intimate thoughts and feelings with anyone, not unless they can help us find her," Meredith said. "I came to you and told you only because I needed your advice. You've simply confirmed that my decision not to tell anyone was the right decision."

Griff sat alone in his study, the room partially restored to normal. Even in a house filled with people, he had never felt so alone. Without Nic, this big house was empty no matter how many people were in it. With each passing hour, he became lonelier, as if Nic was moving farther and farther away from him. They had located where she had been taken—to Shelter Island, a few miles off the Belize coast—but they had arrived too late to save her. And now she was out there some-where at the mercy of a madman. He couldn't bear thinking about what might be happening to her, what sick, evil plan York had made to use Nic as a means of punishing him.

"I killed you once, you son of a bitch," Griff said. "I'm going to kill you again and this time you're going to stay dead!"

A rap on the outer door gained his attention. "Yes?"

"May I come in?" Sanders asked from the other side of the closed door.

"Yes, come in."

When his old friend entered the study, Griff immediately noticed the look of concern in his eyes. "You heard what I said, didn't you?"

Sanders shrugged.

"Don't worry, I haven't lost my mind. I know the real York is dead."

"Do not let anything that happens make you question that fact." Sanders closed the door behind him. "We sent Luke Sentell with Ms. Sinclair to Nic's cabin and they have returned."

"You should have sent someone else with her. I want Luke—"

"He's packing now. It was only a minor delay. You know that Ms. Sinclair's magic seems to work better when Luke is with her."

"And what did Meredith's magic discover at the cabin?"

Griff hoped that perhaps Meredith's unique psychic gifts had come up with something that could help them locate Nic or at the very least give them some small clue that would lead them in the right direction.

"I'm afraid Ms. Sinclair was unable to sense anything significant concerning Nicole's abduction and she did not pick up on even the smallest hint of where Nicole might be."

"I suppose it was a long shot." Griff glanced down at Nic's wedding band where he had slipped it on his left pinkie. Her fingers were long and slender so the ring caught just above his knuckle.

"We are going to find her," Sanders said. "Everything possible is being done."

Griff nodded, all the while twisting Nic's ring around and around on his finger. "She's strong and tough. She's a fighter. But we both know what can happen to her, what she may have to endure before we rescue her."

"Nicole is also a survivor," Sanders reminded him. "She will not allow anything to defeat her."

Griff didn't reply. He couldn't. The words died on his lips as pain clutched his throat tightly. *Do not think about what could be happening to Nic at this very minute. You have to stay sane if you're going to help her.*

When the telephone on Griff's desk rang, he tensed instantly. Sanders didn't hesitate to cross the room and pick up the receiver. "Griffin's Rest. This is Sanders speaking."

Griff could tell from the expression on Sanders's face that something was wrong.

"Yes, Mr. Powell is here," Sanders said. "Will you please hold?"

Griff rose from the comfort of the large wingback chair in front of the fireplace. Sanders placed his hand over the mouthpiece.

"The caller identified himself as Malcolm York."

Every muscle in Griff's body stiffened. "And?"

"The voice is an excellent imitation. *Almost* identical to the real York's." He held out the telephone to Griff.

Willing his intensely chaotic emotions under control, Griff reached out and took the receiver. Every call coming into Griffin's Rest was being monitored so tracing the caller's whereabouts was possible.

"This is Griffin Powell."

"Hello, old friend."

"Who the hell is this?"

"Don't you recognize my voice?"

"No, I can't say that I do."

The man laughed ever so softly. God, how familiar that sound was! If he didn't know better, he would swear . . . No, it wasn't York. York was dead.

"I did so enjoy all our little games," the voice said with just a vague hint of a British accent. The real York had been born in London, but had been educated in boarding schools throughout Europe and had attended college in the United States. "You were always a challenge during our hunts. You became our most popular quarry. And oh how my friends and I enjoyed—"

"I don't know who you are or why you're calling me, but I know you're not Malcolm York."

"And you know this for certain because you think you killed me." He paused for a moment. "Did you ever ask yourself why my body disappeared off Amara and was never found?"

"I figured that pack of dogs York kept on the island ate the flesh off his bones."

"You didn't like my dogs, did you, Griffin?"

Griff shivered. *Don't remember. Push past the memories threatening you.* Whoever this guy was, he knew too much about Malcolm York, about Amara, and about Griffin's captivity not to have been a frequent visitor.

"You're very quiet," the voice said. "Are you remembering what it was like for you and the others on Amara? Or perhaps you're thinking about your wife. I understand she has disappeared and you're scouring the Earth to find her."

Control. Control. Stay in control.

"Nothing to say, Griffin? You came so close to rescuing her, didn't you?"

"You seem to have all the answers. You tell me."

"Of course. Since you want to dispense with

211

the pleasantries, I'll get straight to the point. If you want to ever see your wife alive again, you'll do exactly what I tell you to do."

"How do I know you have Nicole?"

"You know that I sent Anthony Linden to fetch her. She played right into his hands when she ran away from you. I had hoped the letter I sent informing you where you could find Yvette's daughter might prompt you to be honest with your wife and the great revelation would send her scurrying."

Whoever he was, he was a clever bastard. Just as the real York had been. Diabolically clever.

When Griff didn't respond, the caller said, "Listen very carefully. I will contact you again this evening. Please have Yvette Meng and Damar Sanders there with you. My instructions are for all three of you."

"Before you start issuing orders, you'll have to prove to me that you have Nic and that she is alive and well. Otherwise, don't call again."

"If I weren't looking forward to our games, I wouldn't call again and you'd never know what happened to your wife. But I'll give you what you want—proof that Nicole is with me and that she is very much alive and, for the most part, unharmed."

As fury burned hot inside Griff, the son of a bitch hung up on him. He slammed down the receiver, looked at Sanders, and said, "I want this guy, whoever the hell he is. And when we find him, he's mine. All mine."

Chapter 14

Locking the door to ensure his privacy, Griff secluded himself inside his study. He wanted a drink. But he needed to stay stone-cold sober. For the past few hours, he had fought the urge to drown himself completely in glass after glass of his best Macallan Scotch whiskey. If ever there was a time he had a right to get rip-roaring drunk that time was now. It wasn't every day that a man had to face a ghost from his past who presented him with an overdue notice for his sins.

If only he could go back four years, before he fell in love with Nicole Baxter . . .

He had never meant to fall in love, not ever. How could he have asked any woman to accept the man he had become after four years on Amara? But Nic had been different from any woman he had known. Her strength and courage amazed him. Her kind heart and sense of right and wrong endeared her to him. In the early days of their acquaintance, she had disliked him, mistrusted him, and had told him to go to hell more than once. But from the first moment he had touched her, held her, kissed her, made love to her, she had been his. And God help them both, he had not been able to let her go.

Before they married, he should have told her

everything, the entire truth, and given her the chance to walk away, to run from him as fast and as far as she could. But he had been selfish. He had been desperately afraid of losing her. And so he had told her half-truths, shared just enough information about his kidnapping at twenty-two and his years on Amara to partially explain his complex relationships with Sanders and Yvette.

How many times had he promised himself that he would be honest with her, that he'd share even the most sordid details of his past with her? If only he had told her about Yvette's child years ago.

The letter from the pseudo-York had forced his hand. And that had been just what the devious bastard had wanted. Why hadn't he tried harder to stop Nic from leaving him? His guilt and remorse had forced him to allow her to leave the safety of Griffin's Rest.

If he had it to do all over again . . .

Everything was his fault.

Four years ago, he should have let her go. Three and a half years ago, he should have told her the truth. Even six months ago, it might have been too late.

But he had been stupid enough to think that their loving each other would be enough, that he could protect her from the secrets buried in his past without his lies destroying their marriage. Time and time again, when she had been on the verge of leaving him, he had persuaded her to give him one more chance.

Had it been only months ago when he had taken her away to their own island paradise for a second honeymoon, hoping to prove to her that she was more important to him than anyone or anything? Their time there had been almost perfect.

But even then Malcolm York's malevolent shadow had darkened their lives, a faraway threat growing ever closer.

Griff heaved a deep, heavy sigh and closed his eyes. Pain welled up inside him, spiraled through his entire body, and held him captive. Unable to endure the reality of Nic's situation and deal with his guilt, Griff's mind grabbed hold of a memory. Only by escaping from the present into a past time when they had been together, a past where he could have altered the future, could he hold on to his sanity.

Four-and-a-half months ago . . .

The past four days had been great, everything he had hoped for when he and Nic had left Griffin's Rest and flown on their private jet to his Caribbean estate. He had purchased the small island, located southeast of the Bahamas, six years ago and had sent in an architect, a contractor, and a designer to restore the old manor house. During their stay, they had seen no one, other than the two servants he had arranged to remain there to prepare meals and keep the estate running smoothly for the week they would be there. But both Adele and her husband, Horatio, possessed the discretion of highly trained professionals, seldom being seen or heard, blending into the background as if they were invisible. Griff had explained to Adele that this trip was a second honeymoon for him and his wife and the astute lady had understood exactly what he wanted. Privacy and seclusion.

He stood on the balcony overlooking the jagged cliffs that jutted out and then dropped like an uneven gray ribbon to meet the turquoise ocean. A series of tiered patios cascaded downward, each connected by a series of stone steps. The house had been built over a hundred years ago on a magnificent spot of land that took advantage of the spectacular panoramic view from the island's highest point. The estate combined elements of a Southern plantation with a Mediterranean villa, the twelve-thousand-square-foot house built of white stone, with enormous white columns supporting balconies that circled the entire house.

He had brought Nic here on their honeymoon three years ago and they had spent almost a month in their own private paradise. Until Nicole Baxter had become as necessary for his existence as the very air he breathed, he had never believed that such complete happiness existed, especially not for a man like him.

Griff turned and looked into the bedroom, his gaze settling on Nic's sleeping form, her beautiful face buried in the down pillow, her sleek body curled contentedly beneath the sateen cotton sheets. They had made love a few hours ago and both of them had fallen asleep. But his sated rest had been abruptly disturbed by a dream that had quickly turned into a nightmare. In those brief, terrifying moments, Nic had been Malcolm York's captive, a slave forced to do his bidding. And he had been bound in chains, helpless to defend her. Awakening in a cold sweat, he had quietly gotten out of bed.

He didn't know how long he'd been standing there staring out at the vast blue sea, but even now the image of York's diabolical face hadn't completely faded from his thoughts. The man had been a cruel, inhuman monster. And as much as Griff had suffered from York's barbarous treatment, Yvette and Sanders had suffered far more.

Malcolm York is dead, Griff reminded himself. *You know he's dead. You killed him.*

Then why were there rumors floating around all over Europe about a man named Malcolm York being alive and well and rebuilding an empire he claimed had been stolen from him?

A shudder of unease drummed up Griff's spine. The man was not the same Malcolm York. He was a fraud, an impostor using another man's name for reasons that greatly concerned Griff. Why would anyone want to take on the identity of a brutal psychopath?

When the rumors had first begun spreading, he had gone to Europe and taken Meredith Sinclair with him to help in his search for the truth. Hadn't Meredith, the most powerful among Yvette's conclave of gifted residents, sensed that the man was not the real York, that he had assumed the other man's identity to draw Griffin out for a duel to the death? Winner takes all. And the fake York would use the innocent to achieve his goals just as the real York had done.

Meredith did not know his true identity or why he had only now "risen from the dead" to seek revenge.

"Griff," Nic called to him from the bed.

His gaze focused on her. He smiled. "Hello, sleepyhead."

When she stretched like a contented cat in the warm sun, the sheet dropped below her waist, revealing her full, round breasts. Griff's body tightened. He wanted her again. And again. And again. If he lived to be a hundred, he would never have his fill of her.

Without Nicole, his life would be meaningless.

He would do whatever he had to do to keep her safe, to protect her from the past that he had believed to be long dead and buried.

If only he had the courage to be completely honest with her. But what if she didn't understand? What if she could never forgive him? What if she left him?

The time might come when he would have no other choice than to tell her. But now was not that time.

He had told her just enough—that there was an impostor in Europe, flying under the radar, who called himself Malcolm York. And he had explained that this was the reason he had made several trips overseas and why he had shared that information with Yvette and Sanders.

"I didn't want to worry you," he had told her. "But instead, by not telling you what was happening, I made you distrust me."

"Just don't keep things from me. No more secrets. Please, always be honest with me," she had said.

If only . . .

You've told her all she needs to know.

Who are you protecting, Griffin Powell—your wife or yourself ?

Nic tossed back the sheet, rose from the bed and onto her feet—in all her glorious nakedness —and then walked out onto the balcony. His gaze traveled from the top of her head, down her silky neck, and to her luscious breasts. His sex tightened. He scanned her slender waist, her softly rounded hips, the triangle of dark hair between her trim thighs, and then from her sleek legs all the way down to her ruby red toenails. When she drew close, he pulled her around in front of him, pressed her back against his chest, her buttocks against his arousal, and wrapped her in his arms. He lowered his head and kissed her neck.

"I love you," he whispered against her ear.

God, how he loved her!

She sighed as her body relaxed into his. "Tell me that we'll always be this happy."

He nuzzled her neck. "We'll always be this happy."

For her sake, dear God, let it be true. You do your part, Big Guy, and I'll do mine. I swear I'll do everything within my power to keep her as happy as she is right now.

"How long has he been in there alone?" Yvette asked as they approached the locked door of Griffin's study.

"All day. He insisted on being alone," Sanders replied. "After the phone call, he told me to contact you. According to the man claiming to have kidnapped Nicole, he has instructions for all three of us—you, Griffin, and me—when he calls again this evening."

"I should have come sooner, but . . . " She hated to confess that her own selfish concerns had delayed her, that she had gone against her own rules and requested one of her protégés use his

220

"remote viewing" talent as a favor to her. "I asked Adam to help me by trying to project himself to the Benenden School. Since I can't go to England right now and meet Suzette, I thought perhaps . . ." She turned from Sanders's disapproving glare.

Her dear old friend knew her better than anyone else, even better than Griffin did. Sometimes she thought Sanders knew her better than she knew herself because he had the ability to see her for who and what she truly was. He understood that her survival depended on her ability to maintain the alternate reality in which she existed. She visited the real world whenever necessary, but kept her home base secure within the tranquil, unemotional inner peace she had created for herself.

She did not love. She did not hate.

She devoted her life to her students, the young men and women who, like she, were gifted psychics, and because of their special talents were outcasts and misfits in a world that did not trust the transcendental part of mankind's nature. Her only goal in life was to help others, be that the residents of her sanctuary or those associated with the Powell Agency.

"Please do not look at me with such stern censure," Yvette told Sanders. "You, of all people, should understand my need to see this girl, to discover for myself if she is my child."

221

"I do understand." His gaze softened, his expression one of empathetic sympathy. "But if this girl is your child, which I do not believe she is, she will be at Benenden a week from now, a month from now, even a year from now. But Griffin needs you today."

"Of course, you are right. You are always right."

"This man who calls himself Malcolm York will use your desire to find your child to manipulate you," Sanders told her. "Surely you realize he wants to punish you and me as well as Griffin. He has abducted Nicole to punish Griffin. He will find a way to use your missing child to punish you. And I am sure he has something in mind for me also."

"Who can this man be?" Yvette struggled to maintain her composure as memories threatened, like dark ominous clouds before a destructive storm. "Why is he pretending to be Malcolm York? And why is he seeking revenge for York?"

"Those are questions that you should concentrate on. You have six students with various abilities that they can use to help us. Instead of asking Adam to try to transport himself to Benenden, ask him to search for Nicole."

"I asked Meredith for help," Yvette said defensively. "As you know, she went to Nicole's cabin with Luke Sentell this morning and came away without picking up on any leads. She tried, but she and my other students are still learning to control their talents, and I know from experience that it can take a lifetime to master such powerful skills."

"I did not mean to criticize you or imply that you aren't willing to do all that you can to help us find Nicole. I simply thought you might need a reminder about prioritizing your goals."

She longed to lay her hand on Sanders's arm, to simply touch him as an act of kindness, a "thank you, dear friend," expression. But for her there was no such thing as a simple touch. Even when she deliberately blocked other people's feelings, she was never able to completely avoid connecting with them. The more powerful their emotions, the more easily they overrode the barrier she projected between them and her.

"When Griffin first heard rumors about York, I tried to help," Yvette said. "I went against my better judgment and my own rules and asked Meredith for help because at the time she was my most gifted student. None of the others were advanced enough or disciplined enough to help and even now only Adam has progressed enough to be of possible assistance."

"Nic! No, Nic, don't go. Please . . . Nic!" The shouting came from inside Griffin's study.

Yvette and Sanders exchanged concerned looks. "You have a key," she said. "Use it. Unlock the door now."

Without hesitation, Sanders removed his key

223

ring from his pocket, chose a small brass key, and inserted it into the lock. When he opened the door, he paused, intending to allow Yvette to enter first. But the moment she saw Griffin, she stopped immediately. He looked right at her, but did not see her. His shoulders were slumped, his face haggard, his eyes glazed, and tears poured down his unshaven cheeks.

Nicole stood on the main deck of the *Isis*, now docked out at sea, but within viewing distance of a nearby port, and watched the sun set and twilight descend. Surprisingly, Linden had given her permission to explore the yacht beyond her luxurious guest suite. But not alone. An armed guard followed her every step. More than once she had thought about trying to overpower the man and take his rifle, but he would be useless as a hostage, and the odds that she could actually manage to escape were zero. From what she could tell, none of the staff spoke English. There were at least half a dozen armed guards posted at various intervals throughout the ship. And unless she could swim several miles to shore, jumping overboard would accomplish nothing except her drowning halfway to her destination.

Taking note of her surroundings, she concluded that the landmass was due west and that the ship had been sailing south/southwest all afternoon. If her assumption was correct that Linden had originally taken her to an island somewhere in the Caribbean, that meant they were probably now docked near the coast of either Venezuela or possibly Colombia.

So how do you think having some idea of where you are will help you?

It wouldn't, not really. But being able to figure out her possible location gave her the illusion of having at least an iota of control over her present situation.

After sharing lunch with Linden in the elegant wood-paneled dining room, she had not seen him again until a couple of hours ago. She had been lounging in the salon, on the twelve-foot-long sofa situated beneath a row of windows over-looking the main deck. Or were those called portholes despite their square shape? As often as Griff had explained sailing lingo to her on their infrequent yachting trips, she had yet to master ship-speak.

"I'm going ashore," Linden had told her. "While I'm gone, you be a good girl. If you're not, I've left orders that if necessary to shoot you in the foot and then lock you up below deck until I return."

She had wanted to ask him where he was going and what business he had ashore, but she had simply smiled at him as if she didn't have a care in the world. After all, why not play the role she had been assigned, that of a pampered guest?

225

From the luxurious bedroom suite she had been given to the designer slacks and blouse she had found in her closet and now wore, to the respectful way the crew and even the guards treated her, no one would suspect that she was being held against her will.

Concentrating on the colorful beauty of the sky bathed in the remnants of dying sunlight, Nic did her best not to think about why Linden had gone ashore. But try as she might, fear overrode her determination. Would he bring back guests, men she would be expected to entertain tonight? Was he gathering up a new hunting party? Would they be going to another island to participate in their sadistic blood sport ritual? Was that why Jonas MacColl had been brought on board and was now somewhere below deck?

Nic seriously doubted that Jonas had been given a guest cabin with his own private bathroom. More than likely he was locked away in a storage area in the boiler room. Or was it called a generator room or maybe an engine room? Griff had once told her that their yacht, the *Nicole*, was equipped with full electronics, four generators, two 400 horsepower engines, and that most of the equipment had been duplicated for backup purposes. But if he had ever referred by name to that area of the ship, she didn't remember.

Dear God in heaven, what she would give to be aboard the *Nicole* right now, with Griff standing at her side, his arms draped around her. She could see him in her mind's eye, could hear him whisper her name, could almost feel his powerful embrace. She swallowed the lump in her throat, refusing to cry. Tears were useless.

Off in the distance, she caught a glimpse of a motorboat zipping along across the water, heading straight for the *Isis*. Her heart stopped for a millisecond as she held her breath while an unknown terror approached the ship.

Nic considered running back to her cabin when that initial fight or flight moment kicked in and gave her two options. She could run, but she could not hide. She would stay and meet Linden and whatever terror he had brought back with him. Better to get an up-close look at her enemy, face them, and do battle eye to eye, than to wait and let them sneak up and ambush her from behind.

Staying where she was on deck, Nic watched the boat approach and Linden and one other man climb aboard the yacht. From a distance, the man looked to be in his fifties, but she assumed that age because of his silver hair.

Once firmly on deck, Linden searched for her. When he found her standing there looking directly at him, a surprised expression crossed his face. With her shoulders straight and her head held high, she watched the men as they approached, her gaze gliding slowly back and forth between Linden and the other man. As they drew nearer, she concentrated completely on the silver-haired guest who was tall, slender, and attractive. And not nearly as old as she had first thought. With an aristocratic air and a glint in his sinister eyes, he stared at Nic. His piercing look sliced her to the bone.

The man seemed familiar. Had she seen him before? Did she know him?

When he was within five feet of her, his face clearly visible, his features unmistakable, Nic knew where she had seen this man. No, not the man himself, only old photographs of him.

Smiling broadly, Linden seemed to take great pleasure in introducing them. "Nicole, my dear, may I introduce my employer, Malcolm York."

After giving her a moment to respond, which she didn't, he then said, "Mr. York, this is Griffin Powell's wife, Nicole."

CHAPTER 15

Griff paced up and down the hallway outside his study. They had been waiting for hours. Yvette sat on the sofa, her hands in her lap and her eyes closed as she meditated. He wished he could escape from the present reality, that he had the ability to find a peaceful retreat inside his own mind. The solemn, stoic Sanders always appeared unfazed by whatever storm whirled around him.

He stood watch over the telephone on Griff's desk. The others in residence there at the main house—Derek, Maleah, and Barbara Jean—continued their duties as they, too, waited. A couple of times in the past hour, he had heard the soft whir of Barbara Jean's wheelchair close by, hovering, but keeping her distance. She worried about all of them, but especially about Sanders. Griff was glad his old friend had found someone who could love and accept him as he was, and asked no more of him than he was capable of giving. Although very different types of women, she and Nic had become good friends.

With every breath he took, every step he made, Griff struggled to remain in control. From childhood, he'd had a strong, somewhat volatile personality. The discipline of football had taught him how to channel his explosive energy and control his quick temper. The years on Amara, a slave to a madman's whims, had brought out both the worst and the best in him. At the worst of times, he had become an animal capable of untold savagery. At the best of times, he had sacrificed himself to protect others.

If given the chance, he would sacrifice himself for Nicole. He would lay down his life without regret if he could save her.

Just as Griff reached the end of the hallway that opened up onto the foyer, the telephone in his study rang. He stopped, stood there unmoving, every muscle in his body fixed, every nerve vibrating on high alert. Instinct urged him to run. Logic instructed him to remain calm.

As he turned and walked steadily toward his study, he heard Sanders's voice. "Griffin's Rest. Sanders speaking."

When Griff reached the open door of his study, he looked directly at Sanders who held the telephone receiver out to him. Yvette rose to her feet, her gaze fixed on Griff. As he crossed the room, feeling as if heavy ankle weights slowed each step, he forced down his fear and anger, caging it inside himself.

He took the phone from Sanders. "Griffin Powell here."

"Hello, old friend," the man said, his voice a disturbingly accurate imitation of Malcolm York's.

Griff did not reply.

"I have someone here with me who is eager to speak to you," the caller said.

A second later, Griff heard her voice.

"Griff, it's me. It's Nic. I'm all right."

"Nic . . . I—I—" Torn between rage and gratitude, Griff struggled for a few seconds and then quickly composed himself. "Tell me again that you're okay."

"I'm okay for now," she told him. "Griff, he really is Malcolm York. Please believe me."

"I believe you, honey, I believe you." Griff

didn't for one minute believe that the real Malcolm York was alive, nor did Nic. She'd been told what to say. For some perverse reason the man holding Nic captive wanted Griff to believe he was the maniac who had ruled a despotic empire built on human misery.

"He wants me to tell you that my life depends on your cooperation."

"I plan to cooperate. I'll do whatever I need to do to bring you home."

"I'd very much like to come home."

Griff clenched his jaw. "There's nothing I want more."

"I love you, Griff."

Indescribable agony invaded Griff's very being, his body, his heart, his soul. "I love you, too."

"How sweet," the York clone said. "You two want to be together, and being the kind, generous man that I am, I plan to give you what you both want."

"Name your price," Griff told him.

"We'll begin with your cooperation. Agreed?"

"Agreed."

"I'm going to enjoy making you jump through hoops, but of course, as any good master does with a trained dog, I will reward you for your obedience."

"The only reward I want is your promise that Nic won't be harmed."

"I have no immediate plans to place your wife in harm's way again."

Again? What did the son of a bitch mean by that statement?

"What have you done to her?"

"Now, now, you mustn't get upset. I assure you that she's none the worse for wear. And if you want to keep her alive, you'll do exactly as I tell you."

Tamping down the fury boiling inside him, Griff managed to say, "I'm listening."

"I want you to take my wife to England, to the Benenden School in Kent to meet her daughter. I've already contacted the school to alert them that Suzette's mother will be visiting her tomorrow."

The request surprised Griff, but he quickly agreed. "All right, if that's what you want me to do. Yvette and I will leave tonight."

"Ah, that is what I like—immediate capitulation. After you and Yvette meet her daughter and the three of you have a family reunion, I will contact you again."

"I'll want to talk to Nic then, too."

"Perhaps."

"No bargaining on that point. As long as I know Nic's alive and well, I'll keep jumping through hoops for you. And I'll want proof, so that means I talk to her on a fairly regular basis."

"Trying to locate me by tracing my phone calls is futile. We will be staying on the move, so even if you could zero in on where we are, by the time you or any of your underlings arrived, we would already be somewhere else."

Before Griff could respond, his caller abruptly ended their conversation. Griff smashed the receiver down on the base and cursed loudly.

"You spoke to Nicole." Yvette came to Griff, reached out to him, and stopped just short of actually touching him.

"Yes, I spoke to her."

"And she is all right?"

"She's alive and she sounded okay, but . . . I can't think about what she's gone through or what is ahead for her," Griff said, his gaze connecting first with Yvette's and then with Sanders's. "If we have a prayer of rescuing Nic, I have to stay focused on that one objective." He took in and released a deep breath. "I want the jet readied for a transatlantic flight ASAP."

"I'll see to it immediately," Sanders replied.

When Sanders reached for the phone, Griff grabbed his arm. "While I'm gone, make sure the search for Nic continues twenty-four hours a day. He's sending me off on what could be a wild-goose chase."

Sanders nodded.

Griff released his friend's arm and turned to Yvette. "Change clothes, pack a bag, say good-bye to your students. Do whatever you need to do, but be ready to leave in two hours. We're flying to London tonight."

"London? I don't understand," Yvette said.

"Malcolm York wants me to escort you to the Benenden School tomorrow to meet the girl he claims is your daughter."

Linden had marched Nic straight to her cabin after she had been allowed to speak briefly to Griff. The last thing she had heard York say to her husband was *"I have no immediate plans to place your wife in harm's way again."*

Lying son of a bitch. But surely Griff wouldn't trust him.

Linden opened the cabin door, gave her a nudge over the threshold and, chuckling to himself, closed and locked the door. Damn slimy bastard.

Nic came to a skidding halt when she saw Jonas MacColl, unchained and completely naked, standing in the middle of the room. *God in heaven!* After a hasty head-to-toe survey, she tried to keep her gaze focused on his face. Despite bordering on skinny, no doubt due to a lack of adequate nutrition during his imprisonment, he was nevertheless a fine male specimen. Long legs and arms dusted with curly dark hair, well-defined muscles, and a washboard lean abdomen. His shoulder-length brown hair glistened with moisture, suggesting that he had just bathed. A fresh bruise colored his cheekbone and recently dried blood covered the cut on his upper lip.

"I'm sorry about this," Jonas said.

"It's not your fault," Nic told him. "I'm afraid I don't have any clothes that would fit you, but there are some large towels in the bathroom."

"Thanks. I haven't had a chance to look for anything. They just shoved me in here about sixty seconds before you arrived." He turned his back on her and headed for the bathroom.

Nic looked away quickly, but not before she caught a glimpse of his firm buttocks and narrow hips.

There had to be a reason why she and Jonas were being thrown together again. Was he her prize for good behavior or was she his prize?

She walked around the room, visually inspecting the ceiling, walls, baseboards, and furniture, looking for a hidden camera. Just because she didn't find one didn't mean there wasn't one. As she lifted the bedside lamp, checking it for any sign of a bug, Jonas cleared his throat. She lifted her head and glanced at the open bathroom door.

"Well, what do you think?" He gestured to the lower half of his body, now covered from waist to midthigh with a plush beige cotton towel.

"Charming. I understand it's all the rage in Paris this season."

He grinned. "Lady, you're something, you know that? Considering what's happened to you, I can't believe you've managed to keep your sense of humor."

"You're something yourself, Mr. MacColl."

She glanced from his bruised cheekbone to the cut on his mouth. "Even knowing that you can't win, you're still putting up a fight."

"Stupid, huh?" He shrugged his broad shoulders. "But you know that fighting back every once in a while keeps me from totally hating myself."

Nic walked across the room, all the while Jonas never took his eyes off her. When she leaned against him and placed her mouth to his ear, he shuddered.

"There's probably a bug hidden in here somewhere so they can record what we're saying and maybe even a hidden camera," Nic said so softly that she hoped only Jonas could hear her.

He looked her in the eye and nodded.

She slipped away from him and sat on the edge of the bed. He followed and sat down beside her. Keeping her voice whisper soft, she asked, "What do you think this is all about, their putting us together like this?"

"They're getting us used to each other," he whispered. "Sooner or later, they're going to expect us to perform."

Griff's heartfelt plea for her understanding this past Sunday morning replayed in her mind.

"We weren't lovers. Not ever. What Yvette and I did was not making love. God, Nic, it wasn't even having sex, not really. We were forced to perform in front of York."

"Have they made you"—Nic swallowed—"perform?"

236

He looked away from her. "Yeah."

When she laid her hand on Jonas's shoulder, he tensed. "You don't need to be ashamed."

He clamped his hand down over her hand resting on his shoulder. "It was only a couple of times. The first time was because one of the hunters was pissed because I had been able to outsmart him during the hunt and stay alive." Jonas ran his gaze in every direction, and then laughed. "Did you hear that, you sons of bitches?" he yelled, talking to whoever might be listening.

Nic felt his rage. Hell, she shared it.

And then the oddest thought went through her mind.

I'm lucky that they chose to pair me with Jonas MacColl.

Yvette felt ashamed because she was glad that she and Griffin were leaving tonight for London and tomorrow they would drive to the Benenden School and meet a young woman who might be her daughter.

She was allowing emotion to overrule her basic common sense. The York imitator was in charge, pulling their strings, issuing orders that Griffin did not dare disobey. Whoever the man was, he wanted revenge. And since she and Sanders were each as guilty as Griffin of the real York's murder, it stood to reason that they were included in the pseudo-York's plans for retribution.

After changing from a silk shirt and blouse into black tailored slacks and a pale cream linen jacket, Yvette had packed two changes of clothes in a small suitcase and her toiletries in an overnight bag. She had been ready for an hour now and waiting for Griffin to summon her.

"Yvette?" Meredith called as she tapped on the closed bedroom door.

"Yes?"

"Sanders is here."

"Thank you."

Yvette picked up the overnight bag. Sanders opened the door and entered. Without a word, he lifted her suitcase and motioned for her to follow.

Walking side by side to the front entrance, neither of them spoke. After placing her bags in the town car, he opened the back door for her.

"How is he?" she asked.

"How do you think he is?"

"This is not my fault," she said. "As badly as I want to meet Suzette, I did not want it to be like this."

"I know."

Yvette slid into the backseat. Sanders closed the door, rounded the hood of the car, and got behind the wheel.

"Do you think there is even the slightest chance this young girl could be my daughter?" she asked, but before he answered she knew his response would not be what she wanted to hear.

"I do not."

"But if she is?"

"You want her to be your daughter," Sanders said. "She is not. You hope that Griffin is the father of your child, but he may not be. Someday if you do find your daughter or son, will you be able to accept a child that may have been fathered by one of York's friends?"

Sanders did not mince words. He did not spare feelings.

In all these years, they had never discussed the circumstances under which her baby had been conceived. But Sanders had always known that the child's paternity was uncertain.

When she had discovered she was pregnant, she had considered two options—a self-induced abortion or suicide—but had decided she could do neither.

"Only one of Malcolm's friends could have fathered my child—Yves Bouchard."

"You are certain?"

"Yes. Within the time frame when I conceived, I was with only four men. You may recall Bouchard being York's only guest for several weeks. During that time, I was with him once."

Then and now, she had refused to accept the possibility that Yves Bouchard, the brutal fiend who had enjoyed inflicting pain on the boys and young men he raped, could be the father of her

239

child. Although his tastes in sexual partners had not included women, he had occasionally accommodated York's request to watch while he included Yvette in a threesome.

"Yvette?"

"Yes?"

"I believe that someday you will find your child," Sanders said as they drove up to the main house where Griff waited.

"Thank you." Yvette knew that Sanders was thinking of another lost child, one that was buried in his mother's arms, far away, on the island of Amara.

Sanders had no hope of ever seeing his child again.

Griff slid into the backseat beside Yvette. If he would allow her to touch him, she would gladly accept some of his pain again, but he kept a safe distance from her. He did not want her to know his thoughts or sense his feelings. And he did not want her to share his pain.

There had been a time when she had loved Griffin Powell for his kindness, his tenderness, his protectiveness. The part of her capable of caring deeply for another human being still cared for Griffin. He and Sanders were as much a part of her as her arms and legs, as essential to her existence as her heart and lungs. Was it any wonder that she wished for Griffin to be the father of her child?

But there had been two other men other than Bouchard and Griffin.

She vaguely remembered Lunt Anderson, the Swedish cross-country skier who had survived on Amara for less than two months. A sandy-haired, blue-eyed, fun-loving boy of twenty-three who'd been killed on his second hunt. When she had held him in her arms after they had sex, he had trembled like a frightened boy and she had sensed his terror. Poor Lunt. Could he have been the father of her child?

But what if the father is not Griffin or Lunt or even Bouchard?

What if it is the other one?

CHAPTER 16

The *Isis* had docked sometime in the night, hours after two guards had invaded Nic's cabin, shackled Jonas, and taken him away. She had lain awake for a while, her thoughts reaching backward in time to those first few halcyon months after she and Griff first married. Honeymoon happiness. Days filled with great sex and love beyond measure. And the promise of happily-ever-after. She longed to return to that time in her life, to lie in Griff's arms and know that nothing bad could ever touch them. They had been golden then.

As she drifted off to sleep, relaxed by sweet memories, her mind conjured up a final image, her last thought before sleep overtook her. Jonas MacColl.

In the light of a new day, Nic cupped a handful of cold water from the sink and splashed it into her face. As rivulets dripped from her chin and trailed down her neck before disappearing between her breasts, she stared at herself in the mirror. Thirty-six years old. Married, but presently separated. Not bad-looking. Three months pregnant. And the unwilling captive of an insane man obsessed with punishing her husband. Yep, that about summed up who Nicole Baxter Powell was, at least who she was this morning.

But who would she be a week from now, a month from now—a year from now?

Don't look so far ahead. It's counter-productive. Take one day at a time. Concentrate all your efforts on surviving today.

Malcolm York had a plan, one that included Griffin and her in starring roles. Punishment, retribution, revenge. Apparently, his plan included physical and psychological torture. But was killing her part of the plan? Possibly. After all, what better punishment for Griff than to kill his wife?

You're thinking ahead again. Stop it! Griff is going to find you before York becomes bored with tormenting you. All you have to do is stay alive until Griff rescues you. That's your only job—keeping you and your baby alive.

Without warning the cabin door flew open and Anthony Linden swooped in and called to her. Bracing herself for a confrontation, she walked out of the bathroom and into the bedroom where Linden stood, hands on his hips and a surly expression on his face. With his bald head, compact muscular body, and cocky attitude, he looked like a sinister version of Mr. Clean.

Nic laughed.

My God, woman, you must be crazy to be able to laugh at a time like this.

He scrutinized her appearance. "Get dressed and make yourself presentable. Mr. York wants you topside in thirty minutes to meet a guest who is coming aboard this morning."

Nic wasn't laughing now. Her stomach knotted. York was bringing a guest aboard, someone he wanted her to meet. Any way you looked at it, it meant bad news for her.

"I'll be back for you in twenty minutes." Linden practically snapped his heels together before turning to leave.

"I'll be ready," Nic said, doing her level best to sound positively chipper.

Remember, don't think too far ahead. You have no control over what may happen. Don't waste your energy projecting your fears into a future scenario. Your only power is in controlling the way you react. Survival is the name of this game. It is your one and only goal.

On their arrival at Heathrow, Griff and Yvette had been met by the limousine provided by Thorndike Mitchum and chauffeured by one of the UK Powell Agency employees. Griff suspected that Yvette had gotten no more sleep than he had on their ten-hour flight from Tennessee to London. His thoughts had been with Nic as they were his every waking moment. No doubt, Yvette had thought of little else except meeting Suzette York. It was highly unlikely that this young girl was Yvette's daughter. But if by some miracle it turned out that she was, then Griff would have to face the possibility that he was her father. As long as the child had remained missing, possibly dead, the issue of paternity had been unimportant.

Was it so wrong of him to hope Suzette was not Yvette's child, and if she was that he was not the father?

He could not allow anything or anyone to take precedence over Nic. Finding her. Saving her. Bringing her home where she belonged.

As the limo zipped along M25, heading south toward Junction 5, Griff rested his head on the back of the seat and closed his eyes. Why had the phony York sent him on this journey? How did meeting Suzette York play a part in the man's plans for revenge?

He's playing a game, a psychological game, messing with my mind. And he's doing the same with Nic.

But how could Griff win the game when he didn't know the rules and didn't have a clue as to the real identity of his opponent? One thing for sure, the son of a bitch was not Malcolm York. He could call himself Beelzebub, but that didn't make him the devil.

One day at a time, one hour at a time, one minute at a time. One slow careful step at a time, staying sane, keeping the faith. He would find a way to rescue Nic.

Play the game. Learn the rules as you go along. Anticipate York's next move, if possible.

Who the man was was far less important than why he was seeking vengeance. Or perhaps the answer to each was one and the same. If he knew the man's true identity, he could figure out what his motives were.

"How much farther?" Yvette asked.

Snapped out of his musings by her question, Griff opened his eyes and glanced at his traveling companion. "I'm not sure. It's about forty miles or so from Heathrow to Kent." Griff leaned forward and asked their driver, "Where are we and how close are we to Biddenden?"

"We will be turning onto A21 quite soon," the

chauffeur replied. "From there, it is approximately twenty-five miles before we arrive at The West House in Biddenden."

"I had hoped we were closer." Yvette sighed.

"We'll be there soon enough," Griff told her. "Our lunch reservations are for one o'clock."

"Please tell me that she will be there."

"Yes, of course she'll be there."

"Something could go wrong. Plans could change. York may have changed his mind or—"

"York won't change his mind. Everything has been arranged," Griff assured her. "A car will pick up Suzette York at the school and deliver her to the restaurant at precisely one. Mitchum went through whatever channels necessary to expedite matters. Apparently most of the students are still away on their summer holiday, but Suzette has returned to the school per her guardian's request and the headmistress made arrangements for the girl. It seems her guardian prefers the Benenden School counselor accompany Suzette when she meets us today."

Yvette glanced at Griff, a melancholy smile tilting her lips. "Poor Griff. You're here under duress. A part of you must hate me—"

"I could never hate you."

"If not for me, for my child, for the letter York sent, Nic never would have left you. She would be at Griffin's Rest now."

"None of this is your fault," Griff told her. "It's

my fault for not being completely honest with Nic from the very beginning. As for your child . . . She or he is the most innocent of all."

"If Suzette York is my daughter—"

"She isn't."

"But if she is, even if I know in my heart the moment I see her, we will still need a DNA test to prove her paternity."

"Mitchum has a private lab on standby, waiting for a DNA sample from the girl," Griff said. "We will want a DNA test regardless of your gut response to Suzette York. Even if you believe she is your daughter, we need irrefutable proof."

Close to two o'clock that morning, Barbara Jean had persuaded Sanders to go to bed. "Even you are not invincible," she had told him. "You need rest just as we mortals do."

Despite being one of those lesser mortals, Maleah had fallen into the same trap that had ensnared Sanders—the need to work around the clock in the quest to locate Nic. Lucky for her, she had Derek to watch over her, just as Sanders had BJ.

"Here's my plan," Derek had told her. "We split the night shift so we can both get six hours of rest. Ten till four is the first shift, and then four till ten is the second shift. Okay with you?"

She had requested the second shift and Derek had reluctantly agreed. So here she was, five thirty Thursday morning, manning the office, swigging down her third cup of coffee and making arrange-ments for Ben Corbett and Meredith Sinclair to fly to Belize today. Luke Sentell, who usually accompanied Meredith on any Powell Agency related business, was unavailable. He was in London. By personally contacting certain old acquaintances, Luke would do his part to get word out that Griff Powell wanted to see Rafe Byrne.

Luke had flown first class, leaving the Powell jet available for Griff. Purchasing more airplanes for the agency had been shoved on the back burner. But after a brief discussion with Sanders, he had approved Maleah's request that the Powell Agency follow through with Griff's plan to purchase a couple more small used jets. What better time than the present? The seventeen-passenger, 2000 model Astra SPX was being flown in from Atlanta this morning and would be in the air again by noon, off to Belize. The seven-passenger, 2002 Cessna Citation Excel would be delivered from San Diego tomorrow.

Maleah's skepticism didn't stop her from hoping beyond hope that when she visited Shelter Island, Meredith would be able to use her psychic talents to discover something—anything—that might help them locate Nic. Yeah, sure, the odds were not in their favor. The only info Meredith had gathered on her trip to the Gatlinburg cabin was the fact that Nic was pregnant. Apparently

Nic's pregnancy had overshadowed any of her other thoughts this past Sunday. And the "connect with Nic via her hairbrush" session with Meredith and Yvette hadn't been any more successful. But just because Meredith hadn't sensed anything about Nic's abduction didn't mean that while on Shelter Island she wouldn't have a sterling silver moment of clairvoyance. Maleah was willing to try anything and certainly wouldn't rule out using the supernatural. Hell, if she thought visiting a witch doctor would help them find Nic, she'd jump right on it.

Sensing another person's presence in the room, Maleah knew she wasn't alone even before Sanders spoke to her. The guy moved like a phantom, silently maneuvering around the house without being heard and often without being seen.

"Barbara Jean said to tell you that she and Inez will have breakfast ready in about thirty minutes." Sanders approached her desk.

"Okay. Thanks."

His gaze traveled from her computer screen to the telephone on her desk to the nearly empty cup of coffee she held. "Any updates?"

"The Astra arrives this morning. I'm assigning it for Ben and Meredith's use for as long as they need it. If she gathers any info on Shelter Island, they will pursue it wherever it leads. And the Cessna is coming in from California tomorrow. I think we should send Rett to Amara to take a look around, make sure nothing is going on there that we don't know about."

"It would seem you have everything under control."

Maleah never felt completely at ease around Sanders. There was something about the man, something unnerving. He was too quiet, too reserved, too disciplined. Except for the bond that existed between him and Griff and between the two of them and Dr. Meng, and the occasional tender glance he gave BJ, Maleah would swear the man had no feelings. During the time she had known him, she had seldom seen him express any human emotion.

"When do you expect to hear from Griff ?" Maleah asked, breaking the lingering silence.

"I would imagine he will contact me after he and Yvette have seen the girl."

"Do you think she's—?"

"No."

Just a one-word response, succinct and to the point. No discussion. No reason why he believed as he did.

The telephone on Maleah's desk rang. Startled by the unexpected ringing, she jerked at the sound. Without hesitation, she lifted the receiver.

"Perdue," she said.

"Ms. Perdue, this is Jeffries at Powell headquarters. We've just come into possession of some information that we believe could be of vital importance."

Maleah's heartbeat did a nervous *rat-a-tat-tat.* "And that information is?"

"We've been digging into Kroy Enterprises, but it's like swimming in quicksand," Jeffries told her. "Just when you think you've located a reliable source, you discover it's just one more fake lead. Kroy is a riddle inside a puzzle inside an enigma. Dummy corporations. Hidden assets."

"You were able to find out, with very little effort, that Kroy Enterprises owned the jet that took off from McGhee Tyson Sunday morning and that they own Shelter Island," Maleah said. "But we believe that was because someone wanted us to know."

"Well, I can't say whether or not that same someone did or did not want us to find out that there is a hundred-foot-long yacht, a Lloyd's Classification 100-A-1, registered to an M. L. Oclam. But I can tell you that he made it damn difficult to find a link between Oclam and Kroy. We've been searching for anything owned by Kroy, so the yacht almost slipped by us."

"Who is it?" Sanders asked.

Maleah placed her hand over the mouthpiece. "Jeffries at downtown Knoxville headquarters. He's got something."

"Are you still there, Ms. Perdue?"

"I'm here and I'm listening." Maleah's mind whirled with the info, repeating the name

251

M. L. Oclam several times, then she jotted it down. "Is Oclam spelled o-c-l-a-m?"

Jeffries chuckled. "You've already figured it out, haven't you?"

"M. L. Oclam. Just like Kroy is York spelled backward, M. L. Oclam backward spells Malcolm. Surely this guy doesn't think he's being clever. Inverting the letters of a word is child's play. Any intelligent ten-year-old could figure out—" Maleah stopped when she heard Jeffries's laughter. "What?" she asked.

"You'd be surprised how easy it is for highly trained professionals to overlook the name Oclam when they're diligently searching for Kroy."

"Whoever figured it out, give him or her a pay raise."

"That would be Bitsy Chambers, our computer guru."

"This yacht got a name?"

"The *Isis*."

"Lovely. I don't suppose you've been able to track her."

"Oh, yes, we have. She's in the Caribbean Sea, off the coast of Barranquilla, Colombia."

"Thank you, God!" Maleah shouted. "Keep me posted. And Jeffries, give yourself a raise, too. I'm sure Mr. Powell will okay it."

The moment she ended her telephone conversation, she jumped to her feet and almost hugged Sanders, stopping herself just in the nick of time.

"Kroy Enterprises owns a private yacht, the *Isis*, and she just happens to be in the Caribbean Sea off the coast of Colombia right now. What do you want to bet that Nic's aboard that yacht?"

"This could be the break we have been hoping for," Sanders said.

"Should we call Griff ?"

"No, not yet. There will time enough to tell him once we put a plan into motion. We do not know if Nicole is aboard this yacht. Let me handle this"—he paused—"for now."

"Handle it how?"

"The agency has contacts in Colombia."

"Contacts but not agents," Maleah reminded him. "Agents we can trust. Contacts owe their loyalty to no one. They work for the highest bidder."

"If we wait until we can fly in agents, we could lose our chance. If Nicole is aboard the yacht, then we need to act now, not hours from now. And I can promise you that no one outbids the Powell Agency and our contacts know we pay top dollar."

Maleah nodded. "You're right, of course. We can't wait."

Quaint and peaceful, Biddenden, one of many Wealden villages set in the picturesque Kent countryside, was located ten minutes from the Benenden School. Mitchum's secretary had handled their reservations, choosing The West

House for their lunch meeting with Suzette York and the school's counselor, a Ms. Tomasina Hartwood. Ms. Hartwood was a member of the UK Council for Psychotherapy. Mitchum had also made arrangements for their lodging at the George Hotel in Cranbrook.

"The girl has been told that she's to meet a lady who may be her birth mother," Mitchum had explained.

Griff escorted Yvette into the restaurant, housed in a fifteenth-century weaver's cottage, at seven minutes till one, and they were quickly seated at a round table near a huge brick fireplace. When their waiter presented them with menus, Griff informed the man that there would be two others joining them shortly.

"I keep telling myself not to get my hopes up," Yvette said. "But I want this girl to be my child. I want it so desperately."

Knowing the risk he took in touching Yvette, Griff reached out and grasped her hand.

"Thank you," Yvette told him as she eased her hand from his.

"For what?"

"For being you, Griffin, a part of my soul."

Griff looked away, unable to watch the pain in Yvette's dark eyes. He saw his own pain reflected there.

He glanced at the menu, quickly scanning the lunch choices. If Nic was here, she would order the Roast Temple farm label anglaise chicken with wild garlic gnocchi and St. George mushrooms. He could hear her saying, "No matter what these fancy schmancy chefs do to it, they usually can't screw up chicken."

Yvette suddenly tensed. When Griff glanced at her, he noted that her gaze was transfixed at something all the way across the restaurant.

She's here. Suzette York has arrived.

But how could Yvette know for sure?

Griff's gaze followed Yvette's and then he understood why she had instantly recognized the girl. A lead weight dropped into the pit of Griff's belly.

Standing there at nearly six feet tall, with almond-shaped gray eyes, and long, straight brown hair, every feature as delicately beautiful and distinctively Eurasian as Yvette's, the young woman could indeed be Yvette's child.

Griff did not want to admit what he felt at that very moment. But what choice did he have? The girl had his height and his gray eyes. He couldn't deny that she could very easily be his daughter, too.

CHAPTER 17

Linden brought Nic into the empty lounge, indicated for her to sit, and then stood guard at the door, his arms crossed over his chest.

As ordered, she had bathed and dressed and was ready now for presentation to York's guest, who apparently had not arrived yet. Whoever this guy was, he must be an earlier riser. Either that or he had stayed up all night.

"Do you know who York's guest is?" she asked.

"A friend and business associate." Linden barely glanced at her.

"Business associate, huh? Which business—drugs or slaves? Or both?"

Linden glared at her. "I'd keep that pretty little mouth shut if I were you. Better not stick your nose into things that are none of your damn business."

"You don't seem your usual chipper self this morning," Nic said. "What's got you wound so tight?"

That's it, Nic, prod the grizzly bear.

Linden came toward her, his hand raised to strike; but the clearly audible sound of voices outside on deck brought him to a sudden standstill. He lowered his hand to his side and stepped away from her.

"I am delighted that while you were here in Barranquilla on business, you were able to make time to join me on the *Isis* for a few days," York was saying. Apparently he and his companion were close by. "I have a delicious surprise for you, old friend." York laughed. "Of course, I've arranged for your usual entertainment choices. They'll arrive before we set sail."

"Thank you. I can always count on you to see to my every need," the other man said, his accent decidedly French. "But it was your promise of delivering something extra-special that lured me away from business today."

The lounge door opened. Nic rose to her feet, stood straight and tall, and armed herself with every ounce of courage she could muster. She was as battle-ready as she could be wearing a Versace coral silk blouse and cream linen slacks and four-inch Alexander McQueen pumps. York had provided her with a select choice of designer clothing. For all intents and purposes, she appeared to be a pampered guest.

York looked the part of a European playboy with his expertly styled silver hair, glossy manicured nails, and custom-made clothing. At approxi-mately five-ten, he looked even shorter standing next to the six-foot-two, possibly six-three, gentleman with a thick mane of white hair and neatly groomed gray mustache and Vandyke. York's guest was handsome for a man his age, which Nic guessed to be his midsixties, and had probably been drop-dead gorgeous twenty years ago. Where York's sleek, cosmopolitan image seemed somewhat forced, as if he didn't quite fit the part, his guest truly owned his man-of-the-world persona.

York ushered his friend into the lounge, smiling proudly as if he were about to present his guest with something as priceless as the Hope Diamond.

The aging bon vivant stared at Nic, his dark-eyed gaze traveling over her slowly, appraising her worth as if she were on the auction block. A sliver of forewarning spiraled down her spine. This man, for all his attractive, sophisticated appearance was no gentleman. Gut instinct warned her that he was a ruthlessly cunning viper.

"What is this?" he asked, his question edged with contempt.

"Now, now, old friend, there is more to the lady than meets the eye," York assured him. "I have plans for her that you will appreciate. But she is not for your pleasure, of course."

"You have aroused my curiosity, *mon petit* Malcolm."

My little Malcolm? What an odd thing for York's guest to call him. Did this Frenchman know York's true identity? I'd lay odds he does.

Bouchard had used the term as if speaking to a boy and not a man. Did the endearment signify anything of importance? If Griff knew, would it help him figure out the fake York's identity?

"Come here." York motioned to Nic. "I wish to introduce you to a dear friend, a gentleman who visited me often on Amara."

Nic moved forward, her every step forced, as she came face-to-face with someone from her husband's past. Without blinking, she looked him in the eye.

"Nicole, it is my great honor to introduce you to Monsieur Yves Bouchard, well known in our business as *Le Ravisseur*."

The Abductor!

Nic had absolutely no idea who this man was, but it didn't take a genius to figure out that a man whose nickname meant The Abductor was probably in the human trafficking business. "Monsieur," Nic barely managed to say, her heart rate accelerating with each passing moment.

Yves lifted her limp hand to his lips. With iron control, Nic internalized the shiver of revulsion, keeping her hand steady.

"Nicole is the wife of someone you will recall from our many hunting expeditions on Amara," York said. "Yves, this lovely lady is Griffin Powell's wife."

Yves Bouchard's bedroom brown eyes widened in surprise and then he smiled. "You did not disappoint me, old friend. She is indeed the something extra-special that you promised."

"Do you suppose Griffin would still be such

an amazingly cunning adversary on a hunt?" York chuckled softly and winked at Nic.

"He was a superb animal who managed to outsmart those of us who stalked him," Bouchard told Nic. "I've never been on a hunt that equaled the ones when your husband was our prey."

York grabbed Nic's chin between his thumb and forefinger. "And now I have the perfect bait to lure Griffin Powell into my snare and bring him back for one final hunt."

As he rose to his feet, Griffin could not take his eyes off the young woman walking toward their table. Pushing back her chair, Yvette grasped the edge of the table for support as she stood. If Suzette was not who York claimed she was, he had done a mind-boggling job of finding the perfect fake, someone who resembled both Yvette and Griffin. Although her features were not perfect matches for Yvette's, they were similar. The same slanted eyes, although an almost identical gray to the color of Griff's eyes. A small nose, a full mouth, and flawless skin, a shade lighter than Yvette's honey gold complexion. Willowy slender, like Yvette, but much taller, as she would be if her father had been a tall man. Griff was six-four. Suzette was close to six feet.

Only after they arrived at the table did Griff actually look at the woman with Suzette. The middle-aged, petite brunette, dressed neatly in gray slacks and a white blouse, held out her hand to Yvette.

"I'm Tomasina Hartwood." She shook hands with Yvette and then with Griffin. "And this is Suzette."

"Hello." The young girl glanced nervously from Yvette to Griff.

"Please, sit down, ladies." Griff gestured with a sweep of his arm.

Once they were all seated at the table and the waiter took their lunch orders, Ms. Hartwood immediately got down to business. "Mr. York, Suzette's legal guardian, has spoken to her and explained why you are here today, Dr. Meng. She knows that you may be her birth mother."

Yvette didn't respond. She seemed to be in a trance, her body rigid and her eyes downcast.

"We don't want you to feel uncomfortable." Griff focused on Suzette. "And neither Dr. Meng nor I want to upset you, but we do need to ask you a few questions."

"Yes, of course," Suzette replied. "I understand. There are questions that I would like to ask Dr. Meng and"—she looked at Griff—"and you, too, Mr. Powell. Papa told me that you may be my biological father."

Papa did, did he? That son of a bitch!

If this girl was the real deal . . .

Don't take anything at face value. For all you

know, Suzette York is every bit as phony as the imitation York.

"What do you want to know?" Yvette finally found her voice.

"You gave birth to a child who would now be my age. Why did you give her away?" Suzette asked.

It took Yvette several minutes to reply. "I did not give up my baby willingly. My child was stolen from me."

"Oh." Suzette's strikingly beautiful eyes widened and her rosebud mouth opened in a perfect oval.

"Papa found me when I was five. I was living on the streets in Hong Kong, dirty and unkempt, begging in the streets along with other children. I have no memory of my life at that time. I've been told that I probably blocked out . . . " She paused. A lone tear trickled down her smooth cheek. "Papa has been both mother and father to me for as long as I can remember."

"Do you know your actual birth date?" Griff asked, realizing Yvette needed time to compose herself before speaking again.

"No, I'm afraid that I don't. Papa gave me a birthday. He said it was an important date for him. His little sister's birthday. She died when she was just a child."

"And that date is?" Griff asked.

"October first."

Yvette gasped. She had given birth on October first.

"Is something wrong, Dr. Meng?" Ms. Hartwood asked.

"No. Nothing."

"Suzette, would you agree to a DNA test?" Griff asked, determined to unearth the truth as soon as possible. If this girl was Yvette's child—and possibly his child—there would be no simple and easy way to handle the situation. If the pseudo-York was her legal guardian and had brought her up from the age of five, not only would the law be on his side, so would Suzette's loyalty.

"Yes, of course. Papa said that a DNA test would prove whether or not I was Dr. Meng's daughter." She glanced shyly at Griff. "And if I'm your daughter."

The waitstaff brought their food and served them. But apparently only Ms. Hartwood had an appetite. Everyone else picked at their food during lunch. Even when served a delectable dessert of white and dark chocolate honeycomb sorbet—something called a Crunchie—Suzette merely nibbled.

During their meal, Yvette had given Suzette condensed information about her own childhood and teen years, left out any mention of her life on Amara, and told the girl about her profession—psychiatrist—without bringing up anything about being an empath who had devoted herself to students with amazing psychic abilities.

Griff kept his own life story confined to a few

sentences. Born and raised in Tennessee. Played football at UT. Was now a successful business-man.

"Are you two married?" Suzette asked.

"No," Yvette replied. "Griffin and I are friends. I was married once, years ago. I'm a widow."

"And your husband wasn't my father?"

"No, he was not."

"Are you married, Mr. Powell?"

"Yes," Griff replied.

"Do either of you have children?"

"No," they replied simultaneously.

Suzette concentrated on Griff. "I imagined that my biological father would be very tall, like you. And I have wondered if he would have gray eyes, too." She turned to Yvette. "I have dreamed of having a mother. In my dreams she was as beautiful as you are, Dr. Meng."

Moisture glistened in Yvette's eyes. Griff reached over and clasped her hand. He knew that Yvette would sense what he was thinking, that Suzette might well be their child. But damn it all, his gut warned him that when something seemed too good to be true then it usually was.

"Would you allow Dr. Meng to touch you, to hold your hand?" Griff's gaze locked with Suzette's. He noticed a flicker of uncertainty in her eyes.

"Yes, of course." The young woman reached across the table and held out her hand.

"Do it," Griff told Yvette.

Hesitantly, anxiously, after nearly seventeen years of waiting and hoping, Yvette touched the hand of the girl she so desperately wanted to be the baby that had been stolen from her, the baby Malcolm York had never allowed her to see.

Yvette took Suzette's trembling hand in hers and once they connected, the trembling stopped. Griff studied Yvette's face, waiting for any sign that would tell him if she had emotionally recognized this girl as her child. But the transfixed expression Yvette held in place told him nothing.

"I'm afraid I don't understand why—" Ms. Hartwood said, but was cut off abruptly mid-sentence when Suzette snatched her hand from Yvette's loose grasp.

"What were you doing?" Suzette asked. "I could feel you probing around inside me."

"No, you did not," Yvette said. "You were too busy sending me mental messages that I am your mother to have noticed my gentle probing."

"I was thinking about how much I hope you are my mother," Suzette cried loud enough to draw glances from several other customers.

"And I hope that you are my daughter," Yvette assured her in a soft, soothing voice. "I had felt so certain that if I could only see you . . . touch you . . . that I would know." Yvette murmured under her breath, almost inaudible, "But even growing inside me, my baby hid from me."

"But you don't know if I'm your daughter, do you? Seeing me isn't enough. Touching me didn't convince you." Suzette's bottom lip trembled. Tears filled her gray eyes.

"I look at you and I see what I want to see, what is so very obvious," Yvette said. "There is an undeniable resemblance. You could be my child and Griffin's. And when I touched you, I felt a jolt of awareness, but . . . What I was aware of was that you want me to believe you're my daughter."

"Then let's do the DNA test," Suzette said as she shoved back her chair and stood. "Let's do it today. Right now. I need to know the truth just as much as you do."

Rafe didn't know the man's real name. In the underground jungle that he frequented, reputations were far more important than identities. And everyone used aliases, and many, like Rafe, used more than one. Over the years, Harry Northcliffe had proven himself a reliable and trusted source of information, unknowingly helping him locate the Amara visitors that he had systematically sentenced to death during the past sixteen years. The curly-haired, dimple-cheeked little black marketeer kept his finger on the pulse of the treacherous, clandestine realm that existed parallel to mainstream society. Harry was a world traveler, popping up in London, Madrid, Paris, Rome, or wherever information meant money. If you became a marked man, Harry could probably discover who had put out the hit and even narrow down the list of possible assassins. If you needed to get a message to someone who flew under the radar, Harry could deliver without endangering the anonymity of either party. So, when Harry had told a friend who told a friend who told another friend that Harry Northcliffe had a message for a guy named Eddie Castell, Rafe stopped by Harry's favorite London hangout, Frankie's Italian Bar and Grill in Chiswick.

The first time Rafe had met him at the family-style bar and restaurant, he'd found it amusing that a fellow like Harry would have chosen a pub that possessed a 1930s art deco glamour, a place you could bring your mother. But he didn't know the real Harry Northcliffe any more than Harry knew the real Eddie Castell, although he suspected Harry might know him by several of his other aliases.

From the street, the pub wasn't impressive. But the entrance, through a Mediterranean-style terrace with overhead trellises, floral cloths on the round tables, and bright pink chairs, welcomed customers with flair. Once inside, Rafe surveyed the long, shiny black bar, lined with stools, for any sign of Harry. Then he searched the cozy bar rooms, with black-and-white tiled floors, red-checkered tablecloths, and disco ball–type light fixtures. After a brief search, he found Harry in the dining room, sitting at a table near the back wall lined with mirrors.

The moment Harry saw Rafe, he threw up a hand and waved.

Rafe took the chair across from Harry and said, "You're looking well."

Harry grinned. "Clean living. No smoking. No drugs. Just wine and good food." He lifted his glass, saluted Rafe, and finished off the remaining drops of wine.

A waiter appeared almost instantly, proving what Harry always said about Frankie's well-trained staff being top-notch.

"I've ordered us a couple of pizzas," Harry said. "And we have this bottle of Chianti, but if you'd prefer something else to drink . . . ?"

"Chianti is fine."

Harry dismissed the waiter. He poured wine for Rafe and then refilled his own glass. "Are you staying in London for a while?"

"You tell me," Rafe said.

Harry shrugged. "You never stay anywhere for very long, Mr. Castell."

"Nor do you, Mr. Northcliffe."

"No money to be made in rooting yourself in one place."

"So, how are your finances at present?"

"Quite nice. Thank you for inquiring."

"A recent investment payoff?" Rafe asked.

"Through recommendations from friends, I've

reconnected with a former client, one who pays extremely well."

"Good for you."

"He's a billionaire from the U.S."

Rafe didn't have to ask the man's name. He knew.

"I believe he's someone you've done business with in the past," Harry said. "According to his associate, a Mr. Sentell, he is interested in going into a joint venture with you and would like to negotiate terms as soon as possible."

Rafe had not seen Griffin Powell in sixteen years, not since Rafe's release from the Royal London Hospital. Griffin, Sanders, and Yvette had reached out to him, asked him to join them, but he had refused. Nearly six years later, millions of dollars had shown up in a Swiss bank account in his name, a gift from his old Amara comrades. The money had been dirty. Filthy. Soaked in the blood of countless victims. But he had kept it, put it to good use, washed it clean with vengeance. Griffin had collected Malcolm York's ill-gotten billions, through legal and illegal channels for York's widow, and apparently she had turned the bulk of the enormous fortune over to Griffin.

"I assume he wants to set up a meeting," Rafe said.

"At your earliest convenience."

"I'm not sure this is a joint venture I'd be interested in."

Harry shrugged. "Suit yourself. It's nothing to me one way or the other. But if I'm not mistaken, you're indebted to this gentleman. I'd think you would want to repay him."

So that's how it was. After nearly two decades Griffin Powell was calling in his marker. If that was the case, it could mean only one thing—the rumors about Malcolm York rising from the dead were true.

CHAPTER 18

Griff and Yvette left the restaurant in Biddenden shortly after Suzette and Ms. Hartwood said their good-byes. Despite being in tears, Suzette had managed to be polite following her emotional outburst.

"How shall we proceed?" Suzette had asked. "Do I spit in a cup? Or give you a lock of my hair?"

"I've arranged for someone from a reliable lab to come to the school for a sample," Griffin had explained to Suzette before speaking directly to the counselor. "If you need to contact Mr. York, please do so. I'm sure he will give his permission."

Whatever game York was playing, this young girl had a starring role in it. As much as Griff wished, for Yvette's sake, that the girl was her daughter, he remained skeptical. What reason would York have for handing Yvette the thing she wanted most in this world?

As they rode along toward Cranbrook, Yvette in silently composed, eyes-closed state of meditation, Griff concentrated on the man who had kidnapped Nic, the man who had ordered him to bring Yvette to England to meet her long-lost daughter. Why would anyone assume the identity of a monster like Malcolm York? A friend? A relative? An admirer? The real York's closest friends had been as sick and evil as he had been. But only one of those bosom buddies still lived— Yves Bouchard. Griff remembered Bouchard well. Griff had been the man's favorite quarry when York arranged his special hunts. And Rafe had been Bouchard's favorite boy toy. But Griff couldn't imagine Bouchard embracing someone else's identity, not when his own ego was astronomical. If ever a guy was in love with himself, it was Yves Bouchard.

The sadistic Amara guards were all dead. He had made sure that not one of them survived. And only six captives had left Amara alive. Two of the men were dead; at least Griff had been sent copies of their death certificates. But death certificates could be faked, bodies could be switched, mistakes could be made. Would either Fletcher or Papandreou, if actually still alive, have any reason to metamorphose into a Malcolm York clone?

They had hated York, had been as abused as the other slaves, and had helped in killing the guards. Unless one of them was still alive and had snapped and become mentally unstable, and for some unknown psychological reason woke up one morning and decided to become Malcolm York, then Griff could rule out both men.

As for relatives, York had a number of distant cousins, but there were no records of siblings or children. His nearest kin was Sir Harlan Benecroft, a wicked old pervert whose depravity reinforced the theory that personality disorders such as insanity and a penchant for evil did indeed run in families. Sir Harlan had produced one offspring, a son named Ellis. Griff had a copy of his death certificate, too. Ellis Benecroft, renowned as a worthless, womanizing playboy, was last seen alive with a famous supermodel. His and his female companion's charred bodies had been found at the bottom of a ravine in Italy, where Ellis's Lamborghini Gallardo had crashed.

Had Griff overlooked someone? Did York have an unknown sibling? An illegitimate child no one knew about? An admirer who hadn't been a frequent visitor to Amara? If not, then the only possibilities were Yves Bouchard, Sir Harlan, and three dead men.

Griff didn't even notice that the car had stopped until their chauffeur said, "We've arrived at the George Hotel, Mr. Powell."

"Thank you." Griff glanced at Yvette, who had opened her eyes and was looking at him. "Are you all right?"

"I am confused and disappointed," she replied. "But I will be fine."

The chauffeur opened the back door and assisted Yvette out and onto the sidewalk in front of the historic building housing the boutique hotel. Well maintained, the old brick structure sported new windows, the framework painted gray, as were the entrance door and the decorative metal railing around the narrow awning that extended from one end of the hotel to the other. A gray sign stating the establishment's name and depicting a gray knight atop a gray steed hung from a second-story pole.

The interior was warm and welcoming and check-in a quick and easy task. Upstairs, Griff found his room to be more than adequate, with a large bed and a private bath. He placed his suitcase on the luggage rack at the foot of the bed and left the unpacking for later. Yvette's room nearby was smaller than his, with a double bed, crisp white linens, and a dark brown duvet. She had left the door open as if she was expecting him. Standing by the window overlooking Stone Street, her back to him, she apparently sensed his presence.

"Please, come in."

Griffin stepped over the threshold and closed the door behind him. "I've been promised the

DNA results within a few days. The lab understands that no expense is to be spared to expedite the tests."

Unmoving, her slender shoulders straight, her head unbowed, Yvette continued looking out the window. "I was so certain that I would know if she was my daughter."

"But you're not sure. I have to admit that when I first saw her . . . Damn, but she looks like us, doesn't she? At least superficially. Her Eurasian heritage. Her gray eyes. Her height. The fact that she's beautiful."

"If you were my child's father, I imagine she would look a great deal like Suzette."

Griff walked across the room and stood beside Yvette.

"We have no way of knowing my child's true paternity." She turned and looked up at him. "I would like to believe that she is your child. And if not yours, then Lunt Anderson's. I believe he was a good man." She inhaled deeply and exhaled slowly. "Before we left Griffin's Rest, Sanders asked me how I would feel about my child if I knew that she had been fathered by Yves Bouchard."

"And what did you say to Sanders?"

"I had no answer for his question. I refuse to believe that Bouchard . . . No, not him. Never."

"Then what about—?"

"No, not him either."

Griff understood her reluctance to accept the possibility that her child, be that child Suzette York or an almost seventeen-year-old boy or girl out there somewhere still unknown to them, could have been fathered by Yves Bouchard.

Just as York had been, Bouchard was a monster.

But why did she have such strong negative feelings for the only other person who could have fathered her child? Had something he didn't know about happened between them on Amara? If so, then Yvette would tell him if she wanted him to know.

"I'll leave so you can rest for a while," Griff said, regretting that there was nothing he could say or do to make the situation easier for her. When she didn't respond as he turned to go, he added, "I need to contact Sanders for an update about our ongoing search for Nic."

"I hope he has some positive news for you." Yvette continued staring out the window.

Sanders had never lied to Griffin.

"You can't tell him," Maleah Perdue warned. "Not yet. Not until you know for sure that Nic is on the *Isis*."

"If I do not mention anything about the yacht owned by Kroy Enterprises, I will be lying to him by omission."

"Then, by God, lie to him. For all we know, York wants us to think Nic is aboard the *Isis*. He could have deliberately allowed us to discover that the yacht is owned by Kroy. This could all be part of his game. He could be out there somewhere laughing his head off because he believes that Griff thinks we're on the verge of rescuing Nic again."

"Maleah could be right," Derek Lawrence said. "York is playing a game, one where the only rules are his rules. He sees himself as the puppet master, the one pulling all the strings. He had a reason to send Griff and Yvette to England. For all we know, he's setting some sort of trap, either an emotional trap or an actual physical trap."

Sanders owed Griffin far more than his life and he would spend the rest of his days repaying the debt. He had spent the past sixteen years at the man's side, devoting himself to helping Griffin use the vast wealth he had claimed in Yvette's name—York's blood money—to right as many wrongs as possible. In the beginning, the Powell Private Security and Investigation Agency had been little more than a sideline for Griffin, one more small way that he could use York's wealth to do something good. And it had allowed Griffin a diversion from his numerous other enterprises, but more importantly, playing the billionaire playboy detective had been an excellent façade. Each in his or her own way, he—Griffin—and Yvette existed in two worlds at the same time—the past and the present—and only they truly knew each other.

Griffin Powell loved his wife. Sanders understood, as few others possibly could, the living hell in which Griffin now existed. Sanders had loved his wife. Elora. Kind, gentle, sweet Elora. And like Yvette, an empath.

"I will wait." Sanders looked at Derek. "If Griffin contacts me before we find out what is happening on the *Isis*, I will not tell him. But if Nicole is aboard the yacht, I will inform him immediately, no matter what happens."

"I believe you've made the right decision," Derek said.

"Absolutely," Maleah agreed. "Now, if only we'd hear something from our Colombian contacts." She checked her wristwatch. "The operation should be going down right now, shouldn't it?"

"If all is going as planned," Sanders told her.

Nic had just finished dressing for dinner, a command performance, when she heard what sounded like gunfire.

What the hell?

Shouting.

Frantic commands.

The rumble of feet tramping rapidly in a fury of activity.

Repeated gunfire a constant backdrop to every other sound.

Fear tightened Nic's throat. What was happening? Was the yacht being attacked? If so, by whom? Had York anchored there in Colombia on business? Had a major drug deal gone wrong? Or—?

Her cabin door flew open to reveal a flushed Malcolm York standing outside with several armed guards surrounding him. "We're leaving the *Isis* now," he called as he motioned to Nic.

When she didn't immediately respond, he ordered one of the guards to fetch her. Before the man reached her, she snapped out of her momentary shock and walked as quickly as she could in her four-inch, silver sling-back pumps.

With the sound of gunfire echoing all around them, Nic hurried along the deck with York and his guards, but before they had gone more than ten feet, bullets riddled the deck in front of them, stopping them cold. More bullets shattered the windows above them, showering them with shattered glass fragments. Nic barely managed to stifle a scream. She wasn't the screaming type, but then she wasn't accustomed to being fired on without having a weapon she could use to defend herself.

Whoever was attacking the *Isis*, had managed to send a team aboard the ship. She caught glimpses of several armed men who were not part of York's small army of guards. Two of York's soldiers returned fire as York grabbed Nic and dragged her with him in a hasty retreat. A couple of the guards flanked them, back and front, firing repeatedly at the encroaching enemy.

When they reached the starboard side of the yacht, Yves Bouchard met them, along with several of York's guards and crewmen.

"What the hell's going on?" York demanded, his gaze fixed on Bouchard, his tone accusatory.

"This is not my doing," Bouchard assured him.

"Then whose? Certainly not mine."

"At the moment, does it matter? We are in danger," Bouchard said.

York pulled Nic in front of him and draped his arm around her waist. "I have precious cargo to protect."

"And if they are here for her?" Bouchard asked.

"That is highly unlikely. There is no way Griffin Powell could know that his wife is aboard the *Isis*."

Oh my God, was it possible that Griff had come there to rescue her, that the attackers firing at them were his men?

Before Bouchard could respond, two gunmen came from the bow and two more from the stern, effectively blocking their escape. When York's guards reacted to the threat, the raiders gunned them down, leaving only two standing. But only one of the invaders went down from the return fire.

"My God, do something!" Bouchard screamed.

"What do you want?" York asked the men holding them at gunpoint. "Money? Drugs? Name it and it's yours."

Totally disregarding York's question, one of the raiders looked straight at Nic and asked, "Are you Nicole Powell?"

Nic's heart stopped for a second. Were they here to rescue her? If so, where was Griff ? He would hardly be sitting on the sidelines. And if he had sent in anyone as head of an advance team, it would have been Luke Sentell. She didn't recognize any of these men.

Taking a chance on possibly jumping out of the frying pan and into the fire, Nic said, "Yes, I'm Nicole Powell."

When she instinctively leaned forward in an effort to escape from York's grasp, he tightened his hold, slid his hand into an inside jacket pocket, and whipped out a handgun. Before Nic could free herself or the gunmen could react, York placed the muzzle against her temple.

"The lady stays with me or she dies."

Nic closed her eyes for half a second, steadied her nerves as best she could with a 9mm kissing her head, and said a prayer that these guys knew what they were doing.

"You don't want to do this," the team spokesman told York. "This ship is surrounded and I have a couple of snipers waiting for my command."

"Are you sure I can't pull the trigger before one of your sharpshooters takes me out?" York asked smugly. "Your assignment no doubt was to rescue Mrs. Powell, not to get her killed."

Did York actually believe he had nine lives, that he was the real Malcolm York, risen from the grave, and could be reborn a second time? Or was there another reason for his cocky attitude?

"It's your call, Mrs. Powell," the head of her rescue team said.

My call? Do I risk my life? Can they kill York before he kills me? Or do I give up this chance to go free in order to play it safe? It's all or nothing. Am I willing to take the chance? Damn right I am!

Just as she opened her mouth to speak, the sounds of a nearby scuffle warned them that someone was approaching.

"Ah," York said. "I believe my ace in the hole has arrived." He didn't move, not even by an inch, as the sound of footsteps drew nearer. His steady hand held the grip, his finger poised on the trigger.

The rescue team members saw the source of the ruckus first, moments before two men emerged from below deck. The momentary distraction barely fazed the rescuers, who each zeroed in on a target—York, his one remaining guard, and the new guard who had just appeared on the scene.

Nic noticed Bouchard, who had barely breathed for several minutes.

The bastard's scared shitless.

Nic glance sideways.

York's guard who had brought the other man with him from below deck kept his weapon trained on his prisoner. Jonas MacColl, his ankles and feet unbound, but his arms pulled behind him and his wrists cuffed, cast a surly glare at York and then glanced at Nic. The moment their gazes connected, he shook his head.

"Touching, isn't it, how he is trying to protect you," York said to Nic. "I've raised the stakes a little higher. You're a risk taker, Nicole. Otherwise you never would have married Griffin Powell. But are you willing to bet your life and Jonas's that your rescuers can kill me and my guards before we can kill you and Jonas?"

"You son of a bitch!" Jonas lunged forward, his intent obvious. He was heading straight for York.

His guard grabbed Jonas by his cuffed wrists and yanked him backward and down on his knees before kicking him in the back with his booted foot. York's other guard pointed his rifle straight at Jonas.

Jonas grunted with pain, but recovered quickly and looked up at Nic as he struggled to stand. "Don't let him use me to hurt you. If you do, he wins."

"Nicole's hero," York said to the rescuers. "Be sure to tell Griffin Powell how his wife gave up her chance of freedom to save a man who seemed willing to die for her." York laughed.

He was insane. Certifiable.

"Decisions, decisions," York taunted.

"Shut up!" Nic yelled at him. "Just shut the hell up."

What was she going to do? Risking her own life was one thing, but risking Jonas's life, regardless of what he had told her to do, was something else. But there was always a chance that the snipers could take out York and several of the gunmen before they could kill either Jonas or her.

But what were the odds that she and Jonas would both survive?

If I die, my baby dies.

"Mrs. Powell?" the team leader said.

And then with a response caught in her throat, all hell broke loose. One of the snipers fired from his position on shore, killing the guard threatening Jonas. York yowled, his expression one of shocked outrage, his trigger finger reacting instinctively to the impending threat. Jonas lunged forward and barreled into York, the impact altering the pistol's projection, sending the bullet outward instead of inward, grazing Nic's temple instead of entering her head.

Jonas shoved Nic onto the deck, his body a shield between her and York as York aimed and fired a second time.

CHAPTER 19

York owed Anthony Linden his life. The man was a killing machine. He managed to keep the rescue team aboard the *Isis* busy long enough for the one guard left alive with York to help him and Bouchard get Nicole Powell and her would-be savior Jonas to safety on the waiting motorboat portside. Where the boat had come from, York didn't care at the moment. If Satan had spit it out of hell or angels had brought it down from heaven, he could care less. The boat provided an escape route and that was all that mattered. Getting Jonas down the ladder and onto the boat was no easy task, but they managed. If not for the fact that Jonas was a major player in his games with Griffin Powell, he would have left the wounded hero to die on the yacht. And he also knew that Nicole would be more manageable if he kept Jonas alive for leverage.

Linden, their mighty protector, joined them on the boat as gunfire blazed all around them. The man was worth more than his weight in gold. Once on board, he motioned to the young helmsman manning the vessel to take off, and then he turned to speak to York.

"The minute I realized what was happening, I contacted Fernandez," Linden shouted to York over the roar of the outboard motor. "He dispatched a boat from nearby and he's sending enough men to take care of our unwanted visitors and clean up afterward."

As if on cue, two helicopters roared through the sky like giant blackbirds, wings flapping and emitting a repetitive cry. Machine guns rained lead across the *Isis*, along the shore, and inland where the rescue team's snipers and backup soldiers were stationed.

"I'll be sure to thank Lorenzo when I see him again," York said as they headed out to sea in the small motorboat.

Lorenzo Fernandez was a business associate, a native Colombian, someone York could count on to protect him and their mutual interests. A man who possessed his own well-trained army was just the kind of friend to have when one found oneself in such a dangerous predicament.

Linden picked up lifejackets, tossed one to York and another to Bouchard, then he slipped into one himself before throwing a couple of them toward Nicole and Jonas.

York glanced at Bouchard. His sophisticated French friend did not have the stomach for battle. He had always known that sad truth about Yves. The man was soft. He could mete out punishment, but could not handle pain and suffering himself. He enjoyed the hunt, loved the kill, but could never have survived even one hour as the quarry.

"There's a larger boat waiting for us," Linden said. "It will take us to Santa Marta. You can contact Fernandez when we're aboard to discuss future arrangements. I'm sure he's looking forward to making a lucrative deal."

York laughed. "No doubt. He's a greedy bastard."

"Damn it, York," Nicole Powell yelled over the pounding waves and motor's rumble. "Help me." She had ripped apart the bottom of her couture dress and used it as a bandage to soak up the blood seeping from Jonas's gunshot wound. "Did you bring him with us just to watch him die?"

York could understand why Griffin Powell had found this woman so irresistible, why he had claimed her for his own. Despite what she had recently endured, she was not shivering with fear or weeping uncontrollably or begging for mercy. She was angry and belligerent and demanding. She was spitting fire like a she-dragon. He smiled. The lady was a fighter. Her warrior attitude combined with her statuesque body would make her a favorite in the ring, despite her age.

"I brought Jonas with us just for you, my dear," York told her. "It's entirely up to you if he lives or dies. Unless you allow him to bleed to death, which I can do nothing to prevent, then I'll see that he gets medical attention when we're out of danger."

Nicole glowered at him, rage and hatred

286

burning in her dark eyes. But she didn't waste another minute on him, didn't utter another condemning word. Instead she checked Jonas's wound and saw that the blood-soaked rag of silver silk was drenched. She hurriedly ripped her evening gown from above her knees to the shredded edges. After wadding the cloth into a thick pad, she pressed it down on top of the soaked rag at Jonas's side, doing her best to keep the hole plugged and stop the flow of blood.

York could see her talking to Jonas, but couldn't hear what she was saying. However, within seconds, she lowered Jonas onto his back, took one of the lifejackets Linden had tossed toward her, and used it to elevate Jonas's legs. She put on the remaining jacket and lay down beside the wounded man, halfway covering him with her body as she continued applying pressure on the wound.

Watching Nicole, so fierce and brave and competent, excited York. He looked forward to introducing her to her first kill-or-die competition. She would be a champion; of that he had no doubt.

Sanders received the report around midnight that Friday night. Before he ended the telephone conversation, Maleah suspected the worst. Something had gone wrong. There would be no celebration tonight. Derek reached over, took her hand, and gave it a quick squeeze.

"Keep the faith, Blondie," he told her, his gaze

caressing her reassuringly. "No matter what's happened—"

"The rescue attempt failed," Sanders said the moment the phone call ended.

"Was Nic on the *Isis*?" Maleah asked.

"Yes." Sanders stood ramrod stiff, his demeanor philosophic, his voice edged with only a hint of anger. "The team that went in had the upper hand at first, but apparently someone aboard ship managed to get out an SOS and a small army invaded, along with helicopters and machine guns. York escaped with Nicole."

"Then it's definite that Nic is alive and still with York," Derek said.

"Apparently."

"We need to contact Griff now," Derek told Sanders. "You have no choice now but to bring him up-to-date on what's happened."

Sanders nodded.

Maleah wanted to cry, but she didn't. Tears wouldn't change anything. Crying her heart out wouldn't help Nic. She felt helpless not being able to save her best friend. Right now, all she could do was work with Derek and Sanders to gather as much info as possible and hold down the fort here on the home front.

Nic, wherever you are, whatever is happening, please know that all of us who love you are doing everything within our power to find and rescue you.

Maleah added a silent prayer. *God, please watch over Nic and her baby.*

Griffin had already showered and shaved when he took the six thirty call from Sanders that Saturday morning. He had listened while his trusted second-in-command explained what had occurred the day before, the decisions Sanders, Derek, and Maleah had made, and the reasons they had kept him in the dark while the rescue attempt had been made.

Nic had been aboard a yacht called the *Isis*, a ship owned by Kroy Enterprises, the multibillion-dollar international conglomerate spearheaded by the fake York.

"If we had waited . . . " Sanders's voice trailed off.

"You couldn't wait," Griff said. "You did exactly what I would have done."

"I am sorry that the men I sent in were unable to rescue Nicole."

"So am I. But at least we know she's still alive."

Anger, rage, and disappointment brewed inside Griff, mixing with a deadly combination of fear and regret. He had no one to blame but himself. He was responsible for condemning himself to hell and for dragging Nic with him into damnation.

"Tell me what you need, what you want me to do," Sanders said.

"Continue to do what you're already doing. Information is power. Keep searching, keep digging."

"And you and Yvette and the girl?"

"We should have DNA results by Monday."

"You've seen her, talked to her. Do you think—?"

"I think our pseudo-York went to a great deal of trouble to find a young woman whose physical appearance would match that of a child who could be mine and Yvette's."

"But you do not believe she is the child Malcolm York took from Yvette only moments after it was born."

"My gut tells me that this girl is not Yvette's child, but . . . I'm not sure."

"I understand."

"Sanders?"

"Yes?"

"Next time, if there is a next time, contact me immediately. Don't wait until after the fact."

"Yes, of course."

Griff ended the call, slipped his phone into the inner pocket of his jacket, and left his room. He hesitated before knocking on Yvette's door, but tapped softly several times, assuming she had slept no better than he had and was probably awake and dressed. She eased open the door and looked up at him.

Yvette Meng was beautiful. Even in her early forties, she possessed a youthful glow, her creamy skin flawless, every feature as perfect now as it had been the first time he saw her.

"Good morning," Griff said.

She nodded. "You are up very early."

"As are you," he replied. "I'm heading down for coffee. Would you like to go with me or would you prefer to have breakfast in your room?"

"I will go with you." She slipped back into her room for a minute and then returned with a small leather clutch.

When they reached the lobby, the clerk called out to Griff, "Mr. Powell, there's a special delivery for you, sir."

Griff tensed. Sanders had not mentioned a delivery. It wouldn't be from the Powell Agency in Knoxville. And if Powell headquarters in London had sent something, Thorndike Mitchum would have given him a heads-up. Griff walked over to the counter just as the clerk brought out a padded manila envelope and handed it to him.

"Thank you." Griff clutched the envelope, curious about its contents and instinctively wary of the unknown. Whatever the contents, it wasn't good news.

"It looks innocent enough." Yvette glanced at the thin package. "But you think it's from York, don't you?"

"Let's have our coffee and tea in the patio garden," he suggested, then asked the clerk if he could arrange for coffee, hot tea, and some scones to be delivered to the patio area.

"Certainly, Mr. Powell. Whatever you like."

Griff escorted Yvette out to the garden, the morning sun bright, the air crisp and clean, the village's coming-awake sounds echoing all around them.

"Might as well get this over with."

Griff inspected the envelope, noted the name of a London-based private delivery service, and became more convinced than ever that the pseudo-York had sent him a "gift." Without hesitation, he ripped open the package, reached inside, and withdrew the contents—photographs. Half a dozen pictures of Nicole and a man Griff did not recognize. He flipped through the photos quickly, his gut tightening painfully, and then he sat down and laid the pictures on the table.

"That sick son of a bitch!" Griff wanted to rip the photographs to shreds. He wanted to get his hands around York's neck and choke the life out of him. He wanted to believe that Nic was safe, that she was unharmed, that she was untouched. The thought of another man having sex with her, forcing her to surrender to him . . .

"Griffin?" Yvette stood beside him, her small hand draped gently over his shoulder.

"Take a look at these and see for yourself."

Yvette sat beside him and carefully picked up each photograph, studied it, and then laid one on top of the other in a neat stack.

"Look familiar?" Griff asked. "Remind you of anything?"

"These photographs of Nicole and a man chained and bound are all too familiar," Yvette replied. "They mimic the situation when my husband introduced me to you. You were dirty, haggard, and in chains."

"You know what he's trying to tell me with these photos, don't you?"

"I know what he wants you to believe. He is taunting you, playing on your fears and—"

A waiter appeared carrying a tray with two cups and saucers, a small pot of coffee, another of tea, and a plate of assorted scones with jam and clotted cream. He spoke to them, wishing them a pleasant morning, as he placed the tray on the patio table. With his job done, he discreetly left them to continue their private conversation.

Yvette poured Griff's coffee and handed him the cup before she prepared her tea. Griff thanked her, took several sips, and set his cup in the matching saucer on the table.

"He wants me to know that history is going to repeat itself, only this time with my wife and some poor soul he has enslaved as the real York enslaved me."

"No matter what this man who calls himself Malcolm York does, we cannot allow him to win these mental games," Yvette warned. "You have no way of knowing for sure exactly what is happening with Nicole, but you do know that she is a very strong woman. She will find a way to survive, just as you did, just as Sanders and I did, until you can rescue her."

When Yvette set her cup on the table and reached for him, Griff pulled away from her, not wanting her to touch him. He did not want to share the agony ripping him apart inside with anyone, not even Yvette, who could ease some of that pain. Oddly enough, the only thing keeping him halfway sane was his pain.

Griff stood and walked across the garden patio, keeping his back to Yvette. He didn't want to be here, wasting his time with Yvette and her heartbreaking search for a child she would probably never find. He needed to be out there in the forefront, taking part in the search for Nicole. He should have been the one to head up the team that had stormed the *Isis*. He should be tracking down York, not playing the man's foolish games.

Absorbed in thought, he didn't sense Yvette come up behind him until she spoke. "What do you want to do with these?"

He glanced over his shoulder, his gaze connecting with hers before settling on the manila envelope she held. Apparently she had slipped the photographs back in the padded bag.

He grabbed the envelope. "I'll send them to Sanders and see what our lab can come up with. Probably nothing, but you never know."

"I am so very sorry," she told him.

"Yes, I know." He caressed her cheek with the back of his hand.

A slight shiver vibrated through her body, enough so that he felt it.

"Yvette?"

"It's nothing," she assured him. "For a fleeting moment, I felt what you were feeling. You love her desperately, don't you?"

Griffin couldn't respond, could barely breathe.

Held captive by his own emotions, he couldn't manage to focus on the repetitive noise he heard, but when it continued, he realized that his phone was ringing. His gaze met Yvette, each of them fearing more bad news, and then he put the phone to his ear and answered the call.

"Griffin Powell speaking."

"Mr. Powell, this is Tomasina Hartwood, the counselor at the Benenden School. By any chance is Suzette York there at the hotel with you and Dr. Meng?"

"No, she isn't. Why do you ask?"

"I'm afraid Suzette is missing."

"What do you mean she's missing?"

"No one has seen her this morning. We have conducted a thorough search of the school and grounds. She isn't here. We had hoped she might be with her mother . . ." Ms. Hartwood cleared her throat. "With the woman she believes may be her mother."

"Has this ever happened before?" Griff asked. "Has Suzette ever run away?"

"Never! She was at Benenden last year and not once—"

"Dr. Meng and I will let you know if we hear anything from Suzette. I'd appreciate it if you would return the courtesy."

"Most assuredly, Mr. Powell."

Griff slipped his phone into his pocket and turned to Yvette. "That was Ms. Hartwood. Suzette York has disappeared. No one has seen her this morning."

"This is York's doing, isn't it?" Yvette said. "He's taken her away. He's stolen my child from me again."

Uncaring of the consequences for either of them, Griff pulled Yvette into his arms and held her. "Don't jump to conclusions. We don't know that York took her. And even if he did, remember two things—she may not be your child and we know for certain that he isn't the real Malcolm York."

CHAPTER 20

Nicole had no idea where they were—what country, what city or town. They had gone by motorboat somewhere out to sea, staying within sight of land the entire trip. Concentrating completely on doing everything within her power to keep Jonas MacColl alive, she had paid little attention to anything else, but she felt certain the boat had docked within an hour. Wherever they had initially landed had been an isolated cove and not a conventional harbor of any kind. Armed men had met them and escorted them off the boat, two of them lifting Jonas and carrying him ashore. She had tried to pull free from York to go with Jonas, but York had kept a tight hold on her.

"You can see him later," York had told her. "If he lives. They have a doctor here who'll patch him up."

Once inside one of the small, shabby buildings only yards from the shore, York had locked her in a tiny, dark room, no bigger than a broom closet, and left her there. Feeling grimy, her dress ripped to shreds, Jonas's blood all over her, and dying of thirst, Nic had sat quietly and tried to meditate. What else could she have done?

Hours later, York had sent one of the guards to fetch her.

She'd been given a change of clothes—cotton slacks and shirt, both men's clothing and a size too large—a bottle of water, and a couple of slices of stale bread.

They had traveled by jeep caravan—four vehicles, each with an armed driver and an armed soldier riding shotgun. During their journey, she had searched the heavens for any signs of direction, but thick clouds overcast the sky, hiding the stars. She catnapped on and off until they had reached their next destination—a small plane. Nic had recognized the aircraft as a Piper Seneca V, a six-seater, with piston twins and Hershey bar wings.

Sometime during the night, they had landed and had once again traveled by jeep to a wall-enclosed house in the middle of nowhere. Another island retreat? Or a vast compound in Colombia or Venezuela or somewhere in Central America, South America or the Caribbean?

She had asked about Jonas, but had been given no information. York had turned her over to a guard who had escorted her to a room on the upper level. Completely exhausted, she hadn't bothered with checking out her accommodations. She had known that there would be time enough for surveying her prison later, after she rested. Fully clothed, she had dropped sideways onto the bed and fallen asleep instantly.

Nic had awakened when a young girl of no more than twelve had entered the room, placed a tray on a bench at the foot of the bed, and pulled back the heavy curtains to reveal the luminous morning sunshine. When Nic spoke to the girl, the girl stared at Nic with big, round, frightened eyes and scurried from the room as if being chased by demons.

So, there she was in another gilded cage, albeit somewhat smaller than the first one Linden had placed her in several days ago. The stucco walls were a vibrant ocher, the furniture dark mahogany, the floors rust red tiles, and the long, narrow windows draped in decorative black iron bars. No doubt behind one of the two interior closed doors was a bathroom which hopefully contained a shower. She felt as if she could stand under a warm, cleansing spray for hours. But before trying the first door, her stomach growled, which prompted her to glance at the tray the girl had set on the bench. A brightly painted metal tray held a variety of fruits, a half loaf of crusty brown bread, and a glass of what appeared to be juice. And lying there on the edge of the tray, a rectangular-shaped padded envelope caught her eye.

Despite longing for a bath, Nic delayed finding the bathroom. She picked up the envelope and inspected it. Her name had been hand-printed in large bold letters across the width of the package. As she lifted the open flap and reached inside, her hand trembled ever so slightly. She pulled out a thin stack of photographs and stared at the one on top. The date was clearly stamped at the bottom of the picture. If her calculations were correct, it was yesterday's date. But since she couldn't be a hundred percent sure what day it was today, the pictures could have been taken several days ago. Or the stamped date could have been forged.

What did it matter?

Nic stared at the photo of Griff, his hand splayed across Yvette Meng's slender back as they entered what looked like a restaurant. She flipped the photo over and noticed a hand-printed notation: "The West House, Biddenden, Kent, UK."

What was Griff doing in the UK?

Oh my God!

Gripping the photos, Nic slumped down onto the floor. She stared at the top snapshot, her gaze lingering on Griff's big hand touching Yvette so tenderly.

Damn him to hell! Instead of manning a search for her, his wife, Griff had escorted Yvette Meng to England to find her daughter.

Their daughter?

Nic guessed that she now knew for sure exactly what Griff's priorities were. And they sure as hell didn't involve locating his missing wife.

Emotion rose inside her, clenched her throat and threatened to choke her. Her worst fears had been confirmed.

Stop it! You are jumping to conclusions. You are assuming the worst. Who do you think orchestrated this little drama? Who ordered the photographs taken? Who provided you with copies?

Forcing herself to look at the other photos, she flipped through them quickly. She stopped abruptly and stared at the young woman standing in front of Griff and Yvette, a woman Nic didn't recognize at the girl's side.

So this was Yvette's daughter, Suzette York. The resemblance was obvious, and not just a resemblance to Yvette, but to Griff, too. The girl was tall, probably close to six feet, and her eyes were the same strikingly beautiful blue-gray as Griff's.

Nic clutched the photo tightly, wrinkling the corner, as she studied the girl more closely. Griff's child. His daughter.

She dropped the photos to the floor, wrapped her arms protectively around her belly, and vented her frustration and rage with an ear-splitting scream.

The call Griff had been expecting came in shortly before noon. He had spent the past few hours alternating between trying to keep Yvette from going off the deep end, working with the local authorities in their search for Suzette, and consulting with Thorndike Mitchum at Powell's London headquarters. It seemed that no one had seen Suzette since bedtime last night. Apparently, she had simply disappeared sometime before daybreak this morning. Vanished without a trace.

"Mr. Powell?" the unfamiliar voice asked.

"This is Griffin Powell."

"I have instructions for you from Malcolm York."

"I'm listening."

Yvette rose from where she had been sitting on the edge of Griff's bed, rushed over to him, and mouthed the question, "Who is it?"

He shook his head.

"Something that Dr. Meng wants very badly has been misplaced," the man said. "To locate this prized possession and keep it out of harm's way will require ingenuity on your part. If you fail to make the correct choices, all will be lost."

More of York's sick games.

"Continue," Griff said.

"You will find what you are looking for in London. If you follow directions to the letter, do exactly as instructed, you and Dr. Meng can save what she values so highly."

"And if we don't—?"

"I'm afraid the object will be destroyed."

Griff's gut tightened. Would York kill Suzette, a girl he claimed was his beloved ward? Of course he would. Think how much sweeter her death would be to him if she truly was Yvette's child.

"Tell me what we need to do," Griff said.

"For now, check out of your hotel and go to London. Check into the Lancaster London. There will be a package for you at the front desk."

"What do I do with the package?"

The man chuckled. "The contents will be self-explanatory."

"Very well."

"I'll contact you again at seven this evening with further instructions." The caller ended the conversation.

Griff turned to Yvette, hating the fear he saw etched on her lovely face. He slipped his phone into the pocket of his jacket, and then grasped Yvette's shoulders. She sucked in a soft, unsteady breath.

"Were you speaking to York? Did he take Suzette?"

Their gazes met and locked. "Yes, more than likely York is responsible for Suzette's disappearance. But the man on the phone was just a messenger for York."

"Why did York do this?"

"It's all a part of the games he's playing with us." He squeezed Yvette's shoulders. "Listen to me. First of all, you need to remember that we have no proof that Suzette is your daughter. We can't trust York. He wants to see us, me in particular, jump through hoops, and that's what this is all about. Understand?"

Yvette kept her gaze focused directly on Griff as she nodded. "Yes, I understand. But even if Suzette is not our child, she's an innocent in this horrible game York is playing."

"Is she? Are you one hundred percent sure?"

"What are you saying?"

"I'm saying that, given enough time to dig deeper into Suzette York's past, we might discover that not only isn't she your child, but she is no wide-eyed innocent."

Averting her gaze as she shook her head, Yvette pulled away from him. "What does he want us to do?" she asked, her voice little more than a quivering whisper.

"Our instructions were to leave here, drive to London, and check into the Lancaster London. I'm to pick up a package there and wait for further instructions."

With her back to him, her slender shoulders hunched as she bowed her head, Yvette asked, "If we do not obey his commands, he will kill her, won't he?"

"I'm afraid so. But even if we do as he wants, we can't be sure he won't issue an order to kill her anyway."

Leonardo Kasan, aka Rafe Byrne, arrived at Harlan Benecroft's London residence in Regent's Park, an elegant multistory home boasting six-and-a-half-thousand square feet of luxurious, elegant living space. Harlan had purchased the property twenty-five years ago and done an extensive renovation. The Hanover Terrace home was only one of several that Sir Harlan owned, but it was where he spent more than half his time each year. In certain circles, the old reprobate was known as a superb host, catering to his guests' every need. Rafe knew that he would be sucked into a quagmire of aberrant, perverted pleasures this evening and no doubt offered his choice of human delights. Over the years, he had become an excellent actor, pretending to be one of the men he greatly despised, a connoisseur of monstrous debauchery on a level only the very wealthy could afford. His chameleon-like abilities to present himself as the type of person each occasion required had aided him these past sixteen years in his search-and-destroy missions. But he had paid a price—perhaps too high a price—for his brand of justice. With each passing year, he had lost more of his soul, as his heart hardened so much so that his only reason for living was revenge.

An apathetic uniformed butler opened the door and ushered Rafe from the twenty-foot-wide foyer into the massive drawing room on the first floor. Apparently Rafe was not the only guest to arrive early. More than a dozen people populated the twenty-by-thirty-five-foot area filled with upscale blond furniture and decorated in varying neutral shades from palest cream to rich gold. Rafe recognized only three of the other guests—a Savile Row designer who had attended Harlan's dinner party at the Savoy, a well-respected, middle-aged MP whose face appeared regularly in the society columns along with his wife, an American heiress, who had accompanied him tonight. Rafe had hoped Yves Bouchard would have returned to London by now. Bouchard was his main reason for accepting the invitation.

"Mr. Kasan," a bone-thin woman of an indiscernible age said as she approached. Decked out in an obscenely revealing dress worn to expose her rather large, surgically enhanced breasts, she alternated between sipping on a cocktail and puffing on a cigarette. "Please join us."

As she came toward him, Rafe plastered on an I'm-thrilled-to-be-here smile and said, "I'm afraid you have me at a disadvantage. Have we met before, Ms. . . . ?"

Her laugher was as dry and brittle as she looked. "I'm simply crushed, dear boy. Cassandra introduced us last year at one of her intimate little soirées."

Click, click, click. The pieces fell into place. The lady had dyed her hair, going from jet black to platinum, and appeared to have gone under the plastic surgeon's knife once again in a vain effort to maintain a youthful appearance.

"Countess Orlov, I'm delighted to see you again." Rafe kissed the woman's hand with all the gallantry he could muster. The countess was as fake as he was, but no one questioned her authenticity as the widow of a descendant of Russian royalty.

"Come and meet everyone." The countess crushed out her cigarette in a crystal bowl on a nearby table, then laced her arm through Rafe's and led him into the fray.

While she introduced him to the others, he studied each face for any sign of recognition, any connection to Amara, to Malcolm York or to Yves Bouchard. The seven men and five women were all strangers to him, except for the countess, the MP and his wife, and the fashion designer. Doing more listening than talking, acting as if he were interested in their idle chitchat, Rafe zoned out, his mind focused on his recent conversation with Harry Northcliffe.

. . . someone you've done business with in the past . . . is interested in going into a joint venture with you and would like to negotiate terms as soon as possible.

Griffin Powell wanted to see him.

He had already booked a flight out of Heathrow for Monday. He would have left for the States sooner, if not for Harlan's party tonight, an event that could easily continue through most of the day tomorrow. Ingratiating himself to Sir Harlan, gradually gaining the old bastard's complete trust, would eventually give him what he wanted— unrestricted access to Yves Bouchard.

But until then . . .

Apparently, Griffin Powell needed something from him.

If the Malcolm York rumors floating around Europe for the past couple of years had any basis in facts, then Griffin would be amassing an elite army to do battle. Rafe could think of no other reason his Amara savior would have sent for him.

When they had arrived at the Lancaster London, a four-star hotel opposite Hyde Park and Kensington Gardens, the clerk at the check-in counter had given Griff the package he had been told to expect.

"I believe you requested one of our Embassy Suites," the clerk said.

Griff had nodded in agreement. Apparently York had booked the suite for them.

Once they were alone in their elegant private lounge, Griff ripped open the envelope and found one digital snapshot of three young women and a cryptic typed message. He and Yvette recognized only one of the threesome—Suzette, her hands and feet bound and her mouth gagged. The other two girls, approximately the same age as Suzette, had been given the same treatment. Terror radiated from three sets of eyes, clearly discernible in the photo. Oddly enough, the other two girls bore more than a vague resemblance to Suzette.

The note consisted of a single sentence, a comment that Griff had replayed in his mind a thousand times in the past few hours.

One is your daughter, two are her clones, and all three will die tonight unless you make the right choice.

Griff wanted to take the snapshot away from Yvette, but she clung to it as if keeping it near her could somehow save Suzette's life. Standing over Yvette where she sat on the sofa, he clamped his hand down on her shoulder.

"You're making yourself crazy. Put the picture down and stop looking at it. There's not a damn thing we can do until York's guy calls us."

"It's already five past seven," Yvette reminded him. "He said he would call at seven. What if something has gone wrong? What if—?"

The phone rang. Yvette jumped. Griff released his hold on her shoulder, picked up his phone from where he had placed it on the coffee table, and answered on the second ring.

"Griffin Powell."

"You received the photograph and the message?"

"Yes."

"The three girls will be in Hyde Park tonight," the man said. "Each will be taken to a specific location. I suggest you be at the Grand Entrance to the park, at precisely eleven o'clock. I will contact you at that time with further instructions. It will be up to you to choose which girl to try to save first. You will have until the park closes at midnight to attempt to rescue all three of them."

Holding his phone to his ear, Griff listened to the dead silence for several seconds as he digested the caller's instructions. York's minion had introduced Griff to the participants in a life-or-death game to be played out tonight in one of the largest parks in central London.

"Was that—?"

"Yes." Griff relayed the man's message to Yvette as he slid his phone into his pocket.

"What if Suzette is not our daughter? Could it be possible that one of those other girls is our child?" Yvette reached out and grabbed Griff's hand as she gazed up at him through tear-filled eyes. "How can you decide which girl to try to save first? What if you choose the wrong—?"

He clasped her hand. "Stop doing this to yourself. This is what he wants, for us to suffer while we try to make an impossible decision."

"But, Griffin . . . " She choked back more tears.

"For all we know, not one of those three girls in the photo is your child . . . our child."

"But if one of them is?"

"I intend to do whatever I can to save all three girls tonight, but you have to prepare yourself for whatever happens." He leaned down and wiped the tears from her cheeks with his fingertips. "Now go wash your face while I contact Mitchum again and give him an update."

"Please remind him that his men are to do nothing to bring attention to themselves. If York finds out that—"

"Mitchum's agents are professionals. This won't be their first hostage rescue mission. They're not going to do anything to endanger the girls."

Malcolm smiled as he listened to his employee in London report on the progress of the Suzette York kidnapping caper. By now Yvette Meng had to be half out of her mind and Griffin Powell on the verge of acting irrationally. What delicious thoughts. He smacked his lips, almost able to taste the sweetness of the moment. If only he could be there, in Hyde Park, to watch the events unfold.

He hoped that Griffin was as cunning as he had been on Amara, as capable of surviving at all costs. Otherwise, not only would all three girls be killed, but Griffin, a more than worthy opponent, would die tonight and the marvelous games would end far too soon.

CHAPTER 21

Griffin arrived shortly before eleven that night near the Grand Entrance at Hyde Park Corner next to Apsley House. Standing alone close to the Wellington Arch at the southeast corner of the park, he waited for further instructions from the madman in charge of tonight's lethal games. Despite the late hour, this was a Saturday night and the park was far from empty, although not as heavily populated as it would have been earlier in the evening or if a major event was being held there. He had left Yvette at the hotel, along with one of Mitchum's agents to guard her. Griff couldn't be certain that the search-and-rescue game at the park was the only entertainment York had in store for them tonight. It was a wait-and-see situation, one in which they needed to be prepared for anything.

There was no way one man could cover the entire 350-acre park in an hour. And it was highly unlikely that, even with a dozen of Mitchum's men spread throughout the park, each having entered separately at various locations over a period of several hours, they would be able to save all three girls. Griff was working under the assumption that the pseudo-York didn't give a damn about his hostages, not even Suzette, and would willingly sacrifice each of them for his own amusement. Punishing Griffin seemed to be of paramount importance to York, seeing him and those he cared for suffering his only goal.

Planning ahead without any concrete idea of what York had in store for him during the next sixty minutes, Griff had changed into loose-fitting jogging pants, a lightweight hooded sweatshirt, and running shoes. Mitchum had outfitted him with a Kevlar vest, a commando knife in a leg sheath, and a Glock 17 in a hip holster, now covered by the length of his sweatshirt. The last piece of equipment—a skeleton-style earpiece—would allow Griff to communicate with Mitchum.

Griff had spent the past three hours mentally

preparing himself for battle. Psychological battle. Physical battle. No doubt, he would be faced with a combination of the two, one as deadly as the other. A map of Hyde Park, with which he had familiarized himself as best he could, and a mini maglite snuggled side by side in his sweatshirt pocket.

At precisely eleven o'clock his phone rang. "Griffin Powell here."

"Listen very carefully to your three clues," the voice said. "You will find each prize in a different location."

"Okay, I'm listening."

"These clues are in no particular order. It will be up to you to decide where to go first. Who you reach first, second, and third is your choice. And if you reach all three in an hour, you may be able to save their lives." The caller paused and when Griff didn't respond, he continued. "An arrow is centered in the heart of a rose. A snake slithers near elephants. A king leads to a princess."

Griff repeated the three clues, memorizing them, preparing to repeat them to Mitchum once York's delivery boy completed his message.

"That's it?" Griff asked.

"Oh, one more thing—each prize will be guarded."

No big surprise.

"Thanks for the warning," Griff said.

"Good luck, Mr. Powell."

Conversation ended.

Griff checked is wristwatch—11:02. Fifty-eight minutes and counting.

As Griff made his way from the well-lit Wellington Arch entrance, past Apsley House and the Hyde Park Corner Colonnade, the structures bathed in golden light, he spoke quietly with Thorndike Mitchum.

After repeating the three clues, Griff said, "Any ideas off the top of your head?"

"Actually, yes," Mitchum replied. "But I'm putting all three clues into the computer and running a cross-reference with Hyde Park."

"Until something shows up, what are your thoughts? You know London. You've visited Hyde Park, right?"

"An arrow is centered in the heart of a rose could mean the Cupid Fountain in the Rose Garden. You shouldn't be that far away right now. Take a look at your map and tell me exactly where you are."

Griff stopped, pulled out the map and mini maglite, and quickly zeroed in on his location. "I'm on Rotten Row, just past Hyde Park Corner."

"Check your map and locate the rose garden. There's a statue of Cupid in the center of the fountain. There are other statues and fountains, but you want the fountain with Cupid."

"Got it."

"Be careful," Mitchum told him. "I have two

agents nearby who can get to you in five minutes."

"I'm going in now," Griff said, keeping his voice low as he moved steadily toward the target area. "Every minute counts."

Griff ran along the wide, tree-lined bridle path used now not only for horse riding, but cycling, rollerblading, and jogging. The almost four-mile-long road ran parallel along the Serpentine Lake past the Serpentine Gallery and the Princess Diana Memorial Fountain. The Rose Garden was at the east end of the path, close by, requiring only a slight detour from the road. Just as he veered off Rotten Row, he noticed a couple coming toward him from the opposite direction, but they were so absorbed in each other that he doubted they even noticed him.

Locating the circular area surrounding the Cupid Fountain within the Rose Garden had been an easy task. A little too easy to suit Griff as he stopped before entering the circle and gauged every aspect of the scene before him. The garden appeared to be empty, not a person in sight, not a squirrel or bird stirring this time of night. A summery breeze shimmered through the treetops. The hum of nearby traffic rumbled across the park. The sound of distant laughter reminded Griff that there were innocent bystanders still in the park, even this late at night.

A sudden sense of foreboding—an innate gut instinct honed and perfected years ago on

Amara—alerted Griff to imminent danger. Just as an arrow whizzed past him, Griff dove behind a bench, hitting the ground near a line of shrubbery. He brought out his Glock as he quickly gained his bearings. The archer was well hidden in the darkness, somewhere in a cluster of trees, west of Griff's present location.

Without any warning, a shadowy figure hobbled toward the fountain. Even before Griff heard her whimpering, he realized that one of the hostages, her hands and feet still bound and her mouth gagged, had been sent out into plain view.

That meant only one thing.

Knowing he had only minutes, perhaps only seconds, to act in order to save the young woman, Griff crept along the outer perimeter of the fountain area, along the paved walkway backed by trees and shrubbery. Gun in hand, prepared to shoot to kill, he raced toward the lone figure trembling at the edge of the fountain. Within arm's reach of the girl, Griff cursed his timing as an arrow ripped through his hooded jacket and pierced the Kevlar vest beneath. The impact knocked him backward and off his feet. Reeling from the force of the archer's shot, he struggled to recover. With the arrow embedded in the protective vest, he rose to his knees and then up on his feet. But not fast enough to prevent the next arrow from hitting its intended target.

Griff lunged forward, hoping against hope, and

within seconds realized the futility of his rescue attempt. The arrow burst through the girl's neck. Blood gushed from the deadly wound as she fell face forward into the watery bowl surrounding the fountain.

Before he could reach the girl, two dark-clad, armed men rushed toward him and quickly identified themselves as Mitchum's agents.

"I'm okay," Griff told them. "And we can't help the girl. You two go find the archer before he gets away."

"Another agent is tracking him," one of the men said. "Our orders are to take care of you."

"All I need is to get rid of this arrow and move on to the next location," Griff told them. "Time is running out for those other two girls."

Griff didn't want to think about the possibility that he would no more be able to save either of the girls than he'd been able to rescue the first one. He wanted to know if the victim was Suzette, but he couldn't waste time with identifying her now.

After all, in the long run, would it really matter?

Only if one of the three hostages actually turned out to be Yvette's daughter.

" 'A snake slithers near elephants,' " Mitchum repeated the second clue. "The Serpentine Lake is in the middle of the park and stretches westward all the way to Kensington Gardens. But close to the southeastern edge of the lake there is a display of elephant sculptures. There is a serpent and elephants only at that one specific area."

Griff checked the map, ascertained the location of the elephant sculptures, and wasted no time in heading west along Rotten Row. Once again only yards off the bridle path, he found the area mentioned in the second clue. Thirteen life-size elephant sculptures, comprised of what appeared to be willow bands wound around metal frames, meandered almost lifelike among a small bevy of trees. A short distance behind him, the Serpentine Lake murmured faintly. Reflected moonlight shimmered across the water's surface.

The drone of his own pounding heartbeat grew louder inside his head as he surveyed the scene. Another hostage's life depended on him making the right life-or-death decisions. But he was as much a pawn in York's murderous game as the three young women York had chosen to use as bait.

Tonight's game was about far more than attempting to locate the captives and save them; it was about following York's orders, about paying any price to save Nic's life. And no one knew this better than York did.

Cautiously, ever aware of danger lurking in every dark corner, Griff searched for any sign of the next girl and her guardian. Alert to the possibility of an attack, he took no undue chances. But after a five-minute exploration of the area in every direction, Griff decided that the second clue was not the second location chosen for battle. If not here, then where? Apparently the third clue named the spot for the second confrontation.

Returning to Rotten Row, Griff contacted Mitchum. "If you have agents heading my way, stop them. Send them to the location described by the third clue after you tell me where you think that is."

"Bloody hell," Mitchum grumbled. " 'A king leads to a princess.' I believe the king refers to Rotten Row itself. The term is derived from the French *route du roi* or king's road. The third location is probably somewhere near the Princess Diana Memorial Fountain. That's all the way down to the bridge that crosses the lake."

"Then I'd better get moving." Griff refused to give in to the temptation to check his watch. What good would it do to know exactly what time it was?

Before heading off down the path again, he located the memorial and the bridge on the map. If he hadn't kept himself in tiptop shape, there would be no way he could keep up a running pace or manage to reach the bridge, face whatever awaited him there, and then backtrack to the elephant sculptures for the final skirmish, all before the stroke of midnight.

Just as he spotted the memorial fountain up ahead, he caught a glimpse of movement in his peripheral vision on both sides of the path.

Mitchum had said that his agents would be coming in from the west, from the area where the Serpentine Gallery pavilion was located, so he figured the activity to his left was his backup team temporarily keeping out of sight.

The second hostage and her guard would be to his right, somewhere in or around the memorial. The granite circular fountain resembled a narrow river, flowing in two directions from the highest point, swirling and bubbling as the waters joined in a small pool at the bottom. As Griff made his way toward the memorial, he sensed someone watching him. Waiting. Preparing to attack.

And then he saw her. Running. Coming from the roadway, down the pedestrian path between the lake and the memorial. The roar of motorbikes rumbling like a thundering herd of mustangs came to life and within seconds three Triumphs barreled down on the fleeing girl. Griff drew his Glock, took aim, and hit the lead cyclist, hurling him to the ground and sending his driverless bike sailing through the air and into the lake.

Racing like mad, determined to pick off another rider before the two remaining attackers could run down the frightened young woman, Griff saw the reason she hadn't screamed or cried for help. Although her hands and feet were unbound, she remained gagged. Ignoring him as if he didn't exist, as if he hadn't only moments before gunned down their comrade, the two bikers caught up with their prey. Slowing their Triumphs to the girl's running speed, the two bikers flanked her. Less than ten feet away, Griff aimed at the rider on the girl's right, but before he got off a shot, the man ran straight into the girl, knocking her onto the walkway and running the bike over her. He backed up over her and then reversed gears and ran over her again. When the cyclist backed up and revved his engine, preparing for another attack, Griff fired. The bullet hit the guy's shoulder just as his partner on the other bike fired at Griff, missing him by mere inches.

As Griff neared the path along the lake, Mitchum's agents appeared and took out the cyclists while Griff rushed to the severely injured girl. He knelt beside her, felt for a pulse, and finding one, he hurriedly contacted Mitchum. "We found her. She's alive. Barely. She needs medical attention ASAP."

Griff whispered to the unconscious girl, "Hang on. Help's on the way."

He smoothed back her shoulder-length black hair and touched her flushed cheek. Poor kid. She wasn't Suzette York and whoever she was she probably wasn't Yvette's child, but she was somebody's little girl.

"One of you take over," Griff called to the agents. "Mitchum is sending in the medics. I have to backtrack to the elephant statues."

He rose from the pathway and going against

his better judgment, he checked the time—11:44. Sixteen minutes till midnight.

Winded, his heart beating ninety-to-nothing, Griff arrived back at the elephant statues at the southeast end of the lake.

A snake slithers near elephants.

At Cupid's Fountain, the first hostage's guard had used a bow and arrow to attack Griff and kill the girl. At the memorial fountain area, cyclists had chased their victim and run her down, as the paparazzi had chased Princess Diana. If Griff could figure out the method the third hostage's guard planned to use, he might be able to stay one step ahead of him. An elephant gun? Snake venom? Both were highly unlikely.

Think outside the box. Don't think literally. Think figuratively.

He needed to think like a highly intelligent, diabolical madman.

"You're on your own for now," Mitchum informed him. "It will take a good ten minutes for my nearest agents to make it across the park from the vicinity of the Speaker's Corner near the Marble Arch. The ones you left behind at the memorial are handling cleanup and waiting with the victim for our medical team to arrive."

"Got it," Griff said. "Any idea about a connection between snakes and elephants and a way to kill?"

"Nothing plausible," Mitchum admitted. "Then again, our Mr. York could be planning to change the rules mid-game. No way to know."

"I don't see a damn thing. No sign of anyone. There are too many blind spots at this time of night. The moonlight helps and the lights from the pathway and here and there around the lake, but with so many trees and bushes, they could be hiding anywhere."

Mitchum grunted.

"If anything goes wrong . . ."

"Positive thinking, old chap."

Griff chuckled. "Take care of Yvette."

"Will do."

As the tension coiled in his gut, tighter and tighter, Griff surveyed the area and found nothing suspicious. Vigilant on his hunt, noting every sound and smell, watching his back, uncertainty at war with duty, he spent the next ten minutes searching, second-guessing his every move.

He reported in to Mitchum after the first five minutes and was told that the second girl—on her way to the hospital—was still alive.

And then he contacted Mitchum again when there were only six minutes left on the clock. "I'm in the wrong place. I've wasted too much time here."

"You're in the right place," Mitchum told him.

"Then where are they? Are you sure that there isn't another place in the park that 'a snake slithers near elephants' could describe?"

"I repeat, you are in the right place. He's making you wait, hoping to confuse you. Think about it."

"Yeah, okay." With time running out, Griff suddenly sensed someone approaching. Gun in hand, he eased around and came face-to-face with more of Mitchum's agents. "A couple of your guys just showed up."

"Remember that whatever happens, it's not your fault if you can't save this girl. York never intended for any of them to live. You know that, don't you?"

"Yeah, I guess I knew all along. But I had to try. I had no choice other than to give York what he wanted."

The agents flanked Griff's position there on the pathway between the lake and the elephant statues as they waited. Two minutes later—Griff checked his watch—at four till midnight, a woman's voice called out from somewhere nearby.

"Help me, please. It's Suzette, Dad, your daughter. Please, don't let me die."

Dad? Damn! He was not her father.

But what if he was? What if Suzette was Yvette's long-lost baby?

How much pleasure would York derive out of killing Suzette only days before the DNA results proved she was Griff and Yvette's daughter?

Emerging out of the darkness from behind a stand of trees, Suzette York walked slowly past the statues and onto the pathway by the lake.

When she saw Griff, she stopped and held up both hands in a signal for him to stay where he was.

And that's when he saw the snakelike device coiled around her waist and across her hips. A metallic serpent decorated with small dots of explosives wired to a detonator. Was it a timed detonator or a remote detonator? In the years he had spent on Amara, Griff had never dealt with explosives. He had no idea how to defuse the bomb wrapped around Suzette.

"He—he's gone," she called out to Griff. "I'm going to die if you don't help me, but you could die if you try to save me."

Griff turned to Mitchum's guys. "I don't suppose either of you knows how to defuse a bomb, do you?"

The taller, older guy, his dark hair streaked with silver and his tanned face rutted with hard-living lines answered, "I do."

"You do?"

"Fifteen years in the SAS."

What were the odds? But then again, considering that Mitchum would have chosen the best of the best for this mission, maybe the odds had been in their favor all along.

"You know this is above and beyond the call of duty," Griff told him.

"It bloody well is, but I can't just let the girl die, now can I?"

Without further conversation, Griff and the

former SAS soldier exchanged a man-to-man look. Griff watched as the agent approached Suzette, spoke softly to her, and then examined the bomb strapped to her trembling body. Griff suspected that timed or remote, the detonator would set off the bomb at midnight.

Three damned minutes!

"You two need to move back," the agent warned. "There's nothing either of you can do to help me, and if this thing explodes, there is no need for all four of us to die."

Suzette whimpered in fear.

Something deep and paternal rose up inside Griff, urging him to comfort this girl. At that moment, it didn't seem to matter if she was Yvette's child, possibly his child, too. She was a human being, a young girl on the verge of womanhood, her whole life ahead of her.

Griff and the other agent heeded the warning and took cover a good distance away. With each passing second, the weight of guilt grew heavier and heavier on Griff's shoulders. If Suzette and Mitchum's seasoned agent died, it would be because they had been caught in the crossfire between York and him.

The UK Powell agent at his side nudged Griff. When he faced the man, he was handed a pair of compact, high-powered binoculars. "If anyone can do it, Hughes can. I've seen him pull off a blooming miracle more than once."

Griff nodded. "Thanks." He grasped the binoculars, lifted them into place, and zeroed in on Suzette and the man trying desperately to save her life.

Sweat moistened Griff's hands and dotted his forehead and upper lip. Thin rivulets of perspiration dampened his sweatshirt. He watched silently, the only sound he could hear the staccato beat of his own heart.

Two minutes.

What would it do to Yvette if Hughes couldn't save Suzette and the DNA test results proved she was her daughter?

There's still time. It's not too late.

"What's going on?" Mitchum's voice in Griff's ear momentarily stunned him.

"Your man Hughes is trying to defuse a bomb strapped around Suzette like a slithering snake. If my guess is right, he has exactly one and a half minutes to get the job done."

Mitchum grunted. "If anyone can do it—"

"Yeah, I know, if anyone can do it, Hughes can," Griff said. "By the way, was it just a coincidence that one of your agents is an explosives expert?"

"I made a point of bringing in agents with diverse talents for tonight's operation. But it was luck that placed him where he needed to be at precisely the right time."

Lowering the binoculars, Griff stared at his wristwatch.

Sixty seconds.

CHAPTER 22

Encased in fear, despising his own helplessness, Griff again watched through the binoculars as Hughes worked feverishly to disarm the bomb. Seconds ticked by at the speed of light. Or so it seemed. There just wasn't enough time. Two more people would be sacrificed on the whim of a madman.

Who the hell are you, Malcolm York?

Why are you impersonating a dead man?

Why do you hate me so God damn much?

The night closed in around him, a suffocating numbness settling over his body, gluing him to the spot.

How many more people would die because of the pseudo-York's thirst for revenge? Wasn't kidnapping Nicole punishment enough? Didn't York understand that anything else he did, no matter how horrible, would affect Griff in the same way?

You know what he's doing. He is trying to destroy you by degrees, weaken you, and render you powerless, so that when the final battle comes—the battle to save Nicole—you won't have the strength to protect what is most precious to you.

Griff's vision blurred as he stared at Hughes and

Suzette. He closed his eyes, opened them, and blinked repeatedly until his vision returned to normal.

Come on, come on. You can do this, Hughes. You can do it.

Instantly switching for silently cheering Hughes on to begging a higher power for assistance, Griff uttered a heartfelt prayer. He wasn't a man of faith, had cursed God on more than one occasion, had substantial doubts that God even existed. And yet here he was praying.

He figured that in the days to come, he would be doing a lot more praying. What else could a man do when confronted with things beyond his control?

Griff forced himself to watch Hughes and Suzette in those final moments, death only seconds away for both of them.

And then it happened!

The agent at his side slapped Griff on the back. "He did it! Son of a bitch, he did it."

All at once, with less than thirty seconds to spare, Hughes had performed another *blooming* miracle.

Suzette fell against Hughes as he gave Griff and the other agent a thumbs-up signal. To say Griff was relieved would be a vast understatement. Hughes wrapped his arm around Suzette and led her toward a nearby bench.

"Hughes did it," Griff informed Mitchum.

"Damn!"

"We'll meet up with you at the main entrance as soon as we can," Griff said. "In the meantime, get in touch with Yvette, and let her know that Suzette is safe and I'll bring her with me to the hotel once your medics check her out."

"What do you want me to tell Yvette about the other two girls?"

"The truth. One is dead and the other is seriously injured."

With Mitchum's agent keeping watch over the situation, prepared to strike if danger threatened, Griff made his way straight to Suzette. While Hughes studied the snakelike coils set with explosives that wrapped around Suzette's waist and hips, Griff sat down beside her on the bench.

She glanced at Griff, her eyes still wild with fear, her face void of color. "I nearly died. If it hadn't been for . . . " She buried her face against Griff's chest.

He eased his arm up and around her shivering shoulders. His gaze locked with Hughes's for a split second before Hughes returned to the task of freeing her from the deactivated bomb strapped around her.

Yvette retreated to the privacy of her bedroom there at the Lancaster, leaving Mitchum's agent alone in the lounge. She did not know how long it would be before Griffin arrived with Suzette, but she suspected it would be at least another hour. She needed time alone to collect her thoughts.

"Suzette is alive," Mitchum had told her.

"And the other girls?"

He had cleared his throat before answering. "One is dead and the other in the hospital."

If any one of the three girls was her child, then Yvette believed it was Suzette. Telling Griff and her that one of the other girls could be their daughter had been nothing more than a cruel trick York had tried to play on them.

York. But not the real Malcolm York.

She knew, without a doubt, that her husband was dead, had been dead for sixteen years. And yet his ghost still haunted her, his memory alive inside her no matter how hard she tried to destroy it.

Yvette sat on the plush tan sofa and stared sightlessly out the window overlooking the vast expanse of the park. Off in the distance, the central London skyline glimmered with nightlife. Like all big cities worldwide, London never slept.

She had first met Malcolm there in London more than two decades ago. He had been a debonair charmer who had swept her off her feet. She had been a girl of twenty, sheltered from the world, struggling to come to terms with her burgeoning empathic powers. She had been so enamored with the sophisticated billionaire that she had dismissed any doubts she had about him. Telling herself the reason he had not even kissed her and seldom touched her was because he was a gentleman, she had fallen victim to a psychopath. In truth, he had feared that any prolonged physical contact would allow her to see inside his evil soul.

After only a month's acquaintance, he had asked her to marry him.

A soft knock on the bedroom door snapped Yvette out of the past and into the present.

"Dr. Meng?" the guard said.

"Yes?"

"Mr. Powell is en route to the hotel. He should arrive within the next ten minutes."

"Thank you."

Yvette couldn't have known that Malcolm had sought her out for one reason only—because of her empathic abilities. She had been one of six women he had chosen as a potential replacement for the empath he had held captive on Amara for less than a year.

Elora Sanders had died in childbirth.

And Yvette, also, could have died giving birth. Without a doctor, only a midwife in attendance, if there had been any complications . . .

Both she and her baby had survived. She had heard the infant's newborn cries. But she had not been allowed to see her child. The midwife had instructed her to rest, telling her that she could see the baby later. Exhausted from hours of labor, Yvette had fallen asleep.

Later that day, Malcolm had taken great

pleasure in informing her that he had arranged to send the child away, that she would never know where her child was or what had happened to it.

In the weeks that followed her child's birth and disappearance, she had turned to Sanders. If anyone understood the devastating effects of losing a child, Sanders did. He had lost everything that mattered to him. Doing all he could to help her and the others held captive on Amara had become his only reason for living.

Sanders's wife and child had died on Amara. They were buried together on the island. Sometimes Yvette thought that Elora had been lucky, that it would have been better for her and many others if she, too, had died on Amara. Elora had lived in hell for only seven months, but her death had condemned Sanders to a lifetime in purgatory. Yvette had been Malcolm's captive, a slave to his every whim, for six agonizing years.

During the months of her pregnancy, she had convinced herself that Griffin was her baby's father. Even now, all these years later, she still clung to that hope. Not because she was in love with Griffin or ever had been, but because out of the four possible fathers, he was the best man.

The young, naïve Yvette never would have thought it possible for her to take another human life. But on the day Griffin and Sanders had led the captives in a revolt, she had stood with them against Malcolm and helped them kill him. She had no regrets about that day, no guilt, no remorse about her participation in her husband's brutal murder.

"Yvette?" Griffin called to her before he opened the bedroom door and brought her back to reality.

She rose from the sofa and turned to face him, relief spreading through her when she saw that Suzette was with him.

Unable to control her emotions, tears flooded her eyes. She held open her arms, inviting Suzette to come to her for maternal comfort. Without hesitation, the young girl ran to Yvette.

Wrapping Suzette in her arms, Yvette consoled her with tender affection. "You're safe now, sweet girl. You're safe."

Griffin had showered and shaved and ordered coffee while Suzette slept in Yvette's arms where they sat on the sofa in Yvette's bedroom. The guard had taken up his post outside the suite, giving them the privacy they needed. Mitchum had called with an updated report. The hospitalized girl was in surgery, her condition critical.

"What's the situation with the police?" Griff had asked. "Am I going to be held up here in London because of what happened?"

"Your name has not been mentioned nor has Suzette York's," Mitchum had assured him. "I've managed to keep things under control. As far as the police know, the agency was hired by an anonymous voice over the phone to rescue two kidnapped girls. The rescue attempts didn't go off as planned. And I contacted the Benenden School and the local authorities to let them know Suzette has been found."

"I appreciate your handling everything so discreetly. If there are no further complications, I will be going home tomorrow."

Griff finished off his third cup of coffee as he paced the length of the lounge. His mind refused to give him any peace, repeatedly recalling every detail of the hour he had spent in Hyde Park. With his eyes wide open, he could see the arrow shooting into the girl's neck, severing her jugular, killing her before she even knew what had happened. He could hear the roar of the motor-bikes as the riders chased the other girl, running her down, almost killing her.

When he saw the door to Yvette's bedroom open, he stopped pacing.

"Everything all right?" he asked as Yvette entered the lounge, Suzette at her side.

Yvette nodded. "Suzette wants to talk to us."

Griff glanced from Yvette to the young woman who towered nearly half a foot over her, and then focused on their clasped hands.

"Okay." Griff motioned for them to come farther into the lounge and to sit on either of the two sofas that formed an L shape in the corner beneath the windows.

When Yvette sat down with Suzette, still holding the girl's hand, Griff placed his coffee cup on the serving tray and took the chair across from them.

"Go ahead," Yvette urged. "Tell Griffin what you told me."

Suzette looked at Griff, then hurriedly glanced away and stared down at her feet. "My name isn't really Suzette York. And I'm not seventeen. I'm twenty-three."

Griff wasn't surprised. His gut instincts had told him something was off about this girl. She was too perfect a fit, as if she had been created for the sole purpose of posing as their child.

"I suppose my real name doesn't matter, but . . . I was born Kimberly Safford. I have no idea who my father was, but my mother was an actress, of sorts. She died when I was fifteen. I . . . uh . . . I worked as a prostitute until three years ago. That's when this rich guy offered me a new life, a new identity. All I had to do was pretend to be his ward, a kid who was only fourteen."

"Who was this rich guy?" Griffin asked, knowing the answer before she replied.

"His name is Malcolm York."

"What did he look like?"

"Average height and build. Gray hair, actually more silver than gray. And dark eyes. Brown, not black."

"What age?"

"I'm not sure. He isn't young, not in his twenties, but he's not old either. Late thirties, maybe early forties."

"Then he's prematurely gray?"

"I—I guess," Suzette's voice quivered. "I'm sorry. Honest. I didn't realize . . . " She looked at Yvette. "I thought he was a good man, that he actually cared about me. He set up a bank account for me, bought me a car, pretty clothes, and never once did he . . . well, you know—ask me to have sex with him."

"He treated you almost like a daughter," Yvette said.

"Yes, I suppose he did. He even asked me to call him Papa when anyone else was around. And he convinced me that pretending I thought I was your daughter wouldn't backfire on me. He said he'd protect me. He even promised me more money—five thousand pounds." Suzette pulled her hand from Yvette's. "I know it was wrong to lie to y'all, but I wanted to please him. I'm sorry, but the things he gave me were important to me. I didn't want him to take it all away. Besides, he told me that once the DNA test was done, you'd learn the truth."

"He knew we wouldn't be convinced without the DNA test," Griff said.

Still unable to look at Griff, Suzette wrung her hands together as she averted his hard glare.

"Your birth certificate, your adoption papers,

every document proving you are Suzette York were all forgeries," Griffin said. "It would have been only a matter of time before we would have been able to prove that and to prove that you knowingly took part in York's grand deception."

Suzette nodded. "Yes, I know. So what happens now?"

"You go back to being Kimberly Safford," Griff told her.

"What do you think he'll do to me when he finds out that I'm alive?" she asked. "He probably thinks I'm dead now."

"I doubt York will do anything to you. You've served your purpose."

"You don't think he'll come after me?"

"He'd have no reason to do that," Griff assured her.

Finally, Suzette looked squarely at Griff. "What are you going to do—turn me over to the police?"

"No, of course not." Yvette answered her question before giving Griff a chance to respond. "You're as much a victim of York's cruelty as we are."

"You're wrong," Griff said. "Suzette . . . or rather Kimberly, isn't a child. She knew what she did was wrong, that York was paying her to lie to us. She's no innocent."

"He's right," she told Yvette. "I'm no innocent young girl who didn't know any better. I was desperate and stupid and yes, I loved all the clothes and the car and money and I even loved attending the Benenden School. My God, I was rubbing elbows with girls from some of the best families in England."

"You can't turn her over to the police," Yvette said.

"I can, but I won't, if she'll help us."

"I'll do anything you ask," Suzette said.

"I'm not going to turn you over to the police, but I am going to turn you over to Mr. Mitchum, the head of the Powell Agency here in London. He'll question you far more thoroughly than I have and when you've helped us as much as possible, he'll arrange passage for you to wherever you want to go. He'll even provide you with another new identity, if that's what you want."

"Yes." She gasped the word. "Thank you."

A repetitive rapping on the suite door paused their conversation.

"I'm expecting Mitchum," Griff told them as he got up and walked toward the door.

Tall, broad-shouldered, with a lanky, strutting gait, Thorndike Mitchum entered the suite. At six-four, he stood eye-to-eye with Griff. Immaculately dressed in a single-breasted, gray bespoke suit, his wavy brown hair neatly styled, he looked every inch the successful businessman he was.

"Everything all right here?" Mitchum asked as he glanced at Suzette. "No problems?"

"No problems," Griff said. "Did you bring the photos?"

"They're here in my briefcase." Mitchum held up the slender black leather case.

"What photos?" Yvette asked.

"Want me to handle this?" Mitchum asked.

"Go right ahead," Griff told him.

"What's going on?" Suzette jumped to her feet.

"Calm down," Griff said. "We just want you to take a look at some photographs of several different men and tell us if you can identify one of them as Malcolm York."

"Oh." Suzette's face went chalk white.

"Once you've looked at the photographs, you'll leave with Mr. Mitchum and he'll take care of everything for you."

Mitchum set his briefcase on the coffee table, opened it, and removed a thin folder. He closed the briefcase, set it under the table, and opened the folder. Yvette stood and guided Suzette closer to the coffee table. Griff joined them as Mitchum spread out eight photographs.

"Take your time, miss," Mitchum said. "Look at each of these men and tell us if one of them is the man you know as Malcolm York."

Griff's gaze traveled over the photos. He recognized all of the men. Recent photos of Harlan Benecroft, Damar Sanders, Griff's attorney, Camden Hendrix, and Thomas Landry, a British business associate Griff had known for years. The photo of Yves Bouchard had to be at least fifteen years old, the one Interpol had posted on their

Most Wanted site. The final three photos were of dead men: Ciro Mayorga, Ellis Benecroft, and the real Malcolm York.

Suzette looked at each photograph, doing as Mitchum had requested and taking her time.

"That's him. That's the man I call Papa. That's Mr. York."

She reached out, picked up the photograph, and handed it to Mitchum. A gasp caught in Yvette's throat. Griff's gut tightened.

The photo Suzette had identified as the pseudo-York had been taken twenty years ago. The man in the photograph was the real Malcolm York.

CHAPTER 23

Nicole had been confined to her room ever since their arrival. And once again, she had no idea where she was, what country or what continent for that matter. Other than the young girl who had delivered food three times yesterday and breakfast this morning, Nic had seen no one. If Malcolm York was in residence or if his guest, Bouchard, or henchman Linden, were still around, they hadn't paid her a visit. It wasn't that she wanted to see any of them, but she suspected York was playing with her, keeping her in solitary confinement for a reason. It was the not knowing that fueled her imagination, creating several frightening scenarios of what might lie ahead for her. She had tried talking to the servant girl, but the wide-eyed child had refused to interact with Nic, avoiding eye contact, as she hurried in and out as quickly as possible.

Asking questions had proven futile, but she had kept trying. She had asked where she was, asked the girl's name, and inquired about York and Linden and about Jonas MacColl.

Was Jonas dead or alive? He had taken a bullet for her.

Please, God, let him be alive.

Instinct told Nic that she would soon be seeing York.

Yesterday, she had received the packet of photos with her morning meal. No doubt her initial reaction had been exactly what York had wanted. She had taken the photos at face value, seeing what York had wanted her to see—Yvette and Griff with their daughter. But just because the girl bore a vague resemblance to both Yvette and Griff did not mean she was their child, or even that she was Yvette's child. And if Griff had escorted Yvette to the Benenden School to meet this girl, it didn't mean that finding Nicole was not his top priority. Despite the secrets and lies that had stood between them, eating away like acid at the fragile material of their marriage, Nic knew that Griff loved her. Having had more than twenty-four hours to think, she now suspected that York had somehow orchestrated the entire thing. Exactly how he had accomplished that, she didn't know.

Included with the breakfast delivery this morning had been a rectangular box, which the servant girl had placed on the foot of Nic's bed. She had stared at the box for several minutes after the girl left before she had removed the lid and looked inside at the contents. After removing each item and spreading them out on the bed, she had laughed.

But she wasn't laughing now. As the morning had worn on, she had eaten, bathed, dressed in the same baggy men's slacks and shirt she'd been given on the first stop during their escape from the *Isis*, and had spent hours studying the articles of clothing lying ominously across the green and gold striped comforter.

Why would York have sent her such an outlandish costume? There was no other way to describe the items. And where had he gotten the costume? The only explanation was that it had already been here in this house or at a nearby location. Who had it belonged to in the past? She seriously doubted that it had been custom made for her. The knee-high silver boots, decorated with what resembled iridescent scales, looked a couple of sizes too small, as did the sheer undergarment that resembled an unadorned silvery green teddy. The lightweight metallic silver vest, covered with iridescent scales shimmering green, gray, and

343

beige, resembled a knight's breastplate. The last item puzzled Nic more so than any of the others. A diaphanous cape shaped like wings.

With nothing to do but wonder and worry and draw conclusions, Nic finally forced herself to stop inventing theories about Griff's trip to England, about the photos of him with Yvette and Suzette, about why York had sent her the ridiculous costume, and about what York had in store for her next.

She hated feeling helpless, hated being at York's mercy.

So, what was she going to do to pass the time? She didn't have a book to read, no TV to watch, no music to listen to, no knitting needles and yarn, not even a pad and pencil so she could draw or scribble. Taking a walk was out of the question. But exercise wasn't.

What about yoga?

She could start out with some basic stretches and deep breathing exercises. Meditating would keep her sane. Mind over matter.

Nic had very little control over anything in her life at present. But whatever happened, she could control her reactions. York would choose the games and make the rules. There was nothing she could do about that. Whether she won or lost a specific game, she couldn't let him defeat her.

Nic shoved back a couple of chairs to clear an area on the hand-woven rug so that she would have enough room for her exercises. She stood with her feet together, her hands at her sides, and looked forward. She lifted her toes, fanned them apart, and then came back down on the floor. Following the procedure for the "Mountain/ Tadasana" pose, she soon found herself absorbed in the process. Breathe. Relax. Don't tense. She felt her breath rising up from the floor, moving through her legs and torso and into her head. After reversing the process and repeating it several times, she went on to the next step and raised her arms over her head, lowered them, and then exhaled.

As she became totally absorbed in the routine, she moved fluidly from one pose to another. Tension drained slowly away, restoring her mental and emotional balance, refreshing her body and soul. Time slipped away, became irrelevant, so that when she ended with the "Corpse/Savasana" pose, she felt removed from the reality of her situation.

Nic lay on her back, her feet slightly apart, her arms at her sides, with her palms up. After closing her eyes, she inhaled slowly and deeply as her body sank into the surface beneath her.

Before she achieved the ultimate state of pure relaxation, the bedroom door opened and Malcolm York breezed into the room. Nic rose to a sitting position on the floor and looked up at the smiling intruder. She feared the man's smiles far more than his frowns.

"You're quite lovely when you're flushed and your body is damp with perspiration," he told her as his gaze traveled the length of her body.

Whenever he surveyed her in such a blatantly sexual way, she felt violated, as if he had run his hands over her naked body. "Good day to you, too."

She pushed herself up from the floor and faced him defiantly.

York chuckled. "You never disappoint me, Nicole. I admire your fighting spirit. You're going to need that strong will to survive more than ever quite soon."

"Am I supposed to ask what you mean by that statement?"

"I've already given you a clue." He glanced back over his shoulder at the bed. "I see you received my little gift."

"Is that what the ridiculous costume is— a gift?"

"You think it's a costume?"

"Isn't it? The least you could have done was made sure the items were in my size."

"The items I sent you once belonged to one of my favorite champions. She served me well for more than a year. Your indomitable fighting spirit reminds me of hers."

Nic had to admit that he had now piqued her curiosity. She had no idea what he was talking about, but she sensed whoever this champion had been and whatever she had done to deserve the title, the woman was now dead.

York stared at Nic, like a cat that had cornered a mouse and was waiting for it to make a move before pouncing on it. "Nothing else to say? No questions?"

Nic shook her head.

"Aren't you curious?"

Maintaining the sense of peace she had acquired during her yoga exercises, Nic simply stared at him.

"I've ordered a uniform to be special made just for you, Nicole. It should be ready for your first performance in a few weeks. In the meantime, I've arranged for you to begin work with a trainer."

A trainer? Just what did he intend to train her to do?

"I caught that hint of curiosity in your eyes," York told her. "If you want to know more, all you have to do is ask."

Hell would freeze over first. "I think I'll wait and let you surprise me."

His face hardened, obviously angered by her attitude. And then, he did an about-face and laughed out loud.

Griff and Yvette arrived at Griffin's Rest late Monday afternoon. Sanders had picked them up in the limo, giving the three of them time alone to talk on the drive from the airport. Griff had spoken at length to Sanders the day before, condensing the events of Saturday night in Hyde Park and Suzette York's confessions in the early-morning hours following her near-death experience. And Sanders had given Griff a full report on the investigation into Nic's disappearance. Today's private conversation had focused on how the past and the present had collided, placing Nicole in the hands of a monster, and putting everyone the three of them loved in harm's way.

"I have decided to tell Barbara Jean about Elora," Sanders had told them in his usual succinct manner.

"It's past time she knew. If I had told Nic the truth and explained everything to her instead of hiding behind half-truths, she would be here with me now."

At the time, when he had asked Nic to marry him, he had convinced himself that it was best for both of them if she never knew more than he had already told her about his years on Amara. In retrospect, he knew that he hadn't told Nic because he had doubted her ability to understand and forgive. He had been selfish, keeping the whole truth from her because he was afraid to lose her. Not sharing everything with his wife had been the worst mistake Griff had ever made, one that both he and Nic were dearly paying for now.

Yvette, Sanders, and Griff had made a pact when they escaped from Amara, agreeing that before one of them would share any information about the years they had spent as York's captives, they would ask permission of the other two. That pact of silence, along with their shared experiences in hell, had bound them together irrevocably. The humiliating truths of surviving at any cost combined with the painful memories of humiliation and degradation and unforgivable barbarous acts united the three of them and excluded everyone else, even the women that Griff and Sanders loved.

When they drove past the entry gates at Griffin's Rest, Yvette asked that they take her to her home.

"You should stay with us," Griff said. "You shouldn't be alone."

"I will hardly be alone in a house filled with students."

"Come to dinner tonight," Sanders told her. "Barbara Jean will be disappointed if you are not there."

"I dare say that she will be the only one."

"If you are referring to Maleah—" Sanders said.

"I sense Maleah's dislike and distrust whenever I am near her. And I'm sure that Nicole's brother would prefer not to see me while he is here."

"If Charles David blames anyone for what's happened to Nic, he blames me. As well he should," Griff said.

Sanders dropped Griff off first at his request before driving Yvette home. This was where Griff wanted to be, where he needed to be, not halfway around the world chasing ghosts from his and Yvette's past.

And what will you do if York sends you off on another wild-goose chase?

Griff stood on the porch and gazed out at the land surrounding his house, acres and acres of woods and winding dirt pathways and shoreline along Douglas Lake. Home. Seclusion. Sanctuary. Safety.

Where are you, Nic? Are you safe? Are you well?

He could not bear the thought of Nic in pain, of her being raped or tortured or hunted like a wild animal, of her being subjected to any of the horrors that the captives on Amara had endured.

"Welcome home," Barbara Jean said.

Griff had been so engrossed in his thoughts—in the waking nightmare about Nic—he hadn't heard the front door open.

Facing the attractive redhead confined to her wheelchair, he said, "Thank you," and then leaned down to kiss her cheek. "It's good to be home."

She grabbed his hand. "A lot of people care about you and Nic and they all want to help you."

"I know."

Backing up her wheelchair so that Griff could enter the foyer, Barbara Jean said, "Maleah and Derek are in the office. They'll join us for dinner this evening. Charles David went out for a walk half an hour ago. He's been taking a lot of long walks since he got here. Ben and Meredith are back from Shelter Island. She sensed that Nicole had been there, but wasn't able to figure out where she is now. Ben's in the office filing a report."

"I had hoped Meredith would be able to sense something while she was on the island about where they had taken Nic," Griff said. "I know she tried, that she did her best."

"Cam Hendrix has called every day," Barbara Jean told him. "And so have Lindsay and Judd. They all want to do something—anything—to help."

"There's nothing they can do." Neither his long-time buddy and lawyer nor two of his dearest friends could help him.

"They can do what the rest of us are doing. They can pray. And they can keep on sending out positive thoughts and believing that you're going to find Nic and bring her home."

"I hope you're right about that," a voice from behind them said.

Griff spotted the lone figure, wearing jeans and a polo shirt, standing at the back of the foyer, apparently just having come in from the patio. Charles David, his wife's younger brother was tall, dark-haired, dark-eyed, and bore an almost twinlike resemblance to his sister.

"Dinner is at six thirty," Barbara Jean said as she wheeled off toward the kitchen.

Griff faced Charles David, searching the guy's

handsome face for any sign of hostility. He saw none. Was it possible that Nic's brother didn't hate him, didn't want to beat him within an inch of his life?

"How are you, Griffin?" Charles David asked.

Griff didn't denote any hint of sarcasm in the man's voice. "I'm hanging on to my sanity by a very thin thread."

"Hang on tightly. Nicole needs you."

Griff released a deep, whooshing breath. "I'm heading to my study." He inclined his head in the direction. "Why don't you come with me? We can talk in private."

"And share a glass of your best Scotch whiskey?"

"If you'd like."

As they walked side by side down the hallway toward the study, neither of them spoke, not until they reached the open doorway to Griff's private domain.

"Whatever you've done wrong, whatever mistakes you've made, Nic will forgive you," Charles David said. "She loves you."

Griff swallowed hard as his emotions threatened to overwhelm his iron resolve. "I swear to you that I'm going to find her. No matter what I have to do, what price I have to pay, I will bring Nic home."

Yvette had left Meredith in charge when she left for England and had found out only after she had arrived in London that Sanders had asked Meredith to accompany Ben Corbett to Shelter Island in the hopes of picking up Nic's trail.

"Adam managed quite well without either of us," Meredith had explained. "He's a rather remarkable person and far more in control of his talents than I am."

Adam Marlow was one of six highly gifted students Yvette had taken under her wing, giving them instruction and protection. She guarded her young charges as fiercely as any mother tigress.

If only someone had been able to do that for her when she was a young girl . . . before Malcolm York had come into her life. Instruct her, protect her, guard her.

Yvette slipped out of the clothes she had worn on the flight from London, stripped down to her underwear, and walked into the bathroom. Standing in front of the mirror, she stared at her reflected image. Most women longed for physical beauty, would go to any lengths to achieve it. For Yvette, beauty had been as much of a curse as her empathic gifts had been. Few men looked past the surface to see the real woman behind the flawless mask. Inside, she was not beautiful. She was ugly, hideously ugly, her very soul black with sin.

After removing her silk bra and panties, she turned on the shower and stepped beneath the cool, refreshing spray. If only she could wash away the past as easily as she washed the grime from her skin.

Her perfect body had given pleasure to countless men, some whose faces she could no longer recall, many of them Malcolm York's friends and business associates. She had been coupled with dozens of the slaves held captive on Amara during the years she had lived there as York's wife. Sometimes, the man had been brought to her bedroom where she seduced him in order to get inside his thoughts and emotions and report back to York.

"Either you do as I ask or I'll kill him and force you to watch," York had told her.

The first time, she had not believed he would actually kill one of his prized "animals" used in his sadistic hunts. But she had been wrong and her stupidity had cost the slave his life. As long as she lived, she would never forget the moment York had placed his pistol to the man's head and fired.

On special occasions when York entertained certain friends who especially enjoyed sexual voyeurism, she and whatever slave York chose would perform in front of a very select audience.

Some of those poor souls had begged her to forgive them, while others had taken her with savage pleasure and walked away when they had finished without saying a word. And then one evening, York had chosen his most valued captive, a man who had survived numerous hunts, a man who had outsmarted York and his fellow hunters time and time again. On that fateful night, Griffin Powell had been delivered to her bedroom.

She had lured him with her naked body, taken him into her bed, and used her empathic talents to connect to his thoughts. Able to see past the lust that drove him, she had sensed an innate goodness in him, a fierce pride and unbendable strength. And oddly enough, without any psychic abilities whatsoever, Griffin had instinctively known, that despite the fact she was York's wife, she was nothing more to him than a pawn used in his evil games. She had been as much a slave as he.

Griffin had become her friend. He had been her friend then as he was her friend now. In another world, another time, another place, if they had met under different circumstances, then perhaps they could have been more than friends.

But the heart wants what the heart wants. It loves whom it pleases, without regard for right or wrong or for sensible choices and suitable matches. If only Griffin could have loved her. If only she could have loved him.

Perhaps she had never truly loved anyone. She had been infatuated with York, at least in the beginning before she had seen past the glossy façade to the corrupt, despicable creature beneath the surface. The real Malcolm York.

She had cared for Sanders as if he were her brother. Helping her survive the horrors York inflicted on her became Sanders's only reason for living. After losing his wife and child, he had tried to kill York and had been severely punished. When York had brought her to Amara as his new captive bride, Sanders had appointed himself her guardian, just as he had taken on the role of Griffin Powell's mentor, teaching him all he needed to know about surviving "the hunt" time and time again.

Remembering the past serves no purpose. Nothing can change what had happened.

Yvette rinsed her hair, turned off the shower, squeezed the excess water from her hair, and stepped out of the shower. After winding a towel around her head and drying off her body, she slipped into her turquoise silk robe.

Don't think about him. He is dead to you. Dead to anyone who knew the boy he once was.

She eased her feet into her soft house slippers and then sat down at the vanity table. A pair of sad dark eyes stared back at her from the mirror. She did not want to be sad. If Suzette had been her daughter, she would have been happy. Finding her child would give her great joy. Becoming a mother to that child could possibly restore a part of her soul.

What if Suzette had been your daughter and Griffin had not been her father, what then?

No matter who had fathered her child, she would love her . . . or him.

Could you really love a child fathered by Yves Bouchard?

Bouchard, who preferred teenage boys, had surprised her when he had requested that she participate in a ménage à trois with him and his favorite Amara partner.

Yvette removed the towel from her long, straight hair and blotted it partially dry, and then she speared her fingers into her hair, running them through from her scalp to the tips that reached her shoulder blades.

Until the pseudo-York had renewed her hope of finding her child, she had refused to believe that anyone other than Griffin was the father. Now she faced the truth—unless she found her child, she would never know.

But if not Griffin, then please let it be Lunt Anderson.

Never Bouchard!

Somewhere deep inside her, another truth emerged ever so gradually, a truth she had refused to acknowledge, a truth that even now she did not want to accept. Perhaps, she had loved once. Only once. Loved with tender passion, her emotions and his fragile, otherworldly, far removed from reality. He had been a boy of eighteen to her woman of twenty-three the first time York had sent him to her. Such a sweet, gentle boy, his soul as pure as a child's.

Do not do this. Do not remember.

He could be your child's father.

No! Yes. It would explain why your baby could shield herself from your probing, why you could never connect with her in order to discover her paternity.

Raphael Byrne had possessed latent untutored psychic abilities he had refused to acknowledge because he had been taught such things were "of the devil."

Once, long ago, Raphael Byrne had been an angel.

Now, Rafe Byrne was a demon.

CHAPTER 24

She lay beneath him, their bodies joined so completely that they were one. Arching her back, she lifted her legs and wrapped them around him as he lunged into her again and again. Sweet Jesus! *If the loving got any better, he wouldn't be able to stand it. His mouth found hers. Soft, moist, opening for him.*

He grasped her hips, lifting her, pressing her closer as he ground into her. Her nails raked across his back as she came, her breath hot against his neck, her whimpering cries of release sending him over the edge.

Griff loved this woman, loved her beyond reason. He would do anything for her.

Nicole. His Nicole.

"I love you," she whispered as she clung to him in the aftermath of their lovemaking. "I love you so much."

Griff woke abruptly from the sweet dream.

Nic was not lying beside him.

Reality hit him hard.

He flung back the covers and bounded out of bed. Anger coiled inside him, needing to be vented. A good workout in the gym should help clear his mind and reduce his stress level, at least temporarily.

He slipped into sweatpants, an old UT T-shirt, and a pair of athletic shoes, combed his hair with his fingers, and headed downstairs. Before he reached the foyer, he saw Sanders at the foot of the stairs.

"Morning," Griff said. "What's up?"

"We just received Suzette York's DNA results from Mitchum," Sanders replied. "I thought you would want to know immediately."

"And the DNA test proved what we already know." Griff met Sanders in the foyer.

"The young woman is definitely not your child or Yvette's."

"Mitchum is going to have DNA tests run on the other two girls, just to make sure."

"It's being done now."

"Any word on—?"

"The girl in the hospital is hanging on still in critical condition. They have not been able to identify either the hospitalized girl or the dead girl."

"Have you spoken to Yvette this morning?" Griff asked. "I'm concerned about her."

"As am I, but there is nothing either of us can do to help her. Would you like for me to give her the DNA results?"

"Yeah, thanks. And see if Barbara Jean can persuade her to come up to the house later today. If ever we all needed to be together, it's now."

Anthony Linden came for Nic that morning, not Malcolm York. Did it mean that York was no longer in residence or simply that he couldn't be bothered with mundane chores? Upon entering her room, Linden tossed a pair of denim shorts and a skimpy halter top to her.

"You're to wear these today."

"I'll change in the bathroom," she told him.

"Go right ahead." He grinned at her.

She shot him a bird.

"One of these days . . ." he threatened.

She wanted to say, "Bring it on, you son of a bitch," but Nic wasn't stupid. Under most circumstances, she could handle any man who tried to attack her. But Linden wasn't just any man. He was former SAS, a highly trained, skilled warrior with killer instincts. Common sense warned her that she was outmatched.

Without a word, Nic hurried into the bathroom, stripped out of her dirty oversized shirt and pants, and put on the skimpy shorts and stretchy knit halter that clung to her breasts. She doubted anyone would notice that her breasts were fuller now, having increased gradually with her pregnancy. But how long would she be able to hide her condition? Already her belly had begun to swell, just a tiny baby bump, but it was only a matter of time before her body blossomed. Having had so much idle time on her hands the past couple of days, Nic had thought a great deal about being pregnant, about the child growing inside her, about how to protect her baby when she wasn't sure she could protect herself.

By her calculations, she was probably about ten weeks along, but looking back and remembering her last period, she realized that it was possible she was farther along, perhaps closer to three and a half months. If that was the case, then she would probably be conspicuously showing within another month.

The longer I can keep my pregnancy a secret from York, the better.

When she came out of the bathroom, Linden inspected her from head to toe. "You have a great pair of legs. They're so long they seem to go on forever."

"Gee, thanks for the compliment."

"I look forward to the day when someone

teaches you to keep your mouth shut," Linden told her. "Unfortunately, it won't be me, but I'll be around to watch and enjoy vicariously."

She took him at his word, having learned that Linden didn't make idle threats. Not knowing what the outcome of his most recent threat would be, Nic tried not to formulate any theories.

"Let's go. Your trainer is eager to meet you."

"I'm ready."

As he escorted her from her bedroom prison, Linden said, "You have to be dying of curiosity. You must want to know what you're going to be trained to do."

"I guess I'll find out soon enough."

"You may think you're prepared for what's in store for you, but I can assure you that you are not."

Malcolm lingered over breakfast, enjoying being handfed by two delectable young girls, one a dark-skinned beauty from Ethiopia and the other a petite French redhead. The girls had been a birthday gift from Harlan Benecroft a couple years ago when they had both been only twelve. The old man had a penchant for sweet young things, preferring their adolescent bodies and inexperience to nubile women with lush figures who were trained in the art of pleasing a man. But Malcolm preferred the latter, so for the past two years, he had shared the girls with friends who appreciated their immaturity. Now, at fourteen, their bodies blossoming into womanhood, he found them both delightful bedmates.

As he caressed the girl's back, Malcolm bit into the ripe strawberry she held to his mouth. Aisha's body reminded him of an Arabian thoroughbred, dark and lean and sleek. Dusty nipples topped her small, firm breasts. A thatch of wiry black curls formed a bushy triangle between her long, slender legs.

Wanting his attention, Chantal traced her bright red fingernails down the T-shape of his chest hair until they reached the tip of his penis. If he didn't stop her, she would work feverishly to arouse him. He grabbed her by the wrist, brought her hand to his mouth, and sucked on each finger. She curled against him like a contented little kitten, her melon-size breasts pressing against him.

By now, he should have learned how to control his need for a woman. But he managed to abstain for only so long until his desire to fuck overcame his determination to derive complete pleasure only from visual stimulation. To fully come into his own, to embody all that Malcolm York was, he had to learn to find sexual pleasure solely from voyeurism.

The resurrection of Malcolm York had taken years and was still a work in progress. Bringing a man back from the dead was no easy task, but he had proven that if anyone could rise from the grave, the indomitable Malcolm York could. A thirst for vengeance could perform miracles. And once he had reunited his old friends from Amara and punished them for their parts in his death, all would be as it should be. Yvette Meng, Damar Sanders, and Griffin Powell would die by his decree, but not before they had suffered unbearably. And then he could live the life he had been destined to live.

Rafe Byrne gave the guard at the gate his real name and waited for approval to enter Griffin's Rest. Not once in the past sixteen years had the other three Amara survivors tried to contact him. By his own choice, he had declined their offer to join them after his release from the Royal London Hospital. They had used York's blood money to establish legitimate businesses and for numerous philanthropic endeavors. He had chosen a different path in life, taking a share of the money, investing it wisely, and using it to finance his search-and-destroy missions. They were solid, upstanding citizens. He was a renegade.

"Drive on through, Mr. Byrne," the guard said as the massive iron gates swung open onto a tree-lined drive.

He gave the guard a quick midair salute and then guided his rental car into Griffin Powell's private sanctuary. He had kept track of his old friends over the years. Basic information. Nothing more. He suspected that when they had heard about York's old Amara visitors being murdered, one by one, they had known who had exacted revenge for all of them.

Ten years after his abduction and enslavement, Griff had gone home, back to the Tennessee hills, and had established his own little kingdom, protected night and day by an army of elite agents. Had he been able to reconnect with the part of himself that had once been the star of the UT football team, a good old boy who had overcome his poverty-stricken childhood? Had he truly put his Amara past behind him?

Rafe had heard about Griff's marriage a few years ago. Had he told her about Amara, about how he had survived, about the day he had butchered York and chopped off his head? It would take a special woman to be capable of accepting that type of darkness in a man's soul.

Sanders had stayed with Griff, at his side for the past sixteen years, the two of them forever connected. Just as Rafe owed Griff his life, Griff owed Sanders. It had been Sanders, a third-generation Gurkha and great-grandson of an English major and the daughter of a Gurkha officer, who had taught Griff warfare and survival. Did Sanders have a life other than one of loyal service?

Yvette would be here at Griffin's Rest. She had

lived in London for many years, occasionally visiting Griff and Sanders. And then she had suddenly moved to Tennessee, into a home Griff had built for her and a select group of young psychics. Did Griff's wife know about the unique connection between Griff and Yvette? If she did know, then Griff had found himself an exceptional woman, one he looked forward to meeting.

As Rafe neared the main house, he found himself surprised by the simplicity of the structure. Maybe it was a mansion by good old boy standards, but not by billionaire playboy standards. However, he could see where the place suited the man who had built it. Like Griff, the house was large and substantial, a true showplace in a rustic setting, and just as Griffin Powell could be described as a diamond in the rough, so could his home. Rafe grunted. He had read that description of Griff a few years ago, probably in a magazine or newspaper article about the mysterious billionaire bachelor.

He parked the rental car, got out, and before he reached the porch, the front doors opened to reveal a man who had changed very little since the last time Rafe had seen him. Damar Sanders's dark gaze settled on Rafe, studied him, quickly dissected him. As muscular and toned as he'd been two decades ago, his head still shaved, his stance and movements military precise, Sanders came out onto the porch to meet him.

"Welcome to Griffin's Rest."

"Are you a welcome party of one?" Rafe asked.

"I wanted to speak to you privately before you see Griffin and Yvette."

"Keeping secrets?" Rafe clicked his tongue. "I thought the three of you shared everything, but then I suppose three to a bed gets old after a while."

Ignoring his comparison of their close relationship to a sexual one, Sanders closed the doors behind him and motioned for Rafe to follow as he came down the front steps. "I thought we might take a short walk together."

"I'm intrigued by all the mystery." Rafe fell into step alongside Sanders.

"No mystery. I simply thought it best if I explain why I sent for you."

"You sent for me?"

"Griffin asked me to locate you. We need your help."

"Help with what, or should I say with whom?"

"You've heard the rumors about Malcolm York being alive."

Rafe nodded. "Rumors we know can't be true. No man can survive having his head separated from his body."

It had been a long time since anyone had intimidated Rafe, but Sanders came damn near close when he cast Rafe a virulent glare. How could he have forgotten how lethal Damar

Sanders could be? While Rafe had still been in grade school, Sanders had belonged to one of the most elite military forces in the world. It had been said that the Gurkhas were the world's most feared soldiers.

"Sorry," Rafe said. "But I can't believe that you and Griff are taking these rumors seriously."

"We have no choice but to take them seriously. And no, of course we do not believe that York has risen from the dead. But we know for a fact that someone has taken York's identity, someone seeking revenge for York's death, someone with enough money and power to pull off an elaborate hoax."

It took Rafe a minute to wrap his mind around Sanders's revelation. "How do you know this? Do you have any proof?"

"Malcolm York orchestrated Nicole Powell's kidnapping. He is holding Griffin's wife hostage. She's been missing for the past nine days. Griffin has spoken to her briefly and to the man who calls himself Malcolm York."

"Holy hell!"

"We are using every resource available to us to locate Nicole," Sanders said.

"And I'm one of those resources. Now I understand why Griff has called in my IOU."

Yvette had spent the entire morning with her protégés, doing all she could to take her mind off

368

of recent events. Occasionally, she had thought about Suzette York, the girl she had so hoped would turn out to be her daughter. But for the most part she had managed to concentrate on her work with the six talented young people who lived here with her within the security of Griffin's Rest. Of all her students, only Meredith Sinclair could possibly help Griffin in his search for Nicole. But her recent journey with Ben Corbett to Shelter Island had not garnered any new information that could help them locate Nicole. As gifted as Meredith was, she had yet to harness her remarkable psychic energy enough so that she could control it instead of it controlling her.

Barbara Jean had shown up unannounced shortly before noon and invited Yvette to join the others for lunch. When she had declined, Barbara Jean had insisted.

"I will not take no for an answer."

Yvette had allowed the woman to influence her decision for several reasons, the least of which was because Barbara Jean Hughes was her only female friend in Griffin's household and among his agents. Not that she had ever chosen sides nor would she. Barbara Jean was also Nicole's friend.

"All right, but only because you asked me." *And because she knew that Griffin wanted her there.*

Since it was such a lovely day, an unseasonably

cool breeze diluting the sun's warmth just enough to keep the temperature in the low eighties, Yvette decided to walk from her home to the main house. She appreciated the beauty as well as the serenity she found here at Griffin's Rest. The estate grounds flourished with summertime maturity, rich and lush, brimming with verdant life.

As much as she loved living here, she often wondered if she had made a mistake moving from London to Tennessee. In the early days of Griffin's relationship with Nicole, Yvette had hoped that she and Nicole could become friends. They both had tried. But Nicole had sensed there was far more to Yvette and Griffin's past relationship than either had admitted. In retrospect, she wished that she had encouraged Griffin to be totally honest with his wife. If she could, she would change so many things.

Less than halfway to her destination, Yvette spotted two men coming from the opposite direction, each walking leisurely along the path. She paused when they stopped and faced each other, apparently deep in conversation. She was too far away to identify either man, but certainly had no reason for concern. They were probably two Powell agents assigned to duty at Griffin's Rest.

When she drew nearer, she recognized the shorter man as Sanders. He had his back to her as he spoke to his companion. She could hear his voice, but couldn't make out what he was saying.

And then she looked at the other man, really looked at him. She had seen that face only once before, sixteen years ago at Royal London Hospital.

Rafe Byrne was here at Griffin's Rest. Had she conjured up the image of his surgically reconstructed face and transposed it onto the man talking to Sanders? If so, why was it Rafe's sharply chiseled features she saw and not Raphael's youthful beauty?

She closed her eyes and reopened them in an effort to erase the image. But the man talking to Sanders really was Rafe Byrne. Not the twenty-year-old she remembered. Rafe would be thirty-six now. No longer a boy. His shoulders were wider, his chest thicker, his arms and legs more muscular, though still lean. His dark hair, chopped in a shaggy cut, fell loosely over the left side of his forehead and grazed the collar of his casual, long-sleeved shirt.

She had known that this might happen, that Rafe would learn Griffin Powell wanted to see him and simply show up at Griffin's Rest out of the blue. Hadn't she agreed that if anyone on earth could help Griffin find Nicole, that person was Rafe? Wasn't this what they had all wanted?

So why did she want to turn and run, to get away as quickly as possible?

While she stood there staring at him, Rafe undoubtedly sensed her presence. He stopped

371

talking and looked directly at her. His stare was hard and cold. Unfeeling. And in that moment, she knew without a doubt that there was nothing of Raphael left inside this man.

CHAPTER 25

After what seemed like a half-mile walk, Linden escorted Nic through a set of wide-open, twelve-foot-high wooden doors and into a thatch-roofed, block building that reminded her of a barn. The structure stood in a clearing surrounded by jungle, thick with tangled vegetation and vine-draped trees. Midmorning sunlight poured in through the two massive open doors on either end of the building. Rising three rows along the wall, old, wooden, bleacher-style benches covered the entire left side of the interior. The remainder of the forty-by-thirty-foot area was empty—except for a ripcord lean man with tattoos covering his bare chest and arms. Nic suspected that beneath his tight jeans, his legs were similarly decorated. His long brown hair, slick with oil, hung in a pony-tail between his shoulder blades.

Nic paused halfway into the barn. Linden allowed her to stay there as he walked over to the tattooed man she assumed was her trainer. While the two men talked in hushed tones, too quietly for her to hear, she examined her surroundings as thoroughly as possible. That was when she saw the assortment of weapons, consisting of half a dozen knives in various sizes, a machete, three handguns, two rifles, a shotgun, and what looked like a number of billy clubs.

"Come and meet Vartan." Linden motioned to her.

His command gained her full attention as she forced her gaze away from the weapons and directed it at the two men. Hesitating for only a moment, she stiffened her spine as well as her resolve as she approached them.

"Nicole, this is your trainer," Linden told her. "You will be spending a great deal of time with him over the next few weeks."

Vartan sized her up and smiled. "Yes, I see why Mr. York has chosen The Amazon Queen for your name." He turned to Linden. "She seems to be in excellent physical condition. How old is she?"

"Midthirties, I believe," Linden replied.

Again focusing on Nic, Vartan grasped her shoulders. She jerked at the unexpectedness of his touch. But when he ran his calloused hands down her arms, then over her rib cage and waist before tightening his grip as he clutched her hips, Nic didn't move. She barely breathed.

Releasing her, Vartan took a step back, ran his gaze over her from head to toe, and then without any warning, he slapped her hard across the face. Reeling from the blow, Nic struggled to stay on her feet. Stunned by his actions, she couldn't think straight. Then the taste of blood inside her mouth and the burning ache in her jaw shot her quickly from astonishment to awareness. She reacted purely on instinct, years of training coming into play, as she prepared to retaliate.

Wrong move. Think before you act.

Only seconds after going into attack mode, she reversed gears and positioned herself defensively for another hit.

"Excellent, excellent." Vartan clapped.

Alert to whatever he might do next, Nic glared at him. Never again would she let her guard down around this man.

"I'll leave her with you," Linden said. "But remember that Mr. York doesn't want her permanently damaged in any way during your training sessions. Do whatever you need to do to prepare her, but don't forget what a priceless commodity she is."

"I understand."

"Still don't want to ask me any questions?" Linden mocked her.

"No, thank you," Nic said. "I'm sure Vartan can fill me in on everything I need to know."

"Yes, I'm sure he can."

Nic looked at the tattooed man. "I assume my training began with the slap." Combining saliva with the blood on her tongue and lips, she cleansed her mouth by spitting on the dirt floor. "I need to always be on my guard, right? Lesson learned. So, what is lesson number two?"

"Hello, Yvette," Rafe said, his gaze raking over her with casual interest.

"Hello." She hoped her voice sounded calm. "Did you just arrive?"

"Yes, I just got here. Sanders waylaid me at the front door so he could fill me in on why Griffin sent for me." Rafe grunted. "Damn shame about his wife. I was looking forward to meeting the woman who finally tamed Griff Powell."

"We are all extremely concerned about Nicole," Yvette said.

"So this guy who's passing himself off as Malcolm York kidnapped her, huh?"

"Yes." Sensing that Rafe was testing her, Yvette forced herself not to break eye contact. "This man is doing an excellent job of mimicking my late husband, not only by his actions, but apparently he has undergone facial surgery to make himself look like Malcolm."

Rafe cocked an eyebrow. "You've seen him?"

"No, but . . . we have an eyewitness, someone who knows him quite well. When given photographs of eight different men and asked to identify the man she knew as York, she chose an old photograph of the real Malcolm York."

Rafe grinned. "That must have made you three wonder, if only for a few seconds, whether or not you had really finished off York the way you thought you had."

"The real York is dead," Sanders said emphatically. "We have no doubt about that nor should you. You saw him, didn't you?"

"I was in and out of consciousness when Griff rescued me, but yeah, I vaguely remembering catching a glimpse of what was left of York's body and his severed head perched on the end of the machete that Griff had plunged through his heart and used to pin him to the ground. Slight overkill, wasn't it? But I understand what drove Griff to do it."

"I imagine you do," Sanders said. "By all accounts, almost all of York's old friends have met untimely deaths, each killed in a gruesome manner."

The sound of Rafe's soft laughter unnerved Yvette, reinforcing her fear that this man had become as viciously inhuman as the men he had hunted down and killed.

"Yves Bouchard is still around," Rafe said. "And so is Harlan Benecroft. But Sir Harlan is relatively insignificant. Besides, he isn't going anywhere. He'll always be easy enough to find."

"But not Bouchard?" Yvette asked.

Rafe's gaze connected with hers, reminding her that he, too, remembered the night Bouchard had chosen them for his perverted ménage à trois. "I recently saw *Le Ravisseur* again, for the first time in more than sixteen years."

"You've seen Bouchard?" Yvette hoped to never see the man again as long as she lived.

"Where did you see him?" Sanders asked.

"London. At a dinner party Sir Harlan hosted at the Savoy."

"You are mingling with a rather unsavory group these days, aren't you?" Sanders said. "By any chance, did either Benecroft or Bouchard happen to mention Malcolm York?"

"No. But why would they? It's not as if I've managed to gain their complete trust. Not yet."

"But you will," Sanders said. "And the sooner the better."

"Some things can't be rushed. They require patience."

"Not when Nicole Powell's life is on the line," Sanders told him. "Bouchard was York's friend and business associate, and Benecroft is his cousin. It stands to reason that in trying to assume York's identity, the pseudo-York would find a way to associate with both of these men."

"Interesting theory," Rafe said. "And if it proves to be true, it could be quite profitable for me."

"Profitable for you how?" Yvette asked.

While Rafe simply smiled at her, Sanders, who apparently knew exactly what Rafe meant, explained. "Rafe is willing to use his social connection to Harlan Benecroft to help us locate Malcolm York, for the right price."

"You would ask Griffin for money to help him find York so he can rescue his wife?" Yvette stared at Rafe, her disbelief quickly fading as outrage rose to the surface. "What kind of man are you?"

"I'm the kind of man my experiences on Amara made me, the kind of man you think I am—one without a conscience or a heart or even a soul."

After putting her through an hour of what amounted to a series of basic exercises from stretches to push-ups and crunches to squats, Vartan offered Nic a bottle of water and invited her to take a seat beside him on the bottom row of wooden bleachers. She accepted the water and the invitation. After uncapping the bottle and downing several deep swigs, she wiped her mouth. Then she poured water in her hand and splashed it on her flushed face.

The routine he had put her through had been strenuous. If she hadn't been in excellent physical condition, she would be greatly concerned about herself and her baby. But her child was safe, cocooned within her. As long as she was well fed and well rested and didn't receive any severe physical attacks, she and her baby should be fine. At least for now. But once her pregnancy progressed, what then?

Sensing Vartan staring at her, she turned and studied the tattooed man as thoroughly as he was scrutinizing her.

"One warrior recognizes another, eh?" Vartan said.

Although his command of the English language was almost perfect, Nic detected a hint of an accent. Eastern European? She wasn't sure.

"Is that what you are, Mr. Vartan, a warrior who trains warriors for York?"

"I am simply Vartan," he told her. "And yes, that is what I do, train warriors for Mr. York."

"Mind if I ask how long you've worked for York?"

"Two years."

"And exactly what do you train York's captives to do?"

He shrugged. "Some I train for The Hunt. Some I train for The Ring. Others I train for The Execution. Some, like you, I train for all three."

All three? Damn! How lucky can you get? But then, I'm special to York. I'm Mrs. Griffin Powell.

"I know what The Hunt is. But what's The Ring? And what is The Execution?" Nic was sure she was not going to like his answers, but she needed to know exactly what she would soon be facing.

"In The Hunt and in The Ring, you will be paired with a male partner. You must learn to work together in order to survive." Vartan grinned, revealing a set of uneven teeth, the top center incisors gold-capped. "The Ring is nothing more than two couples fighting, sometimes to the

379

death. Sometimes it is like gladiators fighting. And sometimes it is a gun battle, old west-style. It depends on what the clients want."

No doubt these "clients" were like the ones the real York had brought to Amara, men who could pay a high price for their perverted pleasures.

"And The Execution, what is that?" she asked.

"It is an exhibition for a very select clientele. Men and sometimes women who take pleasure in watching a reluctant executioner take the life of a condemned person."

Had she heard him correctly? "Which part are you training me to play—executioner or one of the condemned?"

"Executioner, of course." Vartan laughed. "There is no training for the condemned."

"One more question—who are the condemned?"

He grinned at her, apparently taking pleasure in answering her question. "The condemned are whoever Mr. York says they are."

Griff shook hands with Rafe and immediately knew that this man was a stranger. He had known Raphael, had been fond of the vulnerable young boy so badly abused by York and his friends, but there was no similarity between the boy and the man. Apparently when Rafe Byrne had walked out of the Royal London Hospital sixteen years ago, he had left behind whatever had remained of Raphael. Or perhaps Raphael had died long before then, on Amara, and only the dark side of his nature had survived.

But how could Griff, in good conscience, condemn Rafe? He understood only too well what it had been like on Amara, although his experiences had not been identical to Rafe's. In order to survive, Griff had become a vicious animal, capable of ripping another man apart with his bare hands. He had done unforgivable things, forced against his will to commit the worst of sins.

"It's good to see you again after all these years," Griff told Rafe with complete honesty.

"Yeah, I guess it's good to see you"—he glanced at Sanders and then at Yvette—"all of you. This is kind of like an Amara survivors' reunion, isn't it?"

"That's one way to look at it," Griff said. "Why don't we all sit down and get reacquainted before Barbara Jean herds us into the dining room for lunch?"

"Sure, why not?" Rafe sprawled into the nearest chair, crossed his arms over his chest, and relaxed into the soft leather.

Yvette and Griff sat on either end of the sofa. Sanders waited until everyone else was seated before he chose a straight-back chair at the edge of the room near the double-door entrance.

"Sanders has explained to you about my wife." Griff watched Rafe for any sign of emotion and saw none.

"Malcolm York kidnapped her," Rafe said. "You

want to find York and rescue your wife. That's the situation, right?"

"Yes." Griff nodded.

"You want me to help you find York."

"Name your price."

Uncrossing his arms and leaning forward in the chair, Rafe replied, "No reminders that I owe you my life. No recriminations about why I'd ask payment from an old friend for services rendered and no haggling over money." Rafe grinned. "I like that."

"No point in wasting my time or yours," Griff said. "Not when the only thing that matters is saving my wife."

"What makes you think I can locate York when your entire network hasn't been able to locate him?"

"We've located where Nicole was taken twice," Sanders told Rafe. "The first time, we arrived too late. The second time, the rescue attempt failed."

"Third time's the charm, huh?" Rafe said. "If you've managed to zero in on where your wife was twice, then you'll be able to do it again without my help."

"You're an alternate plan," Griff said. "I believe in covering all my bases. You've been able to infiltrate some pretty exclusive circles around the world during the past sixteen years. My guess is that you either already have access to, or soon will have, to Yves Bouchard as well as Harlan

Benecroft. They're the only two of York's frequent Amara visitors who are still alive. Odds are that the new Malcolm York has ties to both Bouchard and Benecroft and they can lead us straight to him."

"Five million." Rafe stated his asking fee. "A million up front. Two million when I locate York and your wife. Another two million once you've rescued her."

"Deal," Griff said without hesitation.

"You've done well this morning," Vartan told Nic after another hour-long training session. "For the next few weeks, you will train two hours every morning and two hours every afternoon. It is a light schedule, but you are in very good condition and if I work you too hard, Mr. York will not like it. You are special to him, eh?"

"Oh, yes, I'm very special to him."

"I thought so. He has paired you with a champion, one who can help you survive the exhibitions." Vartan motioned to the guards at the front of the barn. "Bring him in. It's time."

Hot, sweaty, and exhausted, Nic wanted a shower and a nap before the afternoon workout session. Apparently Vartan had something else in mind for her—an introduction to her partner.

Oddly enough, when the guards escorted Jonas MacColl into the building, Nic wasn't surprised. On some level, she had known that York had chosen him specifically for her. Wasn't that why he had kept Jonas alive?

"I brought Jonas with us just for you, my dear," York had told her.

Unfettered by cuffs and chains, his overly long hair secured in a short ponytail, and his upper torso bare, Jonas walked a few steps ahead of the guards, his entrance demanding attention. The puckered, healing gunshot wound in his side, the skin around it discolored, reminded Nic that this man had saved her life back aboard the *Isis*.

Nic couldn't take her eyes off him. She was glad to see him, thankful he had survived, and was eager to talk to him.

Vartan motioned to Jonas. "Come, come. Mr. York has chosen your new partner."

Jonas came forward, stopped, and looked straight at Nic before he cast his gaze to the dirt floor.

"I believe you already know each other, but I will introduce you all the same," Vartan said. "Nicole, this is Jonas. Jonas, this is Mr. York's pet, Nicole. You will train together every day and take your meals together. If you do well together in your first exhibition, you will be allowed to share quarters." Vartan laughed as he slapped Jonas on the back. "It's been awhile since you had a woman, hasn't it?"

Jonas didn't so much as flinch.

"You will stay here. Rest. Talk. Enjoy a couple of hours of free time," Vartan said. "Food will be brought to you soon. And I will return this afternoon and work you both very hard."

Jonas stood tall and proud, not moving, not speaking, and Nic followed his lead, both of them waiting for Vartan to exit the building.

Once they were alone, the guards and Vartan no longer inside the barn, Jonas looked at Nic.

"How are you?" she asked him. "I wasn't even sure you were still alive."

"It takes more than a bullet to kill a tough old country boy like me." He inspected her from head to toe. "Fetching outfit you're wearing, Mrs. Powell."

She appraised his appearance, noting that his only clothing was a pair of cotton knit shorts. "Are the rest of your clothes in the laundry today?"

Jonas grinned. "It's good to see you, Nicole. I've worried about you."

"I'm okay. No major catastrophes since we last saw each other."

"When they told me I was going back into training today, I figured they'd have you waiting for me, that York had put us together."

"I'm glad," Nic said. "I understand that you're a champion."

Jonas snorted. "I'm a wounded champion. If I'm put to the test before this wound heals, I could be more of a liability to you than an asset."

"Vartan said something about training me for the next few weeks."

"Did he explain what he's training you to do?"

"A triple whammy. I get the prize behind all three doors—The Hunt, The Ring, and The Execution."

"Son of a bitch! I'm sorry. I wish I could—"

She pressed her index finger across his lips. "Shh . . . Don't. We're not going to waste any energy on things we can't change. If we're going to survive, we'll have to focus completely on what we can do to stay alive."

CHAPTER 26

Yvette and Sanders had watched while Rafe made his deal with Griffin. His business there at Griffin's Rest was complete. When issued an invitation to spend the night, he had declined.

"I'd prefer not to waste any time. The sooner I begin my search, the better my chances of locating York. If your jet is available, why not fly me back to London this evening?"

During lunch, Yvette had avoided looking at Rafe, and unless he said something to her, she hadn't spoken to him. And later, when Griffin had invited Rafe to his study to finalize the monetary details of their arrangement, she had taken the opportunity to slip away and return to her home.

Yet all the while, she had known he would come to her.

For the past two hours, she had waited with anticipation and dread.

What would they say to each other after all these years?

Before he rang the doorbell, she sensed his presence. At least that one aspect of their former relationship had not changed. On Amara, she had always known when he was near and she had suspected that because of his latent "talents" that he so vehemently denied, they had connected on a transcendental level.

Yvette had been meditating, preparing herself as best she could, for the moment now at hand. She opened the door to the past, desperately longing for Raphael to appear. But Rafe Byrne stood there, a man she did not know, a man she feared.

"May I come in?" he asked.

"Yes, of course."

"I'll be leaving in a couple of hours. Griff's eager for me to earn my fee."

When she did not respond, he looked around inside the wide foyer, his gaze pausing on first one and then the other of the two arched doorways, one leading to her students' quarters the other to her private apartment.

"Why did you leave London and move here?" he asked.

"Griffin offered me a home here, a safe,

secluded place where I could bring my students."

"His offer must have been a dream come true for you."

"In a way, I suppose it was." Yvette inclined her head toward the hallway leading to her apartment. "Would you care for something to drink? Tea? Coffee?"

"Got anything stronger?" he asked as he followed her down the hall.

She opened the door to her living room and invited him to come inside with her. "I have wine and there may be a beer in the refrigerator. I can go see."

"Who do you keep the beer for, Griffin or Sanders?"

"I occasionally entertain friends and that includes Griffin and Sanders. The beer is for anyone who wants it."

"Skip the beer," Rafe said as he inspected her living room. "Nice place. Griff takes good care of you with Malcolm York's money."

"Griffin has put that money to good use."

"Yeah, I suppose he has. I've always wondered about something though . . . why did you turn over York's millions to Griff ? Or need I ask?"

"You must know why, so what is it that you're really asking me?"

"You handed over your sizable inheritance to Griff because you loved him. And you're still in love with him, aren't you?"

Rafe's accusation momentarily stunned her. She had thought he knew that she couldn't have kept York's money, that for her it would have been impossible. But she had known Griffin would do only good with the money that had been obtained in the most horrendously evil ways.

"My God, I've rendered you speechless." Rafe's laughter filled the room, sucking up all the oxygen, making her gasp for air. "Surely you didn't think I wasn't aware of how you felt about him."

"Why would you care how I feel about Griffin?"

"I don't. Not really. Just curious."

"Of all the things that I thought you might say to me, I never imagined you would—"

"He's not in love with you," Rafe told her. "He never was."

"No, he was never in love with me, but Raphael was in love with me, wasn't he?"

She thought perhaps retaliating with an accusation of her own might conclude the subject of love, but she was wrong.

"That poor, pitiful boy loved you beyond all reason," Rafe admitted. "And he was fool enough to think you felt the same."

"I wasn't in love with Griffin or Raphael or any other man during those years on Amara. I cared for Griffin and for Sanders . . . and for Raphael. But what does any of that matter now? I care for

389

Griffin and Sanders as if they were my brothers."

"And Raphael?"

"Raphael is dead, isn't he?" *Please tell me that he's not dead, that some small part of him still exists deep inside you.*

"Long dead. I buried him on Amara."

"Why did you come here, Rafe?"

"Griffin Powell summoned me."

"No, I didn't mean why did you come to Griffin's Rest. Why did you come here to my home to see me?"

"I came to say good-bye."

He moved toward her. She felt a moment of sheer panic, but managed not to cringe when he reached out and caressed her cheek with the back of his hand. Flashes of intense emotions bombarded her. Anger. Hatred. Resentment. Regret. And lust.

"Feel it," he told her. "Feel all of it."

She jerked away from him, saving herself from the emotional injury such intense feelings would cause. With several feet separating them, she stared at Rafe, silently questioning him, understanding the answer without any response. *You hate me. And yet you want me.*

"I never meant to hurt you," she told him. "I only wanted to help you, to protect you as best I could. I did what I did because I cared, because I knew that without giving you a reason to live, you would give up."

"Then I suppose I owe you my life as much as I owe Griff, don't I?"

"You don't owe me anything. I did what I did for Raphael, not for Rafe."

He smiled, the expression almost frightening. "Why is what I've been doing these past sixteen years so different from what Griff did on Amara? He single-handedly killed several guards, didn't he? And he spearheaded York's murder."

"Griffin did what was necessary to free us from York and our captivity on Amara. And he has spent the past sixteen years trying to make the world a better place, using York's fortune in a positive way."

"And isn't the world a better place without Tanaka, Di Santis, Klausner, Sternberg, and Mayorga?"

"Yes, of course. But killing those men gave you the only kind of pleasure you're capable of feeling now. You wanted me to know that horrible truth, didn't you? That's why you touched me. So that I could . . . Oh, Rafe, how terrible it must be for you."

"What's wrong, Yvette? Can't you work your magic on me now and heal me, make me capable of feeling hope and trust and love again?"

"I'm sorry. I'm so very sorry."

"All out of miracles, huh? That's okay. Having human emotions would just get in the way of what I have to do. Yves Bouchard is still alive.

And so is Harlan Benecroft. I'll need to use them to find Griff's wife. Then once they've served their purpose . . . "

While she stood there looking at him, tears in her eyes, her heart breaking, Rafe gave her a final bittersweet smile, and then turned and walked away.

Nightfall was fast approaching. The sun's dying light set the western horizon ablaze. Fiery red and flaming orange melted together around the descending orb, announcing day's end. The overgrown jungle, heavy with humidity and damp from the afternoon rainfall teemed with life and yet smelled of rot and death. Blood-sucking mosquitoes searched for victims. And half a dozen armed hunters tromped through the tangled undergrowth, each man eager to bag the most challenging animal and claim the ultimate prize.

Griff paused by the shallow stream, knelt down, and cupped a handful of water. After drinking his fill, he splashed his leather-tan face and dirty, sweat-drenched torso before rising to his feet.

Repetitive bursts of gunfire shattered the quiet, muted hum of the steamy jungle. Birds flushed up into the sky by the dozens. Griff ran away from the abrupt clatter of the hunters' high-powered rifles and their triumphant yells.

Apparently at least one of the hunters had scored a hit, killing the prey he had been tracking for hours. Four captives had been sent out earlier today. Jules, Perry, Carlisle, and Griff. Knowing each man as he did, Griff figured that Perry would have been the easiest to find and kill. The young Canadian had been on Amara a little over a month and lacked the survival skills to keep him alive on his first hunt. Griff and the others had done their best to help him, but there was only so much you could do to train a guy in such a short period of time.

Hurry, sundown. Darkness couldn't fall soon enough.

If he could make it past nightfall, he would live.

York's hunts always concluded at the end of the day whether or not the hunters had killed one of their human quarry. But that seldom happened. York always made certain that at least one of the captives sent into the hunt was weak and vulnerable. His goal was to keep his wealthy friends and business associates happy so that they would become repeat customers.

Griff knew the jungle on this godforsaken island, knew how the hunters thought, knew how to stay alive. Damar Sanders had tutored him, teaching him survival techniques that he had learned as a Gurkha. But even the smartest, most cunning prey could be killed. All it took was one mistake.

As he went deeper into the forest, the sounds of celebration faded, but Griff didn't relax. He wasn't safe. Not yet. Just because one of the hunters had made his kill, didn't mean the other three would stop tracking the other captives.

A barely discernible crackle of human footsteps on the jungle floor alerted Griff to imminent danger. One of the hunters was nearby. He'd lay odds that it was Mayorga. The cunning Spaniard was a seasoned hunter, having traveled the world over on hunting expeditions, beginning when he was a boy and had accompanied his father. Griff had heard him bragging to the others about how he had learned from the best—his papa.

The bullet whizzed over Griff's shoulder, the shot barely missing him. He dove into the thicket, the brambles and thorns nipping his bare back, chest, and arms. His heart pounded. His pulse quickened. A rush of fear-induced adrenaline pumped through his body.

If Mayorga zeroed in on him, he would be unable to defend himself against a rifle. He lived or died by his wits, as did all the captives on Amara.

The hunter was close. Griff could not only hear him, he could smell him.

Griff waited. Sweating profusely, barely breathing, he peered into the oncoming darkness and spotted the rifleman. Not Mayorga. A new visitor to Amara, some guy named

Brzezinski, who right that minute had his back to Griff.

Acting immediately, Griff came up on his feet and lunged into the clearing. Tackling Brzezinski with the force of one of his former UT team-mate linebackers, Griff took the man down to the ground and ripped his M-16 away from him. Bounding up and over the hunter on the ground, Griff aimed the gun at him. Every instinct urged him to kill.

Pitch blackness suddenly surrounded Griff, blinding him. Where the hell was Brzezinski? Why was there no hint of moonlight?

You can't kill him, Griffin. If you kill one of my hunters, I'll kill Yvette. Or perhaps I'll kill Sanders or execute three or four of your dungeon mates. Malcolm York's voice echoed through the darkness, seeming to come from every direction.

Where are you, you son of a bitch? Show yourself, damn you!

Griff's eyes popped open as he awoke from a recurring nightmare. Only recently those old dreams had returned, memories that plagued him in his sleep. Every waking moment, he fought the images his mind conjured up about Nic being subjected to the horrors he and many others had suffered on Amara. But his subconscious would not allow him any peace.

The bedroom lay in darkness, with only narrow

slices of moonlight slipping through the shutters. Griff stared up at the ceiling, his eyes unfocused, his mind and body recovering from the all-too-real nightmare. He tossed back the covers, got up, and slipped on his robe. The digital alarm clock blinked the time—11:50 P.M. He'd been asleep less than an hour.

Glancing back at the bed, he imagined Nic lying there.

She smiled at him, opened her arms, and invited him to come to her.

If only . . .

But the bed was empty, as empty as his life without Nic.

Barbara Jean Hughes was his friend and lover. Her generous spirit and loving heart had reawakened a part of Sanders that he had believed long dead. During the first few days of their acquaintance four years ago, he had felt an immediate attraction to her, one he had tried to deny. She physically resembled Elora only slightly, but in so many ways, she reminded him of his late wife. There was gentleness inside Barbara Jean, an innate kindness, just as there had been in Elora.

He could never forget Elora and their infant son, both buried on Amara. They were ingrained in his memory forever. They were a part of his heart and soul. And he could never love another woman the way he had loved Elora, the way he still loved her. Love does not end with death.

Sanders cared deeply for Barbara Jean. Perhaps he loved her. He knew that she loved him. She accepted him as he was, never expected more from him than he could give, and never questioned him about his past.

But she deserved to know the truth.

"Are you awake?" he asked, keeping his voice whisper soft.

She stirred beside him in the bed they had shared for three and a half years, reached out, found his hand in the darkness, and said, "Yes, I'm awake."

He squeezed her hand. "I do not want to ever lose you."

"You won't. I'll never leave you."

He released her hand, eased back the covers, and turned to sit on the side of the bed. "Nicole needed to know the complete truth about Griffin's past, about his years on Amara, and his relationship with Yvette. If he had been totally honest with her, she never would have left him."

"I'm not Nicole," Barbara Jean said. "I don't need to know more about your past."

Sanders flipped on the bedside lamp and glanced over his shoulder. Barbara Jean lifted herself into a sitting position.

"You do know how much you mean to me," he said. "I do not deserve you. I would not blame you if—"

"What's wrong, Damar? You're not acting like yourself."

"Do you mean that I am not acting secretive, aloof . . . even emotionally distant?"

"You're worrying me by saying these things."

Sanders stood, rounded the foot of the bed, and sat down beside Barbara Jean. "I was a Gurkha soldier as my father and his maternal grandfather had been. My father's father was an Englishman, therefore my surname, Sanders." He took her hand in his. "You know all of this, of course. But you do not know anything about Elora."

"You don't have to do this," Barbara Jean said. "Not for me."

The corners of his lips lifted in a melancholy smile. "If not for you, then for me. I want you to know."

She squeezed his hand. "Then tell me."

"I met Elora in Singapore. I was assigned there and she was working at the British Embassy. She was the most beautiful woman I'd ever seen and I think I fell in love with her at first sight." Sanders closed his eyes as the memories swept over him like a gentle tide caressing the shoreline. "We married less than two months later."

"A whirlwind courtship," Barbara Jean said.

Sanders looked at her and nodded. "We were so happy, so in love, so unaware of the hell that fate had in store for us."

"It's too painful for you. Please, you don't—"

"Elora was an empath."

Barbara Jean released a soft sigh. "Like Yvette."

"Yes, like Yvette. But only a handful of people knew. Elora hid her talent quite well and used it rarely," he said. "We had been married two years when Elora met Malcolm York at an embassy function of some sort."

"Oh, my dear . . ." Barbara Jean lifted Sanders's hand and brought it to rest against her chest.

"A few weeks after she first met York, he invited us to what we believed was a fund-raiser for a Singapore orphanage, held aboard York's yacht. It was a very exclusive party, but we didn't suspect anything, not until we awoke the next morning, locked in one of the guest cabins. Our drinks had been drugged, my champagne and Elora's virgin cocktail."

"York had kidnapped you."

"He had kidnapped Elora because somehow he had discovered she possessed empathic abilities. We never knew how he found out," Sanders said. "I was kidnapped because I was with Elora. And of course, York soon discovered that he could manipulate Elora by threatening me."

"And control you by threatening Elora."

Sanders nodded.

"Only days before the party aboard York's yacht, Elora had told me that she was pregnant."

Barbara Jean lifted Sanders's clenched fist to her mouth and brushed her lips across his knuckles.

"Once we reached Amara, they separated us. I was placed with the other male captives and Elora was taken to York's house. He used her to gain information from his business associates without their knowing that when she touched them, she was able to absorb their thoughts and feelings.

"I was trained for the hunt and in those months before our child was born prematurely, I took part in three hunts and managed to survive. Each time I survived, I was allowed to visit Elora. Three times in five months."

With the retelling came renewed pain. Memories he had strived so hard to bury deep inside him rose to the surface with agonizing clarity.

"The night before Elora went into labor, York had granted a request from his guests who had come to Amara for the next hunt. These three men asked for Elora. They were intrigued by her beauty and the fact that she was pregnant."

Sanders swallowed hard.

"No more, please, no more." Barbara Jean leaned forward and wrapped her arms around him.

He embraced her, rested his head against her heart, and surrounded with the strength of her love, he managed to continue. "York's three guests raped Elora. They brutalized her. I did not know what was happening, and even if I had known, there would have been nothing I could have done. The following day, she went into labor with only a midwife in attendance. My son was born dead. Elora hemorrhaged to death."

Tears streamed down Barbara Jean's cheeks as she clung to Sanders, holding him with all her might.

"I was allowed to see them, Elora and our son, the day York buried them. I went into a murderous rage and York had me beaten so severely that I didn't recover for weeks."

"My poor darling." She caressed the back of his neck.

"A few months later, York brought his bride to Amara. Yvette might have been York's wife, but she was as much a prisoner as Elora had been, as I was. And York soon learned to use Yvette to control me. That's when he put me in charge of training the new slaves who were brought in for the hunt. I did what I could to help the new captives stay alive, but it wasn't until Griffin was brought to Amara that I saw the chance to train a champion, someone who could survive long enough to help me with my plans to kill York."

"Killing York was your idea?"

"Does that shock you?"

"No." Barbara Jean kissed his cheek. "I'm glad you had Griffin to help you and that you were able to save Yvette. And I understand why you and Griffin and Yvette share the bond that you do."

Sanders lifted his head, and then he reached up

and placed his open palms on either side of her face. Holding her with the utmost tenderness, he said, "You are a very special lady . . . my lady. I love you . . . I love you very much, Barbara Jean."

CHAPTER 27

For the past two weeks, Nicole's life had consisted of morning and afternoon training sessions with Jonas as her supportive partner and Vartan as her strict trainer. Although she didn't like Vartan, she had found that she didn't hate him. The man was like a robot, programmed for one task. He trained her as he would have a prized Thoroughbred being prepared for an important race, and he treated her accordingly. After that first day, she had realized that Vartan's sense of right and wrong was somewhat skewed. He did as he was told and danced to York's tune regardless of the consequences. And then there was Jonas MacColl. The more time she spent with the former NASCAR driver the more she liked him. Her instincts told her he was a good man, someone she could count on no matter what they had to face in the weeks or months ahead.

Nic believed that she was probably about four months pregnant and thankfully still was not showing except for a small baby bump and a slight increase in the size of her breasts.

Apparently, no one had noticed or if they had, thought nothing of it. Of course, she hadn't gained any weight due to excessive exercise and meals of lean meat, vegetables, and fruit. As far as she knew, she and her baby were healthy. But they were not safe and would never be safe as long as she was York's captive.

During the fourteen days she had spent at this tropical compound, she had seen York only once. He had stopped by to watch a training session three days ago and afterward had taken her aside and instructed her to write a note to her husband.

"You will write exactly what I tell you to write. Nothing more. Understand?"

She had written the note.

"Thank you." York had taken the dictated message, folded it, and placed it in his pocket. "I'm excited that your first hunt will be this Saturday. It won't be anything major, only two hunters. You and Jonas will be paired together, of course. I have guests arriving on Friday, one a business associate and the other a friend of my friend Bouchard."

York had grasped Nic's chin. "I want you alive for a while longer, so don't disappoint me. I could care less about Jonas. He can be replaced. Remember that." He had looked Jonas over from head to toe. "I'll give her to you for the next three days, in case they are your last three on Earth. Enjoy her."

As York had walked away, his taunting laughter resonating all around them, neither Jonas nor she had said a word.

For the past three nights, she and Jonas had shared her room, an armed guard outside the locked door.

Jonas had slept on the floor each night.

Griff ripped open the vinyl-coated envelope that had just arrived at Griffin's Rest via international courier service. The return address on the envelope was for a London-based business, Kroy Enterprises. Sanders had hand-delivered the package and remained with Griff. Inside the thin eight-by-ten padded bag, Griff found a hand-written note and a glossy four-by-six photograph. He removed the note first.

"It's from Nic," Griff said. "It's her hand-writing."

My dearest Griffin,

I am alive and well and will remain alive as long as you follow York's instructions. If you love me, please do whatever he asks you to do. I miss you terribly and long to be with you.

All my love,
Nicole

Griff held out the note to Sanders. "What do you make of this?"

Sanders took the single piece of paper, read it hurriedly, and said, "This does not sound like Nicole. York dictated the words to her."

"I agree. Any other instinctive insight into why he sent this particular message and why he sent it now?"

"After two weeks of silence, without a word from York, apparently he has decided what your next challenge will be. This message is a reminder that you must do as he demands. I would say that you can expect to receive a call from him very soon."

"We have to be prepared for anything."

"Yes, we do," Sanders said.

Griff slipped the photograph from the envelope and studied it. Nic in shorts and a halter top, her hair damp with perspiration, stood facing a bare-chested man. They were both smiling.

He flipped over the snapshot. Four words had been printed on the back of the photo. *"Nic with her lover."*

Griff cursed silently, knowing damn good and well that if Nic was having sex with the man in the photograph, it was not consensual. Their smiles had nothing to do with them being lovers. He could not allow York to manipulate him, to make him think Nic was being unfaithful to him. Messing with his mind was all part of York's master plan.

"He's had her for nearly a month now," Griff

said. "God knows what she's been through. We should have located her by now. With all the info we've collected on Kroy Enterprises, why hasn't any of it led us back to York again? We had two chances to rescue Nic and blew them both."

"We will keep digging until we find another link that takes us directly to York. And next time, we will not fail."

"What the hell is taking Rafe so long to find out something and get back to us?"

"As for Rafe . . . give him time. I have no doubt that he will eventually play a role in our rescuing Nicole."

"We both know that the longer Nic is in captivity, the more difficult it will become for her to simply live from day to day."

"And for you as well," Sanders said.

"My personal hell is unimportant."

Sanders pulled the envelope and the photo from Griff's tight grasp, and then glanced at the picture. "Nicole looks well. That is what you need to see in this photograph. Nothing else should concern you. Not the man. Not Nicole's smile. Not what York wants you to assume."

"Yeah, that's what I keep telling myself."

Malcolm rose from his seat at the head of the table. "Gentlemen, please continue with your breakfast. I have to place an important business call to the United States. Once that's done, I'll introduce you to your guide. He will take you into the jungle for today's hunt. Since it is the first time for both of you, I have decided to join you, at least for a part of the day."

He had instructed the guide to make sure if either hunter tracked down Nicole Powell, he should not be allowed to kill her, but he could take her for the night and exact whatever punishment he preferred.

Thirty-year-old playboy Peter Curnow had inherited a fortune from his wealthy parents who had died in a tragic house fire when Peter was twenty and supposedly away at Oxford. Half of Europe suspected the amoral Peter had, if not lit the match, paid someone quite well to torch the family home. The handsome, blond, adrenaline junkie's death-defying exploits around the world were legendary. York had known Peter would jump at the chance to hunt human prey; it was just the sort of sport that would excite him.

York's other guest, Frederick Strauss, an Austrian-born financier and Bouchard's new business associate, who stood barely five-five, was a chubby troll with thinning brown hair and round, shiny, dark eyes that moved continuously, like a vulture searching for its next meal. At twenty-nine, he had already made a sizable fortune and became infamous for his savagery in dealing with anyone who crossed him.

Both men had paid handsomely to participate

in today's hunting session, an experience he hoped would prove to be immensely enjoyable for each of them. If so, they would become two of his many repeat customers.

After leaving his guests in the dining room, Malcolm slipped away into the den at the back of the house on his small private estate in Ecuador, just across the Colombian border. Of all the compounds where the hunts were held, this one was his least favorite, but one favored by his associates in Colombia. If all went as planned, he would leave on Monday and take Griffin Powell's wife with him. He had given her his most experienced warrior as her partner and put her through two weeks of extensive training with Vartan, all in the hopes she would survive her first contest without incident. He suspected that, if necessary, Jonas MacColl would die to protect her.

He wanted Nic to experience everything, to learn what it meant to be a slave, at the mercy of her master. And he longed for Griff to know what his wife was going through every day, every night, with every breath she took. But he did not want Nic to die. Not yet. Not until the time was right.

Closing and locking the door behind him, Malcolm ensured his privacy. His personal business with Griff was no concern to his guests.

He placed the call. The phone rang four times.

"Griffin's Rest," the man said. "Sanders speaking."

"Hello, Sanders. How are you today?"

Momentary silence.

And then, "I want to speak to Nic," Griffin told York.

"I'm afraid your wife is unavailable at the moment," Malcolm replied. "She's still in bed with her lover. But I'll allow you to speak to her again very soon, after you've completed your next assignment."

"I want to speak to her now."

"It is not going to happen today. I don't want her upset, not today of all days. She and her partner are participating in her first hunt. It should be quite an experience for her. I'd much rather her speak to you after she's lived through such an exciting adventure."

"If anything happens to her—"

"You'll do nothing. You can't save her. You have no idea where she is. But I promise you that I'll do what I can to keep her alive for as long as possible, but only if you continue to follow my instructions."

Malcolm loved being able to make Griff squirm, and one day soon he would make the big man beg. For years now, his ultimate goal had been to acquire enough power to humble the great Griffin Powell and exact revenge against him and Sanders and Yvette for what they had done on Amara.

"What do you want from me now?" Griff asked.

"I want you to go to Amara."

"Why?"

"I have my reasons. And I don't want you to go alone. I want you to take Sanders with you on a sentimental journey."

"And what do we do once we are there?"

"Remember the past."

"We don't need to go to Amara in order to remember," Griffin said.

"Humor me." Malcolm smiled. "Leave today, as soon as possible. I'd like you to arrive by sometime tomorrow morning. I want you to stay at the hotel you had built on the site of my old home. I'll contact you in a few days with further instructions. Oh, and one more thing—I want Sanders to take Barbara Jean Hughes with him."

"And if we refuse?"

Malcolm laughed. "I don't think you'll do that, will you, knowing what is at stake if you refuse my request?"

Outfitted in loose-fitting khaki cargo pants and an oversized long-sleeve shirt, Nic sat down on the wooden bench beside Jonas to lace up her hiking boots.

"No matter what happens today, stay with me," he said. "I've participated in a couple of hunts here at this compound in the past. Although the jungle changes constantly, there are only a limited number of acres on York's estate and they're surrounded by the river on three sides and guarded around the clock on the remaining side. There's water and food, if you know where to find them. And this is far from my first hunt. If you'll trust me, I promise that I'll make sure you survive."

When she glanced up at Jonas, he tossed her a small amber bottle. "Rub this on your face and neck and hands and anywhere else you can."

She uncorked the bottle, took a whiff of the foul-smelling liquid, and frowned. "What is this stuff?"

"It's the native version of mosquito repellent. Old Pepe, one of the groundskeepers, slipped it to me. He sort of owed me a favor."

Without a word of protest, Nic poured a handful of the atrocious concoction into her palm and hurriedly spread it over her face and neck.

"Out there where we're going the mosquitoes are huge and vicious," Jonas told her. "I've come off these hunts looking like I have measles."

Despite the seriousness of the situation, Nic managed to smile.

Jonas picked up the cotton slouch hat lying between them on the bench and put it on her head. "It's going to be hot and humid and muddy after all the rain. You're going to get awfully tired so we'll rest when we can, but if I say we keep going, that means we don't stop for anything. They'll send us out before noon and give us about a thirty-minute head start before the hunters begin tracking us."

411

Before Nic could reply, movement near the barn doors caught her attention. Four armed guards escorted three other couples inside, each of the six people outfitted with boots, hats, and khaki pants and shirts. Anyone seeing them from a distance wouldn't be able to tell them apart. They would all look alike, including Jonas and her. One set of captives consisted of a woman and a man; the other duos were comprised only of men.

"Looks like we're not the only captives being hunted today," Jonas said. "Two hunters and eight quarry. I'll take those odds. My guess is that York wants to give you more than a fighting chance to stay alive."

"What about the others?" Nic asked. "There's another woman over there and she looks awfully young and scared and she's about half my size."

Jonas's expression hardened as he grasped her shoulders. "When the hunt begins, you can't worry about anybody except for yourself and your partner. Staying alive until nightfall is your only goal. It doesn't matter what happens to anyone else. If you forget that fact for one minute, you're in trouble."

For a split second Nic hated Jonas for what he'd said. He'd sounded so cruel and heartless. But common sense quickly replaced sentiment and she understood the necessity of setting aside human decency and compassion. Today she would become an animal being stalked by human predators determined to kill her. At the end of the day, no matter what she had to do, she had to be among the survivors, she and her baby.

"I understand," Nic said.

He nodded and loosened his tight grip on her shoulders.

A few minutes later, Vartan entered the barn and, speaking Spanish, issued orders to the guards. They quickly rounded up the four teams and herded them into the central courtyard in front of the house. Nic kept her gaze down as she stood by Jonas, her hands clammy and her pulse racing.

When she heard York's voice, she glanced up, but kept her head lowered. Two men flanked York, both relatively young, one tall and fair and handsome, the other short, stocky, and dark, with the face only a mother could love. Each sported a shiny new rifle. Nic thought they were Ruger M77s, no doubt provided by York, but she'd need to inspect the weapons more closely to be a hundred percent sure. And she sure hoped she didn't get close enough to either hunter to find out anything else about his weapon.

York and his guests chatted, their laughter at odds with the impending horrors the eight captives would soon face. At that moment, Nic thought about Griff and what it must have been like for him on Amara before each terrifying hunt. How had he managed to survive for four years?

Suddenly, Vartan shouted as he held up a

413

revolver, aiming it toward the cleared pathway that led into the dense forest. "The hunt begins now." He fired the gun.

Without hesitation, Nic followed Jonas onto the pathway, running as fast as possible. He stayed several feet ahead of her, but within sight at all times. The other six captives lagged behind, but two of the men were catching up quickly. For what seemed like days but was probably only an hour or so, Nic ran until her lungs ached, her feet throbbed, and her mouth felt parched. Jonas had kept them on the narrow pathway that snaked crookedly through the forest while the others had veered off into the jungle.

When she reached the point where she doubted she had the strength to continue, Jonas slowed his pace, reached back, grabbed her arm, and brought her to an abrupt standstill. Staring at him, she opened her mouth to speak, but he slapped his hand over her mouth and shook his head. She nodded, understanding that she shouldn't make a sound.

Jonas led her slowly through a dense thicket of verdant foliage, their bodies pressing against the limbs, stretching them to the breaking point. Smothered by the oppressive heat and the cocooning coppice, Nic tried to ignore the panic rising inside her. Sunlight shimmered randomly high above them, the majority of light blocked by the towering trees, with only shards of shadowy illumination dotting the undergrowth beneath their feet.

Nic struggled to keep up as Jonas took her farther away from the cleared pathway. Just as she began to wonder how long they would be trapped in the lush tropical weald, the thicket gradually cleared enough so that she could see the savage beauty all around her and hear something other than her own frantic heartbeat. Forest insects hummed, the unique sounds blending together to create background music for the jungle. In a nearby tree, a couple of colorful parrots fluttered their wings and higher up a spider monkey swung from one limb to another.

Jonas slowed as he approached a shallow stream trickling smoothly over large slick rocks. He motioned silently to her and then knelt down on the muddy ground by the stream. He cupped his hands, delved them into the water, and brought the water up to his mouth. Nic joined him, grateful not only for the chance to catch her breath, but to be able to quench her thirst.

Without warning, Jonas grabbed her upper arm, hauled her to her feet and placed his index finger in the center of his lips, signaling silence. Her gaze shot from side to side as she listened for whatever sound had alerted Jonas to danger. The crackle of breaking limbs and the dull thud of footsteps plodding over the gray, mud-soaked earth warned them that someone was nearby.

Was it a fellow captive running for his life or one of the hunters tracking his prey?

Jonas pulled her along with him away from the stream and through a small grove of Podocarpus trees, several reaching over sixty feet high. As the approaching footsteps drew closer, Jonas pushed Nic up against the three-foot-round tree trunk, fluted and twisted with age. With his lean body pressed protectively against her, her chin touching his shoulder, they waited. Silently. Barely breathing.

The footsteps halted.

Oh, God, had one of the hunters tracked them and now knew where they were? Was it only a matter of minutes, perhaps seconds, before he aimed his rifle directly at them? Once he had them in his sights, running would be futile. You couldn't outrun a bullet.

The explosive rifle shot thundered through the jungle. A single human cry followed. And then another gunshot.

Nic clamped her teeth together, effectively trapping the scream vibrating in her throat. It took her a full minute to realize that neither she nor Jonas had been hit. She snapped her gaze up and connected with his. They shared an unspoken "poor soul" thought and yet at the same time she knew he was as grateful as she that they had not been the targets, that they were still alive.

CHAPTER 28

The Powell jet took off shortly after one that afternoon, their final destination Amara. The small South Pacific island had once been the scene of bloody, inhuman atrocities perpetrated by a group of extremely wealthy, supercilious monsters. Now the island was a vacationer's paradise, with a luxury resort complex overlooking the ocean.

Even though she had not been included in York's invitation, Yvette had insisted on going with them to Amara.

"Whatever he has planned for you and Sanders, I should be there with you, to help you if possible," she had told Griff when he'd tried to talk her out of coming with them.

Realizing how important it was to Yvette, Griff had finally allowed her to join them; but he suspected that her presence wouldn't be required. York had already put her through her trial of fire in England where her hopes of finding her long-lost child had been brutally destroyed. So now it was Sanders's turn. Griff didn't know what York had planned for Sanders, but he suspected it would somehow involve the two women he loved. Yvette's child was her Achilles' heel; Sanders's weaknesses were his memories of Elora and his affection for Barbara Jean.

Griff opened his laptop, intending to spend the next few hours going through all the updated information from Powell headquarters concerning their ongoing search for Nic. But before he tapped the first key, Sanders sat beside him.

"Barbara Jean is napping," he told Griff. "She has not been sleeping well lately."

"I'm truly sorry that she's being dragged into my fight with York."

"Our fight," Sanders corrected him. "If this man is intent on avenging Malcolm York's death, then Yvette and I are equally guilty of his murder. Perhaps I am more guilty than either of you since I formulated the plan to kill him."

"But I'm the one who chopped off the bastard's head."

"Enough guilt for all of us, right?"

"More than enough."

Neither of them spoke again for several minutes. Griff thought of Nic. Always Nic. And he knew that Sanders was thinking of Elora. Always Elora.

Finally breaking their silence, Sanders said, "If only we could figure out who the fake York really is."

"If only," Griff agreed. "But knowing that he has to be someone with a connection to the real York, someone who knew him and admired him, perhaps even loved him, hasn't helped us discover his true identity."

"Is it possible that someone actually loved such a monster?"

"Another monster."

"All of York's closest friends are dead now, everyone except Yves Bouchard," Sanders said. "But we've ruled out Bouchard. Rafe has seen the man recently. Whoever is impersonating York has gone to the trouble of having cosmetic surgery to alter his appearance."

"He has York's face."

"And I suspect he is as psychotically evil as his namesake."

"Kroy Enterprises was formed five years ago," Griff said.

"Harlan Benecroft and Yves Bouchard were two of the major investors."

"Along with Malcolm York."

"Which probably means that the pseudo-York came into existence around that same time."

"I thought so, too, but so far no evidence has come to light to substantiate that theory," Sanders said. "Benecroft and Bouchard could have simply used York's name when they founded Kroy Enterprises. But we have nothing that irrefutably proves the reincarnated York came into existence precisely five years ago. He could have been around years before that or—"

"Or he could have come to life only a couple of years ago when we first heard the rumors about Malcolm York being alive."

"There are too many variables in the York equation. The only thing we know for certain is that he is not the real Malcolm York. We do not know this man's true identity and we do not know how he was connected to York. We can speculate about when he became the resurrected York, but we cannot pinpoint a year."

"And we don't know whether he is the man in charge and is the one pulling the strings or if someone else is the mastermind and he simply chose a willing participant to undergo facial reconstructive surgery and take on the role of Malcolm York."

"If that's the case, then the man's true identity is relatively unimportant."

"What does your gut tell you?" Griff asked.

"The same as yours, I imagine—that this York is no one's puppet."

"I think he really wants to be Malcolm York."

"Yes, I agree," Sanders said.

"Maybe he already believes he is the real York."

The deserted thatch-roofed hut looked inviting, a place to escape from the oppressive late-afternoon heat, but Nic knew it was a deadly trap. Without slowing down, she kept pace with Jonas as he avoided the partial clearing and stayed inside the relative safety of the woods. Every muscle in Nic's body screamed in pain, reminding her how badly she needed rest. The blisters on her feet had burst, leaving raw flesh rubbing against her cotton socks. Even though she had reapplied the native mosquito repellent, dozens of the bloodthirsty little beasts had left red marks on her skin, itchy bites that begged to be scratched. Pausing long enough to catch her breath, she gazed straight up, searching the patch of visible sky through the canopy of treetops. She couldn't see the sun, but she did see streaks of scarlet and fuchsia overlaying the azure blue and suspected that daylight would soon be fading. Wildflowers grew in profusion in the jungle. Patches of orange, red, white, and yellow blossoms had flashed by in her peripheral vision while she'd been on the run for what seemed like days on end. Jonas had known which flowers, which plants, which berries were edible and they had stopped several times during today's hunt to eat and replenish their strength. When he had eaten a variety of insects, Nic had passed on the offer to join him. She didn't think Baby Powell wanted nourishment from such wild delicacies.

Up ahead near the riverbank, Jonas stopped unexpectedly. From where Nic stood several feet away, all she saw was the flickering sunlight dancing on the water. Jonas glanced over his shoulder, held up his hand in a Stop signal, and then stepped back far enough for her to see the body lying facedown in the mud.

It's the young woman she had seen earlier that day.

Forcing herself to stay put instead of rushing forward to find out whether or not the girl was dead, Nic waited to see what Jonas intended to do. Using the tip of his boot, he nudged the small body. No sign of life. He inserted his foot under the woman's midsection and turned her over. Nic's stomach lurched when she saw that part of the pretty girl's face had been shot off.

Jonas motioned for Nic to back up and away from the river. Just as she took the first tentative steps backward, repetitive blasts of gunfire erupted downriver, probably less than a quarter of a mile away. Apparently one of the hunters was zeroing in on the dead woman's partner.

Every instinct Nic possessed urged her to help the other captives, but logic dictated her actions. There was nothing she could do to help anyone else. She would be lucky to end the day alive.

Nic turned and ran for her life.

Jonas caught up with her a few minutes later as they headed away from the direction of the gunfire. Without speaking, communicating with expressive looks and easily understood hand signals as they had done all day, not even a whispered word between them, they slowed their pace and trudged deeper into the forest. Nic longed for rest, but rest would have to wait. Jonas would let her know when he felt it was safe enough for them to stop.

She wondered how many captives were dead.

Two that she knew of, one from this morning and the woman by the river. Possibly three or more were dead now, after the recent shooting spree. Without any set rules to follow and no limit to the prey they could kill, the hunters wouldn't stop until the end of the day.

A two-word prayer replayed over and over in Nic's mind.

Hurry, sundown.

As darkness descended, the hum of the jet engines lulled Griff into a quiet, reflective state of mind. He glanced across the aisle where Sanders sat with Barbara Jean, his arm draped around her shoulders. Over an hour ago, Yvette had reclined her seat, closed her eyes, and was now either in deep meditation or she had fallen asleep.

Tomorrow morning, they would arrive on Amara. Griffin had visited the island on a number of occasions during the construction of the resort complex, but he had not been back there for more than five years. He had leveled York's spacious, sprawling mansion overlooking the ocean as well as the dungeonlike prison where the slaves had been kept. Every semblance of Malcolm York had been wiped off the face of Amara. Everything except the graveyard.

After killing York and escaping sixteen years ago, neither Sanders nor Yvette had ever returned. Each of them dealt with the past in their own way. Griff had chosen to face the demons and dared them to destroy him. He had fought the debilitat-ing memories, had conquered his fears, and had found happiness with the woman he loved. Ironic that York's "ghost" possessed the power to take away the one thing he now treasured above all else.

Without Nic, he had no life.

When he found her and brought her home . . . ?

He would take her to his island where they had spent their honeymoon, where earlier this year, they had made love day and night, reaffirming their commitment to each other. But even then, rumors circulating in Europe about Malcolm York had concerned him.

Six years ago when Griff had purchased the Caribbean island, both Sanders and Yvette had questioned his reasons for doing so. He wasn't sure either of them would ever understand. Owning the island, remodeling the old manor house, and creating good memories there had been one way in which he had tried to overcome the past. What happened on Amara had taken away a part of his soul that he could never recapture. In some odd way, being able to enjoy spending time on another island, one that he owned, that he controlled, proved to him that he could conquer the horrific memories of Amara.

Either you conquer the bad memories or they conquer you.

When he found Nic and brought her home, would she ever be able to conquer her memories of being York's captive?

Falling in love with Nic, refusing to give her up, and then marrying her had put her at risk. Only at the time, he hadn't known just how terrible that risk would be. From the very beginning of their relationship, he had been selfish. He had never been in love before, had never needed a woman the way he'd needed Nic. If only he had known then the price she would pay for loving him, for being his wife, he would have given her up for her own sake.

He could still hear York's voice taunting him. *"I'm afraid your wife is unavailable at the moment. She's still in bed with her lover."*

If Nic had been forced to have sex with another man, Griffin knew they were not lovers, no more than he and Yvette had been. But he also understood that, in time, Nic might bond with this man, as he had bonded with Yvette. The thought of another man touching her, having sex with her, sharing the horrors of captivity with her enraged Griff.

Now he truly understood how Nic must have felt when he had finally told her the complete truth about his relationship with Yvette.

If you're out there, God, please listen.

This man, whoever he is, help him protect Nic.

Griff ached deep inside. Deeper than his heart. Soul deep.

York had sent Nic out today, to be hunted down as if she were an animal. *I don't want her upset, not today of all days. She and her partner are participating in her first hunt. It should be quite an experience for her.*

Nic was smart. She was in excellent physical condition. She was a survivor. And York wouldn't want her to die this soon. Griff had to believe that all those pluses added up to Nic having a damn good chance of surviving the hunt and being alive at the end of the day.

At twilight, Nic found herself slowing her pace, but she didn't dare stop. If she stopped, she would fall to the ground and be unable to get back up on her feet. During their trek away from the hunters, Jonas had guided her through brambles and tall grass, under bushes and around trees, urging her on with backward glances. Now in the semi-darkness, she could barely see him up ahead of her, his broad shoulders silhouetted in the last rays of sunlight fighting through the tangled roof of treetop greenery.

If they could make it just a little while longer . . .

Nightfall was fast approaching.

And then in what seemed no more than minutes, darkness surrounded them and Nic could make out only Jonas's shape even though he was only a couple of feet ahead of her.

Suddenly she heard the trickle of water. But being unable to see beyond her outstretched hands, she could not immediately locate the source. Something told her that they had circled around the compound and were now back near the stream ambling down the low, sloping hillside. Unexpectedly, Jonas reached out, grasped her wrist and pulled her along with him. Grateful that he had found the stream and was pausing for a drink, she knelt beside him. He lifted his cupped hands to her mouth and poured water onto her parched lips. He repeated the process several times, and then placed his mouth close to her ear.

"Look up," he whispered.

Craning her neck backward, she lifted her gaze toward heaven. Countless stars twinkled above them in the vast night sky, like pinpricks of light shining through a piece of black velvet.

What an amazing sight.

Jonas pulled her down beside him onto the damp earth and put his arm around her. She settled against him, thankful for his support. The buzzing chorus of what had to be a million crickets serenaded them.

"It's nightfall," he told her. "The hunt has ended and we're still alive."

Nic slid her arms around him and buried her face in his shoulder. She wanted to cry. She wanted to laugh. She wanted Griff to be the one holding her. But she was far too exhausted to laugh or cry. And with Griff thousands of miles away, she took comfort in the arms of Jonas MacColl.

CHAPTER 29

Four days at the Paradise Resort without a word from York. Four days of waiting. Griffin divided his time between tending to business and marathon walks every morning and evening. Yvette had not left the hotel since their arrival, but she had joined Sanders, Barbara Jean, and him for dinner each evening. Sanders had done the exact opposite. He had escorted Barbara Jean on afternoon excursions to explore the island, but they had not ventured out alone. Two of the six Powell agents temporarily assigned to bodyguard duty on Amara went with Sanders and Barbara Jean whenever they left the hotel.

Half a dozen photos of Nic lay spread out on the dining room table in Griff's penthouse suite. Afternoon sunshine flooded the room through the wall of windows overlooking the ocean. The light shimmered across the photos, spotlighting them with a bright sheen. As much as he had wanted to rip the pictures into shreds and burn them, he couldn't. The candid snapshots, no doubt taken by one of York's flunkies on his command, were all he had to prove that Nic was still alive. He loved the photographs as much as he hated them.

Griff downed the last drops of the water in the bottle he'd been nursing for the past half hour while he had been conducting business via telephone and e-mail. He had been able to delegate a great deal to others, but some matters required his personal attention. Employees around the world depended on the large network of Powell corporations for their livelihood. He had people counting on him, people Nic would not want him to let down while he was scouring the globe for her.

Those damn photos called to Griff as if they possessed some type of magic power. He should have stuffed them in an envelope and locked them in the safe, not left them nearby where they posed a constant temptation.

Slamming shut his laptop, he cursed under his breath. Frustration had begun eating away at him, the waiting and not knowing like droplets of acid dripping continuously into his mind. But that was what York wanted—for Griff to go slowly but surely out of his mind.

He shoved back the desk chair and stood, took several deep, huffing breaths, and crossed the room. Standing by the dining table, he stared at the photos. He reached down and picked up the one of Nic with York, apparently taken the night after Nic's first hunt. She looked exhausted, her expression blank, her face streaked with dirt and perspiration, her clothes filthy and tattered. York stood beside her, a rifle strapped across his shoulder, a triumphant smile on his face.

Goddamn it, he looked just like the real Malcolm York. Whoever had given him his new face had been a talented surgeon.

Griff's gaze zeroed in on Nic's hand clasped in York's as he held their arms up in a gesture evoking "the winner and today's survivor" for the camera.

There on the third finger of her left hand was her engagement ring. Odd that York allowed her to wear it.

Griff kept Nic's wedding band anchored just above the knuckle on his pinky, the only finger the ring would fit. Using his thumb, he twisted the ring around and around, remembering the day he had placed it on Nic's finger.

Their wedding day.

Nic hadn't wanted a big fancy wedding. He could have given her a wedding fit for a princess, but that wasn't what she'd wanted.

"I had the white gown, the bridesmaids, and the flower girls when I married Greg," she'd told him. "I was young and starry-eyed and put more thought into the wedding than I did the marriage. With you, it's different. I'm different."

And so they had gotten married in a little chapel in Gatlinburg. Barbara Jean and Sanders had been their witnesses. And they had spent their wedding night in a rental cabin, the one he had eventually bought as a gift for her, the same cabin where she had gone the day she left him.

If he could go back to their wedding day or the day before or the night he had proposed, he would tell her everything about Amara and his relationship with Yvette. If he could do it all over again, he wouldn't keep any secrets from Nic. But there were no do-overs in this life. You got one chance to get it right.

Griff laid down the photo he held and carefully chose another, looked at it, and then took his time studying the other four. All the snapshots were of Nic. One with York and two with the man York insisted was her lover taken the night after the hunt. Three were of Nic alone and apparently taken before the hunt, perhaps several days before. The last photo he looked at, the one he couldn't put down, showed Nic, wearing shorts and a halter top, sitting on a wooden bench. She wore no makeup, her hair was pulled back in a loose ponytail, and although she faced the photographer, she appeared to be looking beyond the camera, her thoughts far away.

Had she been thinking about him? Had she been wondering why he hadn't found her, why he hadn't rescued her? Or had she been remembering the two of them together, just as he was doing right now? Had she been thinking about the first time they made love? Their wedding night? Their honeymoon?

There had been a lot of women in Griff's life, before he'd been abducted and shipped off to Amara and in the years after his escape from York's hellhole.

He remembered some of the women, recalled several with fondness, and had genuinely liked many of them. But until Nicole Bellamy Baxter had stormed into his life with her take-no-prisoners attitude, he'd had no idea what it felt like to need a woman the way he needed air to breathe. From the moment they first met, they had mixed like oil and water. She had disliked him on sight, both personally and professionally. And although he'd found her undeniably attractive, he had figured her for a ball-bashing bitch.

As an FBI agent, Nic had been all about law and order, following the rules, doing everything by the book. Griff, by his very nature, was a rebel— always had been and always would be. He lived by his own rules and did whatever was necessary to see justice served. They had locked horns more than once whenever the Powell Agency had taken an interest in one of the bureau's cases.

And then the inevitable had happened.

He would never forget the night they made love for the first time. Every detail, every word, every touch, every sensation was imprinted on his brain.

"It'll just be sex," she'd told him.

"Sure, honey. Whatever you say."

But it hadn't been just sex for them, not that night, not ever.

He never forgot to use a condom, but he'd forgotten that night. Afterward, they had been concerned that she might be pregnant. But it hadn't happened. Now, he almost wished it had. After they'd been married for a while, they had decided they wanted a child, but try as they might, Nic hadn't conceived.

Considering the hostility they had felt when they first met, who would have ever thought they would wind up madly, passionately in love, married, and wanting children? He wasn't sure who had been the most surprised by that turn of events. Nic or him?

"God, woman, I love you," Griff said aloud. "Whatever you do, don't give up. I'll find you. I swear I'll find you."

Once again, Nic had no idea where she was. They had left the jungle compound yesterday morning and the jet had landed at a private airstrip shortly before dawn. Neither Jonas nor their trainer, Vartan, had traveled with her. She had tried questioning York about their destination and about Jonas, but he hadn't been forthcoming with information about either.

"You have experienced the thrill of the hunt," York had told her. "It is time for you to prepare yourself for the next phase of your captivity."

And that was all he had told her.

While still nighttime, York had whisked her from the airplane straight to a waiting limousine with shaded windows. Wherever they were, the climate certainly wasn't tropical. When she had deplaned, she had felt a definite chill in the air. She suspected they were in a big city somewhere. As the limo had zipped along a well-paved road, they had passed through block after block of well-lit streets. After at least a thirty-minute drive, the car had pulled up in front of an old house on the outskirts of town, a two-story stone-and-brick residence flanked on either side by what appeared to be deserted buildings. Upon entering the house, York had turned her over to a stern, sullen-faced woman, whom Nic had suspected wouldn't hesitate to kill her if ordered to do so.

Nic had been confined to her room since their arrival, a small, dark room on the second floor. As soon as old Sourpuss had left her alone, she had explored the bedroom and the tiny connected bathroom with antiquated fixtures and no windows. And then she had checked out the single window in the bedroom, which she quickly discovered couldn't be opened. Numerous coats of paint over the years had glued the window permanently shut. At daylight, she had peered through the window in the hopes of figuring out where the house was located. No such luck. The only thing she'd been able to see was a garbage-strewn alley and the backside of other run-down buildings.

During the examination of her new quarters, she had discovered a basket filled with small bottles of water and juice and a loaf of crusty whole grain bread. The corner armoire, a seen-better-days antique, had been empty. Apparently there was no heat in the house, at least not upstairs in her room. She had pulled a blanket off the bed and wrapped it around her shoulders, plopped down in the single chair in the room, and curled her feet up and under her on the ratty floral cushion.

She must have fallen asleep for quite some time. Glowing sunlight now swept over the room, casting pale shadows on the dingy walls and brightening the rough wooden floors. Every instinct she possessed urged her to rebel, to scream and pound on the door or to break out the window, tie the bedsheets together, and escape. But common sense reminded her that acting irrationally would only get her killed. No doubt York had the front and back entrances guarded, so risking her life to climb out the window and possibly make it down into the alley would be futile. Screaming and pounding on the door would be stupid and gain her absolutely nothing, but a sore throat and bruised fists.

Admit it, you got used to having Jonas around all the time, to never being alone. You can't let solitary confinement make you stir-crazy. It's probably part of York's master plan. He wants to unbalance you by changing tactics, taking you from semi-luxurious quarters in a tropical setting, with Jonas at your side 24/7, to a drab room in a colder climate, with you isolated and alone.

York's voice echoed inside her head, his last comment replaying repeatedly—". . . prepare yourself for the next phase of your captivity."

Did the "next phase of your captivity" mean The Ring or The Execution? Did it really matter? Unless Griff found a way to rescue her, she would face both eventually and each would end in someone's death.

But it damn well wasn't going to be her death. She was going to live!

Nic paced the floor, back and forth, back and forth. Her head ached. Her stomach fluttered. The stress created by her intolerable situation was getting to her. The stress was understandable, all things considered, but it was counterproductive, and perhaps even harmful.

Don't do this to yourself. Think about your baby.

How much longer would she be able to hide her pregnancy? By her own calculations she was between four and four and a half months. She had heard that women begin showing sooner with a second pregnancy, that often with a first baby you didn't look pregnant until you were close to six months. God, she hoped that would be true for her.

Her stomach fluttered again, as if a tiny butterfly had awakened inside her and was testing its wings. What an odd feeling.

Nic stopped in the center of the room, laid her hand over her belly, and gasped when she realized that her unborn child was moving inside her.

Oh my God!

Almost indiscernible little ripples pulsated with life, a life that she and Griff had created. Their baby.

Tears gathered in Nic's eyes. Overwhelming emotion flooded her senses.

Damn it, she hated weepy women. She had prided herself on not being one of those silly, weak females who cried at the drop of a hat. But . . .

"Griff, I wish you were here to share this moment with me." Only she heard her soft, heartfelt whisper.

A peculiar feeling of contentment came over Nic suddenly, as if somehow she actually was sharing this moment with Griff. She walked over to the chair, picked up the discarded cotton blanket, wrapped it around her like a shawl, and curled up in the chair.

If only she had told him about their baby.

She had no idea why it had taken her years to conceive. She and Griff had undergone testing procedures only to be told there was no physical reason why Nic couldn't get pregnant.

The first time they had made love, neither of them had been in their right mind. They'd been wild for each other. They hadn't even made it to her bedroom. There had been no soft music, no candlelight and no sweet words of love. Only raw passion. Afterward, she had reminded herself that it had just been sex.

Nic smiled. Yeah, but it had been damn good sex.

She caressed her belly. "Your daddy is a wild man in bed. And he's told me I'm pretty wild, too." She laughed. "That's not something you'll ever hear me say when you're old enough to understand."

With her arms wrapped protectively around her middle, Nic closed her eyes. She could almost feel Griff's big hands caressing her, his lips on hers, and then his tongue spiraling down her throat. She shivered.

"I love you, Griffin Powell. I swear that if I live through this captivity and make it back to you, I'll never leave your side ever again."

Sanders stood by the grave, his gaze riveted to the monument that Griffin had ordered erected years ago. He had stayed far away from Amara for the past sixteen years. And in the four days since they had returned, he had deliberately avoided coming to this small cemetery where his wife and son were buried. He was here now, at Barbara Jean's insistence.

"You have to go," she had told him. "Don't you think Elora would want you to say good-bye to them?"

"I said good-bye a long time ago."

"I don't think you did."

Standing here this afternoon, with memories whirling around him like hovering spirits, he knew Barbara Jean had been right. He had never said good-bye, had never let go. He had kept Elora alive in his heart all these years, leaving no room for anyone else. And yet, he still couldn't cut the ties that bound him to his wife. He reached out and laid his hand on top of the white polished marble stone. Even in the warmth of tropical Amara, the monument felt cold to the touch.

He had asked Barbara Jean to come with him, but she had insisted he visit Elora's grave without her. His bodyguard waited a discreet distance away at the front entrance to the cemetery, giving him the privacy he needed to be alone with Elora . . . and their son.

He thought of his wife often, kept her pictured in his mind as she had been the first time he saw her. Young, beautiful, carefree. But he seldom thought of the child, their child. A little boy, born too soon to survive in this hard, cruel world. York had allowed him to see the baby, tiny little thing, so small he could have fit in the palm of Sanders's hand. And yet perfectly formed. Ten fingers. Ten toes. Angelic features so like Elora's.

Sanders knelt by the graveside, his eyes dry, his heart gripped with unbearable pain. He stared at the dates and the inscriptions and an excerpt from a love poem chiseled into the face of the stone.

Elora Sanders, beloved wife of Damar Sanders
Infant Boy Sanders
I love thee with the breath, smiles, tears,
of all my life!—and, if God choose,
I shall but love thee better after death.

Yvette had chosen the poem. He vaguely recalled having told her that Elizabeth Barrett Browning had been Elora's favorite poet.

As he placed his hand on the grave, his mind whispered the final line of the poem. *And if God so choose, I shall love thee better after death.*

"I still love you," he said aloud.

And I love you, my darling. He heard her voice as plainly as if she were at his side, a voice from the grave, from the haunting memories that consoled him. She would never leave him.

Sanders rose to his feet. He wouldn't come here again. Elora was not here. She was in his heart, a part of him forever.

As he turned to walk away, he caught a flash of movement in his peripheral vision. Something or someone had slipped behind a nearby palm tree.

"Who's there?" he called.

No response.

Perhaps it had been an animal of some sort. He walked toward the enormous old tree, its large fronds gently rustling in the balmy breeze off the nearby ocean. As a woman ran out from behind the tree and rushed away from Sanders, he caught a whiff of her delicately scented perfume.

It couldn't be. His senses were playing a trick on him. He only thought he could smell Elora's perfume.

Acting on impulse, he followed the woman who managed to keep at least twenty feet ahead of him. She was slender and petite, her shoulder-length reddish blond hair shimmering in the sunlight.

"Wait," he called out to her.

She seemed not to have heard him.

His mind was playing tricks on him. Just because he had thought he smelled Elora's perfume . . . just because the woman reminded him of Elora . . .

Sanders walked faster, trying to catch up with her. He called out to her again just as she reached the iron gate on the far side of the small cemetery. And then just as she opened the gate and walked out onto the crowded street, she paused and turned and looked at him.

It was Elora!

But that was not possible. This woman could not be his Elora.

"Elora." He cried her name.

She ran away before Sanders could reach her. He stood by the open gate and searched the busy street. She had simply disappeared.

His bodyguard caught up with him. "Mr. Sanders, are you all right?"

"I am . . . yes, I am all right. I thought I saw someone I knew."

Whoever the young woman was, she was not Elora. Just because she had been wearing Elora's perfume . . . just because she looked like Elora . . .

He had been thinking of his wife, remembering her, and he had allowed himself to see what he wanted to see. There was no other possible explanation.

CHAPTER 30

Ten days in solitary confinement had taken a toll on Nic. She had seen no one except old Sourpuss, who had brought a basket of food items to her every morning. But as she marked off the days, counting sunrises each morning, she had reminded herself that there were much worse fates than being alone. Little had she known just how prophetic that thought would be.

Nic looked at the costume Sourpuss had delivered, along with specific instructions. "You are to bathe and then dress in those garments. Do so immediately."

She had showered, washed and dried her hair, and left her dirty clothes lying on the bathroom floor. Now, standing naked by the bed, she picked up the first item of clothing. Initially, she thought it was a blouse or jacket of thin white cotton, but after slipping it on, realized it was meant to be a dress. The material was soft to the touch and so sheer that it was almost transparent. The gold braid-edged hem fell to mere inches below her butt and the one-shoulder bodice had been constructed so that her left breast remained uncovered. No matter how she rearranged the material, even flipping the dress from front to back, it had not altered the configuration. If she wore it backward, her right breast was bare.

The other items lying on the bed were not technically garments. She picked up the two gold armbands and snapped each around a bicep. The next item was a pair of gold-studded, fingerless white leather gloves. She laid them aside and lifted a gold helmet, amazed at how lightweight it was. It set on her head like a hat, sculpted to reveal her ears, leave her entire face visible, her forehead untouched, and it draped around the base of her head in the back.

My God, was she supposed to be decked out as if she was going to a Halloween party? The dress was a provocative version of an ancient Greek gown and the armbands and helmet reminiscent of a female warrior.

Damn! That was it. York had sent her an Amazon Queen costume. That fact alone told her one thing—tonight was the night she would be introduced to The Ring. But where was Jonas? Wasn't he supposed to be her partner?

Nic ran her hand over her body, from full bare breast to the nicely camouflaged swell of her stomach. The dress's loose, flowing construction adequately hid her round, slightly protruding belly. At almost five months, she was fortunate not to be twice this size. But was she too small? Shouldn't she be showing more than she was? If the baby inside her wasn't moving occasionally, she would worry that something was wrong.

"Little one, I'll do everything I can to protect you tonight."

The bedroom door opened without warning. Nic expected to see Sourpuss, but instead of the prune-faced old woman entering, Anthony Linden strode into the room. She should have known that York would send his rabid alpha dog to get her.

"You look rather fetching," Linden said as his gaze slid over her, pausing to appreciate her large, naked breast. "I had forgotten just how voluptuous you are."

"I'm disappointed. I thought you'd never forget anything about me."

He glared at Nic. "Still have a smart mouth, I see. I'd have thought being hunted like an animal would have taken you down a peg or two. Apparently not.

444

Perhaps tonight's event will. You won't be running to survive. You'll be fighting to survive."

"I assume that means I'll be introduced to The Ring this evening." *Whatever you do, don't show him any fear. You know that you're scared half out of your mind, but he doesn't.*

"How astute of you." Linden grinned.

She hated his vicious smile.

"Mr. York is quite eager to see how well you perform," Linden said. "The tickets for tonight's event sold for ten thousand each and required an invitation from either Mr. York or one of his trusted friends. I'm told there will be a hundred and fifty people there tonight."

A hundred bloodthirsty people wanted to watch a fight to the death between two sets of warrior opponents and had paid dearly for that right. Nic knew she shouldn't be surprised by how viciously depraved some humans were, others like York and Bouchard whose wickedness set them apart from the average sicko.

"Put on your gloves, Amazon Queen," Linden told her. "We have a limousine waiting."

Nic picked up the gloves, slipped them on, and marched out of the room, her head held high as she prayed she wouldn't throw up all over her pretty little costume.

Griff's patience had run out days ago. They had been in Amara for nearly two weeks. No word from York. If the son of a bitch didn't contact him soon . . . He'd do what? York had him right where he wanted him. Caught by the short hairs and going slowly out of his mind. The waiting had gotten to them all, even the normally cheerful Barbara Jean and the ever calm and composed Yvette. But the person Griff worried about the most was Sanders.

"I saw a woman at the cemetery," Sanders had told him the first day he had visited his wife's grave. "I swear to you that she looked like Elora. I know my mind was playing tricks on me, but she was even wearing Elora's perfume."

If seeing the Elora look-alike had happened only once, Sanders could have chalked it up to a trick of the mind. But it had happened again at various places around the island. The second time had been at the hotel's Olympic-size swimming pool. The third time, the woman had been getting into a car that drove away from the hotel. And then it had happened again today. This time Griff had seen her, too. Sanders had joined Griff for his afternoon walk-off-steam jaunt away from the hotel, through the busy tourist market, and back around by the western beach. But each time the woman had appeared, she had disappeared before Sanders could reach her.

This evening, Griff had ordered dinner for four to be delivered to his suite. Not only did they need one another's companionship now more than ever, but they needed to demystify the Elora sightings. Griff and Sanders had a pretty good idea what was going on, but Sanders hadn't discussed their theory with Barbara Jean.

"I think you should return to Griffin's Rest," Griff told Yvette. "There's nothing you can do here except waste your time. That seems to be all we're doing."

"I would prefer to stay," she replied. "After all, how much longer can he make us wait? He is simply building up the tension so that he can make a big production of issuing you the next challenge. Like the real York, this man seems to love the dramatic."

"Do as you please," Griff said. "I can't leave nor can Sanders and Barbara Jean. We're trapped here until York decides it's time to end the waiting game."

"We have a delicious meal waiting for us." Barbara Jean indicated the feast spread out on the dining table, and then picked up the open bottle of merlot and poured the rich, red liquid into four glasses. "I'm hoping we can get through one meal without any mention of York."

Sanders reached over and grasped her hand. She snapped her head around and stared at him, and when he said nothing, she burst into tears.

"Please, don't . . . " Sanders rose from his seat, leaned over Barbara Jean's wheelchair, and put his arms around her.

She pushed him away and buried her face in her hands.

"This is York's doing," Sanders said. "The woman who looks like Elora. He sent her here to torment me. It's all part of his elaborate scheme."

"Sanders and I agree on this," Griffin said. "In some way, this phantom Elora is part of whatever York has planned for us here on Amara."

Barbara Jean lifted her head, brushed the tears from her face, and looked at Griff. "I'm not sure I can do this, whatever it is. I thought I could, but . . . "

Sanders's hand hovered over Barbara Jean's shoulder, but he did not touch her. His gaze met Griff's and Griff felt his old friend's pain and frustration.

Sanders was a man torn between the past and the present, between the ghost of the woman he loved and the flesh-and-blood woman who loved him.

"You can do whatever needs to be done," Griff told Barbara Jean. "You'll do it for Nicole, not for me or for Sanders."

Barbara Jean looked right at Griff. "You're right. I'll do whatever I have to do to help Nic."

Griff smiled. "I know you will. That's why we're all here, allowing York to torment us with the waiting and the not knowing. None of us are in a good place mentally or emotionally."

"Thank you for trying to make me feel better." She returned his smile. "I'm afraid I've lost my appetite." She wheeled herself away from the table. "I think I'll go back to my room and rest for a while."

"I will go with you," Sanders said.

"No, you stay here," she told him. "I'd like some time alone."

The moment Barbara Jean's bodyguard closed the outer door of Griff's penthouse suite, Sanders slammed his right fist into the palm of his left hand. "It is this goddamn fucking island. It's cursed. That's why he made us come back here."

"The island is not cursed," Yvette said. "We are."

Rafe Byrne had watched the first gladiatorial battle with cold detachment, feeling little sympathy for the competitors and only a vague interest in the spectacle. As Sir Harlan's guest, he was one of a select group attending tonight's debacle—the slaughter of two human beings by two superior combatants. He was present tonight for one reason and one reason only and that was to further ingratiate himself to Benecroft.

The first event had pitted two men against two other men, each in costume, the pairs equally matched. They had fought for nearly an hour, with a three-minute rest period every fifteen minutes. The match had ended with all four men wounded, but no one dead.

The ringmaster made an announcement, explaining that since there was no obvious winner—no one dead—the guests would be allowed to choose which couple lived and which couple died. Within minutes the decision was made, the spectators obviously having a clear favorite. The winners stepped aside as four guards entered the ring and forced the losers onto their knees. Holding each man in place with his head yanked backward, the guards then motioned to the winners to strike their deadly blows. A chant rose up from the observers and grew louder and louder with each passing second.

Kill. Kill. Kill.

While the audience's excitement built into a frenzy of anticipation, their voices shaking the rafters, the champions plunged small stilettos into the doomed participants' jugulars. As the blood gushed, spraying the guards and the champions, the crowd went wild with shouts and cheers.

"Quite a show, my boy, quite a show." Sir Harlan slapped Rafe on the back. "Didn't I tell you that you'd love it? Nothing like it to get the juices flowing."

Rafe forced a smile.

"I have arranged for us to meet Bouchard for a late-night snack after tonight's main event. We'll have our pick of some choice little tidbits."

"You're always the consummate host, Sir Harlan."

The old bastard laughed with gusto, enjoying himself immensely.

"I didn't know that Monsieur Bouchard was here tonight," Rafe said.

"He arrived back in London only this morning. Came in for tonight's entertainment." Harlan indicated with a wave of his hand, his index finger halfway pointing the direction, where Bouchard could be located. "Yves has a front-row seat. He relishes an occasional blood splatter. I've heard him remark how much he enjoys the smell of fear and excitement that he can experience only if he's close to the ring."

Rafe's gaze followed the trajectory of Benecroft's finger as he searched for Bouchard. Sitting in the center front row, the debonair Frenchman threw back his head and laughed at something his companion had said. The man sitting beside Bouchard cocked his head to one side, giving Rafe a clear view of his face. For a split second Rafe didn't believe his own eyes.

It can't be!

He stared at the man's familiar face.

It is him. It's Malcolm York.

Nic heard the roar from the spectators, sounding more like a thousand onlookers than a mere one hundred. Since Linden had brought her down into the underground auditorium, she had been kept secluded in a small holding room. And then a few minutes ago, two muscular guards had escorted her to the double doors leading into the entertainment chamber. Two sets of crescent-shaped rows of deluxe theater seats circled a raised center stage that resembled a huge boxing ring. As she watched the murders of two captives condemned by the ruthlessly cruel audience, another set of brawny guards directed her partner to stand at her side. When she glanced his way, she almost smiled.

Jonas MacColl, also in costume, stood on her left.

They shared a brief look, each conveying to the other how good it was to be together again, to know they were both still alive.

"You two are the main attraction this evening," one of the guards told them. "You had better put on a good show if you want to live to fight again."

All four guards laughed.

The frenetic celebrations in the auditorium gradually quieted to a low rumble as the bloody bodies of the defeated were dragged out of the ring and straight past Nic and Jonas. Following closely behind, the match's champions treaded quietly, their heads bowed. It was only then that Nic noticed the two people she assumed were their opponents, a woman and a man in costumes, standing on the opposite side of the massive double doors. The woman's gaze met Nic's and they shared a moment of mutual fear and sympathy. Both of them knew that in only a few minutes they would have to try to kill each other.

Mercy God in heaven, help me.

Nic did not want to kill anyone, except maybe York and Linden, but certainly not this willowy blonde with frightened blue eyes.

"Showtime," one of the guards said.

"Let's go." Another gave Nic a rough nudge.

Jonas grabbed her elbow as they were led across the brick floor and into the theater. To avoid looking at the rowdy crowd, Nic shifted her gaze from her partner to the spotlighted ring and then up to the plaster ceiling above them. A chill settled over her when she saw that more than two dozen iron hooks hung from the rafters.

What was this place? Or what had it once been?

Leaning close to her ear, Jonas said. "Survive at all costs. It's going to be kill or be killed."

The assembly of barbaric thrill seekers cheered as she and Jonas and the other couple were taken to opposite sides of the ring and led up separate sets of stairs. As the announcer introduced them, Nic noted that their costumes somewhat fit their ring names. Khan wore dark trousers, a wide leather belt, a triangle-shaped helmet trimmed in fur and was bare-chested. White Witch was decked out in white bikini briefs, a white pointed hat, and a white knee-length cape that tied at the neck and left the woman's breasts bare. Mountain Man, aka Jonas, wore ragged cut-off jeans, secured with rope instead of a belt, and a red bandanna tied around his neck. His head was bare and his long hair looked as if it had been combed with an eggbeater.

The first fifteen-minute round was unarmed combat. Fists and feet. Within a few minutes, Nic realized how ill-equipped her opponent was for this type of fight. She fought like a girl—scratching, biting, and pulling hair. Although those tactics could be effective if properly applied, it took Nic all of five minutes to put White Witch flat on her back and subdue her in a chokehold. The onlookers yelled for Nic to kill her adversary. Shouts of "Strangle the bitch" reverberated in the stylish decorated underground hall. Apparently Jonas and his opponent were more equally matched and at the end of the first segment, both men had bloody mouths and were battered bodies.

During their brief break, when they were given water to drink, Jonas grasped Nic's wrist. "You'll be fighting Khan next. Use whatever skills you have to kick his ass."

I'll be fighting Khan? Crap. Holy crap.

Nic didn't have time to think about White Witch, although she knew that Jonas would have no trouble handling her. She was too damn busy trying to keep Khan from landing a body blow. If she wasn't pregnant, a fist to her gut would hurt like hell and knock her to the floor, but if Khan landed a blow to her stomach, it could injure her baby. She managed to use some fancy footwork to avoid being hit—at least for several all-important minutes. She moved forward and then back, took a side step, and then circled. But she could avoid her enemy's blows for only so long. She was playing defense, but soon she'd have to go into offense mode.

Khan threw a straight punch. Nic threw a hook to his forearm and followed with several punches to his midsection. Having taken him off guard, she quickly followed up with a jab to his groin. While he doubled over in pain, she moved in close enough to stomp his toes. He hollered several obscenities, sucked in enough air to drain a ten-by-ten room, and then came at her with rage in his eyes.

Apparently Khan knew some karate moves, but she could tell he was far from being a pro. But then so was she. She knew the basics, enough to defend herself, but not having used her martial arts skills in a good while, she was a bit rusty. When she got back home, she needed to do something about that. Why she hadn't continued to practice, she didn't know. Too busy? Maybe, but she had always found time to keep her marksmanship skills sharp. Unfortunately, that skill wouldn't help her any tonight. She didn't have a gun handy.

If she could continue successfully evading Khan's punches for a few more minutes . . . If she could manage to glide in and out of his range . . . If she could—

And then the inevitable happened. Khan landed a blow—to her jaw. She reeled back, staggered like a drunk, and then went down, down, down to the floor.

When she came to, Jonas was splashing water in her face. She didn't immediately realize where she was and what had happened, but as she became more fully alert, she sighed with relief when she saw that they were on the sidelines during break time.

"It'll be you and White Witch again," Jonas told her. "I went as easy on her as I could, but she's pretty bruised up. If the crowd wants her dead, there is no way you can save her. Remember that. Save yourself."

The third round went fairly quickly, at least for her. She let her challenger get in a few scratches and a couple of punches that landed on her arm, and then she simply grabbed White Witch's long blond hair, pulled her head downward, and kneed her in the face. Dirty fighting, but effective. By the time the fifteen-minute bout ended, Jonas had gotten the upper hand and knocked out Khan.

The final bout could end only one way—two people would die. Either she and Jonas killed their opponents or beat them so badly the crowd demanded their deaths or vice versa.

Can I do this? Can I actually kill another human being in cold blood?

You have no choice. If you don't kill her . . .

As if reading her thoughts, Jonas said, "Take a good look at the White Witch. She's dead already. The crowd really doesn't want to see any more of her until the moment you kill her."

Nic swallowed. Would she have to plunge a dagger into the other woman's jugular the way the first team members had done to each of the defeated?

The final round began, Jonas and Khan fighting to the death. Nic had taken out White Witch in less than five minutes and now waited on the far side of the ring. She occasionally glanced toward White Witch, who lay huddled in a collapsed ball, her head bowed, her small, high breasts covered in blood.

Nic continued watching until the final moment when Jonas sent Khan reeling, down onto the floor, stunned, perhaps bordering on unconscious.

The spectators yelled, "Kill him!" over and over again, until the chorus of their combined voices obliterated every other sound, even the thundering beat of Nic's heart pulsing in her ears.

One of the guards walked into the center of the ring and handed Jonas what looked like a short sword, the blade no more than sixteen inches long.

Oh my God!

Jonas stared at the sword for a couple of seconds before taking it.

Nic held her breath.

Jonas stood over Khan's still body. The man

was still breathing. She could see the rise and fall of his chest.

Jonas clutched the sword's grip in his hand, the blade pointed downward, and without hesitation, he lunged the blade into Khan's chest. Using every ounce of his strength, he pushed the sword into his enemy more than halfway up to the hilt.

The crowd went wild.

Suddenly, Jonas pulled the sword out of Khan's chest, leaving the dead man lying in a pool of his own blood. He stormed across the ring, grabbed Nic's arm, and dragged her to the opposite side where White Witch sat hugging herself and rocking back and forth. Before she realized his intent, Jonas thrust the sword into her hand, held his hand over hers, and forced her to thrust the blade into the pitiful woman's chest.

White Witch raised her head, her eyes wide with shock, her mouth gaping open as she took her last breath.

Jonas pried Nic's fingers from the sword and caught her with one arm as she fell against him.

The cheering crowd, many giving them a standing ovation for their performance, faded away, their shouts a rumbling echo in Nic's ears as Jonas lifted her bloody hand in his and lifted their arms in a show of triumph.

CHAPTER 31

The phone rang shortly before nine that morning. Griff answered without hesitation. To his surprise, the voice on the other end of the line belonged to his wife.

"Griff, it's me."

Momentarily overcome by an odd mixture of shock, happiness, and relief, he couldn't speak.

"Are you there? Did you hear me? It's Nic."

"I'm here. God, sweetheart, it's so good to hear your voice."

"I know. Yours, too. But listen, please. York is giving me only a few minutes. It's a reward for my success in The Ring tonight."

"What the hell is The Ring?"

"A fight to the death in front of an audience. It's sort of a cross between the spectacle put on by the World Wrestling Federation and the gory Roman gladiator events."

"God damn, Nic."

"I'm okay. I survived, with help from my partner." She paused for a moment. "Griff, York is ready to give you instructions for what he wants you and Sanders to do there on Amara."

"Yeah, sure." He lowered his voice and asked softly, "Do you have any idea where you are?"

"Yes. How is Yvette?"

Yvette? Why had Nic mentioned—? London. Yvette had lived in London for years. Was that what Nic was trying to tell him?

"Yvette's fine, honey."

"I love you, Griff."

"I love you, too."

York's muted chuckles enraged Griff. "How sweet," York said. "Ain't nothing like true love, is there?"

"Not that you'd know a damn thing about love," Griff said.

York burst into full-fledged laughter. "What's that old saying about if you can't be with the one you love, then love the one you're with? Nic's partner is taking really good care of her in the loving department. What about you? How's the sex with Yvette these days?"

"It won't work. I don't believe you and I'll bet Nic doesn't either," Griff said. "You might as well give it up."

"Believe what you will." York snorted, signifying his aggravation over not being able to rile Griff. "Are you and Sanders ready to participate in an extraordinarily special game that, once completed, will keep Nicole alive and take you one step closer to being with her again?"

"We're ready. We've been ready for the past two weeks, ever since we arrived on Amara."

"You sound frustrated."

"Just pissed that you've wasted two weeks of my time," Griff countered.

"Even knowing your wife's fate is in my hands, you can't help being an arrogant son of a bitch, can you, Griffin?"

"I'd say it takes one to know one, Malcolm."

York chuckled, the sound toxic to Griff's senses. "Are you finally beginning to see things as they are and not as you believed them to be? Have you finally realized that I am Malcolm York?"

"If you need for me to believe that you're the real York, then I'll believe it."

"Very wise of you."

"I want my wife. I want Nic."

"Patience, patience."

"I've about run out of patience."

"One more challenge for you and one more for Nic," York said. "And if you both do well and please me, then you'll get the reconciliation you want."

"Name my final challenge."

"You're eager to do what I want. I like that."

"Stop screwing with me and just tell me what it is that I have to do."

"I want you and Sanders and Yvette to suffer as I have suffered, to know what it is like to lose what you hold most dear."

"Yeah, I get it," Griff said. "You must have suffered a whole hell of a lot when I chopped off your head."

461

Silence.

Damn! Had he pushed York too far?

In a cold, harsh, barely controlled voice, York said, "At sunset today, I want you, Sanders, and Ms. Hughes to be on the beach at the far side of Amara, the eastern side. Come alone, just the three of you. If you bring along anyone else . . . if my people see any of your bodyguards . . . well, let's just say that the consequences will be deadly."

"Okay. Got it. Sanders, Barbara Jean, and me on the eastern beach at sunset. What else?"

"That's all. Just be there. And tell Sanders to be prepared to make a sacrifice in the name of love."

"What the hell do you—?"

York hung up on him.

Nic and Jonas had been whisked away after their performance in The Ring and taken aboveground to the first level of what appeared to be some sort of business. Linden and two guards had escorted them hurriedly into an elevator and up to a second-story office, sleek and modern with glass and chrome furniture and a bank of expansive windows. The big-city nighttime skyline had spread out before them, sparkling with lights, alive with the hustle and bustle of life. Despite aching all over, her jaw unbearably painful, and peculiar twinges pinching her stomach, Nic had drunk in the sight, desperately wanting to know where she was.

462

"And Khan and White Witch are dead. We killed them."

"I killed them," he said.

She took several hesitant steps toward Jonas, and then stopped when she was close enough to reach out and touch him. "I suppose I should thank you for making the decision for me. I can tell myself that I wouldn't have killed her, but I know better. It might have taken me a little longer to do it, but . . . "

"It's all right." Jonas tucked his open fist under her chin and lifted her head so that she would look at him. "You've got quite a bruise there on your jaw. You're going to feel like hell for several days. But we'll probably get some time off before we're put on exhibition again."

"I wish I could get out of this damn costume. It's dirty and torn and smeared with blood and I'm cold, damn it."

Jonas reached around behind her and yanked the spread off the bed. With gentle concern, he folded the spread and wrapped it around her shoulders as if it were a winter cape.

"If you won't lie down, then sit down. You look like you're about to topple over."

Nic bunched the edges of the spread near her throat, walked across the room, and sat in one of the chairs. She felt sick to her stomach. Her head hurt, her entire body ached, her jaw was sore, and the twinges in her side had increased in degree and frequency. It wasn't the baby. It couldn't be. She hadn't taken any blows to the stomach. But her body had moved and stretched in ways it hadn't been forced to do in years. And she was no twentysomething kid any longer.

"At least you got to talk to your husband tonight," Jonas said as he sat in the other chair.

Nic glanced at him and smiled. "York wants Griff to think you and I are lovers. And he wants me to believe that Griff is having an affair with his friend Yvette."

"Your husband knows better, just as you do."

Nic stared at Jonas. "You look pretty silly sitting there in nothing but a pair of cut-off jeans and a red bandanna around your neck. Aren't you cold?"

"I'm chilly, but I'll be okay."

A cramping ache gripped Nic's belly.

It's nothing to worry about. I'm tired. I'm hungry. I just survived an hour of hand-to-hand combat. All I need is some rest. A good night's sleep and I'll be fine.

Jonas must have noticed her wince. "What's wrong?"

"Nothing really." She tried to smile. "I hurt all over, but that's to be expected, right? I did just get beaten up a few hours ago."

"Yeah, you did. Look, we're both battered and bruised, totally worn out, and we're cold. The sensible thing is for you to go to bed, cover up, and try to rest, maybe even get some sleep if you can."

"You want me to take the bed and leave you nothing but the floor. I know you're trying to be a gentleman, but really, Jonas, there's no way I'm going to bed unless you do, too."

"Are you sure?"

"I'm sure."

"You know you can trust me not to . . . well, you can trust me to continue being a gentleman, even if we sleep together." He grunted. "That didn't come out the way I meant it to."

Nic stood up. "I trust you, Jonas. I trust you with my life."

As she walked toward the bed, Jonas called out to her. "Nic, wait up."

She glanced back over her shoulder and the expression on his face frightened her. "What's wrong?"

He rushed to her, grasped the spread from around her shoulders, and groaned. "God, Nic, you're bleeding. There's blood on the spread and it's all over the back of that damn dress."

"No, no . . . I can't be bleeding. I can't be . . . " She dropped to her knees, wrapped her arms around her body, and cried, "Oh, please, God . . . not my baby."

CHAPTER 32

Thorndike Mitchum cursed when he stubbed his toe on an out-of-place chair as he made his way across the dark bedroom. Once in bed for the night, he seldom had to get up and go to the loo. Apparently tonight was an exception. Just as he hobbled toward his bed, his phone rang.

"Bloody hell," he mumbled to himself.

Managing to make it back to the bed without further mishaps, he sat, turned on the lamp, glanced at the clock, and picked up his mobile phone from where he always placed it on the bedside table. He didn't recognize the number, but being in his line of business, he had learned not to dismiss the possibility of a middle-of-the-night emergency. Of course, almost five in the morning, he realized, wasn't quite the middle of the night.

"Mitchum here."

"Griffin Powell gave me your number," the voice said.

"Did he? In reference to what, may I ask? And couldn't this conversation have waited until morning?"

"Griff instructed me to ring you first if any information I unearthed involved the necessity of a manhunt in Europe, specifically the UK. As for why I'm contacting you—it concerns Griff's wife. And no, this conversation—"

"Would you please identify yourself."

"Rafe Byrne."

"Ah, yes, I suspected as much."

"Unfortunately, we've already lost several hours. I was delayed. I couldn't break free from my companions without arousing suspicion."

"Get to the point, man. You said this involved Nicole Powell and a manhunt."

"I saw Mrs. Powell last night," Rafe said. "At a secret upscale fight club arena in Clerkenwell. Griff's wife was one of the combatants in a rather spectacular show, with a kill-or-be-killed conclusion."

"Am I to assume that Nicole Powell was not killed?"

"You assume correctly."

"And I also assume that Nicole is no longer at this arena. Do you know where she is now?"

"Somewhere in London," Rafe said.

"That's not much help to us."

"Somebody knows something. Send in the clowns to round up the usual suspects."

"Quite humorous, Mr. Byrne."

"Yeah, I'm a regular funny man."

"So it would seem."

"Listen up, okay? When you talk to Griff, downplay the facts as much as possible. And even if you think there's not a snowball's chance in hell of your locating his wife, lie to him and tell him there is."

"I do not need you to tell me how to do my job, Mr. Byrne. Or how to be a friend to Griffin Powell."

Nic awakened slowly, groggily, her brain fuzzy and her head hurting like hell. Where was she? What had happened? Why did she feel as if she'd been hit by a Mack truck?

Something—or someone—stirred beside her. Strong arms held her, drew her into the warmth of a male body.

Griff. She was home, lying in bed with her husband, his strong arms embracing her. She sighed with pleasure.

"How are you feeling this morning?" the male voice asked.

Not Griff's voice.

Nic turned and looked into Jonas MacColl's brown eyes.

"Oh." She uttered the one word.

When he lifted his hand to her face, she shivered. He hesitated before caressing her cheek. "Do you remember what happened?"

Nic nodded. "The Ring. We killed two people." Lifting herself up into a sitting position, she brought the sheet and blankets up to cover her naked breasts. And then suddenly, the rest of the night came swooping down on her like a banshee, screeching a death warning. "My baby. I was bleeding. I don't remember what happened. I must have passed out." She grasped Jonas's naked shoulders, uncaring that the covers slipped to her waist. "Did I lose my baby?"

"No, you didn't. And I don't think you've bled any more," he told her. "You did pass out, but I don't think it was from blood loss. You'd been through hell and then you thought you were losing your baby. I . . . uh . . . I cleaned you up as best I could, using the bedspread. And then I put you to bed. I found a couple of blankets in the dresser. And I've checked on you every couple of hours, just to make sure."

Nic stared at Jonas, her guardian angel, and smiled.

"Before you freak out, I need to tell you that you're completely naked. Your dress was soaked in blood and—"

Nic grabbed his face between her open palms and kissed him. A quick thank-you kiss right on the mouth.

"If you were saying thanks, then you're welcome. But I didn't save your baby. The Good Lord did that. All I did was do my best to look after you."

"I should have told you that I was pregnant, but . . . I know I can't hide it from York for much longer."

"How far along are you?" He glanced down

toward her belly, completely covered by the sheet and blankets. "You've got quite a little baby bump there."

And then apparently realizing how personal his comment had been, he cleared his throat and said, "I'm sorry, but I couldn't help noticing when I took off your dress."

"It's all right," she told him. "I'm sure you were a gentleman."

"Well, my actions were gentlemanly, but I can't swear to you that my thoughts were."

Nic smiled. "I'm not sure exactly how far along I am. Almost five months, I think, maybe four and a half. I hadn't gotten around to seeing a doctor before York sent Anthony Linden to kidnap me. I had just realized I was pregnant a few days before that. I'd missed a couple of periods, but . . . " She shrugged. "Griff and I had been trying for nearly three years to have a baby."

"He must be going out of his mind worrying about you and the baby."

"Griff doesn't know I'm pregnant. I didn't tell him." But Maleah could have told him. No, Maleah would have kept her secret. She would have kept the truth from Griff.

"I guess it's probably better that he doesn't know."

"Yes. This way, if anything goes wrong . . . " She swallowed fresh tears. "I'm not going to lose this baby." She laid her hand over her belly.

"Griff will find me. He'll never give up. I know my husband."

"I believe you," Jonas said.

"I know that if you were my wife, I'd move heaven and earth to find you."

Before Nic could respond, Anthony Linden barged into the room without even a second's warning. But that was Linden's style—brash and bullying. The guard who followed Linden tossed a couple of thin cotton robes on the foot of the bed.

"Get up. You'll be allowed to shower and dress this morning. There are clothes in the bathroom for each of you. You can shower together or separately."

"Separately," Jonas said.

Linden grinned. "Tired of her already?"

"Go to hell." Jonas threw back the covers, got out of bed, and looked Linden square in the eyes.

Linden snapped his fingers and the guard accompanying him pointed his rifle at Jonas.

"You have thirty minutes to shower and get dressed. We're leaving here this morning," Linden said. "It will soon be time for Nicole to prepare herself to participate in another of Mr. York's entertainment events."

Amara's eastern beach was off-limits to the tourists because of the dangerously rocky shore-line, with fifty-foot drops off from the cliffs above the ocean. On the drive to the far side of the island, Griff thought about his telephone conversation with Thorndike Mitchum.

"You were correct in assuming the clue your wife gave you indicated she was in London. Rafe Byrne saw Nicole last night in Clerkenwell. That's in central London, south of Finsbury."

"Yes, I know. I took Nic to a club in Clerkenwell a couple of years ago. A place called Fabric, I believe."

Griff knew that Mitchum had downplayed the situation, no doubt wanting to spare him the gory details of Nic's to-the-death fight in The Ring. Either the pseudo-York had expanded the entertainment selections for his wealthy clientele or there had been aspects of the real York's business enterprises that Griff hadn't been exposed to while held captive on Amara.

"I sent in an elite team to the location where Byrne saw your wife. During the day, the upper levels house several businesses, apparently all of them legitimate. The lower subterranean level once housed a rather large meat cellar and that property is a rental, presently leased to Kroy Enterprises. The place was, as we expected, empty except for a clean-up crew."

"I assume they were questioned."

"On the scene," Mitchum had told him. "We checked them out, naturally. They're employed by the Scrub and Clean service that specializes in that sort of thing. Most of them knew absolutely nothing about what goes on in the cellar. A couple of the guys said they had heard it was some sort of fight club."

"No leads on Nic's whereabouts?"

"Sorry, no. But I've put every available agent on a citywide manhunt for Mrs. Powell."

"Thanks. I know you'll do all you can, but let's face facts. London is a mighty big city and the odds of locating one woman are slim to none."

Griff veered the hotel van he was driving off the main road and onto a bumpy, narrow dirt lane that wound downward to the beach area. Ignoring the posted warning signs—DO NOT ENTER— Griff angled off to the left, bypassing the blockade cones. He parked the van at the end of the pathway.

"We'll wait here," Griff said. "I see no point in getting out until we hear from York."

"I don't see anyone else here," Barbara Jean said from her position in the backseat.

"Let's hope no adventurous tourist accidentally shows up." Griff hit the Down button to lower the van's windows and allow the ocean breeze to cool the interior while they waited. "I don't want York thinking we've disobeyed orders."

"How would he know?" Barbara Jean asked.

"We assume York has a few spies here on Amara," Sanders replied. "That's why we couldn't risk posting our agents anywhere near this place."

Griff turned around and glanced at Barbara

Jean. "Thank you for doing this. I know it can't be easy for you."

"What do you think York has in mind for us?" she asked.

"I have no idea," Griff said. "But you can be sure that it won't be pleasant."

"We're all risking our lives." Sanders looked over his shoulder, his gaze settling on Barbara Jean, his face expressionless. "This York is as bloodthirsty and insane as his predecessor."

She leaned forward, reached over the seat, and held her hand out to Sanders. Without hesitation, he grasped her hand.

"I am sorry that you are involved in this," Sanders told her. "York included you because he knows you are important to me and that he can use you to hurt me."

"I know." She squeezed his hand.

Griff's phone rang.

The sound of the surf only yards away and his own rapid heartbeat inside his head faded into the background as he answered the call. "Griffin Powell."

"On time and following instructions," York said. "That's good."

"What next?" Griff asked.

"Eager, aren't you?" York laughed. "Anxious to get this—whatever it is—over with as soon as possible."

"Quite right. We'll begin. In a few minutes

you'll see a boat coming near the shoreline. When the boat approaches, you are to take Ms. Hughes out onto the beach and leave her there alone."

"That's not going to happen."

"Then I'll kill Nicole today."

"You won't do that."

"Are you willing to take that chance? I prefer not to kill your wife, at least not until the two of you are reunited, but I assure you that if my instructions are not followed, I will kill her."

"I can't ask her to—"

"Yes, you can and you will."

"If she agrees, then what?" Griff asked.

"Then you return to the van and wait with Sanders for further instructions."

Griff pocketed his phone and turned to Barbara Jean.

She spoke before he did. "What does he want me to do?"

"If you refuse, I'll understand," Griff told her.

"What is it? Just tell me."

"We're to wait until we see a boat approaching the shoreline and then I am to carry you onto the beach and leave you there alone."

"No!" Sanders shouted the single word.

"Yes," Barbara Jean said in a soft yet adamant tone. "We are going to do exactly as he has requested. I trust that if it is possible, you and Griff will save me from whatever York has planned."

"There has to be another way." Sanders clung to her hand.

She pulled her hand out of his grasp and looked at Griff. "Listen. I think I hear the boat now."

Griff saw the bowrider approaching the shoreline. Then it stopped a good twenty feet out and sat there like a blue-striped white rocket ready for takeoff. One driver and one passenger, both male, dived overboard, leaving the anchored Stingray floating in the ocean.

"We need to go now," Griff said as he opened his door and got out of the van.

He opened the side door, leaned inside, and gently lifted Barbara Jean up and into his arms. She draped her arm around his neck, offered Sanders a farewell smile, and closed her eyes.

Griff carried her onto the beach, his big feet burrowing into the loose sand. When he stepped onto the hard-packed sand nearer the ragged shore, walking became easier. The two boatmen had swum ashore and stood in front of Griff, their arms at their sides. Both were equipped with railguns and titanium scuba dive knives in lanyards strapped to their legs.

"Put her down," one of the men told Griff.

"She can't walk."

"Sit her down on the beach," the other man said. "Then return to your vehicle and wait."

Griff hesitated.

"Do it," Barbara Jean said.

He eased her carefully down and onto the beach. "I'm so very sorry."

"It's my choice."

Griff glared at York's flunkies. The evening sunlight bounced off their deadly, thick-barreled spearguns, manufactured for hunting deep-sea big game.

Anger and desperation coiled inside Griff like a cobra preparing to strike. After sixteen years of freedom and possessing great power and wealth, he had almost forgotten what it felt like to be forced into submission. At the moment, there was little he could do except follow York's orders. But the day would come—and soon—when he would get his chance to strike back. He had killed Malcolm York once; he could do it again.

When he reached the van, Sanders was waiting outside behind the vehicle.

"You just left her with them?"

Griff nodded. "York will call again. Someone" —Griff scanned the cliffs above them—"is keeping an eye on us and reporting to York. He can see us, but we can't see him."

"So what now?"

"We wait."

"Goddamn it, Griffin, look at her sitting out there on the beach!"

"She's all right, at least for now."

"Listen." Sanders pointed out to sea. "It's another boat."

Griff followed Sanders around to the side of the van and they watched as this boat came as close to the rocky shoreline as possible. A man sat behind the wheel, and the two passengers, a man and a woman, sat in jump seats in the rear. With the boat idling, the male passenger helped the female to her feet, and then the two of them dove into the water and swam toward the beach. One of the two men on shore walked over and stood behind Barbara Jean while the other man met the newcomers. The man grasped the woman's arm and dragged her out of the water and up on her feet. After he handed her over to the waiting guard, he returned to the ocean and swam back out to the boat. The guard marched the soaking wet woman across the beach toward Barbara Jean and forced her to sit down in the sand. The two women, now seated about fifteen feet apart, stared at each other.

One of York's henchmen stood behind each woman.

"What the hell?" Griff grumbled.

"It's her," Sanders said, a barely discernible quiver in his normally steady voice. "It's Elora."

"Are you sure it's the same woman you've been seeing around the island?"

"Yes, I'm sure. She's the spitting image of Elora. Her face, her hair, even her body. It's as if . . . I know. I know. You don't need to remind me that she isn't Elora."

A sickening feeling hit Griff in his gut as he realized that somehow York intended to pit Barbara Jean against the Elora look-alike. "Whatever happens, don't forget that your wife is dead. Whoever that woman is, she is not your Elora."

Griff's phone rang.

"Yeah, York, what next?" he asked when he answered the call.

"Please place Sanders on the line," York said. "My next instructions are for him."

Griff eased the phone from his ear and held it out to Sanders. "He wants to talk to you."

Sanders grabbed the phone. "Damar Sanders speaking."

"Hello, Sanders. Don't you want to thank me?"

"For what?"

"For bringing Elora back to you. You believed she was dead. You believed I was dead. And yet here we both are quite alive."

"That woman out there on the beach, whoever she is, is not Elora. And you can call yourself Malcolm York, you may even believe you are York, but I know the real York is dead, just as my wife is dead."

"Oh, ye of little faith. Wouldn't you like to have Elora back again? Hold her, kiss her, make love to her?"

Sanders did not respond.

"You can have your wife back, your beloved

Elora. Or you can choose Ms. Hughes. But you can't have them both. You have to decide which one is going to live and which one is going to die."

Chapter 33

"Don't do this," Sanders said.

Griff had never heard Damar Sanders beg, but he was begging now.

Without saying another word, Sanders handed Griff his phone.

Griff slipped his phone back into the belt holster. "Tell me."

"He intends for one of them to die. I have to make the decision. I have to choose between saving Barbara Jean and saving Elora." Sanders cleared his throat. "The woman who looks like Elora."

"And that's who she is," Griff reminded him. "She is a woman who looks like Elora. My guess is that she had some cosmetic surgery done, just as York did. If she looks that much like Elora—"

"She does. She looks just like her."

"She looks the way Elora looked twenty years ago," Griff said.

Sanders heaved a heavy, resigned sigh. "Yes, the way she looked the first time I saw her."

Griff curved his hand over Sanders's shoulder.

"What do you have to do to indicate which woman you've chosen?"

"I simply walk across the beach and get her."

"You cannot save them both," Griff told him. "York has deliberately placed you in an unthinkable position. As harsh as it may sound, you can't let your concern about a woman you don't even know affect your decision. That's Barbara Jean out there, damn it. That's the woman who loves you. The flesh-and-blood woman who has shared your bed for the past three and a half years."

"Do you think I do not know that?"

"Then for the love of God, do what you have to do, what York is forcing you to do. We'll deal with the consequences later."

"There has to be a way to save both—"

Griff grabbed Sanders and turned him so that they faced each other. He looked down at the shorter man and gave him a hard shake. "If you don't do what that fucking crazy York has told you to do, you won't just be putting Barbara Jean's life in danger, but Nic's life, too. Damn it, man, are you willing to risk the lives of the women we love to save a woman who is nothing more than an illusion?"

Sanders pulled away from Griff, his black eyes blazing with fury.

And then Griff's phone rang again.

Sanders stared at Griff as he answered, "Yeah, York, what is it?"

"I forgot to tell Sanders something rather important, something that might affect his decision."

"There is no decision to make. He knows the woman isn't Elora."

"Perhaps she isn't." York sighed dramatically. "Let me speak to him."

Griff held out the phone. "The son of a bitch is enjoying every minute of this. He's prolonging the inevitable."

Sanders took the phone. "Yes, I'm here. Yes, I'm listening."

Griff watched the play of emotions crossing Sanders's face and couldn't imagine what York had just told him to make him go pale. Sanders dropped Griff's phone on the ground and walked away toward the beach, but stopped abruptly long before he reached the two women.

Griff came up behind Sanders. "What the hell did York say to you?"

With his gaze glued to the Elora look-alike, he replied, "York asked me if I'd ever thought about the possibility that the dead baby buried with Elora was not our child, that our child lived, that the baby was a girl and—" Sanders's voice cracked.

God in heaven! York was as sadistically cruel as the real York had been, a man who derived immense pleasure from the physical and emotional agony of others.

"That woman out there is not Elora," Griff said. "And she is not your daughter. This is one of York's tricks. Do you hear me?"

"But what if . . . I wasn't with Elora when the baby was born. I saw the dead infant the day Elora was buried. Isn't it possible that Elora could have had a daughter and she lived and York took her away exactly as he took Yvette's child from her?"

Griff didn't know what he could say or do to convince Sanders that York was lying to him. Under normal circumstances, Sanders was the voice of reason, the logical thinker who cautioned Griff about allowing his emotions to control his actions. But when a man was offered a miracle, even the hope of a miracle, he could be forgiven for thinking with his heart instead of his head.

"You know the right thing to do," Griff told him. "You know York is lying to you. You have only one choice and that is to save Barbara Jean's life."

Sanders didn't respond.

Griff watched as his dearest friend on Earth walked alone toward the two women, knowing that he could save only one of them. Never in the past had Griff ever questioned Sanders's ability to make the right decision. Not the popular decision or the politically correct decision, and sometimes not even the strictly legal decision. But always the right decision.

Helpless to do anything except observe, Griff thought how at odds the beauty of nature surrounding him was with the events unfolding before his eyes.

Sunset colors in vivid hues of red, orange, lavender, and pink caressed the western horizon behind him, and the dying embers of light cast golden shadows across the beach. Amara possessed the same tropical splendor of other South Pacific islands, and to the visitors who vacationed here, it truly was paradise. But sixteen years ago, Amara had been hell on Earth where the condemned had overthrown Satan in a bloodbath. They had slaughtered York and his loyal servants.

Griff couldn't help wondering if Yvette had been right when she'd said that Amara was cursed.

Sanders stopped ten feet away from where the two women waited, each knowing her fate lay in his hands. First one guard and then the other removed his scuba dive knife from the lanyard strapped to his leg. Barbara Jean's clasped hands rested in her lap. With her head bowed and her eyes closed, she appeared to be praying. Griff felt certain, knowing her as he did, that she was praying for Sanders and not for herself. The other woman looked straight at Sanders, her arms lifted to him in a pleading gesture. Tears poured down her cheeks.

Griff knew what Sanders was thinking. *Is it possible this young woman is my daughter?*

York had upped the ante. The woman Sanders

loved versus his daughter. He had given Sanders a fictional scenario, a "what if " hope, placing him in an impossible situation, with an unimaginable choice to make.

She isn't your daughter. She's some poor girl that York transformed into the image of Elora. Use your brains, man, the way you always do.

With each passing moment, tension built, the conflict in Sanders's soul playing out in front of Griff. And there wasn't a damn thing he could do to change what was about to happen. He could do nothing that might risk Nic's life. Despite how much he loved Sanders and Barbara Jean and Yvette, Nic came first. Always. If he interfered, York would kill her.

Sanders moved slowly toward Elora, his gaze soaking in every aspect of her face and body. No doubt memories of his long-lost love enveloped him. He paused in front of her. Elora's guard placed his knife at her throat. Barbara Jean's guard did the same.

Griff held his breath.

The ocean waves splashed onto the shore. Birds circled in the twilight sky. A cool breeze drifted in off the sea. Nightfall was fast approaching.

"I am so very sorry," Sanders said, his gaze devouring Elora.

And then he turned and rushed toward Barbara Jean. He dropped to his knees in front of her and pulled her into his arms.

Thank you, God.

The man guarding Barbara Jean stepped back and slid his knife into the sheath strapped to his thigh. But Elora's guard brought his knife down and across her throat, cutting a deep, bloody line from ear to ear. Then he leaned down and stuck his knife in the sand to clean it before returning it to the lanyard.

Sanders kissed Barbara Jean's forehead and cheeks. She clung to him, crying.

York's two hired assassins walked away, dove back into the ocean, and swam toward their anchored bowrider.

Griff ran to his friends, reaching them just as Sanders pulled away from Barbara Jean and rose to his feet.

He turned to Griff and said, "Take care of her for me."

Griff nodded, then knelt down and lifted Barbara Jean up and into his arms while Sanders walked over to where the other woman lay dead, her blood soaking the sand around her. He dropped to his knees, reached out, and turned her over from where she had dropped sideways onto the beach. With trembling fingers, he reached out and lifted a strand of long, strawberry blond hair from her face. Tears pooled in his eyes.

He pulled her up and into his arms and held her, rocking her back and forth, as if she were a child in need of comfort.

CHAPTER 34

He admired himself in the mirror. His image reflected the man he had been twenty years ago. Wealthy, sophisticated, handsome. Now, as then, he was at the top of his game. He was invincible. Indestructible. Immortal.

He was a god among men.

Griffin and Sanders and Yvette thought they had destroyed him. They were wrong. Much to their regret, they now knew the truth. Malcolm York had risen from the ashes like the proverbial phoenix. He would have his complete and absolute revenge against them soon enough. But for the time being, he was having far too much fun playing with them, tormenting them, watching them unravel at the seams.

York ran his slender fingers over his lean, hairless chest, down to his navel, and then he moved upward, pausing to rub his nipples with the pads of his thumbs. His penis twitched.

He was hard. He needed relief.

But you must try to remember that you prefer to watch and achieve fulfillment without ever touching a woman. You derive the most pleasure from their humiliation and pain.

He turned so that the woman could see him naked and aroused, the braided leather whip in his hand. Her eyes grew wide with alarm. He lapped up her fear with the gusto of a hungry cat consuming a bowl of cream.

Barely controlling the urge to use the whip himself and then screw the bitch unmercifully, York handed the whip to the muscular young man awaiting his command.

York stepped back and took a seat on the thronelike chair across the room. "Begin. Now."

The naked youth cracked the whip twice and then lashed the young woman's delicious buttocks again and again and again. Welts formed on her smooth flesh, red, swollen, oozing rivulets of blood. She whimpered and squirmed, but could not escape. The rope binding her wrists together hung over a large hook in the ceiling, forcing her to balance herself on her tiptoes.

When she whimpered, he smiled. And when she began screaming, he laughed.

"Enough," York called out as he rose from the chair and walked across the room.

He shoved the man aside, and then reached down and wiped the blood from a long, narrow gash on her left butt cheek. Placing his finger to his lips, he licked off the blood, savoring the coppery taste.

"Fuck her," York ordered as he snapped his fingers.

He moved aside, and the young man came forward to do his bidding. An adrenaline rush surged through his body, blood engorging his penis and making it throb wildly. He watched with envy, hating himself for wanting to change places with his slave.

He was Malcolm York in every sense of the word. In looks, in speech, in presence, and in deed. But unlike his former self, the reincarnated York desired physical contact with women, not to simply watch another man beat them and screw them. But he was determined to overcome this one last defect that prevented him from a complete and total metamorphosis into the Malcolm York he had once been.

And will be again!

They flew out of Amara that night.

Sanders had not uttered a single word since they had left the beach. Neither Griff nor Barbara Jean had tried to force him into a conversation. Griff suspected that Sanders was not the only one in a state of shock. Barbara Jean had been only seconds away from death and he had been forced to stand by and watch the slaughter resulting from Sanders's decision.

On the drive back to the resort, with Sanders in a near-comatose state and Barbara Jean weeping quietly, Griff had contacted his local head of security who resided on Amara year-round and explained there was a cleanup job on the eastern beach.

"I want the woman's body sent directly to London," Griff had said. "Contact Thorndike Mitchum for procedural instructions."

Mitchum would handle everything with his usual efficiency and take care of all the necessary paperwork required to ship a body into the UK, presumably for burial. His second call was to Mitchum, detailing the situation and requesting a DNA test be done on the young woman.

"You have Sanders's DNA on file," Griff said.

His third call had been to Yvette, apprising her of recent events.

"Do you think Sanders will allow me to help him?" she had asked over the phone.

"Doubtful."

"Do you think there is even the slightest possibility that the young woman may have been Sanders's daughter?"

"No," Griff had said adamantly. "But it may take the DNA results to completely convince Sanders."

Four hours later, they were aboard the Powell jet, heading home to Griffin's Rest. Going home to lick their wounds, recuperate, and find a way to be thankful they had lived to fight York another day.

Yvette had drugged Barbara Jean's tea, per Griff's instructions, and he had carried her into the plane's bedroom two hours ago. She would sleep for hours, giving her a much-needed escape from reality. He hoped she wouldn't have any nightmares.

When he had emerged from the bedroom, he had found Yvette sitting beside a silent and withdrawn Sanders. She hadn't been talking to him or even touching him, just sitting there with him.

Griff longed for sleep, just a few hours' reprieve from the never-ending hell in which he existed every waking moment. But restful sleep wouldn't come, only snippets of snoozing on and off. He dozed off, thinking of Nic. He awoke, thinking of Nic. Wondering. Worrying. Tormented by images of her in captivity. He knew only too well the psychological damage being subjected to such depravity could cause. Even after sixteen years, he had not fully recovered from his experiences on Amara. A part of him would always be that wild, murderous animal that York's inhuman treatment had created.

Griff leaned back and closed his eyes.

He felt Nic's presence, as if she were there with him. She was so much a part of him that he would never again be a whole person without her. Love could create a bond that was more powerful than life itself, even more powerful than death.

A smile played at the corners of his mouth as he remembered the first time Nic had come to Griffin's Rest. The reason she, Special Agent Nicole Baxter, had joined forces with him on the Beauty Queen Killer case had been because they were the only two people the killer had personally contacted. He could hear her saying, "I don't like you. And we both know that I do not find you irresistible." He had called her Nicki. She hadn't liked it. He had known she wouldn't.

On that very first visit, she had met Sanders and Barbara Jean and Maleah. By the way she and Maleah had hit it off, he should have known they would eventually become best friends.

While working on the BQ Killer case, he and Nic had butted heads continuously. During one rather heated conversation, they had summed up their opinions of each other.

"You're an arrogant, egotistical, womanizing bastard who thinks the rules others live by don't apply to you," she had told him in no uncertain terms.

He'd shot right back at her. "I don't like women who need to prove they can do everything a man can do and do it better. I like being a man, and I prefer women who enjoy being female." That particular incident had ended with him grabbing her and her telling him not to ever touch her again.

He should have known then and there that he had met his Waterloo.

Griff chuckled softly as the warm memories comforted him.

"May I sit with you?" Yvette's question jerked him back to the reality of the moment.

He opened his eyes and looked up at her. "Sure.

Sit." He patted the wide leather seat beside him.

"You were thinking about Nic, weren't you?"

"I was remembering how we detested each other in the beginning. God, she was magnificent. Not like any woman I'd ever known."

"You'll get her back." Offering him a sympathetic glance, she sat beside him.

"Will I?"

"There has to be a happy ending for one of us. I would say you and Nicole have the best chance for that happening."

Griff stared across the aisle at Sanders, sitting alone, his eyes open but unfocused, his body as rigid as a marble statue. Only God knew what was going on inside the man's head.

"He's not going to let either of us in, is he?"

"Not yet. But eventually, he will turn to us. And hopefully, he will allow Barbara Jean to help him. She can be his salvation, if only he will let her."

"Nic was my salvation," Griff said. "She's everything to me."

"York is not going to win. We will not let him take any more from us. Nicole is going to live and the two of you will be together again."

Griff prayed that Yvette was right. "You deserve to be happy, too. You need someone." Without thinking, he reached over and clasped her hand.

She shuddered.

"What's wrong?" he asked as he withdrew his hand.

"Nothing. I'm all right."

"You were thinking about Rafe, weren't you?"

Yvette gasped. "God, no. What made you think such a thing?"

"Because I was there on Amara with the two of you, remember. I know how you felt about Rafe and I know how much he loved you."

"That sweet, wonderful boy named Raphael died on Amara," Yvette said. "Rafe Byrne is as much a monster as Malcolm York."

"You don't believe that."

"No, perhaps I don't believe him to be the kind of monster York was, the monster this resurrected York is. But Rafe is cruel and heartless. There is no love or compassion in him. And . . . he hates me."

"I'm sorry. I shouldn't have mentioned his name. I didn't realize . . . " Griff groaned. "I'll shut up now. Why don't you go lie down on the sofa and try to take a nap?"

She patted his hand as she got up, a faraway look in her eyes. "Wherever she is, whatever she is going through, Nicole loves you, too, just as much as you love her."

"I know," Griff said. "I know."

Nic couldn't be a hundred percent sure, but her gut instinct told her that she was finally back in the United States, somewhere in the northwest. Colorado or Montana or Idaho or Wyoming. The magnificent view she saw through the windows of her room all but screamed Rocky Mountains. She had accompanied Griff on a fishing trip to Montana the first year of their marriage and had marveled at the majestic beauty of the region. The Rocky Mountains were different from her beloved Smoky Mountains, but each was equally magnificent.

If she was right about her location, she couldn't help wondering why York had brought her here. This was the United States of America, with laws to protect its citizens against people who trafficked in drugs and humans. Slavery had been abolished in this country a century and a half ago. But as a former FBI special agent, she knew that some of the darkest, most heinous crimes occurred in civilized countries. Criminals existed just below the radar, part of an underground society that protected its own.

Nic forced herself to sit in the comfy chair by the double windows overlooking a nearby mountain stream, the semi-barren mountains a backdrop to endless rows of evergreen trees. The day before yesterday, she had almost lost her baby. Only by the grace of God had the bleeding stopped, but she lived in fear that it might start again. She had to stay as calm as possible and take every available opportunity to rest. Controlling the restless need to pace back and forth in her rather comfortable cage, Nic concentrated on her breathing. Yoga deep breathing. Soothing. Peaceful.

Anthony Linden had accompanied her and Jonas on the trip here, but there had been no sign of York. The jet had landed in the early morning hours and they had been transferred to waiting SUVs. Linden had taken her with him and Jonas had been shoved into another vehicle. After their arrival at the sprawling, log cabin–style lodge set in the middle of the back-of-the-beyond, Linden had deposited her in a rustically upscale room on the second floor. By her calculations, that had been approximately two hours ago.

Since being locked away, she hadn't bothered to explore her jail. She was tired and weak and frightened. She feared for her child's life. She felt like screaming. But what good would that do? She needed to vent her frustration, to beat on the walls, to stomp her feet, to break out a window. But instead, she sat curled up in the big easy chair and stared out the window.

Where was Jonas? What had Linden done with him?

Why had York separated them again? Or had keeping them apart been Linden's idea?

She wanted Jonas with her . . . needed him.

Oh, Griff, my wanting Jonas, my needing him so desperately, isn't a betrayal of my love for you. I swear . . .

Had this been the way Yvette had felt about

Griff ? Not love. Not sexual desire. But the need for human companionship. A man she could trust to help her and not to hurt her. Someone who understood the hopelessness she felt.

Every muscle in her badly bruised body ached. Her swollen jaw had turned purple and was sore to the touch. Her arm and shoulder sported jagged pink bite marks inflected by the White Witch during their battle in The Ring. Misery settled inside her like a lead weight.

She could not—would not—give in to the abject despair that threatened her sanity. Tears choked her as she fought the melancholy wrapping seductively around her.

And then, like a flickering light in the darkness, her baby kicked. Just a teeny-tiny little punch, as if saying to her, "Hey, Mom, I'm okay."

"Hello, right back at you." Nic rubbed her belly, caressing the gentle slope of her abdomen that cradled her unborn child. "I'm okay, too, sweetheart. Just missing your daddy and wishing we were back home in Tennessee with him."

Listen to me, baby. No matter what happens to me, you have to hang in there. You hear me. You have to fight for life. You are Griffin Powell's son or daughter. You are strong and brave. You are a survivor.

And you are a precious gift from God.

CHAPTER 35

They had returned to Griffin's Rest a week ago, all of them mentally and emotionally drained, but Sanders most of all. He had gone back to work immediately, as if nothing had happened, taking charge of his professional responsibilities and refusing to discuss what had taken place on Amara, not even with Griff or Yvette. His relationship with Barbara Jean had been irrevocably altered by their experience on the beach. He had left their shared bedroom suite on the first floor and moved into an upstairs bedroom. No one had questioned either of them. And the entire household had been tiptoeing around Sanders as if he were a bomb set to explode with the least provocation.

Charles David had returned to San Francisco while Griff had been in Amara. Maleah had persuaded him to go home. After all, he hadn't been helping Nic by staying at Griffin's Rest and at least at home he would have his work to keep him occupied.

Each day Griff expected to hear from York. A phone call. A special delivery package. A fax or e-mail message. But apparently, they were back to playing the waiting game. Nic had been kidnapped nearly three months ago. He could count the days, the hours, and the minutes since he had last seen her driving away, leaving him and all the lies she couldn't forgive far behind her. Griff tried not to think about what Nic had been enduring these past three months, but he couldn't continuously fight his own nightmarish thoughts. Awake or asleep, Nic was always on his mind.

As he stepped out of the shower, he heard his phone ringing. He grabbed a towel off the rack, draped it around his hips, and opened the door to his bedroom. His heartbeat accelerated. Was York calling him with instructions for a new and even more deadly game?

Mitchum's name showed up on the caller ID.

Griff answered. "What do you have for me, good news or bad news?"

"Information," Mitchum replied. "We have the DNA test results on the woman from the Amara beach."

"And?"

"And we have dug up some interesting info about the young lady."

Half an hour later, Griff met with Sanders, Yvette, and Barbara Jean in his study. He had debated about whether or not to meet privately with Sanders and had decided that they each had a vested interest in the information Thorndike Mitchum had relayed to him.

"The DNA results came in on the Elora look-alike," Griff said, his gaze focused on Sanders, who showed no emotion whatsoever.

No one said a word.

"The young woman was not your daughter," Griff told Sanders.

Sanders did not react in any way.

Barbara Jean gasped.

"Thank goodness," Yvette said.

"Her real name was Alisa Mistretta. She was born and grew up in London, was in trouble with the law from the age of twelve and was arrested for prostitution the first time when she was fourteen. Mitchum wasn't able to locate the surgeon who altered her face to resemble Elora's, but the photos of her presurgery show a rather pretty girl who bore little resemblance to Elora. Even her hair was dyed that particular shade of reddish blond. Alisa had brown hair."

"I think we all knew that she was simply another of York's diabolical tricks." Yvette said, and then turned to Sanders. "You must have known in your heart that she wasn't your child."

Sanders did not respond.

"That's all the info Mitchum had," Griff said. "Now we all know the truth."

"If you will excuse me, I have work to do." Without another word to anyone, Sanders walked out of the study.

"He just needs time," Yvette said.

"I'm not sure that's all he needs," Barbara Jean

said. "Neither Sanders nor either of you has been able to completely let go of the past. You're all bound to it by some invisible cord that you refuse to cut. God knows I can't begin to understand what y'all went through on Amara, but I do know that until you cut that cord, all three of you are doomed."

Stunned by Barbara Jean's vehement outburst, Yvette and Griff stared speechlessly at her as she wheeled herself out of the study.

Another damn costume!

Nic stared at the Annie Oakley outfit hanging in her closet. In the week since her arrival at the hunting lodge, she hadn't seen either Linden or York. Her day-to-day needs had been taken care of by closemouthed, obedient servants who provided her with decent food, clean clothes, and escorted her for an afternoon walk outside every day.

The costume had been delivered this morning, along with a note: *"Proper attire for your performance at The Execution is essential."*

When someone knocked on the closed bedroom door, Nic nearly jumped out of her skin. The servants didn't knock. Linden certainly didn't.

"Nicole, it's me, Jonas," the voice on the other side of the door called to her.

As Nic rushed to the door, it opened. And there stood Jonas, in jeans and plaid shirt and sporting a short beard and mustache just beginning to

503

form on his handsome face. Behind him stood two armed guards.

"May I come in?" Jonas asked.

"Yes, of course."

When he entered, the guards closed and locked the door.

"I am so glad to see you," Nic told him. "I had no idea what had happened to you."

Jonas looked her over from head to toe. "You're looking healthy. How are you?"

She patted her tummy, which seemed to be enlarging a little every day. "We're fine."

"No more problems?"

She reached out and grasped Jonas's hand. "Come sit down and tell me everything you know about where we are, why we're here, and what's going on. And I need to know more about this upcoming event that York calls The Execution."

"I don't know much," he said. "But what I know isn't good for either of us."

"I suspected as much." Nic nodded toward the closet. "I have a costume for the event. A cowgirl outfit—fringed leather skirt and vest, western-style boots, and the cutest little wool felt cowgirl hat you've ever seen."

"The Execution is similar to The Ring in that it's a show for an audience, only not in a ring. From what I understand, there is always a theme to The Execution. The one I participated in had a Civil War theme. I was decked out in a Johnny Reb costume and the man I killed was in Yankee blue."

"Then it's like a play that ends in death. Real death."

"Pretty much." As they sat down on the edge of the bed, Jonas took both of her hands in his. "There were three acts to the play, with three people killed. Two opening acts and then the main event. My guess is that you'll be the main event."

"And it's kill or be killed just like in The Ring."

"These things go on all the time, around the world," Jonas told her. "Most people never know anything about them. There is an underground society of really sick, twisted wealthy people who get their kicks in the most perverted ways possible. Human bondage. Men and women, boys and girls being bought and sold as sex slaves. Hunters tracking and killing other human beings. Watching opponents fight to the death. Having a front-row seat to the murder of one person by another."

Nic squeezed Jonas's hand. "You're going to be one of the acts in this Execution play, too, aren't you? You'll be expected to kill again."

"So will you." He brought her hands to his lips and kissed each. "You have to do it, Nic. You'll have no choice. If you don't kill the condemned person, they will do it for you and then either kill you or punish you in some horrible way."

"I don't know if I can—"

Jonas grabbed her by the shoulders. "You can

and you will." He glanced down at her stomach. "You'll do it, if not for yourself, for your baby."

"I don't know how much longer I can hide the fact that I'm pregnant, and I have no idea what York will do when he finds out."

"He'll use your pregnancy to his advantage, to control you and to torment your husband."

"But Griff doesn't know."

Jonas looked at her questioningly, then asked, "When York finds out, how long do you think it will be before he tells your husband?"

Griff took the call from Rafe Byrne that evening while he was standing on the patio. He had eaten dinner alone in the kitchen, a plate left by Mattie before she'd gone home for the day. Both Sanders and Barbara Jean had been conspicuously absent, as had Derek and Maleah.

"I was beginning to wonder if I'd paid you a million dollars for nothing," Griff said when he answered his phone.

"There was no point in contacting you until I had some useful information."

"And you have some now?"

"Sir Harlan has invited me to fly over to the States with him in a couple of weeks. He's taking part in what he refers to as a marvelously unique hunt. He didn't come right out and say it, but he didn't leave much doubt as to what we will be hunting."

"Did he say where this hunt is taking place?"

"No, but he did tell me that each of the chosen quarry is very special to our host. Two males and two females. And he's invited Bouchard. There will be just the four of us so it'll be one-on-one in the hunt, or so Sir Harlan says."

"Two males and two females. And Nic will be one of the two females."

"That's my guess."

"There's more, isn't there?"

"Nothing more that the old bastard shared with me," Rafe said. "Just a gut feeling I have."

"Tell me."

"I think the prey we'll be hunting is a select group—maybe you and Sanders and Yvette and Nicole."

CHAPTER 36

By her calculations, Nic was six months pregnant on the day of The Execution ceremonies. Her fringed A-line skirt fit loosely and her leather vest and billowy gingham blouse adequately camouflaged her pregnancy. She was afraid that if either Linden or York looked at her closely today, they would notice the slight fullness of her face and the increase in her breast size. If it happened, it happened. She had known all along that it would be only a matter of time before she could no longer hide her condition. But she had hoped beyond hope that before that happened, Griff would have found her.

Traveling by horse-drawn wagons, she and five others, including Jonas, sat huddled together in the wagon bed, with an armed guard riding shotgun and two guards, on horseback, flanking the wagon. Not only were she and the other participants in today's exhibition dressed in costume, but so were their guards. They all looked as if they had stepped off a western movie set. The five men wore decorative leather chaps over their pants, Stetson hats on their heads, and their belts sported big silver buckles. And they had beards and mustaches in varying degrees of growth. Nic and the one other woman had been decked out to resemble the Queen of the Cowgirls, Dale Evans, in fancy attire more suitable for the silver screen than the real old west.

Nic understood why no one felt chatty on the ride from the hunting lodge. Three people were doomed to execution today and three assigned the role of true life executioner. It was better not to know one another, not to share any personal information with the person you would have to kill. Or with the person who would kill you.

They arrived at their destination thirty or so minutes after leaving the hunting lodge. Without a watch, Nic guessed at the time by checking the position of the sun. She figured it was mid-to-late morning. The bumpy road, more dirt than gravel, led directly into the little town, but not just any town—a ghost town. The main street consisted of six dilapidated buildings on one side and three on the other. All except two were wooden structures weathered to gray over the years and in various states of ruin. One was a two-story brick with boarded arched windows, and the other a one-story brick with a ramshackle wooden porch. In the distance on a nearby hillside, a couple of other old buildings, possibly once a schoolhouse and a church, nestled snugly beneath towering evergreens, a weed-infested cemetery planted halfway between them.

The entire town was alive with costumed people: cowpokes, saloon girls, gunslingers, sheriffs, schoolmarms, and gamblers. Nic counted the townsfolk as the wagon rolled along Main Street. By the time the driver stopped the wagon on the outskirts of town, she had counted more than twenty people. Who were they? Surely they weren't all York's captives.

The guards lowered the back of the wagon, ordered them to get out, and quickly divided the men from the two women. She and Jonas exchanged hasty good-bye glances before she and the other woman, a raw-boned brunette only a couple of inches shorter than Nic, were escorted to a nearby shade tree. Their hands were cuffed behind them and attached to shackles hanging from the side of the tree. From where she stood manacled to the tree trunk, she had only a partial view of Main Street, but she could hear the jubilant celebration taking place in the old ghost town.

She glanced at the woman beside her and wondered if she should say something to her. But before she had a chance to decide, one of the guards came for the woman. Nic watched as he released the brunette from the cuffs and dragged her away, forcing her to march in front of him.

A few minutes later, a riotous roar rumbled down the street from the little godforsaken town. Cheers and shouts preceded what sounded like a loud drumroll. And then the crowd quieted. The eerie sound of someone whistling sent shivers through Nic. She didn't recognize the tune, something chillingly melancholy.

Time seemed to stand still.

The sun warmed the earth.

The autumn breeze cooled the air.

A gunshot rang out. And then another.

Boisterous shouts and delirious whoops followed.

Every muscle in Nic's body stiffened. She knew the first execution had taken place. One down and two to go. Jonas would be the next executioner and then it would be her turn. How long would it be before they came for her? How long before she would have to commit murder?

"You'll do it, if not for yourself, for your baby," Jonas had told her.

The second execution had taken place a good while ago, the noise from the townsfolk, York's honored guests, quieted now to a low rumble.

What are they waiting for?

With each passing moment, Nic became more nervous and less certain that she could actually kill another human being in cold blood.

You can do it. You have to in order to save your life and your child's life.

The sun hung high in the sky, directly overhead. Midday.

She saw the guards approaching and knew the time had finally come. One man removed her cuffs, pulled her away from the sheltering tree, and the other man strapped a gun belt around her lower waist. Inserted in the single holster now strapped to her leg rested what Nic suspected was a .45 Colt revolver. My God, was it an authentic weapon or a reproduction? She had handled one of the big old revolvers a few times, a weapon effective for power and control by the user.

As the two guards led her into what she figured had once been a bustling mining town, another drumroll resonated loud and strong, announcing the main event for today's execution ceremonies. When they were able to see her, the onlookers, a dozen or so on each side of the street, cheered

511

her slow, dramatic march up the street to face her opponent.

Whoever the poor man was, would he have a fighting chance? Would he have a gun? And if he did, would it actually be loaded?

When she had gone a third of the way into the center of town, one of the guards stopped her, and then both moved away from her, leaving her alone in the street. Her heart raced like mad, booming in her ears. She felt hot. Sweat dotted her brow despite the mild temperature. Her hands grew moist with sweat.

Nic looked right and left, searching the crowd for any sign of York. The damn egotistical son of a bitch, decked out in cowboy finery, stood front and center, a big smile plastered on his face. He looked right at her, threw up his hand, and waved. Could she draw the revolver and shoot York before the guards either tackled her or shot her? If only . . .

Suddenly the whistler trilled another tune, one Nic immediately recognized. The theme song from the old movie *High Noon*.

You've got to be kidding.

Like the exciting hunts for humans and the bloody fights in The Ring, today's reenactment of an old west gunfight possessed all the pomp and ceremony York's rich clients expected.

As the whistler completed his rendition of "Do Not Forsake Me, My Darling," two guards escorted Nic's challenger down the street from the other side of town.

She squinted as they approached, trying to see the face of the man she was expected to kill. Just as the guards moved away and left the gunslinger alone, Nic got a clear view of his face.

No! It can't be. Please, God, no.

The man standing less than fifteen feet from her was Jonas MacColl.

This was York's doing, just another sadistically cruel maneuver in his game of revenge. He knew she wasn't a killer, knew how difficult it would be for her to execute an innocent person. And now he was making it impossible for her.

She couldn't shoot Jonas.

She glanced away, staring into the crowd at York. The son of a bitch laughed when their gazes met.

Her hand hovered over the holster flap, itching to undo it, and then pull the revolver and aim it at York.

She looked straight at Jonas. *I can't do this,* she wanted to shout. But the look in his eyes told her that he expected her to kill him.

Fear and frustration induced a strong rush of adrenaline that flooded through her system. Her gaze momentarily settled on Jonas's holster. He had a gun. He could shoot her. But he wouldn't.

And then suddenly, before she realized what was happening, Jonas pulled his revolver from the holster. It was in that moment when she reacted by mimicking his actions, their guns then pointed at each other, that Nic knew without a doubt that Jonas's gun was not loaded.

She knew then what she had to do, regardless of the consequences. She did not want to make the ultimate sacrifice, but she could see no other way to end this.

Asking God and Griff and her unborn child to forgive her, Nic whirled around, aimed, and fired.

The crowd gasped in shock. Jonas ran toward her as the four guards took aim straight at Nic. He lunged toward her as the guards opened fire, their bullets riddling his back when he protected her from their attack.

Jonas took her down to the dusty ground with him and covered her body with his. "Why did you do it?" he asked her.

Blood trickled from the corner of his mouth.

"Jonas? Oh, Jonas."

He lay on top of her, his body a heavy, protective weight.

Nic closed her eyes.

And then the weight of Jonas's dead body disappeared. Nic opened her eyes to see a man standing over her. He reached down and dragged her up and onto her knees.

"No!" she screamed.

"You thought you killed me, didn't you?" Malcolm York said. "I'm afraid you shot my bodyguard. Poor fellow is dead. He died to save me just as Jonas died to save you."

York tucked his index finger under her chin. "What's different about you, Nicole?" He grabbed her and dragged her to her feet, then whipped apart her vest and ran his gaze over her body. "You're getting fat." And then as if suddenly realizing the truth, he laughed. "You're pregnant. What a delightful turn of events. Is MacColl the father or dare I hope you're carrying Griffin Powell's child?"

Looking right at him, Nic spit in York's face.

CHAPTER 37

"It's time for the final game," York told Griffin. "I can't keep your wife alive much longer. She has become more trouble to me than she's worth. She's quite a feisty little bitch, isn't she?"

Griff clutched the phone with white-knuckled anger. "Name the time, the place, and the terms. Just you and me, York."

"Now, don't be selfish. We can't leave Sanders and Yvette out of all the fun we're going to have, now can we?"

"I'm the one you want. It's my wife you're holding captive."

"Yes, I want you, Griffin Powell. I want your head stuffed and mounted over my fireplace."

York laughed, the sound edged with hysteria.

The man was insane, every bit as insane as the real York had been.

"And I want to gut you while you're still alive and make you suffer till you beg me to kill you."

"What a bloodthirsty devil you are, Griffin. But we all have our dark side, don't we? That sweet little wife of yours certainly has hers."

"Tell me what you want. But before I agree to anything, I want to talk to Nic again."

"I'm afraid that won't be possible. You see, she's being punished for an unforgivable crime. The crazy bitch actually tried to shoot me."

That's my Nic. "Good for her."

"No, actually, it's bad for her, especially in her condition. I've had to put her in solitary confinement. Bread and water only, unless of course she can kill and eat the rats in her cell."

Griff's face heated with rage. His hand trembled. "What do you mean, her condition?"

"Oh, that's right, you don't know, do you?" York chuckled. "I could send you some photographs, but since you'll soon be visiting me, you can see for yourself. Nicole is pregnant."

"I don't believe you."

"As I said, you will soon be able to see her swollen belly. How does it feel, knowing the child your wife is carrying could be her lover's baby?"

"You're lying. Nic isn't pregnant."

"Oh, she's pregnant, all right. But I can't say

just how pregnant. It's hard to tell about these things. She could be far enough along for the baby to be yours. How about that, Griff ? I not only have your wife, but I may have your unborn child, too."

"No, I don't believe any of this."

"As I said, you can see for yourself. I'm inviting you and Sanders and our lovely Yvette to join me and my guests for the hunt of a lifetime. An exclusive guest list. And the prey will be premium quality—the three of you and Mrs. Powell, too, of course."

Griff had known there would be a final showdown, that in the end York would want to kill him. Go ahead and try, you son of a bitch. The real York tried for four damn years and I outsmarted him every time. I can outsmart you, too.

"I want you to fly to Colorado tomorrow and land at the Denver International Airport," York told him. "There will be a car waiting for you. You'll find instructions in the glove compartment. I'll have a small plane at a private airstrip ready for you and your dear friends. Don't try anything stupid. If you do, I'll be forced to kill Nicole."

The last thing Griff heard was the sound of York's maniacal laughter. Long after York had hung up, Griff still clutched the phone in his hand.

York had lied to him. Nic wasn't pregnant.

But what if she was?

What if the baby isn't mine?

517

Griff stormed out of his study.

"Sanders! Barbara Jean! Maleah! Derek!" He fired off the four names in rapid succession.

Sanders barreled around the corner, followed by Maleah and Derek, all of them coming from the office.

"What is it?" Sanders asked.

"What's wrong?" Derek and Maleah questioned simultaneously.

"York called. He wants us—you, Sanders, and me and Yvette—to fly to Denver, Colorado, tomorrow. If you choose to go with me—"

"Of course we will go with you," Sanders assured him. "He wants all of us. He won't be satisfied with only you."

Griff nodded. "Please contact Yvette and let her know that I've heard from York and explain that he has a special hunt planned, with the three of us and Nic as the quarry."

"Oh my God," Maleah said.

Barbara Jean arrived several minutes after the others. "Is something wrong?"

"York called with marching orders for Griff," Maleah explained.

Before Barbara Jean could respond, Griff zeroed in on her and said, "I want to speak to you and Maleah in my study now. Please."

"Yes, of course," Barbara Jean replied.

Maleah seemed hesitant, but said, "Yeah, sure."

Griff waited for the two women to move ahead

of him, and when they did he followed them to his study and closed the door.

"York told me something that I didn't want to believe. I called him a liar. But I don't know if he really was lying." He looked back and forth between the two, hoping that one of them could tell him what he needed to know. "I have to ask you both, as Nic's best friends, if she shared a secret with both or either of you before she left Griffin's Rest, something that, at the time, she didn't want me to know."

"No," Barbara Jean said instantly. "Nic isn't the type to keep secrets, especially not from you."

Maleah remained silent. Griff looked at her.

"What about it, Maleah?" he asked.

"What did York tell you?"

"He told me that Nic is pregnant."

Barbara Jean gasped. Maleah swallowed.

"He claims that he doesn't know exactly how pregnant she is and doesn't know if the baby is mine or the man he keeps referring to as her lover."

"The baby's yours," Maleah told him.

Griff felt as if he'd been punched in the gut.

"Then she is pregnant?" he asked. "She was pregnant when she left Griffin's Rest?"

"Yes. She just found out for sure a couple of days before and she wanted to wait until things calmed down around here before she told you."

Griff stared at Maleah, his emotions all over the

place. He was happy. He was sad. He was angry. He was hurt. He was racked with guilt and remorse.

"Why didn't you tell me? All these months and you knew and didn't tell me?"

"You may not believe me, but I didn't tell you because Derek and I agreed that—"

"Derek knows?"

"You've had just about all you could handle dealing with Nic's kidnapping and the sick games York has forced you to play. The last thing you needed was to know that Nic was pregnant. I didn't tell you for your own sake."

"Damn it, Maleah, you had no right to . . ." Griff swallowed a gut full of tears.

Struggling to keep his emotions under control, he turned away and walked over to the window.

Several minutes later, he said, "Maleah, see to it that the Powell jet is ready to leave for Denver first thing in the morning."

"Yes, sir."

When he heard Maleah exit the den, he slowly turned to Barbara Jean. "If you love Sanders, and I know you do, then make tonight count. There is no guarantee that he or Yvette or Nic and I will come back alive."

CHAPTER 38

Sir Harlan had kept the location of The Hunt top secret, so it wasn't until their jet had landed at the Missoula International Airport, that Rafe realized he was in the United States. He had wanted to get word to Griff ASAP, but found it impossible to get away from his traveling companion. The old buzzard even went into the men's room with him. While in a private stall, Rafe had managed to get out a quick text message. Two words: *Missoula, Montana.*

The driver who met Rafe and Sir Harlan had loaded their bags in a Land Rover and informed them their trip would take less than an hour. Sir Harlan chatted nonstop for the first thirty minutes, then dozed off, giving Rafe time to soak up their surroundings in peace and quiet. He'd never been to Montana. But from the view out of the SUV windows, he could tell why people raved about this state. The farther away from Missoula they were, the more scenic the landscape as they rolled along on US-93 South. Autumn in all her splendor. The boy he had once been would have loved capturing all the colorful beauty on canvas. Raphael had been an artist with the soul of a poet.

"We are going to a rather exclusive hunting preserve that our host, Malcolm York, owns,"

Harlan Benecroft had told him before they left London. "Some people actually prefer hunting deer and elk and bears, but we will be hunting the most deadly creatures on Earth—humans."

The Cessna Citation, a small eleven-seat jet, landed on a private airstrip in a valley cradled between snow-capped mountains, the foothills gleaming golden in the evening sunlight. When Griff stepped off the plane first, he breathed in the crisp, cool autumn air. A muscular, medium-height man, wearing sunglasses and a black Stetson waited at the bottom of the passenger steps.

"Hope you had a pleasant flight, Mr. Powell," the man said with a slight British accent.

Griff descended the steps, Yvette directly behind him, and Sanders following her. As he glared at their greeter, he caught a glimpse in his peripheral vision of an armed guard standing beside a silver Land Rover.

The minute Griff's feet hit solid ground, he turned to assist Yvette, who grasped his hand, more for moral support than for any other reason. Once Sanders joined them, their escort came forward, removed his sunglasses, held out his hand and smiled at Griff.

"Welcome to Montana. It's a pleasure to finally meet you, Mr. Powell."

Griff ignored the man's outstretched hand.

He dropped his hand to his side and said, "The lodge is only a short drive from here. Mr. York is eager to see you again." He glanced at Sanders and nodded. "Damar Sanders. I've heard almost as much about you as I have about Griffin Powell." Then his gaze settled on Yvette. "May I say, Dr. Meng, that you are even more beautiful than Mr. York described you."

"Where is York?" Griff asked.

"As I said, he is eagerly awaiting your arrival at the lodge. He has instructed me to handle you three with kid gloves. It seems you are extra special guests."

"And just who are you?" Griff asked, but suspected he already knew.

"Oh, so sorry. I should have introduced myself. I'm Anthony Linden."

Anthony Linden, the former SAS agent who had gone rogue and become a killer-for-hire. Employed by York and working under his direction, Linden had viciously murdered Powell agents and members of agents' families earlier that year, all part of York's plan for vengeance.

When Linden didn't get the responses from them that apparently he had been expecting, he glowered at Griff and said, "Shall we go? I'm sure you're eager to see your wife again after all these months. I'm afraid she is a little worse for wear, but she is still alive."

At the mention of Nicole, Griff tensed, but

quickly regained control, determined not to react to this vicious butcher's taunting comments.

Nic stood under the warm shower, savoring the moment, enjoying the chance to cleanse herself. She had no idea how many days had passed since Jonas had been killed and she had tried to shoot York. Three? Five? More?

Afterward, she had thought for sure that York would issue an immediate order to execute her.

"I should kill you for what you tried to do, but considering this new and most interesting discovery"—he had glanced at her belly—"I believe I'll keep you alive until I reunite you with Griffin, as originally planned."

Keeping her alive was all he had done. She had been put in a shed somewhere away from the hunting lodge, a log structure without running water or electricity and no furniture, not even a cot on the floor. And no heat. The guard who had escorted her to her rustic prison had provided her with a two liter bottle of water, a loaf of bread, and a wool blanket. She hadn't seen the light of day, except through cracks in the walls since he had locked her away. She had been forced to relieve herself in the shed, creating a foul odor. The mice and insects with whom she shared the tiny six-by-six-square-foot hovel hadn't seemed to mind. During the day she'd been cold and had kept the blanket wrapped around her shoulders.

At night, when she suspected the temperature dropped to well below freezing, she had nearly frozen to death as she had huddled in a corner and prayed for the warming relief of morning.

Since the bottle of water was nearly empty and there were three stale slices of bread left in the wrapper, she had begun wondering if York would actually let her starve to death or if her meager supplies would be replenished. Then less than an hour ago, when one of the guards had opened the door, she had assumed he would toss her more bread and water and leave her to rot. But he had ordered her to step outside. He hadn't needed to ask her twice. Although extremely weak, she managed to stagger to the door, but the moment the sunlight hit her, she squinted from the overwhelming glare. She hadn't seen sunlight in days, so it took her eyes several minutes to even begin adjusting.

No one had told her why she was being given a reprieve and she didn't ask. She didn't care. For now, she was back in her room inside the lodge.

After lathering and rinsing her hair, Nic opened the shower door and grabbed one of the fluffy white towels, wrapped it around her head, and reached for another. After drying off, she slipped into the baggy maternity jeans and bulky long-sleeved sweater that had been hung on the back of the bathroom door. No underwear. No socks or shoes. And no cosmetics—not even a deodorant stick.

But she did find toothpaste and a toothbrush. Strange how people took little things for granted, something as simple as being able to brush their teeth.

Nic walked into the bedroom, sat on the rug in front of the rock fireplace, and towel-dried her hair. After having endured the freezing cold in the shed, the heat from the burning logs felt wonderfully warm and cozy. During those first twenty-four hours in primitive solitary confinement, she'd been emotionally numb after what had happened during The Execution event in the old ghost town. She still couldn't believe that Jonas was dead, that he had sacrificed himself to save her. And her baby. He had known he was destined to die that day and had possibly accepted his fate, but dear God, dear God . . . She had cried all night that first night. Cried for Jonas and for herself. Cried because she had been cold and hungry and frightened. And alone, so alone.

With each passing day, as desperation and hopelessness settled heavily on her heart, Nic had struggled not to give in to the depression threatening to claim her.

If Griff didn't find her soon, it would be too late. Although she knew her baby was still alive, she feared for that little life growing inside her. York wouldn't keep her alive indefinitely, and if she lived to give birth, what would happen to her child?

Surrounded by nature at its finest, the world alive in the most fundamental way, with mountains and valleys as clean and pristine as they had been a hundred years ago, Griff studied the scenery for a reason far more important than mere appreciation. Soon, tomorrow or the next day, he would have to survive out there in the wild, in the open grasslands, the woods, along the creeks and rivers and perhaps even in the mountains. He noticed that Sanders was soaking it all in just as he was, familiarizing himself with the terrain. They were veterans of warfare on Amara. It would be up to them to outsmart the hunters and keep Nic and Yvette alive until nightfall.

What makes you think nightfall will end the hunt? This is not Amara, and despite what that fool believes, he is not Malcolm York.

In the end, their ultimate survival would depend on one thing—the prey killing the hunters.

The driver turned the Land Rover onto the circular drive in front of the two-story lodge and parked in front of the massive front porch. A balcony ran along the length of the huge log house, as long and wide as the house itself. Two rock-and-wood wings on either side of the central structure jutted out about twelve feet, giving the building a shallow U-shape.

Linden and the driver quickly exited the Land Rover. They hurried to open the back doors of the SUV, and wasted no time ushering Griff, Sanders, and Yvette out of the vehicle. While the driver slid behind the wheel and drove away, Linden marched the three of them to the foot of the steps leading up onto the porch.

"Wait here," Linden told them.

Before Linden's feet hit the porch floor, the double front doors opened and four men emerged, one at a time. Griff instantly recognized Harlan Benecroft. Older, fatter, but otherwise unchanged. And directly behind him, Yves Bouchard, came to a halt at his friend's side. Still devilishly handsome, if somewhat eroded by age, Bouchard, too, had changed very little in sixteen years. Although Griff had expected the third man to be part of this select group, seeing Rafe Byrne being so chummy with the enemy bothered Griff.

The fourth man exited the lodge. He was the spitting image of the real Malcolm York. Except, there were subtle differences. He was shorter, but only by a couple of inches. And his shoulders were not as broad. The silver color of his hair was a shade lighter and not natural.

York snapped his fingers and a woman stepped out from behind him and stood at his side.

Nic!

Griff wanted to run to her, grab her, hold her.

He didn't move; he just looked at her.

"Welcome to Big Valley Hunting Lodge," Malcolm York said. "We are delighted that you could join us. Everything has been prepared for your visit. Your rooms are ready and I've scheduled the first hunt for tomorrow morning."

Griff barely heard what York said. He couldn't take his eyes off Nic. Without makeup, her full, pregnancy-round face pale, her long dark hair uncombed, and the ill-fitting sweater she wore barely covering the swell of her belly, she was the most beautiful thing he'd ever seen.

"Griffin, you'll share a room with your wife, of course. Sanders, you and Yvette have your own rooms," York said. He pulled Nic from where she waited at his side and pushed her a couple of feet in front of him. "Nicole, my dear, why don't you go say hello to your husband."

Nic stumbled in her eagerness as she came flying down the steps. Griff rushed toward her and caught her as she fell. She grabbed hold of him, wrapping her arms around his neck and holding on to him for dear life as he lifted her up and into his arms.

And then he kissed her.

CHAPTER 39

"I hate to break up this little lovefest," York said, laughter in his voice, a voice all too similar to the real Malcolm York's slightly accented, baritone voice.

"You two will have all night together. But for now, I'd like for all of you to join us in the lounge so we can go over my plans for tomorrow's hunt."

Reluctantly, Griff lifted his mouth from Nic's. He looked into her teary eyes. "I love you," he whispered. "You and our baby."

With teardrops trickling from the corners of her eyes, Nic told him in a barely audible voice, "We love you, too."

When York instructed Linden to show his guests into the lodge, Griff set Nic on her feet, but kept his arm securely around her waist. Sanders entered first, followed by Yvette. As she passed by Rafe, she brushed his arm in what appeared to be nothing more than a slight misstep on her part.

"I'm so sorry." She mumbled the apology to Rafe as she followed Sanders into the building.

The lounge covered an area in the center of the lodge approximately thirty-by-thirty square feet, a huge room filled with leather sofas and chairs, Native American artwork and colorful blankets, one hanging on the wall above the eight-foot-wide fireplace. The floor-to-ceiling windows covering an entire wall revealed a breathtaking panoramic view of the nearby mountains.

York pranced into the room like a glorified show horse. "Sit, please, everyone."

The three hunters and the four human prey took seats around the room while York remained standing, taking center stage in his grandiose one-man act. Griff kept his arm around Nic. She held his hand in a death grip.

"This prehunt meeting won't take long," York said. "You will be able to go upstairs to your assigned rooms very soon. Dinner will be provided, of course, in your rooms. And your clothes for tomorrow's hunt are now being delivered. The weather is a bit nippy, the predicted high for tomorrow is fifty-five, but it won't be much above freezing at dawn when you'll be heading out, so I'm allowing you long sleeves." He grinned wickedly, enjoying every moment of his speech.

"I say, dear boy, I'm unaccustomed to rising that early," Harlan Benecroft said. "You should know that I'm not a morning person. Can't we postpone this hunt until a decent hour, say nine or ten?"

"Griffin, Nicole, Sanders, and Yvette will be awakened at dawn and given an hour's head start. See how generous I can be?" He glanced from one of them to another. "We have eight hundred acres here, but of course, you will not be given free rein of the entire ranch. There are guards posted at strategic points to make sure you stay within the proper boundaries."

"Sir Harlan, Mr. Bouchard, Mr. Kasan, and I will return to the lodge at noon for lunch and then resume the hunt at two. At nightfall, the hunt will end. If the hunt is successful . . . well . . ." He laughed. "Those of you who are still alive tomorrow night . . . well, actually, I don't expect any of you to survive."

"If Yvette manages to survive, I should very much like to renew our acquaintance, at least for one night," Bouchard said. "I have some unfinished business with the lady."

"If she survives, she's yours," York said. "For one night. But after that, my beautiful wife will be mine to do with as I please. And unless I change my mind, it will please me to strangle the life out of her."

"That would be such a waste. I have no doubt that, even as old as she is, Dr. Meng would fetch a high price in certain markets," Harlan Benecroft said. "If she isn't killed tomorrow, you really should—"

"Damn it, old man, you have no right to tell me what I should or should not do." York glared at Harlan.

"You always were a hothead. Never would listen to anyone else," Harlan said. "You should have been spanked more as a child."

"And you're the reason children commit patricide!"

Harlan's face turned red as he huffed loudly. "Damn it, boy, did you forget to whom you're speaking?"

York seethed silently for several minutes, the entire room waiting for him to explode. But instead, he said in a strangely calm voice, "Linden, arrange for our special guests to be shown to their rooms." He glanced from Bouchard to Rafe. "Gentlemen, I do apologize. Would you mind giving Sir Harlan and me a few minutes alone to finish our conversation in private?"

Griff had no idea what the problem was between Benecroft and York and didn't care whether they worked it out or not. Actually, he would like nothing better than for the two of them to kill each other.

Sanders and Yvette were led away by guards, but Linden escorted Nic and Griff up the stairs and down the hall to a second-story bedroom.

"Enjoy your night together," Linden told them. "It will be your last."

Ignoring what Linden believed to be a prophetic comment, Griff slammed the door in the man's face, and then pulled his wife into his arms.

Holding her at arm's length, his hands gripping her trembling shoulders, Griff inspected Nic from her disheveled hair to her bare feet. All the while, she could barely take her eyes off his face, his expression so filled with love and concern.

"I'm all right," she told him.

"No, you're not, but you will be as soon as I get you out of here and back home where you belong." Circling his arms around her, he hugged her to him.

She laid her head on his shoulder. "I'm sorry I didn't tell you about the baby. I was going to, but . . . I should have told you the minute I knew I was pregnant. And I never should have left Griffin's Rest. This whole thing is my fault. Oh, Griff, I'm so sorry about—"

"Shut up, damn it." He grasped her face, cradling her cheeks with his palms as he tilted her head and kissed her again.

She gave herself over completely to the savagely passionate kiss. Then moments later, when Griff slowly lifted his mouth and pressed his cheek against hers, he said, "I drove you away with all my secrets and lies. If this is anybody's fault, it's mine, not yours."

"We can share the blame. But there's something else, something wonderful, that we can share." She took his hand in hers and pressed it against her belly. "Let me introduce you to our baby."

Griff's hand quivered as he lifted Nic's sweater and touched her swollen stomach. "When I think about what you've been through . . . what you must have endured . . ."

She laid her hand over his. "Don't. Please. I do

not want to think about these past few months or talk about them. Not tonight. Tonight, all I want is to be with you."

One last night before we die.

She didn't say the words aloud. If she did, Griff would tell her that they were not going to die tomorrow, that he was going to turn the tables on York and save them all.

But what if he doesn't? What if he can't?

He can. He will.

But if the worst happened tomorrow, at least they would have had this one last night together.

Apparently York and Sir Harlan had resolved their difference. At dinner that evening and afterward in the lounge while the five of them enjoyed their host's fifty-year-old brandy, the two men appeared to be, once again, the best of friends.

During the meal, tomorrow's hunt had been the main topic of conversation. Pretending he was as enthusiastic as they about stalking and killing humans took little effort on Rafe's part. All he had to do was think about replacing Griff and the others with York and his cohorts. Something Rafe had every intention of doing. But he needed help to accomplish the reversal of roles in tomorrow's reality play and that meant getting in touch with Sentell tonight if at all possible.

"I was wondering if it would be safe for me to

take a short nighttime stroll around the property?" Rafe asked.

"Quite safe." York swirled the golden mahogany liquor in his glass. "As long as you don't venture too far away from the lodge itself. There are some wild animals out there, but probably not as wild as the animals we'll be stalking tomorrow."

Everyone laughed, even Rafe, who, for the time being, had to continue the pretense that he was Leonardo Kasan, a man as ruthlessly perverse as they were.

"As for any other types of danger," Linden said, "there are guards posted around the clock, a quarter of a mile out, in all four directions."

"I'll be sure not to lose sight of the house," Rafe said as he rose from his chair. "I'm keyed up about tomorrow's hunt. It will be a first for me. I need something to help me relax. I believe some of this fresh mountain air will help me sleep like a baby tonight."

"Quite right. Quite right," Sir Harlan said as he casually saluted Rafe with his brandy snifter and then downed the last drops of the Rémy Martin cognac.

"If you gentlemen will excuse me, I'll run upstairs for my coat before I head out. And if I don't see you before morning, sleep well and have sweet dreams about tomorrow's hunt."

As Rafe headed upstairs to retrieve his coat, he smiled when he heard Sir Harlan say, "Didn't I tell you what a splendid fellow Leonardo is?"

"I find him interesting," Bouchard said. "Sometimes, I feel him watching me and I do not know what to think."

"Perhaps he fancies you," York said, humor in his voice. "He may not know that as a general rule you prefer much younger bedmates. But then, your tastes are somewhat eclectic, aren't they? A little of this, a little of that."

"I say, if I liked men, I'd be tempted by Leonardo," Sir Harlan told them.

With the sound of the men's laughter following him up the stairs, Rafe hurried into his room, grabbed his jacket, and rushed outside as quickly as possible. He needed fresh air, all right, something to cleanse the filth from his mind.

After taking a turn around the house, Rafe ventured farther out, seeking a secluded spot, away from the prying eyes of either those inside the lodge or the sentinels guarding it. He needed complete privacy to make a phone call. As the nighttime wind whirled around him, he turned up the collar on his coat, and then tapped in the memorized number, one he would later delete from the throwaway phone.

He didn't have to wait long before Luke Sentell answered. "Talk."

"This is Rafe Byrne. I know where they are, Griff and the others. I'm here with them, only

I'm slated to play on the home team for the next big game."

"And?"

"We're between thirty-five and fifty miles southwest of Missoula, Montana. We drove past the towns of Lolo and Florence. And then we turned off on a gravel road somewhere between Stevensville and Hamilton and drove maybe fifteen to twenty miles to a place that York calls the Big Valley Hunting Lodge. The ranch covers eight hundred acres, but the hunt will be confined to a much smaller area. And FYI, the place is crawling with guards. They're posted everywhere."

"That's enough info for us to find the place. When we get there, our first order of business will be to take care of the guards."

"You'd better get your butt in gear, Sentell. The hunt starts tomorrow, an hour after dawn. If you and your men don't get here with some real firepower—"

"Do what you can until we show up," Luke told him. "I have a team on standby here in Denver. Griff said you'd come through for him. He sent us to Denver two days ago so we would be ready to move as soon as you contacted me."

"I hope you and your team are as good as Griff thinks you are. My guess is you'll have to wipe out a small army of at least twenty men, possibly more."

"Can do," Luke said. "See you tomorrow."

●●●

Nic lay in Griff's arms, blissfully happy, refusing to let tomorrow intrude on their reunion. They had made love in a frenzy of physical and emotional need. Griff had tried to take things slow and easy, to be extremely gentle, but she had wanted his passion, and had been as desperate for him as he was for her.

When their dinner had been delivered, Griff had met the guard at the door and taken the tray. Later, he had devoured the thick stew and crusty bread. When she had stopped eating after only a few bites, Griff had encouraged her to eat more and somehow she managed to clean her bowl, all the while hoping she wouldn't throw up later.

She didn't want to tell Griff that she had been living on bread and water for days now.

Refusing to think about anything except being with Griff, she curled up against him and kissed his shoulder. He slid his hand over her hip and then cupped her butt as he nuzzled her ear.

"I love you," he told her again. He'd been saying those three words repeatedly, but she never tired of hearing them.

He laid his big hand over her rounded belly. "And I love you, too, almost as much as I love your mama." He lifted himself up and then leaned down to kiss her stomach.

Nic speared her fingers through his thick blond hair as he laid his head beneath her breasts. Griffin was such a handsome man—tall, muscular, broad-shouldered, and ruggedly masculine. And he had the most remarkable blue-gray eyes. Would their child resemble him or her or would he or she, like most children, be a unique combination of each parent? Would their son have Griff's beautiful gray eyes and her dark brown hair? Would their daughter have her brown eyes and Griff's blond hair? One thing for sure, he or she would be tall. Griff was six-four and she was five-eleven.

"Penny for your thoughts, Mrs. Powell."

She smiled. "Just wondering what Little Miss or Little Mister Powell will look like."

"She'll look just like her mama and be the most beautiful little girl in the world."

Nic playfully pulled Griff's hair. "He will look like his father and be the most handsome little boy ever."

Griff lifted himself up and over Nic, bracing his hands on either side of her shoulders so that he kept the weight of his body from pressing down on his unborn child. Nic slipped her hand between them and wrapped it around Griff's erect penis.

"Woman, what am I going to do with you?"

"You're going to make love to me again, that's what you're going to do."

"Is that an order, ma'am?"

"Yes, it is."

Griff took immediate action. He rolled over and

off her. And starting at her forehead, he kissed a meandering trail downward, over her cheeks, mouth, chin, and throat. Pausing at her swollen breasts he laved each tight nipple until Nic thought she would scream.

He lifted his head for a moment. "I'm not hurting you, am I? Your breasts aren't sore or—"

"As long as you treat them gently, you won't hurt me."

He looked into her eyes. "I swear to God, Nic, I will never hurt you again."

"And I'll never leave you again. Not ever."

Griff's facial muscles tightened, as if he was in pain. He closed his eyes.

When he slid his hand between Nic's legs, urging her to part them, she spread her thighs. Returning his attention to her breasts, he licked and sucked, while he stroked her intimately until she climaxed.

Shuddering with release and panting rapidly, she reached out for Griff, but he gently turned her onto her side and began a kissing and licking assault on her back and buttocks. Enjoying every decadent moment, Nic made no protest as he covered every inch of her body, loving her, worshipping her with sensual tenderness. And when he eased her onto her back as he positioned himself between her thighs, she opened to him, giving herself freely, knowing it was what he wanted. He slipped his tongue inside her. In and out, lapping, stroking, pressing, and then sucking gently. Nic's hips lifted off the bed as her body shattered with a second orgasm.

While the aftershocks still rippled through Nic, singing along every nerve ending, Griff lifted her up and on top of him so that she straddled his hips. He bucked up and entered her slowly and carefully. Taking him deep inside her, she melted around him. Giving her control, he allowed her to set the rhythm. Within minutes, tension began to build again, spiraling tighter and tighter so that when Griff came, her own explosive release followed his by mere seconds.

She slid off him, fell backward onto the bed, and nestled against him. When he slipped his arm around her, she laid her head on his shoulder. They rested there together, listening to each other's breathing, savoring the sweet inertia that follows fantastic sex.

"Griff ?"

"Hmm . . . ?"

"There hasn't been anyone else," she said in a barely audible voice. "No sex with—"

"I'm glad, for your sake," he told her. "But you have to know that if . . . if it had happened, it wouldn't change anything for us, about the way I love you."

"I know. I understand so much more about . . . things. You and Yvette and . . . " Nic sucked in a labored breath. "There was a man . . . "

542

"You don't have to tell me anything."

"We didn't have sex. York thought we did, but we didn't. Jonas was a kind, decent man, one of York's captives. He was good to me. I cared about him. He—He died saving my life."

Griff kissed her forehead and held her in his arms as she cried.

CHAPTER 40

Shortly before dawn, one of York's guards woke them, told them to dress quickly, and be prepared to leave the lodge at daybreak. Griff and Nic didn't talk much while they washed off and put on the long-sleeved, bright orange jumpsuits York had provided. No shoes, no socks, and no coats. Not only would they be unarmed, they would be barefoot and cold—and glowing like jack-o-lanterns on Halloween night. If Rafe hadn't been able to contact Luke Sentell, they would be on their own today, with only Rafe to help them. It had been sixteen years since Griff had partici-pated in one of these sadistic hunts. He was older, his reflexes not as quick, his jungle warfare instincts not as sharp, and his survival skills somewhat rusty. But this time around, he had a lot more to lose than in the past. He had a wife and a child to protect. And so help him God, that's what he intended to do.

When the guard returned, Griff kissed Nic hurriedly before they were herded up, along with Yvette and Sanders, and forced down the stairs and outside into the cold. Griff halfway expected York to be waiting for them with a farewell message, but he was nowhere to be seen. Four other armed guards watched over them until the dawn light appeared, pink and red blossoming in the eastern horizon against an indigo sky.

"Let's go," the man in charge told them.

Lined up single file, they followed as one guard took the lead, two brought up the rear, and the other two fell into step on either side of them. They were marched about a quarter of a mile from the lodge, past what had once been open cropland and deposited on the edge of a wooded area.

"You have one hour," the lead guard told them. "Make the most of it."

The guards waited. Apparently their orders were to make sure the quarry scurried into the woods and didn't backtrack toward the lodge.

"For now, we'll stay together," Griff said as he grasped Nic's arm and guided her from the clearing.

Sanders and Yvette followed and no one spoke again as they traveled deeper into the forest, not until at least ten minutes later. Surrounded by towering evergreens, a mix of pines, spruce and cedars, and golden aspens, Griff halted and gathered them closely together.

"If we stay together, it will be almost impossible not to leave a trail of some kind," Griff said. "And my guess is that York has a tracker on his payroll, someone familiar with the territory."

"I agree," Sanders said.

"The hunters will come out together, the four of them, and probably stay together most of the morning, but Rafe will break away from the others as soon as he can. And unless he was able to contact Luke, he's all we'll have on our side."

"Rafe planned to contact Luke last night," Yvette said.

All eyes turned to her.

"You touched Rafe and picked up on what he was thinking?" Griff asked.

Yvette nodded. "As we were ushered into the lodge yesterday, I touched him briefly. He allowed me to read that one thought."

"Let's hope he managed to do what he planned," Griff said. "But until we know for sure and see some sign Luke and his team have arrived, we have to stay one jump ahead of York and his friends." He nudged Nic toward Sanders. "I want you to take Nic and Yvette. Keep them with you if at all possible."

"No, I don't want to leave you." Nic grabbed Griff's arm.

He pulled her around and in front of him. "I'm going to make a couple of false trails so they may think that we split up. It's possible that they will decide to do the same so they can pursue us separately. If that happens, the tracker can't go with all four of them, so I'm hoping York will keep him close by. Once Rafe is on his own, I can meet up with him and find out where things stand."

He could tell Nic wanted to protest. But she didn't.

"Not now, but once you're away from here, do whatever you can to get your clothes filthy, smear them with mud, do whatever possible to dilute the bright color."

And then he hugged Nic good-bye and waited until she disappeared with Sanders and Yvette into the woods. Once the others were out of sight, he worked quickly, going due west, deliberately breaking small limbs off shrubs and disturbing the landscape as subtly as possible, leaving a clearly discernible trail. Once that was done, he back-tracked to the spot where he had parted with the others and headed toward the mountains. He tromped through the woods and into an open field scattered with small boulders, the grass a golden brown and red clover growing in profusion.

After creating two separate trails that might divert the hunters, as a single group, from following the true escape, Griff took refuge behind a seemingly endless wall of stately tamarack trees. He placed himself behind the wide trunk of a single tree—and waited.

● ● ●

Rafe had joined the mighty hunters for an early-morning breakfast.

"I want to speak to Mr. Hirt," York had explained as he'd risen from his chair. "He's an expert tracker. However, I don't plan to put him to work until this afternoon. No sense ending the fun before it even begins."

There had been no way for Rafe to let Griffin know that he'd been able to contact Luke Sentell last night and that the cavalry was on its way. For all he knew, Sentell and his elite warriors were already in Montana, possibly on the outskirts of the lodge, preparing to work their way through the army of posted guards.

After York had left to speak to his tracker and Sir Harlan and Bouchard excused themselves, Rafe lingered in the dining room, nursing a second cup of coffee. Once on the hunt, he had to make some sort of excuse and break away from the others.

Intending to return to his room for his coat and to take the pistol and boot knife from his suitcase and hide them beneath his quilted hunting jacket, Rafe left the dining room and headed toward the stairs. He had managed to hide a Beretta Cougar 9mm and a double-edged boot knife and sheath beneath the bottom lining in his bag that he'd personally carried aboard York's private jet when he had boarded with Sir Harlan in London.

As he passed by the lounge, he heard Yves Bouchard's voice. "Does he truly believe that he is Malcolm York?"

"I don't know," Harlan replied. "In the beginning, he could differentiate between fantasy and reality. He was enjoying the game, and happy and excited as he planned and plotted Griffin Powell's doom. I applauded him, supported him . . . was even proud of him for the first time in his life."

"*Oui*, I also," Bouchard said. "But now, *je suis inquiet*. Since faking his own death and returning to life as our old friend York, your son has gained much power and great wealth. He is to be feared, *n'est-ce pas vrai*?"

"Yes, I'm afraid you're quite right to be concerned. Ellis inherited a sizable fortune from his grandmother and was independent even as a teenager. But at least while he was still Ellis Benecroft, I had some influence over him. Now that he is Malcolm York, he seems to think he does not need to show me the proper respect a son owes his father."

"If he becomes a threat to Kroy Enterprises, how far are you willing to go to stop him?" Bouchard asked.

Rafe stood perfectly still outside the lounge, barely breathing for fear he would be noticed. But the information Sir Harlan was unknowingly sharing with him was far too important not to risk being discovered eavesdropping.

Malcolm York was Ellis Benecroft!

Ellis was Sir Harlan's only child, reported killed in a horrific car crash, along with some famous supermodel, five years ago. Sir Harlan had identified his son's watch and rings, and the dental records had confirmed the corpse's teeth a match to Ellis's. But records could be falsified, doctors paid off or threatened.

"I can't sanction killing my own son," Sir Harlan said. "But I would not seek retribution if someone else did what was necessary."

"If it becomes necessary, I will handle the arrangements."

"I daresay that Mr. Linden would be willing to do the deed, for the right price, of course."

"*Mais bien sûr*," Bouchard agreed. "He owes his loyalty to the highest bidder."

"I didn't realize when I allowed Ellis to spend so much time with Malcolm when he was a boy that the two would bond so completely. While my son merely tolerates me, he truly hero-worshipped Malcolm and apparently longed to be just like him."

"And now he has fulfilled his own wish, has he not? He has transformed himself into the man he idolized, assumed his life and . . ." Bouchard huffed disgustedly. "To think that I encouraged this folly, that I considered the idea of Ellis pretending to be York a highly entertaining adventure. But what happens next, after today's hunt, once he has avenged his hero's murder? How long before he sees the two of us as threats because we and we alone know his true identity?"

Sir Harlan was silent for a few moments, then said without a hint of emotion, "Then you will see to it that what must be done is done."

Rafe didn't wait around to hear more.

Griff watched as York entered the clearing. Holding his breath, he didn't so much as flinch as York walked past him, no more than twenty feet from the stand of tamaracks protecting Griff.

Rafe Byrne followed closely behind his host, but paused, glanced around, and called out to York, "You two go on. My gut tells me that at least one of them went toward the mountains."

"You believe they separated, all four of them?" Anthony Linden asked.

"I think it's possible. It would have been the smart thing to do."

"Then by all means, follow your instincts," York said. "I'm doing the same. Linden and I will go downstream. Sooner or later, they'll be searching for water."

Rafe came toward the row of skyscraping tamarack trees, but went no farther until York was out of sight and earshot. Choosing a small boulder for a chair, Rafe sat down and surveyed the area in every direction. Griff slipped out from behind the massive tree trunk where he had been hiding, and the moment Rafe saw him, he rose to his feet.

"Where are the others?" Rafe asked.

"I sent Nic and Yvette with Sanders. I'm fairly certain that he's taking them the long way around back toward the lodge, at least as close as he can go without running into the guards. If he sees any sign of danger, he'll keep moving."

Rafe unzipped his quilted jacket, removed the Beretta and the boot knife from the inside zippered pockets and gave them to Griff. "This was the best I could do."

"Thanks." Griff checked the handgun, glanced at the four-inch double-bladed knife, and shoved both into the pocket of his jumpsuit. "What about Luke Sentell?"

"I spoke to him last night," Rafe said. "Smart move having him and his team waiting in Denver. My guess is that they're already here at the ranch and making their way toward us."

"Thank God. We might have had a fighting chance against the four hunters, but not against York's brigade of guards. But it could take Luke awhile to get to us. How many guards do you think they'll have to take out first?"

"My estimated guess is at most twenty-five, but only half of those will be on duty."

"You and I should split up," Griff said. "It's time for the hunters to become the hunted."

"I want Bouchard," Rafe said.

Griff nodded. "Agreed. And I want York."

"He's all yours."

As Griff turned to leave, Rafe called to him. "Griff ?"

"Yeah?"

"There's something you should know about York, about who he really is," Rafe said. "I overheard a conversation between Benecroft and Bouchard this morning. Want to guess who York was in his former life? It sure as hell wasn't the real Malcolm York."

His pulse rapid, his heart pounding a loud beat, Griff stared at Rafe. "You found out who York really is?"

"Do you remember Ellis Benecroft, Sir Harlan's bratty kid? I saw him on Amara a couple of times, always following York around like a puppy."

"Ellis Benecroft is supposed to be dead, burned up in a fatal car crash in Italy nearly five years go."

"He's not dead. He apparently faked his death, with some help from Sir Harlan. It seems that the fourteen-year-old kid who idolized York found a way to fulfill his teen fantasy of being just like his cousin while at the same time bringing Malcolm York back from the dead to seek revenge against the people who killed him."

Yves and Harlan had grown weary of the hunt within two hours. Stopping on a rise overlooking a narrow branch of the river running through the property, Yves opened his canteen and downed several large gulps of water.

"We're getting old, my friend," Harlan said as he eased himself down onto a small smoothly rounded boulder rising out of the ground. "These wilderness hunts are a young man's fun and games."

"I agree. And where is the sport in using a tracker? Malcolm never resorted to such unsportsmanlike conduct. I believe I shall stay at the lodge after lunch today. Let York and Linden have their fun."

"Quite right, quite right. I'm in complete—" Harlan stopped midsentence when he heard gunfire. "Listen. Do you hear that?"

"I imagine York has spotted one of the captives," Yves said.

"No, I don't think so. Listen. The gunfire is continuing."

"*Mon Dieu*! What do you think is happening?"

"It must be York's guards firing at someone." If that was the case, it could mean only one thing. "They must be under attack."

"By whom?"

Harlan shook his head. "Someone other than our unarmed quarry, that is for certain."

"But how is this possible?"

"I don't know. The hunt was a by-invitation-only event. But if the lodge is under attack, it means someone betrayed us, betrayed York."

"Should we return to the lodge or—?"

"The gunfire is coming closer. They are closing in all around us."

With his rifle drawn, Yves turned in a circle, searching in vain for the raiders. And then from out of nowhere, a shot rang out and Harlan felt the impact of the bullet as it entered his shoulder. Another pierced his leg. Screaming in pain, blood pouring from his wounds, he couldn't manage to hold on to his rifle as he dropped to the ground.

The last thing Harlan heard before the third and final bullet hit him was Rafe Byrne's voice shouting, "Bouchard is mine."

Luke Sentell tossed Sanders a rifle, an M-4 Carbine, like the one he and the two members of his twelve-man team carried. Nic noticed that each of the two soldiers also had an M16 hung over his shoulder.

Nic motioned to Luke, indicating that she wanted a weapon.

"Give her the M16," Luke ordered one of his team members. The guy immediately handed her the rifle, the M16A2, a lightweight, simple to operate general assault weapon with a thirty-round magazine.

"Got one for you, Dr. Meng, if you want it." Luke said.

"I—I don't know. I've never fired a gun." Yvette

stared at the weapon the soldier offered her.

"Take it," Nic told her. "I'll give you a quick tutorial on the way."

"On the way where?" Yvette asked.

"To help Griff and Rafe," Nic said. "We can't leave you behind and we can't spare anybody to stay here with you."

Nic grabbed the other soldier's M16 and handed it to Yvette. "Odds are you won't have to use it. But just in case."

"Thank you." Yvette's hand brushed Nic's as she accepted the rifle. "Oh . . . "

"Yeah, you got it, didn't you, what I'm feeling?" Nic offered Yvette a closemouthed half smile. "When this is all over, you and I are going to be friends."

Before Yvette could respond, Nic turned to Luke. "I assume the other members of your team are busy taking care of the rest of York's guards. Griff and Rafe are more than a match for the hunters, but with Rafe the only one armed—"

"Griff's armed," Luke told her. "A couple of my guys found him and Byrne. They took out Harlan Benecroft. Now, Griff has gone after York. And they turned Bouchard over to Rafe."

Yvette gasped.

Nic glanced at her. "Don't think about it."

"But Rafe will butcher him," Yvette said.

"Do you really care?" Nic asked. "Bouchard is scum of the earth."

"I care for Rafe's sake, not for Bouchard's," Yvette explained.

"I think it would be best if you two stayed here." Luke glanced from Nic to Yvette. "You're both armed and I'll leave Cusimano here with y'all." He hitched his thumb toward the grizzly, rawboned warrior sporting a thick black beard and mustache. "You're obviously pregnant and I'm sure Griff would skin me alive if I let you—"

"You're not letting me do anything," Nic told him. "This is my fight as much as it is Griff's or yours. I'm the one York has held captive for months. I'm the one Anthony Linden kidnapped. If you think I'm going to stay here and do nothing, then—"

"Excuse me, Mrs. Powell," Luke said. "For a minute there, I forgot who I was talking to."

They separated into two groups. Sanders joined up with the two men from Luke's team, while Nic and Yvette went with Luke. As they hiked back along the same trail they had originally taken, Nic felt uneasy, some sixth sense warning her of danger. Although there were only two hunters—York and Linden—unaccounted for, there were more guards, their exact number unknown. Half an hour out, they began running across dead bodies. By the time they reached an open field spreading out toward the mountain range and guarded by sky-high, golden tamarack sentinels, they had passed four bloody corpses, each no doubt one of York's hired men killed by Luke's elite team.

Nic had no objection to Luke taking the lead. After all, he was the one with all the experience, a former Special Forces soldier. Her only objection had been Luke's intention to leave her behind with Yvette and a bodyguard.

Yvette was scared, but she hid her fear well. Nic was afraid, but not as much for herself as for Griff. Anthony Linden was a highly trained assassin. If Griff went after him . . .

He would go after York first, but what were the odds that Linden wouldn't be stuck to York like glue? York and Linden would know by now that the game was over, that the Big Valley Hunting Lodge had been invaded by a trained team of rescuers.

Staying together, single file, at least five feet between them, Luke led and Nic brought up the rear, leaving Yvette in the middle. As they neared a small clearing along a lake surrounded by thick, heavy woods, Luke halted. He glanced over his shoulder, looked past Yvette, and made direct eye contact with Nic.

Luke said, "Let's backtrack a piece and—"

Nic strained to see what Luke was trying to hide from them. And then Yvette screamed.

Damn it!

Nic grabbed Yvette and shook her. "Shut up!" Nic told her in a rough whisper. "We're already visible enough as it is in these damn orange jumpsuits, even if we did coat them with mud. You don't need to announce our presence."

Yvette trembled, shivering as if the temperature had suddenly dropped to zero. "I'm sorry."

Nic released her and walked up beside Luke who had gone into protective mode, his M-4 Carbine ready for attack. And then Nic saw why Yvette had screamed. Lying there on the river-bank, like a gutted and cleaned fish, lay a man, his rather handsome face unmarked. He had been partially skinned, leaving bare muscles exposed. His body had been ripped open, possibly while he was still alive, and his penis had been cut off and stuck in his mouth. Fresh blood covering the area around where his scrotum had once been indicated that the man had been castrated shortly before they had come upon his mutilated corpse.

"Bouchard." Nic said his name under her breath. Rafe Byrne's doing, no doubt. Yvette was too late to stop Rafe from exacting his barbaric revenge.

Yvette heaved a couple of times and then vomited. Nic walked over to her, grasped her arm, and led her up the riverbank and away from Bouchard's butchered remains. When they were more than thirty feet from Luke, halfway hidden behind a couple of new-growth pines, Nic knelt and used one hand to scoop up some water. And then she gently splashed it into Yvette's face.

"Take some deep breaths," Nic said quietly.

Yvette wiped the cool water drops from her face. "I'll be okay. It's just . . . "

"Yes, I know. Not a pretty sight, was it?"

"How could he—?"

Gunshot.

Close by. Upstream.

Luke?

"Stay here," Nic whispered.

Wide-eyed, Yvette stared at Nic and mouthed the words *I will.*

Nic slipped into the woods, circled back around, and crept close enough to see that Luke had been hit. Blood oozed from his shoulder as he crawled on the ground toward the thick underbrush. She blamed herself. Luke had been so preoccupied with watching over her and Yvette that he probably hadn't been fully alert to an approaching enemy. She searched for the shooter. A flicker of movement caught her eye. Just as the man took aim to fire again, she saw him.

Got him.

Did he plan to wound Luke again, to make him suffer, or did he intend for this to be the kill shot?

Nic said a prayer, ironically asking God to make her aim accurate as she brought the M16 up against her shoulder.

Anthony Linden was less than fifty feet away on a wooded rise that sloped toward the lake. Without a second thought or a moment's hesitation, Nic aimed and fired. The bullet hit Linden in the side of his neck, tearing his jugular in its upward trajectory. She sucked in deep breaths as her heartbeat boomed and her steady hands began to tremble.

Mercy God.

Had Linden not seen her and Yvette? Had he come up on Luke after they had gone downstream so that Yvette could compose herself away from Bouchard's corpse? Or had he mistakenly assumed neither she nor Yvette was a threat to him? The man might have been a sadistic assassin, but he was no fool. But then again, maybe he hadn't done any in-depth research on her and didn't know that she was a crack shot.

What did it matter now? Linden was dead, wasn't he? He couldn't have survived.

She intended to check Linden's body, just so there would never be any doubt in her mind. But first she had to find Luke. She didn't want him taking any potshots at her by mistake.

Circling back around halfway to where she'd left Yvette, Nic emerged from the wooded area into the clearing by the lake and, rifle in hand and ready to defend herself and her party, she moved toward the last spot she had seen Luke. She found him, a few feet away, lying on his belly, his shirt blood-soaked, his M-4 aimed straight at her.

"Luke," she called to him.

He lowered the rifle.

She hurried over and knelt beside him. "How bad is it?"

She shoved back his jacket and tore at his shirt, ripping it apart so she could inspect the wound. "Went through my shoulder," Luke said. "Hurts like hell."

He looked up at Nic. "Where's Yvette?"

"Downstream a piece."

"I didn't see it coming," Luke admitted. "I should have—"

"It was Linden, not some two-bit guard," Nic told him.

Luke grimaced. "Did you get him?"

"Yeah."

"You'd better make sure."

"I will, but we need to take care of your shoulder first."

She zipped up his thick, fleece-lined jacket and pressed her hand down over the wound. He winced as she applied pressure. He lifted his hand and slipped it under hers.

"Go get Yvette."

"I'll take a look at Linden on my way."

When she found Linden's body, she kept her rifle ready, but once she got a good look at him —and checked his pulse—she didn't waste any time moving on toward Yvette.

As she approached the spot where she had left Yvette, she didn't see her, but she heard an almost indiscernible sound coming from nearby.

Damn it, surely one of York's men hadn't—

Yvette and Rafe Byrne came out in the clearing. Nic released a relieved huff. "Where's Griff ?" she asked.

"Gone after York," Rafe said. "I saw Linden. You take him out?"

Nic nodded.

"Revenge is sweet. Isn't it, Nicole?"

Griff tracked York into the foothills and down through the woods and grassland, all the way back toward the log-cabin lodge. The afternoon sun splattered light and warmth in every direction, no doubt bringing the temperature up to somewhere near fifty. The sunshine felt damn good. His feet bled from gravel cuts and underbrush scrapes. His stomach growled with hunger. And not one minute passed that he didn't think about Nic. Was she safe? Was the baby all right? Where was she right now?

York had to know that he couldn't escape, that it was only a matter of time before his elaborate hoax would come to an end. Did he actually think that if he made it back to the lodge, he could get away and escape punishment? Griff had no intention of allowing Ellis Benecroft to beg and plead his way out of a death sentence. The man was responsible for the deaths of Powell agents and members of their families. He had ordered Nic's kidnapping, put her through months of torment, endangered their child's life, emotionally tortured Yvette and Sanders, and had forced Griff to jump through hoops for his personal pleasure.

With the lodge in sight, Griff stopped to study the situation. He had no idea where Luke and his men were or where Nic, Sanders, Yvette, and Rafe were. He knew Benecroft and Bouchard were dead. But that left Anthony Linden. Had he returned to the lodge, waiting to meet up with York so the two of them could make a run for it?

And then he saw movement on the opposite side of the lodge. Four people came into full view. Yvette and Rafe flanked an obviously wounded Luke Sentell, supporting his weight as they all but carried him up the porch steps. Nic, rifle in hand, playing watchdog, followed them. As Griff made his way toward the lodge, his pace picking up speed, he caught a flash of light in his peripheral vision. Old instincts kicked in. He took cover behind a cluster of evergreens and visually searched for the light. When he saw it again, he knew someone had set his sights on the foursome walking up the lodge's front porch steps.

He had to act quickly.

Griff made his way back into the wooded area and across to the other side of the lodge. He spotted the rifle first as sunlight reflected off the polished wooden stock. And then he saw the shooter. York, aka Ellis Benecroft. The man apparently preferred the polished wooden rifle stock for its texture and beauty and in the past hadn't thought it necessary to use a camouflage-painted stock.

Moving in on his quarry, silently and with deadly intent, Griff approached York, knowing he had to act quickly. York's finger pulled back on the trigger just as Griff got a clear shot.

Two rifle shots rang out simultaneously. York never knew what hit him. Griff opened fire and riddled Ellis Benecroft's dead body with bullets, making sure that this Malcolm York was every bit as dead as his predecessor.

Leaving York's shredded body behind, Griff charged out of the woods and toward the lodge. As he drew near he saw Luke propped in a porch rocking chair, Rafe flying down the stairs, and Yvette huddled over Nic's body lying on the porch floor.

York's bullet had hit Nic!

As Rafe ran toward him, Griff met Rafe as he approached the sprawling log-cabin lodge.

"She's alive," Rafe told Griff. "Go to her. I'll find the shooter."

"He's dead," Griff said as he hurried toward the front porch.

Rafe turned and followed.

Griff laid his rifle aside as he knelt beside Yvette and looked down at Nic. She looked up at him and tried to lift her arm. He clutched her hand and squeezed.

"I'm here, Nic. I'm here," he told her.

Holding the phone in a tight grip, Luke called out to Griff. "I've got a chopper on the way. They'll airlift her to the nearest hospital."

"You hear that, Nic. You hang in there. You're going to be all right."

"What about the baby?"

Griff glanced at Yvette who held Rafe's quilted jacket over Nic's belly, applying pressure to the wound. With tears in her black eyes, Yvette shook her head.

Griff screamed silently, the sound inside his head, as he lied to Nicole one last time. "The baby's going to be fine."

"Promise?" she asked only seconds before she drifted into unconsciousness.

CHAPTER 41

Griff sat at Nic's bedside, holding her limp hand, waiting for her to regain consciousness. He wanted to see her open those beautiful brown eyes, wanted to see color back in her cheeks, wanted to . . .

He lifted her hand to his lips.

Nic had been transported from the Big Valley Hunting Lodge to the Community Medical Center in Missoula by CareFlight air transport. Once at the Level III trauma center, she'd been rushed into surgery. Every hour of waiting had been torment beyond Griff's worst nightmares. A constant source of encouragement, Yvette had been at his side during Nic's surgery. Sanders had stayed behind with Rafe Byrne and Luke's team to clean up the carnage before the local authorities arrived. And he had put in a personal call, on Griff's behalf, to the governor. The official story line was that several of the guards at the lodge had gone on a killing spree. There would be loose ends to tie up. Luke's second-in-command would handle the situation while Luke recovered from surgery. As far as anyone was concerned, Griff, Nic, Sanders, and Yvette had been guests at the lodge and Nic and Luke were victims of the guards' murderous rampage.

Nic moaned.

Griff kissed her hand.

Her eyelids flickered.

He leaned down and kissed her forehead.

She opened her eyes.

"Hello, beautiful."

"Griff ?"

"Yeah, honey, it's me."

"What happened?"

Griff swallowed. "Don't worry about anything. Just rest. We have time later to—"

"My baby!" She clutched Griff's arm and struggled to lift herself into a sitting position. "Where's my baby?"

"Nic, calm down." Griff grasped her shoulders

gently and eased her down onto her back. Her eyes wide with fear, she asked, "Is our baby dead?"

Tears pooled in Griff's eyes. "No, he's not dead. By some miracle our son survived. The doctors performed a C-section. He's tiny. Not quite three pounds."

"It's a boy?" Nic smiled. "We have a son?"

"We do."

"Where is he? I want to see him."

"He's not here," Griff said. How could he tell Nic that the doctors gave their child less than a fifty/fifty chance of survival? "He needs special care and we're making sure he gets it. He was transported in an incubator to one of the top-ranked pediatric hospitals for neonatology in the country."

"Where?"

"Palo Alto," Griff told her. "The Lucile Packard Children's Hospital at Stanford."

"You should have gone with him."

"A specially trained doctor, nurse, and respiratory therapist went with him. And you and I will go to Palo Alto together just as soon as you're well enough."

"But he's all alone. I want you to go—"

"I'm not leaving here without you. Besides, he's not alone." Griff debated whether or not he should tell Nic that Yvette had gone with their son. He had no idea if Yvette's empathic abilities would work on a newborn infant, but if there was any chance . . . He decided that telling Nic could wait. "He won't be alone once Maleah and Derek and Barbara Jean get there. They left Knoxville a few hours ago and are going straight to Palo Alto."

"How soon can I get out of here?" Nic asked.

"If you behave yourself and follow doctor's orders, maybe a week. But when you leave here, you'll have a nurse with you around the clock. Understood?"

"I don't care if you hire a staff of doctors and nurses to watch over me twenty-four-seven, as long as I can be with our son." She lifted her hand to Griff's unshaven cheek. "Tell me about him. Everything. Did you count his fingers and toes? Are his lungs developed? What are the odds that we might still lose him?"

"He's got all the essential parts. Arms, legs, fingers, toes, eyes, nose, mouth, and ears. And screw the odds. Our boy's a fighter, tough as they come. He's going to make it. Look what he survived before he was even born."

Rafe Byrne watched Yvette through the nursery window of the neonatal unit at the Lucile Packard Children's Hospital. Griff and Nic's infant son rested in an incubator, a large Plexiglas box with a mattress inside. The baby was tiny, helpless, born too soon, and struggling for life. Yvette stood guard over the child, apparently having been given special permission to visit him in the unit.

Rafe wasn't sure why he was here. When he'd left the Big Valley Hunting Lodge, well in advance of the local law enforcement's invasion, he had intended to return to Europe, either London or Paris. But instead, he had booked a flight to Palo Alto and come by taxi to the hospital. He had wanted to see Yvette, to say a final farewell.

But now that he was here . . .

What was she thinking as she looked so lovingly at Griffin Powell's son? Was she thinking about her own child, the one Malcolm York had stolen from her? Was she wondering if she had a son, a boy almost seventeen, out there somewhere in the world? Was she thinking that perhaps this little boy wasn't Griff's only son?

Rafe knew, had always known, that Yvette wanted Griff to be her child's father. But what if he wasn't? What if . . . ?

During the months of Yvette's pregnancy, Rafe had hoped the child was his, the living, breathing proof of their love. God, he'd been such a fool. Yvette had never loved him.

But that fact did not change the possibility that he could have fathered the child she had given birth to on Amara.

For the past sixteen years, Rafe's goal, his singular reason for living, had been to kill York's closest friends and business associates, the men who had visited Amara frequently and enjoyed the entertainment their host provided. Now they were all dead—Tanaka, Di Santis, Klausner, Sternberg, Mayorga, Yves Bouchard, and Harlan Benecroft. And Griff had, for the second time in his life, killed a monster named Malcolm York.

Rafe had thought that once he had exacted his revenge and they were all dead, he would feel something. If not joy, at least satisfaction or perhaps relief that the job was done. But oddly enough, he felt nothing. He was empty inside, void of human emotion.

That's not true. You still feel something for Yvette. Otherwise you wouldn't be here.

He didn't love her. He was no longer capable of love. But seeing her again had stirred up old memories, memories he had believed long forgotten. A naïve young man's passionate love. His foolish hope that a child born of that love existed.

Was it possible that Yvette's child was still alive, that York hadn't killed the infant? If so, what had he done with the baby? Where was Yvette's son or daughter? And was he her child's father?

Rafe took one last look at Yvette and said a silent goodbye before walking away without speaking to her.

Jonas Sanders Powell weighed four pounds and six ounces. His parents had named him after Damar Sanders, the man who had saved Griff's life on Amara, and Jonas MacColl, the man who had died to save Nic and her baby. At two months, his perfect little head was covered with dark hair and when Nic held him in her arms, he looked up at her with beautiful blue-gray eyes, identical to his father's.

Griff and Nic haunted the neonatal unit at the hospital, spending as much time with their son as the staff allowed. They spent their nights together in a suite at the Stanford Park Hotel in Menlo Park, the Peninsula's only five-star Diamond hotel. Griffin Powell went first-class, no matter what the circumstances. He had showered Nic with love and attention, and kept a nurse on duty around the clock the first month after her surgery.

A homecoming was planned for the day after Joe Powell weighed in at a hefty five pounds. It would be a return to Griffin's Rest for his parents and a royal welcome party for the young prince.

Unable to choose from a list of three god-mother candidates, Nic had asked Aunt Maleah, Aunt Barbara Jean, and Aunt Yvette to share the honor. Uncle Damar and Uncle Derek shared godfather duties with Nic's brother, Uncle Charles David.

Alone in their suite each evening, Nic wrapped in Griff's arms, the two of them more in love than ever, they had talked about the months they were apart, and about Griff's past on Amara, his relationship with Yvette, her experiences being held by York, and her relationship with Jonas.

When, once again, Griff had taken all the blame for Nic's kidnapping, she, once again, had reminded him that she had played a part in what had happened.

"I shouldn't have left you. I should have stayed at Griffin's Rest and worked things out with you. I should have tried to understand about Yvette. I do now."

"Because of Jonas MacColl?"

"Yes, because of Jonas. I wasn't in love with Jonas, just as you weren't in love with Yvette, but I cared about him, and if he had lived . . . "

"He would have been your friend and you would have wanted him to be a part of your life."

"Yes."

"We're going to have a good life from here on out, you and me and Joe."

"And maybe before I get too old, we might give Joe a baby sister."

"If that's what you want, then I'll do my best to accommodate you, Mrs. Powell."

"And have fun doing it."

"You bet."

"No more secrets," Nic had said. "Promise?"

"I promise. And no more lies or even half-truths."

"Agreed. But in the future, if I ever ask you whether or not a certain pair of jeans makes me look fat, remember that the only acceptable answer is no, even if it is a lie."

Laughing, thankful for his many blessings, Griff had pulled his wife into his arms. "Nic, darling, I don't care if you get so fat you have to wear a tow sack. I'll still think you're beautiful."

"Good answer, Mr. Powell, very good answer."

Nic and Griff brought Joe home on New Year's Day. Every room in the house at Griffin's Rest remained decked out for Christmas, even the nursery that Nic had overseen long distance, with Maleah and Barbara Jean handling the day-to-day details with the interior designer. Countless presents, most with Joe's name on them, were piled beneath a twelve-foot spruce by the fireplace in the living room.

The house was filled with family and friends, everyone there to celebrate a belated Christmas, Joe's homecoming, and the renewal of Nic and Griff's marriage.

Maleah and Derek had set a wedding date in April.

"Nothing elaborate. That's not my style. But I do want you to be my matron of honor," Maleah had told Nic.

Sanders and Barbara Jean were working on resolving their problems, but they had decided to sleep apart until they were certain of their future together.

"I don't expect him to ever forget Elora or to

stop loving her, but I deserve more than he's given me," Barbara Jean had said.

Nic wasn't sure how things would work out for them, but she believed that Sanders was much too smart to risk losing the best thing that had ever happened to him.

Upon their arrival, Yvette had met Nic with a smile, the two women having set aside past difference. And later Yvette had admitted how much she envied Nic.

"You have everything. A wonderful husband who loves you and a beautiful child you will bring up together."

Without hesitation, Nic took Yvette's hand. She didn't care if the woman read her mind, sensed her feelings, or absorbed some of her happiness. "You are a beautiful woman and an exceptional human being. You deserve to be happy, to find love, to share your life with someone. That's my wish for you."

"You are very kind, Nicole, but I do not believe it is meant to be."

"Never say never."

Later that evening, as Nic stood over her son's crib, Griff came up behind her and wrapped her in his arms. They stayed there in the nursery for a long time, simply watching their son breathe, his little chest rising and falling in a steady rhythm. They had come so close not only to losing each other, but the child who had been conceived in their love, the child they now thought of as their precious miracle.

The past lay behind them, the misery and unhappiness, the horror and torment. Neither would ever forget, but they would never again allow the past to overshadow the present, each having learned valuable lessons about under-standing, forgiveness, acceptance, and the power of love.